merging paths

merging paths

VINCE BAILEY

IngramElliott

Merging Paths
A Curtis Jefferson novel

Copyright © 2022 Vince Bailey

All rights reserved. No part of this publication may be reproduced, stored in a retrieval system, or transmitted in any form or by other means electronic, mechanical, photocopying, recording or otherwise, without the prior written permission of the publisher.

Published by IngramElliott, Inc.
www.ingramelliott.com
9815-J Sam Furr Road, Suite 271, Huntersville NC 28078

This is a work of fiction. The names, characters, places, or events used in this book are the product of the author's imagination or used fictitiously. Any resemblance to actual people (alive or deceased) events, or locales is completely coincidental.

Book design by Maureen Cutajar, gopublished.com
Cover design by: H.O. Charles

ISBN Hardcover: 978-1-952961-09-0
ISBN Paperback: 978-1-952961-10-6
ISBN E-Book: 978-1-952961-11-3

Library of Congress Control Number: 2022945203

Subjects: Fiction—General. Fiction—Historical. Fiction—Paranormal. Fiction—Suspense. Fiction—Western and Pacific States. Fiction—Myth & Legends. Fiction—Visionary and Metaphysical.

Published in the United States of America.
First Edition: 2022, First International Edition: 2022

The *Curtis Jefferson* series
BY VINCE BAILEY

Path of the Half Moon

Winner of the Arizona Authors' Association Literary Award and the Chanticleer International Book Awards for Paranormal and Supernatural Fiction. Book one in the series, *Path of the Half Moon* is a paranormal historical fiction tale set in a remote detention facility for wayward boys in the early sixties. Curtis is an African American youth whose character and physical endurance are tested by a murderous inmate and a century-old Apache curse.

Courses of the Cursed

Finalist in the 15th Annual National Indie Excellence Awards. Book two in the series, *Courses of the Cursed*, brings back Curtis Jefferson as he continues to be challenged by his nemesis, Harvey Huish, while a café owner struggles with a premonition that her nephew will be the victim of a treacherous plot. The parallel stories share a common theme: the curse of Fort Grant.

Merging Paths

Merging Paths is the exciting conclusion to the colorful, intricate world presented in this unique paranormal series. Curtis Jefferson's closing tale of the century-old curse of Fort Grant follows our hero as he escapes from the fort, endures a perilous desert crossing, and evades a rogue lawman who is bent on ending Curtis's life.

Dedication

I dedicate this third and final book in the series to my family and friends who have fueled my creative efforts with their continuing encouragement and genuine excitement over new developments in Curtis's perilous journey. Thanks to their abiding interest in his tale, I felt compelled to produce a concluding installment that addresses the unresolved issues raised in its series forerunners, *Path of the Half Moon* and *Courses of the Cursed,* and to do it with the same entertaining panache that defines its predecessors. Thanks, as well, to a growing readership for their patience in spite of their hunger for finality. I trust they will find some captivating closure with this writing.

merging paths

A Presence Abroad

The wheels of a beige Ford pickup chattered along the otherwise deserted washboard road for several miles before a smooth stretch finally silenced the annoying floorboard din. Ezra, the nearly nodding driver, raised and cocked his head as if to listen more intently for a sound no longer stifled by the clatter underfoot. Perking up, he released the pressure on the gas pedal and glided the aging rattletrap to a dusty halt at the right shoulder of the unpaved county road. Engine still idling, the old Apache shaman shifted the truck into neutral, set the hand brake, and clambered out onto a wide running board. He craned his neck until his entire weathered face cleared the top of the cab. Facing south, he tipped his nose upward, sniffed the stirring air, and growled softly like a perturbed hunting hound.

"Something…something *human* has entered my desert," he muttered to a nonexistent passenger.

He reached down into the cab, then rose back up clutching a severed arm, using the stiffened dead palm as a visor to shield his eyes from the low morning sun. His enhanced animal vision allowed him to see clearly for more than a mile, but it was his sixth sense that enabled him to "see" several miles beyond the rocky knolls that dotted the horizon. At length, he drew his canine features into a wry smile, and he licked his lips upon identifying the intruder.

"It's the black boy Curtis Jefferson!" he exclaimed with surprise. "He's a bigger fool than I thought. Who in their right mind would abandon the safety and security of those walls after what he's seen of the outside?" he continued, addressing no one. "He's certainly outlived his usefulness to me. Come to think of it, I've never dined on African cuisine, and I am, after all, quite the culinary adventurer. Still, I must put that novelty on hold while I have more pressing business elsewhere. I'll keep an eye out and bide my time with this dolt while the desert has its way with him for a while."

And with a "humph," Ezra, phantom chief of the ill-fated Aravaipa clan, ducked back into the cab and motored up the road northward, toward Phoenix.

Catchin' Up (Interlude One)

"So, this stuff with me all happened in a day and a half, right around the time Isabel sent ol' Ezra packin' back to hell with a pound of lead in his hide."

The statement was startling on several counts. I could tell Curtis had broken off from the story right away by the stark change in his tone. His voice went from monotone while narrating to loud and commanding as he was directly addressing me. But aside from the tone and the volume, I was startled because, once again, he was answering a question that had been building in my mind—answering as if I had asked it aloud. The combined shift and the nearly clairvoyant response to my thoughts struck me momentarily dumb.

"You remember that turkey shoot, don't ya, Vince?" Curtis asked in reaction to my silence.

"Let me see," I answered, pretending to strain for the recollection. "You mean the time she blasted the old shaman nine times and blew off his arm?"

"That's the time." Curtis chuckled. "I thought maybe you forgot."

"Not likely," I countered. "That part of the story stuck out like a fly on a wedding cake. Listen, Curtis," I added thoughtfully, "you don't have to test me. I'm soaking this all up. I just get a little lost on the timing of things. You know, the way the episodes overlap and all. But I'm getting this down in my mental notes."

"I'm glad to hear that 'cause, to be honest, I get kind of mixed-up myself."

"That so?"

"Yeah, it's like everything right around then started happenin' so fast and furious, lots o' stuff started runnin' together—I had the vision of Ezzy and the lieutenant after I got drugged, then Leon and the boys rescued me, then I went to that weird church service, then I found Randy hangin' from the rafters, then I led ol' Harvey down to…well, you know," Curtis said.

"Yeah, I know. Sounds like way too much to handle."

"It was pretty confusing at first, I gotta admit. But, during the year between then and now, I've had a lot of time to sort of put things together and make better sense of them."

"Well, you sure seem to have a handle on it all now, right down to the details. In fact, you've given a few specifics that make me wonder."

"Wonder away right now, writer-boy, 'cause I don't want to get interrupted later."

"Okay, I wonder about how you know all these particulars involving Isabel and Ray. I mean, you were still behind the wall when most of that stuff happened with them, right?"

"Good catch. Yeah, I got most of those parts from the chats I had with them—back then and since."

"Kenny too?" I pressed.

"Yeah, but you gotta understand, I've been working my sixth sense overtime on this stuff for the better part of a year, and sometimes I just fill in the gaps for good measure. Got it?"

"Yeah, I guess," I muttered.

"Now, where was I?"

"You were recapping how you dispatched Harvey Huish. Then there was the fire."

"Oh my God, yes!" he exclaimed. "That was the worst of it—knowin' that those four cavalry guys were in there burnin' up. I hate to even think about it, much less tell it."

"What an awful way to go out," I said. "Did you ever come to understand why the lieutenant did that—burned himself up with the others like that?"

"Best I can guess is that there was no other way out for 'em. They couldn't get discovered as they were, and they couldn't leave the fort 'cause that was part of the curse. I guess the lieutenant figured that burnin' a body into nothin' was the only way the *never-dyin'* can get truly dead."

"What does *that* mean?"

"I'm not sure, but it seems like the four of them stopped gettin' older ever since the massacre—somethin' to do with the curse, I guess, and the way time got all fucked up in that place."

"What do you mean by the *never-dying*?" I wondered aloud.

"At first, I thought *it*—you know, the whole *never-dyin' thing*—was some sort of punishment for bad things they'd done, part of the curse, in other words. That would sure fit for Jeb and the doc. But that wouldn't explain the lieutenant or especially Marcus—no way."

"I get your point—but what, then?" I pressed.

"Let me tell it the best I know how. Take ol' Jeb. Now, there was a bad character if there ever was one—bad and ignorant."

"Yeah, you got him pegged. A grave robber—that's about as low as they come," I said.

"Then there's the doc—sharp as a razor, but slimy as a jar o' toad eggs."

"I'm with you on that one too."

"But take the lieutenant—not a mean bone in that man's body…"

"Are you forgetting about the time he took a razor strop to your backside?" I interrupted.

"Strict ain't the same thing as mean," Curtis observed thoughtfully. "Ya know, there's a part in the Bible that says the Lord whips every son he loves. The lieutenant thought I was lyin' to him—and I was. He was keepin' me on the straight and narrow, kinda like my daddy would have done. No, the lieutenant was a good man, at least to a point."

"And what does that mean—'to a point?'"

"Two things: he drank way too much. The guy was single-handedly keepin' the bourbon business propped up."

"Hmm. Okay, you said two things. What's the other?"

"Decidin' on any ol' thing. If there was more than one way to go about somethin' at all, the guy would go into full-tilt mode. Hell, he'd starve before he could decide between oatmeal and corn flakes for breakfast."

"That's right!" I recalled. "The history said that his indecision sort of set up the massacre. And since he was the author of the manuscript, he was confessing his fault, in a way."

"I guess, but he was in no way to blame for what happened there. Those devils from Tucson that did the killin' were the guilty ones, plain and simple."

"True enough," I agreed. "But from the way you tell it, the notion that he was guilty haunted him for his entire long life. He sounds like a really sad character, Curtis."

"I suppose he was sad, but he was a lot of other things too," he murmured, as if thinking out loud. "I jus' keep thinkin' about how he saved my life—twice, when you think about it. I count him as a hero before anything else."

"That seems fitting," I said. "Heroic and tragic at the same time."

"But now, when it comes to Marcus, well, there was nothin' sad about that man at all," said Curtis, more cheerfully. "That guy was always grinnin' an' crackin' a joke or hummin' a tune. Man, I think Marcus could light up a cemetery on a moonless night jus' by bein' there."

"I guess it was lucky that you had some good friends like Marcus and Randy to make up for the evil that came your way from the others—not to mention the protection you got from the lieutenant."

"I can't keep myself from thinkin' that none of those folks were real friends—or even real enemies, for that matter—though they sure seemed so at the time."

"Do you mean they weren't real friends or enemies because they weren't *real* at all?" I finally blurted out.

"They were real all right," he asserted quickly, as if startled by the question. "They ate and drank and burped and farted jus' like you and me."

"You know, you and Randy had a lot of discussions about the devil's hand in all of this Fort Grant voodoo. Do you think those characters were sort of like the devil's playthings?"

"I think you're close, Vince, but I don't believe any true explainin' is possible for the strange survival of those spooky dudes," Curtis replied. "To me, they seemed like actors in some creepy-ass movie. But if I had to give the short answer, I'd say the two sewer rats were trapped there because of their dark deeds; the lieutenant was caught there because of his damned wafflin'. Maybe Marcus was there because of his blind loyalty to the lieutenant. Who knows for sure?"

"It seems to me that the fire was the lieutenant's rebellion against his own indecision," I continued to speculate. "Maybe only such a firm and final act could possibly break the time-hold on them. Maybe he gave them all a way out."

"Yeah, I think you're probably on to somethin', Vince. But, then again, maybe they were carryin' out a mission."

"And what mission would that be?" I challenged my friend.

"To educate," said Curtis.

"They sure gave you an education. And two of them turned out to be friends," I said.

"No, not really friends. See, the reason I say that again is because they seemed like they were just sort of actin' out roles, just like you said. Fact is, I only had one best buddy in that whole place that was real."

"Let me guess." I nearly squealed. "Leon Hawkins!"

"Right on the money again, bright boy." Curtis grinned. "See, ol' Leon, he stood watch over me, rescued me, took me to church—not to mention that he gave me some provisions, pointed me in the right direction, and helped me over that wall before all the state fuzz come swarmin' around. Yep, he saved my ass and busted me out. I'll be forever beholden to that boy."

"How long was he in for?" I asked.

"Not sure about that, but only a few hard cases were ever in for longer than a year."

"Then he's probably out. Ever try to look him up?"

"Yeah, for one of those chats I was talkin' about," he muttered. "Let's just get back to the story."

"Sure, I just thought…"

"I said we need to get back to the story before I lose the thread," he growled impatiently. "Let's see…I'd just gone over the wall that morning, maybe an hour before dawn. It was pretty easy to go unnoticed, what with all the attention on that fire…"

Sonoran Crossing

Curtis had put a good ten miles between himself and Fort Grant on the first day of his flight. Fear of pursuit pressed him from behind, and the wide azure sky opening before him seemed to beckon the boy onward in his stalwart march eastward across the barren expanse. The dual stimulants of adrenaline and the colorful brightness of the new day drove the sleepiness from his eyes, and the bill of his Dodgers cap sheltered him from the late-morning sun. His strength and stamina had sustained him early in the day. But, in the first hours after midday, lack of sleep from the eventful night before and the draining effect of a glaring sun predictably drew the onset of utter exhaustion. A dull ache in the left side of his rump reminded him of the stitched-up gash in the fleshy cheek, another symptom of profound weariness. The pain jogged his memory of being attacked by a devil-dog outside the fort, just the night before. Was that overgrown coyote actually Ezra, the Apache chief, in his demon form, as the lieutenant had suggested? Curtis purposefully dismissed the thought in order to keep focused.

It was pure serendipity that his leaden plodding brought a lone mesquite into view. Curtis aimed his faltering progress toward the promise of shade that punctuated the horizon. Within five minutes, he reached the solitary source of shelter in an ocean of sand and gravel. He slipped under the bright-green umbrella, sat cross-legged with his back resting against the craggy trunk, and began to nod.

That unplanned nap turned out to be another grace of sorts. Curtis awoke at dusk, refreshed and with a clear enough head to take stock of his circumstances. He sipped from the plastic jug that Leon had rinsed out and filled with water for him. Half of the life-sustaining liquid was already consumed, which was more than troubling. After supplying him with the water and two stale tortillas purloined from the mess hall, Leon had pointed Curtis eastward, advising that there were some truck farms and small ranch communities lying at the southern foot of the Pinaleños, some thirty miles away. Simple math told him the water would not hold out for that distance if not rationed more carefully.

The clarity that the nap had brought also presented him with a strategy. The relative cool of the early evening air made him realize that nocturnal travel and diurnal rest would use less water and energy on a desert march. He knew that to be true; it was James Garner's approach when presented with a similar predicament in a first-season episode of *Maverick*. In addition, night movement was less likely to be detected if any search for him had yet been launched.

He arose, stretched, and nibbled a few bits of the stale flour tortillas that had crumbled in his pockets. The illuminating remnants of sunset allowed him to make out the looming shapes of the Pinaleños in the gathering gloom, giving him his bearings. He broke a long-dead lower branch from his leafy host to use as a walking stick and then resumed his eastward march with a newfound vigor.

The living desert at twilight took on an entirely different character from its austere, sunbaked counterpart. The granite and mica expanses twinkled under the rapidly waning light like jeweled carpets. Stimulated by the cool promise of dusk, tiny kangaroo rats and collared lizards hungrily pursued their insect prey. They darted to and fro between the wispy clumps of creosote brush. Diamondback rattlesnakes buzzed out their warnings from time to time, shaking their beaded buttons like miniature maracas at the sound of Curtis's crunching footsteps. He shook his walking stick in a defiant answer at each encounter.

"Piss on you, snakes—you don't scare me!" he cried out repeatedly to bolster his own bravery as much as to provoke their cautioning rattles for reference to their whereabouts. But a singular sense that the darkened desert might serve up other perils besides serpents played on the boy's deepest fears.

The evening trekker soon began to question his travel tactic as the glow in the west became more and more muted and his route between creosote bushes became less and less well defined. The deepening darkness confounded his navigation, and he tripped over annoying tufts of brush and exposed roots. Before long, Curtis finally halted and propped himself beside a stout paloverde tree that stood guard at the edge of a wide wash. He reckoned that he'd hiked for about an hour since leaving the mesquite tree. An intuitive guess told him that he'd covered approximately a mile and a half at the pace he'd maintained. It was not anywhere near the goal he had set himself for a comfortable lead on the pursuit he assumed would soon be mounted for him. He had to press on, despite the debilitating darkness.

He resumed the eastward march, slowing his pace and scanning the land in front of him with his walking stick, much like a blind man would. For all intents and purposes, he was a blind man, for the black velvet gloom that descended like a drapery of India ink upon the desert air rendered him so. In fact, the boy's progress was so dramatically hindered, he considered abandoning his night-movement plan after a couple hours of stumbling along. At the rate he was moving, he would burn more time and gain considerably less ground than during the previous morning's march. Was James Garner's invincible Bret Maverick character wrong? Was that even *possible*?

His dark eyes flashed about, searching for some semblance of cover to hide in until dawn, when a wink of brightness beaming from the east attracted his attention. There, between two peaks of the Pinaleños, the teasing glint of light began to grow, throwing out a blanket of soft illumination over the desert floor. It was, of course, the natural time and place for a moonrise, but Curtis deemed it a miracle. In a short span of time, he could see even better than before, and he quickened his step to resume his earlier sunset pace.

Curtis enjoyed his relief from discouragement for a couple of hours, until a troubling tickle from his sixth sense could no longer be ignored. It was a sense that he was not alone in the desert that night—that another presence was watching from a well-kept distance. That disquieting notion caused Curtis to halt momentarily and ponder. He closed his ebony eyes, and the image of the Ezra, the old Aravaipa chieftain, once again surfaced briefly. The boy shuddered but continued his trek undeterred.

He had traversed nearly ten miles of desert without incident before the moon finally settled behind the Galiuro Mountains a couple of hours before dawn. Rather than blindly thrash through the brush as before, Curtis laid himself out in the soft sand of a broad wash and napped for an hour before resuming his eastward trek as the glimmer of predawn once again illuminated his path. The troubling sense of being surveilled and stalked seemed to evaporate with the dawn. He'd covered another two miles before the heat of the morning sun drove him to the cover offered by a copse of paloverde trees. There, satisfied with his progress, he napped, nibbled, and sipped the entire sunlit day away.

The desert sojourner awoke from the last of multiple snoozes about a half hour before sunset. It seemed a bit too soon to strike out again, and the interlude provided a needed opportunity to once again consider his precarious circumstances. His tortilla bits had run out during the course of the day. More critically, his water supply was down to less than a pint. He would have to refrain from drinking any more than a few miserly sips from the plastic jug on the upcoming leg of the journey if he was to ultimately survive the desert.

Then what? Whatever the fields beyond the desert held in store was still a troubling matter that he sensed would be crucial. But that concern was easily eclipsed by the immediate survival challenge that was testing his resolve at every turn.

He rose to set out before sunset, knowing he'd have to cover considerable ground before complete nightfall. He had learned enough from Randy about the erratic behavior of the moon to know that he could not depend on it to rise at the same time it did the night before—maybe sooner, maybe later. He could no longer recall the gist of the lesson in lunar behavior that Randy had shared with him.

As he rose to move on, his right calf, then his left, cramped painfully—a sure sign that dehydration was setting in. The pain from the muscular convulsions was excruciating, and he whimpered a bit as he massaged each leg vigorously through his jeans with heavily muscled hands. No one was there to detect the plaintive little cries of weakness—of mounting desperation—and yet…

He reluctantly broke the vow he'd made just a few moments earlier, and took a swig of water. Conservation tactics would not help if they crippled him. In time, the cramping of each calf subsided, and he struck out on what he hoped would be the final leg of his crossing.

———

The night's march netted Curtis several more miles without incident, though the haunting sense of being followed from afar resumed around midnight. For Curtis, that nagging perception conjured the illusory image of a coyote loping behind him in the darkness but never closing the gap. Once again, that foreboding image faded with the coming of a faint glimmer in the eastern sky.

It was nearly dawn when an obnoxious humming took up residence in Curtis's head—no doubt a symptom of dehydration that was growing louder by the minute as the weary sojourner stumbled forward in a fugue state. The buzz grew steadily along with a dull ache in his brow, another sign of critical thirst. The water had run out several hours earlier, but the boy clung stubbornly to the handle of the empty plastic jug, flirting with the desperate notion of saving his own meager production of urine to stave off the inevitable. His eyesight blurred intermittently, but he did not veer off course as he plodded toward the lavender band of predawn light in the east. Daybreak was imminent. Curtis halted his resolute march and cast his gaze about in search of cover to shelter him from the looming sunrise. His hazy vision focused on several dark blots on the glowing horizon. Trees, and big ones by his best reckoning, pierced the edge of dawn some distance away.

Striking out again toward the promise of shade, the boy tried to shake off the dread of enduring an entire day without as much as a single sip of precious water. But after a minute or so of hiking toward the trees, a curious sound seized his attention, and he halted once more. He listened intently. The irritating hum had built once more with his advancing steps until it had evolved into a shrill whine, much like the metallic whirring of a cicada song. It suddenly occurred to Curtis that the sound was not emanating from his skull. It seemed to come from the direction of the line of trees for which he was bound. He struck out again with some enthusiasm in his step. As the whine increased in volume, it signaled a vague sense of the familiar. It was only a teasing hint, but one thing was certain: the sound indicated some human mechanism, and Curtis began to imagine that the tree line that was coming into view held something more than the promise of mere shade.

Then, as he drew nearer, it registered that the abnormally large trees were not of the desert variety. What he saw was a neat row of cotton-woods—trees that grow in river bottoms, in flood plains, and on ditch banks. The familiarity of the whirring sound suddenly made sense. He'd heard it dozens of times before when he and his friends had gone swimming in the canals near Jacobs Well the previous summer. It was the sound of a deep-well turbine pump. It was the sound of life-saving water!

Curtis tried to restrain himself, but his quickened gait soon developed into an ungainly trot as clumps of salt cedars drew into view. He closed the distance between himself and the tree line in a matter of minutes, and, as he trudged up the incline of a raised berm, the scene that unfolded was as he had imagined it would be. The pump was the first sign of civilization to grace Curtis's senses. The sight of it buoyed his spirit—a cylindrical apparatus, about six feet tall and two feet in diameter, perched upon a concrete pad like a mechanical Buddha. But it was the sound of it—the whine had built into a turbine-fed banshee wail—that stirred his association of the shrill noise with water. As he topped the raised berm, the sight did not disappoint: as expected, the screaming electric Buddha was fully engaged in drawing a bountiful twenty-five hundred gallons of precious water from below the desert surface with every passing moment.

The gurgling water spewed and splashed from twin ten-inch outlet pipes, each of which diverted the spillage to a concrete catch basin situated on either side of a concrete diversion wall that doubled as a footbridge. From each of the basins, the water flowed in opposite directions—north and south—via identical shotcrete canals.

Curtis successfully quelled an urge to jump in and swallow great drafts of water. Oblivious to the fact that he was crossing a gravel service road at the top of the berm, he approached the canal bank, knelt reverently at the edge of the southernmost basin, dipped his plastic jug until it was half-filled from the bubbling flood, and raised it to his dry, cracked lips. The water was warm, having been drawn from a hot subterranean mineral spring, but its life-sustaining succor pleasured him to the core. As much as he wanted to, he kept himself from gulping to avoid regurgitation.

After a few moments of imbibing, as the sips of refreshment began to quench his desperate thirst, he indulged himself in a long-overdue bath. He plunged, fully clothed, into the warm, chest-deep water with a broad Curtis Jefferson grin. The buoyancy of the water gave utmost rest and relaxation to his weary limbs as he settled in up to his chin and planted a foot on the smooth concrete bottom to keep from drifting with the current. Drinking and bathing. Not surprisingly, these simplest of physical pleasures erased all concerns regarding the hardship and suffering of the previous hours and days. For Curtis, life was good again. All that was lacking was a bar of soap and a rubber duck.

That was a more-than-well-deserved relief from Curtis's ordeal and a victory lap. After all, he had won. He had beaten the vast, uninhabitable Sonoran wasteland with all of its unbearable heat, its spiny plants, its insect denizens, and its ravenous predators. He had kept his wits through the fog of confusion. With a little help from James Garner, he had devised a strategy and maintained it through shifting tactics and sheer perseverance. For once, the boy who had always depended almost solely on his physical strength and speed to get by could take pride in knowing that his cerebral acumen had done much to preserve him as well.

Curtis grasped the bill of his Dodgers cap and dunked his head under the swirling pool as if being baptized in the enjoyment of his own glorious triumph over the desert crossing. He broke the surface, cleansed of desert dust and the patina of salt from dried sweat that had coated his skin.

It was a revival of sorts—one that was, however, doomed to be short-lived.

The physical relief from the drudgery of the three-day trek and the comforting massage of the warm, bubbling cauldron were rudely interrupted by a thunderous wave of sound that instantly obliterated any hope of continued rest and relaxation—a sudden crescendo of rumbling and rattling that surged in volume so that it overwhelmed even the deafening scream of the turbine pump. Although the earthen canal bank blocked his view of the service road above, Curtis immediately recognized the unmistakable sound of a fast-approaching set of wheels chattering over a washboarded travel path. Fortunately, the same steep bank that obstructed his view of the unanticipated intruder conversely concealed his own presence from the sight of that nameless driver. Nevertheless, the boy instinctively slid downward in the swirling pool until his head was again completely submerged.

The sounds traveling through the underwater world were completely transformed from those above. The shriek of the turbine pump became a muted whir, and the rumble and rattle from the car on the road above became a gentle timpani roll—one that was dying away.

In any event, the boy had submerged himself reflexively without taking the obligatory deep breath that would sustain him. Though his lungs were well conditioned for a lengthy holding period, they burned almost immediately, and Curtis surfaced as quietly as possible, but more from the burn of curiosity than from the carbon dioxide fire in his chest. He gazed upward and beheld the typical cloud of dust that would follow in a traveling car's wake. More to the point, he could hear the idling of a motor whose sound was not traveling. The car had stopped there at the pump.

Had he been spotted already, or was it just some *zanjero*—a ditch boss checking the flow of the irrigation water? Either way, the boy-fugitive could not afford even an innocent chance encounter. He drew in a deep draft of air, lifted the foot that held him against the current, and slipped once again beneath the surface, allowing himself to be taken up by the strong downstream undertow—to be whisked away from the eyes of the unwanted presence by the swiftly coursing water.

Haunted Taunt

"C'mon, Kenny," Ezra implored, "open your eyes. I brought a friend who wants to visit with you."

Kenny huddled on the padded floor of his cell, tucked in his usual fetal position, eyes slammed shut.

"I know you can hear me," the old *brujo* persisted. "Every time your handlers do that sadistic shock treatment on you, it makes it easier for me to get onto your wavelength. It's getting so I can almost call on you at will, although walking through walls and bars still requires a lot of psychic energy—twice as much when I bring a comrade, like now. For that effort alone, you should pay me the courtesy of a warm welcome. Besides, aren't you the least bit curious about who it is that's come to see you? Such a good friend should not be ignored like this. It's bordering on rude, Kenny. It's just not like you."

The heap on the floor that was Kenny Armenta began to shudder. It wasn't enough that he was falsely accused of murder and locked away in a mental institution. The mute, defenseless Native American was also being tormented by his mortal enemy. He squeezed his eyelids shut all the more to counter Ezra's tempting entreaty.

"Well, if you can't see him, I'm pretty sure you can *smell* him, at least."

Indeed, the sickeningly sweet smell of smoked meat filled the air of Kenny's cell. His stomach began a slow crawl up his throat.

At length, the ancient chieftain sighed. "Okay, Kenny, have it your way. C'mon, Eduardo, let's go. We can tell when we're not wanted."

Predictably, the reference to Kenny's friend and ally was the lure that could not be resisted. His eyelids flew open like spring-loaded window shades, and the sight that the old Pima jewelry maker beheld made him wish he'd continued his stubborn refusal. Ezra stood before him in his quasi-human form, a twisted grin blooming across his face. He wrapped his remaining arm around the torso of what appeared to be an inanimate corpse in such a way as to support the stiffened body in a standing pose alongside his own. The naked cadaver's skin appeared to be mummified, though it was actually the charred remains of Officer Cruz. Kenny's stomach muscles began to convulse.

"See, Kenny? I brought Eduardo to see you, although he's not very talkative right now, is he? Speechless, maybe—at the occasion of seeing his old friend again, I suspect. Are you surprised at his transformation?" The ancient Apache chuckled maniacally. "I knew you would be. He's really quite the crispy critter. I bet you wonder how he got this way, don't you?"

Kenny began to sob. His gaze was frozen on the horrifying sight of his friend's defiled corpse. He tried to convince himself that he was hallucinating, but the image being burned into his brain appeared all too real. He sobbed harder.

"Okay! Okay! I'll tell you. You don't have to cry about it."

A few weak little yelps escaped Kenny's quavering mouth as Ezra continued his loathsome monologue.

"Did you ever play that kid's game where a blindfolded player searched for something you hid? Hucka-bucka-beanbag, it was called—or something like that. No?"

Kenny managed to block out the visual assault, but Ezra's taunting voice invaded his skull, seeming to grow louder.

"Anyway, when the blindfolded seeker gets near the hidden object, you're supposed to say, 'You're getting warmer.' When he's straying, you're supposed to say, 'You're getting colder,' and so on. Now, when they get really close, you say, 'You're hot,' or 'You're really hot,' or 'You're burning up!' You get the picture, don't you?"

Kenny just moaned.

"Fact is," Ezra continued, "our friend Eduardo kept getting warmer. Before long, he got hot. Actually, he got so close, 'You're burning up!' didn't quite express how near he'd come. How else can I say it? He *self-*

combusted." The weathered medicine man paused for effect. "I did provide the fuel, I must confess. But the fire was of his own making—his and yours."

A blood-chilling image suddenly flashed into Kenny's mind—that of a man ablaze running a pathetic race with himself down a darkened road, apparently trying to escape the prolonged torture and horror of his own inevitable death, but unable to outrun it. Pieces of the victim's clothing peeled off in flaming tatters—patches of orange light, like fireflies, left in a slipstream of smoke. The dark irony of that imagery—a desperate but futile sprint to nowhere—seized Kenny by the heart, and a spontaneous scream escaped his lips.

"Shut up!" Ezra commanded loudly. "You'll summon that loathsome guard, Odie, and then I might have to hush him up as well. Now, be quiet!"

The admonition cut Kenny's outburst short. He fell obediently silent.

"Listen, Kenny, I'm going to explain something to you, and I hope you take it to heart and give up these feeble attempts to expose me."

A coerced calm held Kenny in abeyance.

"You know I have no tribal quarrel with the River People. The Apache have always tolerated the Pima, even though our ways of survival differ greatly. We have deliberately turned a blind eye to your relations with the loathsome Desert People. So I do not take the same pleasure in killing one of your tribe as I would in spilling the blood of a Tohono O'odham, whom I esteem on the same level with pigs or dogs. That should be clear to you by the fact that I obviously enjoyed the murder of your Papago wife, but only rendered you mute on that occasion. But you should know that those of us who operate on both sides of the veil are charged by our lord below with strict secrecy. At your behest, Eduardo here was seriously threatening that mystic secrecy—one that allows spirits like me to intervene furtively in the corporeal world. Clearly, Officer Cruz's enthusiasm for connecting me with Primrose's slaughter could only be halted by his untimely death."

Kenny let loose with a long and loud sigh that ended with a weak little yelp.

"Now, do not mistake this explanation for an expression of remorse. I found your friend's propensity for noble acts quite nauseating. He was also initiating a flirtation with a white woman and, as you must know, our lord below frowns upon any fraternization between the races. Given his activities, I felt Eduardo deserved a taste of the infernal welcome wagon—hence the heinous way in which I dispatched him."

Ezra loosened and withdrew his arm from the charred cadaver and stepped aside, allowing it to teeter and fall facedown onto the padded floor. Kenny sobbed again.

"I'm telling you all of this, Kenny, as a warning. If you say or do anything more to attract attention to me, you'll make me regret that I spared you that night. Don't get me wrong; I don't want you to forsake your hatred for me—just find some other way to express it. Truth be known, I spared your life in order to kindle an exquisite hatred in you—someone heretofore completely devoid of that revered quality. You, Kenny, are one of my finest works—a complete conversion from innocence. Your sudden obsession with malice has even gained me some favor with our lord below. I wholeheartedly encourage you to continue to abhor me as deeply as ever—just do something else with it."

Ezra paused and chuckled for a moment.

"Perhaps you could turn it on yourself. This is your fault, you know. If you hadn't indulged in that disgusting intertribal marriage, none of this would have come about. Yes, I do believe suicide is a fitting end for you, Kenny. Your immobility makes it difficult, I admit, but the instruments available in this environment abound. Someone with your creativity could surely find a way. For instance, a simple pencil snatched from Odie's pocket could be deadly if plunged into the brain through a nostril or an eye socket. Painful for an instant, I imagine, but over in a split second. No suffering. And, after all, why anyone would want to go on living in this miserable state is beyond me. Suicide seems like a logical end to your lowly circumstances, Kenny. It's just a thought. You should ponder these things carefully, though."

A sudden rattle and clang signaled to Kenny that someone—someone corporeal—was entering the cell.

"Hey, Kenny—what's up?" It was Odie, the orderly. "I heard you scream earlier, but I couldn't come right away. I was right in the middle of sub-duing…or securing…a prisoner. I mean…a patient. Anyway, what's the matter, and what the hell is that horrible smell?"

Kenny opened his eyes and glanced around. As expected, there was no Ezra and no charred cadaver, although the putrid stench of burnt meat still hung in the air.

"As if you could tell me," Odie scoffed.

The orderly was down on hands and knees to be on Kenny's level. Kenny's gaze was stolen by a tiny wink of yellow color emitting from Odie's T-shirt pocket. It was just as Ezra had said. It was a pencil.

Risen

Betty Wood began to rise, ever so slowly, through several layers of a deep subconscious state. She drifted in a sea of nightmarish memories as she slowly regained some semblance of sentience. Upon rising to a certain level of semiconsciousness, her cerebral turnings were suddenly assailed by dual images that threatened to be real: one of a face, appearing in muted moonlight to be burned beyond recognition, with charred flesh stretched tight against prominent facial bones, forming a hideous death mask that seemed to be overwhelming her thoughts. Following several moments of trying to escape that loathsome vision, it suddenly dropped from view. Then, as she raised her gaze, she found to her alarm that the dreaded specter had been replaced by an apparition even more chilling. Looking upward, she beheld the monstrous image of an immense man-beast. The fearsome form stood upright in the same subdued moonlight, towering over a groveling Betty. The beast had the shape of a human, yet otherwise exhibited the features of an animal: dark hairy torso, elongated canine snout, outsized claw-like hands. It was stalking her, it seemed, with smoldering eyes aglow. Again, Betty tried to look away—to purge the petrifying image from her sight.

At that point, after nearly three days of lying comatose in a patient bed at the University Hospital, her buoyant spirit, seeking escape, finally brought her to the surface of awareness as she opened her watery eyes with a little yelp. The still air of the darkened room was a battleground of competing odors. She inhaled the dank, musty smell that diseased people seem to carry about with them like an aura of imminent death: the pungent tang of medicinal ointments and analgesic unguents—camphor, isopropyl alcohol, eucalyptus, and menthol. It was a stiflingly dense atmosphere that hung over Betty like a redolent blanket, and she fought off a brief wave of nausea.

"Betty, can you hear me?"

The words sounded as if they came from a distance, but Betty recognized the voice immediately. It was that of her boss, attorney Stephen Robson.

"Yes…Stephen," she replied with a groan.

"Oh my! I am so delighted at seeing you awaken, young lady. We thought for a while we'd lost you, you know."

Betty forced a smile at Stephen's term of endearment for her. He'd called her "young lady" since she'd signed on with the law firm about ten years ago, and he had continued to do so even as she'd advanced in years.

"Whu…what happened? Where am I?" Betty wondered aloud.

"You're in the hospital, my dear—the intensive care unit. According to the X-rays, you apparently sustained a couple of blows to the skull that would have likely killed a lesser person. You were lucky indeed— or blessed, I should say, with a hard head," Stephen said. "I've been keeping watch over you for quite a while, and, I must say, this chair was not designed for sleeping in."

"But how…"

"The particulars are a mystery. I hoped you'd be able to tell us. But I should summon the nurses and let them know you are awake. Don't worry—I'll stick around until they're finished with all their poking and prodding. We have much to talk about—that is, if you feel up to it. In the meantime, I'll give your sister a call and let her know you've awakened."

Stephen rose from his chair and stood beside the bed. He pressed the call button, took Betty's hand, and squeezed it.

"I'll be right outside," he murmured soothingly. "It's good to have you back in the land of the living."

The Fugitive

The muted whirring of the turbine pump sang a tuneless one-note aria under the surface of the water, a hum that was dying away as the strong current carried Curtis swiftly downstream on a southerly course. Lying in a prone position and battling his own natural buoyancy by blowing air out of his mouth, the boy sped along, submerged and almost completely weightless. In fact, in that floating state, his only sense of travel was the diminishing whine of the pump.

The young fugitive's lungs began to burn for want of fresh air, but he was determined to put as much distance as possible between himself and the stranger upstream. Then, just as his willpower threatened to give out, his rump bumped against an obstruction at the ditch bottom. A sharp pain from the blow to his sutured injury shot through his entire body as he sensed a sudden but slight falling sensation. He broke the surface gasping and sputtering, then turned to see the source of the rude collision. It was a weir—a sort of submerged dam or baffle for restraining the rate of flow and maintaining a certain depth in the canal. The step down in the water level provided some momentary concealment for Curtis as he caught his breath. He clenched his teeth to keep from crying out over the throbbing in his rump. The weir was the perfect hiding spot and vantage point—a watery wall from which he could spy and not be spied. He rested for a moment, gripping the top board of the weir and working up his nerve to face the unknown. At last, the boy slowly raised his head so his eyes were just above the water level for a glimpse upstream.

The canal had carried him some eighty yards downstream, so the unobstructed view of the intruder was clear in the brassy morning light. It was as he'd suspected: a *zanjero*, a ditch rider. Curtis recognized the signature pistachio-colored truck as that of the Water Users Association. The *zanjero* was merely checking the flow from the turbine pump and the water level against anticipated draw from local irrigators. It was highly unlikely that he'd seen the boy or much cared if he had. The ditch rider's presence was a welcome relief in lieu of the much-feared appearance of a San Pedro County sheriff's cruiser. The boy was also thankful that the truck was parked pointing in a northerly direction, away from his present position.

He watched warily as the ditch rider methodically dipped a long metallic rod called a weir stick into the water to gauge the level at its source. Then, pausing from his task, the old man bent over slowly and picked something up from the ditch bank.

"My water jug!" Curtis hissed out loud. "Sonuvabitch—I left it there!"

Next, the *zanjero* snagged a small object floating in the backwash from the water's edge with his weir stick.

"Jesus." Curtis moaned. "It's my Dodgers cap."

To the *zanjero*, it was just garbage—flotsam to clog the gates and grates. He flung the precious vessel, the cap, and Curtis's walking stick into the bed of his pickup, then took a curious gander downstream.

"Shit!" the boy whispered as he ducked. "I'll bet he spotted me."

But if the ditch rider's eyes were sharp enough to detect that scarcely perceptible movement, his disinterest was soon expressed with the cranking of the truck's engine and an idling departure down the service road in the opposite direction. Curtis was more than relieved to see the dusty wake of the vehicle disappear in the distance.

The boy waited a good ten minutes before cautiously clambering up the canal bank to put his soaking wet, sneaker-clad feet on dry land. He was amazed at how heavy his saturated blue jeans felt as the sopping wet clothes produced an unwanted clammy feeling.

Regardless of the chilly discomfort, Curtis was eager to acquaint himself with his new surroundings. He looked eastward, beyond the row of cottonwoods and tamarisk to the horizon where an early sun was just commencing to blink a waking eye from behind the peaks of the Pinaleños. A new radiance was falling upon a huge expanse of cultivated land that stretched out before him on a slightly lower plane. An alternating arrangement of carved furrows and raised earthen beds projected a coffee-colored gridiron effect from the sprawling acreage under the dawning light. *Melon fields*, he surmised correctly from the hint of green that was winking from some early sprouts.

Curtis then turned his gaze in a southerly direction and became startled by the sight of a small farmhouse planted on a barren strip of land between the canal and the melon field, about a hundred yards distant. Alarmed by his exposure to a couple of north-facing windows, the boy quickly withdrew behind a thick copse of salt cedars, and continued his surveillance of the remote dwelling from that place of concealment.

The house was a simple ranch-style structure with a white stucco exterior and a brown asphalt-shingle roof. Curtis assumed that north elevation to be the rear aspect of the house, as it presented only two small casement windows, a bel-air style door, and a tiny covered patio. The western exposure presented a common drive-through carport arrangement. Most importantly, it was a parking port that was currently unoccupied.

The boy retreated deeper into the tamarisks and began to take stock of his circumstances as he stripped down to his boxer shorts and hung his soaking clothes on branches where they would catch the new morning shafts of sunlight. All thoughts over the previous three days had been devoted to survival. He'd given little or no consideration to what he, an escapee, would do once he reached a community, but that time had come. He considered the remote place a good location to hole up for a short time. He had more than abundant water and good cover for shade that doubled as a blind from any more passersby along the service road. But his hideout would only be good for a day at best for multiple reasons.

He eyed an adjacent diversion gate and surmised from the path of its flume that its purpose was to divert irrigation water from the canal to flood the lower-lying melon patch. Perhaps that day, but more likely the next morning, men would come to open the gate and water the field. Already, the siphon tubes for feeding the individual furrows were laid out in a row along the ditch bank, a sure sign of imminent activity, the kind that was certain to produce an unwanted encounter. Curtis was painfully aware that any sighting of a black kid skulking around on his own, out in the middle of nowhere, was bound to raise alarms.

Then there was the familiar inner gnawing that defied any resistance the boy could possibly muster. Since his thirst was nearly quenched, the legendary Curtis Jefferson appetite awakened with a vengeance.

That line of contemplation was provoking Curtis to face some pretty compelling questions regarding his continued state of freedom. It was clear that he would have to find a village or small town before long in order to find sustenance, but in which direction? An easterly course had served him well up to that point, and it seemed plausible that greater concentrations of humans might be found beyond the furrowed fields in that general direction. What then? If the townsfolk spotted him, would they know him to be a fugitive? Would his hunger drive him into being recaptured? Could he use the cover of darkness to conceal himself? Would there be any kind of sanctuary there? Perhaps a church—a kindly priest or pastor might feel compassion upon hearing the boy's sorrowful story and give him quiet, temporary refuge and some food.

That was it—he had a plan. Curtis would strike out to the east at dusk, search for a village, hope to stumble across one before daylight, and hunt for a church—preferably one with a kitchen and a large, walk-in pantry—tell his story, confess his sins, and become a monk—at least for a while until the heat blew over. It was a fine plan. It had a good Richard Kimball kind of feel to it. And when it was all over, he would resume his pursuit of Olympic boxing gold and live happily ever after.

With his confidence bolstered, exhaustion began to creep up on Curtis. He found a dense salt cedar thicket, and, in that pocket of green, he sat with is back propped against a wall of verdant tendrils and quickly nodded out.

———◆———

The whir of a vehicle's engine revving then dying to an idle rousted Curtis from a shallow doze. He rose abruptly with the sudden realization that daylight was rapidly waning, and he immediately focused his attention on the nearby farmhouse. A pair of headlights glaring from the attached carport died, allowing the last remnants of a westering sun to reveal some color and detail—just enough to identify the vehicle as a Water Users Association truck—the *zanjero!*

It made sense, of course. It was a common practice for the WUA to provide housing and sometimes acreage along their easements as payment to their ditch bosses in lieu of a salary. Curtis detected some movement as the occupant emerged from the truck. Only a bright white Stetson hat and white cotton shirt were discernible in the gathering gloom as the man vanished through a side door. Twenty minutes passed as the twilight matured into nightfall.

A troubling detail arose, one that had slipped past the boy's notice up to that point: a light shining from the bel-air window had been burning since before the *zanjero* entered the house. Had it been left on all day? Before the boy could resolve the question in his mind, another pair of headlights suddenly appeared behind the *zanjero's* truck! The ditch rider reemerged from the house and disappeared at the rear of his vehicle with the slam of a car door. The pair of headlights panned left, then headed straight onto the service road, beginning a slow but ominously certain approach toward the boy-fugitive's hiding place.

Curtis was momentarily paralyzed, torn between equally strong instincts to keep hidden and to flee, but also burning with curiosity as to the nature of the new intruder. He dropped to a crouch, opting to wait, if only for a few more seconds, as the car drew nearer.

His curiosity was satisfied, but not pleasantly so, as a third light blazed forth, its brilliant beam cutting the night air like a luminous blade. A side-mounted spotlight could only have meant it was a patrol car, probably a sheriff's deputy, given the remote location. The beam panned back and forth, first sweeping a wide swath of the canal bank, but it soon settled on the copse of trees where Curtis was hiding. The intensely focused candlepower penetrated the foliage like an X-ray, and the boy was certain that his silhouette was exposed. His choice was clear. Curtis broke cover like a flushed jackrabbit and started on a quick canter down an embankment and into the clear, flat melon field below.

Reasoning on the run with the clarity of an adrenaline rush, Curtis surmised his own duplex advantage: his stalker's patrol car was cruising the opposite side of the canal and, with no navigable crossing in sight, was unable to follow the fleeing boy on four wheels. The second advantage was obvious: the indisputable fact that there was no biped on the face of the earth that could close a lead on a sprinting Curtis Jefferson, least of all some overweight deputy in clunky cowboy boots.

Unaware or indifferent to Curtis's superior running ability, the duty-driven deputy immediately halted his cruiser the second his beam exposed the boy-fugitive, exited the vehicle, and ran across the footbridge at the diversion pumps. He scrambled down the embankment with more agility than an average overweight deputy in cowboy boots. The *zanjero* was apparently left behind in the car to work the spotlight, which he did quite accurately, keeping the beam trained on the fleeing boy.

Curtis had put nearly a hundred yards of cultivated ground between himself and his pursuer when the deputy reached the edge of the field, knelt, and let loose an explosion of number six shot from a twelve-gauge shotgun. At that distance, the pellets lost their lethal velocity, but the lead hailstorm that peppered the boy's back sent a message that stung in more ways than one.

"Holy shit!" Curtis yelped, nearly stumbling from the shock of the blast. "You guys are playin' for keeps!"

Memories

After a lengthy examination period, the orderlies wheeled Betty's hospital bed to a private room. Stephen Robson entered the room a short time later.

"Is there anything I can get you, young lady?" he offered.

"Actually, yes," Betty replied in a weak voice. "I think this bed rises up, but I'm not sure how to go about it."

"My unfortunate familiarity with these hospital beds makes me an expert in this field." Stephen chuckled as he stepped up to her bedside and reached for the control pad. A whirring motor kicked in as the upper portion of the bed raised Betty into a sitting position.

"That's good," she said. "Makes me feel almost human." Betty squinted from the morning light that washed the room as Stephen occupied a visitor's chair next to her bed. "Thank you again for being here, Stephen," she offered meekly. "I know how valuable your time is."

"And that time could not be spent in a more deserving way," he replied without hesitation. "Your worth to our team—and to me personally—is, and always has been, quite priceless."

Betty stifled a groan. What Stephen said was indisputable, but it was never expressed so openly.

After an awkward silence, the elderly lawyer cleared his throat. "How are you feeling, my dear?" he asked uncomfortably.

For some unknown reason the "my dear" gave Betty the chills.

"I've got a dull headache, and I'm dying of thirst. All they'll give me are these damned ice chips. They say I've got everything I need in the IV drip."

"I'm sure the medical team knows what's best, Betty. But what I'm asking is…are you up to talking about the event that put you here?"

"I'm perfectly up to it—there's just one problem. I don't have any recollection of an 'event' that put me here. Not even a clue."

"That's understandable. The doctors say that the trauma to your brain did some damage. Their hope is that it is temporary." Stephen paused to let Betty absorb that unwelcome bit of news. "Listen," he continued at length, "maybe you can recall your activities leading up to the incident. Whatever happened occurred three nights ago. It was a Friday, so you were working in the office that afternoon. I saw you last when I left around 4:30 p.m. or so."

Betty was a bit mystified at Stephen's acute interest in her "event," but she submitted to his inquiry nevertheless. "I remember working on some assignments that you gave me, and I got a phone call from that tribal cop Eduardo Cruz—not much after that."

"Now, we're getting somewhere," said Stephen. "Can you recall what you discussed with Officer Cruz?"

"Something about the Kenny Armenta case, but the particulars are pretty blurry."

"Try to remember the details, Betty. What did he say?"

"We both know that he was convinced that Kenny did not kill his wife, and I think he was following some alternative lead. What that lead was, well, I'm not sure if he even shared that with me." Betty's eyes glazed over, and she shook her head. "I'm drawing a blank."

Stephen Robson frowned. "I don't want to plant speculations as fact memories, Betty, but I'm going to divulge some bits and pieces that I know to perhaps help jog your memory. Is that all right with you?"

"Yes…I guess…I guess so," Betty stammered. "I mean yes, of course."

"Is there a problem?"

"I don't know. I'm not sure how to explain it."

"Take your time," Stephen attempted to calm Betty.

"Intellectually speaking, I want to remember, of course. But deep down inside, I feel some resistance. It's like a part of me does not want to remember." There was a slight tremble in Betty's voice. "I have to tell you, Stephen, this is beginning to feel more like an interrogation than a conversation."

"I do apologize for the tone, my dear." (Betty experienced another chill at "my dear.") "I've cross-examined too many hostile witnesses through the years. It's become habitual." He forced a comforting Perry Mason sort of smile and continued. "Once I've divulged my own information, you'll understand the gravity of the situation."

"Then, please, let's continue," Betty conceded.

"All right then, I'm going to suggest that when you got off the phone with Officer Cruz, you drove your car out to the reservation," Stephen said.

"Why would I do that?"

"To meet up with Eduardo Cruz, is my guess."

"Whatever for, and how…how do you know this?" Betty stumbled over her words.

"What your reasons were I hope to eventually hear from you. I don't have the vaguest notion what they were. What I am certain of are your movements that evening, at least up to a point." Stephen paused in anticipation of Betty expressing some recollection. Her extended silence, however, compelled him to press on. "My certainty derives from a conversation I had with your sister, and also the fact that your abandoned car was discovered by the side of County Road 144, about a half mile west of Highway 75."

Betty suppressed a slight resentment that Stephen had gone so far as to question her sister, but she continued to work with him.

"If I left my car out there, how did I get here?" she asked with great wonder.

"That's an entirely different mystery. But let's stay focused on your rendezvous with Officer Cruz first."

"I think maybe you're stretching just a bit with the 'rendezvous' reference, Stephen." She made no effort to hide her indignation. "If I was meeting Officer Cruz, it was part of an assignment that you gave me."

"Of course that's the case, and I apologize for my poor choice of terms. But let's not mince words. Do you remember any of this?"

Betty frowned, as if the effort to recall was painful. But then her face brightened.

"I do recall driving now. I'm going really fast down an open stretch of desert highway. It's like it's late afternoon or evening—almost sunset, in fact."

"That's good. Now, do you remember anything about meeting Cruz?"

"No—what makes you so certain that I met him at all? And what does he have to say about all of this?"

Stephen scowled. "Now, you've forced me to get to the heart of the matter." Once again, the elderly lawyer paused before continuing, as if hesitant about what he was about to disclose. "Betty…um, Cruz was murdered out there where you two met up."

"Oh my God—no!"

"I'm afraid it's so. In fact, his corpse was found on the hood of your car."

"Jesus, Stephen…"

"That's not the half of it. You see, Cruz's body was nearly burned beyond recognition, and the coroner could find no other cause of death. In other words, someone drenched him in gasoline and set him ablaze. Betty, Eduardo Cruz was burned alive! Is that what your mind refuses to remember?"

The image of the hideous death mask from her previous nightmare flashed before her, and she immediately pushed it into a place beyond recollection. Suddenly, she began to sob, uncontrollably so. Stephen offered her the box of tissues that housekeeping had left.

"Betty, I'm sorry to upset you like this, so soon after your own traumatic episode. You must think I'm being terribly insensitive, but I just want you to be prepared."

"Prepared?" Betty choked. "Prepared for what?"

"Consider it all: a reservation cop is murdered in a particularly heinous way, and you were likely the last person, besides his assassin, to see him alive. Now, once the Gila River police find out you're awake and aware—let's just say you're going to get some visitors pretty soon. They're going to be pretty eager to get this resolved quickly, before the feds get involved and the press comes sniffing around."

"They wouldn't suspect that I had anything to do with this, would they?" Betty's tone shifted in an instant. An attitude of self-defense so quickly supplanted her prior grieving that the reversal made Stephen blink. "I mean, we've both seen what can happen in a rush to judgment—innocent people get convicted for expediency's sake," she continued.

"They're certainly not going to charge you with anything—they don't have any evidence. But they are going to be more aggressive with their interrogation than I was here. And, as much as I sympathize with your memory loss, it's not going to play too well with them. I'm afraid they're just going to see it as an evasion, my dear."

There it was: "my dear" again.

"The doctors will corroborate my condition. Besides, if they're not charging me, I don't even have to answer their questions."

"I like that you're thinking like an attorney, but don't behave like one in front of them. I'll be here to take that role. Right now, the presumption of your innocence depends on your willingness to cooperate. We just need to anticipate what they're going to ask you—besides what I've already presented here—and how you're going to respond."

"Once again, I am at a disadvantage, Stephen, because I don't recall the incident. What's more, I don't know what information they have or what approach they're going to take." Betty's exasperation was obvious.

"My guess is that they're going to be most interested in your mysterious escort."

"Mysterious escort?"

"Your knight of the dark realm, Betty—your *deliverance.*"

"I'm starting to get tired of the cryptic innuendoes, Stephen."

"Sorry. I hoped that the hinting might stimulate some recollection."

"Well, it's not working. I certainly don't know what you mean about a 'mysterious escort,'" Betty said.

"No, I don't suppose you would, all things considered. But the Pima police have already heard the stories, and they've probably already jumped to some hasty conclusions about the mystery man who brought you here."

"Naturally, I would assume that an ambulance brought me here, given my condition. Apparently, that's not the case?" Betty asked.

"No, not at all. It seems you got here under the strangest of circumstances. The way the orderlies tell it, a big black luxury car pulled up on Friday night and parked in a dimly lit spot in the lot adjacent to the emergency entrance. The driver never got out, but instead leaned on the horn until the aides came running. As they tell it, the rear door was already open when they reached the car, and you were lying on the back seat, unconscious. Of course, they rushed you into the ER. However, one of them lingered behind to get the info on your condition."

"But?"

"But, unfortunately, the driver tore off before he could get a name or description," Stephen said.

"So, nobody got a look at this shadowy stranger?"

Stephen shook his head. "Not even a fleeting glimpse. And, needless to say, someone who goes to such pains to hide his identity is going to draw suspicion to themselves."

"And then to me as well—if only by association…" Betty mused.

"Too true."

"I won't be much help with this little enigma either. I don't even know anybody with a black luxury car—at least not since Will died. But, to me, it doesn't add up that someone would burn Cruz alive, then go to the trouble of saving me at the risk of being identified. If I were the rez cops, I'd try to focus on whoever wacked me in the head. That should be their most likely suspect."

"I couldn't agree more. Unless or until you can ID that person, however, their attention is going to be on you." Stephen turned his palms up and nodded. "You now know everything I do. At least you won't look completely like a deer in the headlights when they come to question you. And, given my connections with the tribal council, I'll be sure they contact me before they come. I won't act as your attorney—at least not yet. But I will be here to advise you during their questioning."

"Thank you, Stephen," Betty said with a sigh. "That's a great comfort to me. I know how busy you are."

"It's the least I can do under the circumstances, my dear." Again, the "my dear" made Betty shudder inside. "If you begin to recall any of the details relating to Friday night's events, call me. Now, is there anything else I can do for you before I leave?"

"Yes, Stephen, there is one thing."

"And what is that?"

"Say 'my dear' again."

"Whatever you say, my dear." Stephen complied, a little puzzled.

Betty winced, but then a light came up in her eyes. "Now say, 'We'll have to take a rain check on our little date, my dear!'"

Night Flight

Though weak in the knees from the shock of that first shotgun blast, Curtis kept his footing and began to run a serpentine pattern to elude the beam of light while adding another ten yards to the gap before the second blast rang out. That time, the rain of pellets fell harmlessly to the left of him. He veered in that direction, dancing with the light shaft and bracing for a third discharge.

But, instead of an extended assault, the spotlight went dark, and the night went silent. Assuming his antagonist realized he was out of range, Curtis slowed his flight from a sprint to a quick trot, regaining his wind and shaking his head in amazement at the grave turn his predicament had taken. He was not merely being pursued for recapture—he was being hunted. As his friend Leon had predicted, the authorities had connected the fire and apparent deaths back at the infirmary to Curtis, given his past record, and were therefore treating him as a killer at large. There would be a number of lawmen, like the one he'd just encountered, who would shoot first and ask questions later. It was not just Curtis's freedom that was at stake. It was his life.

Trying to collect his thoughts, the young fugitive reduced his pace to a jog. It was a moonless night, and the gloom that had descended over the field was almost palpable. He jogged on eastward for a quarter mile before slowing to a walk, but his mind continued racing. Since he'd been spotted, the pursuit would be relentless, and he wondered if continuing in the same direction he'd been headed when flushed out was the best strategy. Once he had achieved what he felt was a comfortable distance beyond shotgun range, he turned northward. Cloaked in darkness, he resumed a sustained trot in that direction, leaving his stalkers far behind in short order.

After covering about a half mile of cultivated field, Curtis suddenly felt the familiar crunch of granite gravel under the soles of his shoes. He had crossed over into the margin of the desert. It was ideal terrain for losing any pursuer—the rocky landscape laced with deep arroyos and rugged ridges was dotted with clumps of cactus that would deter any low-riding, two-wheel drive police cruiser. He continued to trot into the rough country for a couple hundred yards until he felt sufficiently safe to slow his pace to a brisk walk.

Curtis walked for over an hour into the dark, moonless desert, wondering if any kind of sanctuary would materialize for him and, if so, in which direction it might lie. The authorities knew his general whereabouts, and a full-scale manhunt would be initiated in the area by morning. Already, radios would be crackling and telephones ringing with the news: the escapee had been spotted near the Pinaleño foothills. At daybreak, the volunteer sheriff's posse would be mobilized. A dozen or so pseudolawmen, most of them armed to the teeth, would comb the desert terrain on horseback pretty thoroughly. In any case, it would be open season on the boy-fugitive. And even if he somehow managed to elude the trackers and hawkeyed spotters, he would be spending the heat of the day on the run with no water to fuel his flight.

With so many discouraging thoughts swirling about in his skull, Curtis felt overwhelmed. He looked up into the vast depths of the starlit skies and cried out, "Lord, God in heaven, help me. Show me which way to go. Give me a sign!"

As if in answer, Curtis suddenly detected a low hum in the distance—barely discernible but growing steadily in volume. His eyes traced the direction of the sound and glimpsed a slight glow dancing on the horizon. As the sound intensified, so did the brightness of the glow. The hum raised and lowered in pitch like a motor revving and idling. Curtis realized right away that that was not the message from God he had expected. Quite the opposite, in fact: that was the approach of his shotgun-toting tormentor equipped with the appropriate vehicle for the desert terrain—a four-wheel drive jeep!

In desperation, the boy began to run in the direction opposite the ascending volume of the whirring motor, hoping to find an arroyo too deep and too steep for a jeep to navigate. Instead, he tripped over a barrel cactus and fell face-first into a clump of prickly pear.

"Ah, shit! What else?" he cried out, getting up and brushing the spines from his cheeks. "What the hell have I done to deserve this?" Casting his eyes aloft again, he tried a heavenly aimed suggestion. "You can't let me die here, Lord. I'm gonna be the heavyweight champion of the world…remember?"

He pressed forward in the dark until he reached an embankment that seemed steep enough to be daunting even for a jeep. At the top of the embankment, Curtis encountered an even greater obstacle for any vehicle: another canal—a large ditch, really, not too wide that he couldn't jump across, but an insurmountable barrier for a jeep. He hurdled across the gurgling water but lost his footing as he landed on the opposite slope. He tumbled down the embankment and sprawled out onto a flat plane at the bottom. *Too flat*, he thought, *and too well-graveled*. Curtis raised his head just as a pair of headlights not ten feet from his face switched on and blinded him in the glare of the high beams. He scrambled to his feet on that county road and raised his hands facing the car.

"I surrender," he moaned pathetically. "Please, don't shoot me!"

Mass Communication

Father Frank Cullen had just finished placing the proceeds from the evening's offering in the office safe of Saint Timothy's parish in Jacobs Well when he finally acknowledged a vague disruption at the edges of his thoughts. He just couldn't seem to shrug off an undeniable sense of disturbance but neither could he identify it. No, it was not the usual pang of doubt that often accompanied the aftermath of a Mass performance. That was different. What he felt then was more like an annoyance of sorts—perhaps something trivial that was amiss, like a needling hangnail in his well-manicured life.

He clasped the carved wooden beads of his rosary in the pocket of his black trousers and patted the leather-bound notebook where he kept his homily notes, which was resting within reach on the office desk. He felt reassured that he had everything with him. He shrugged his muscular shoulders as if someone were present with him to see, then rose to begin the process of locking up the church for the night.

The five o'clock Mass had gone long, and though only a smattering of parishioners attended the Saturday evening service, the gregarious priest always "gave them their money's worth," as he wryly put it. His treatment of the Latin prayers and chants was masterful—a reflection of his adoration of the Tridentine Mass. But it was his homily that consistently seized the attention of his flock. In the tradition of the master of the parable, he would create a way to draw some day-to-day relevance from the readings, more often than not using a current sports story or news event as his medium, then roar some related moral challenge at the rafters that would stir the most listless of the assembly into at least a whisper of heartfelt hosannas. The charismatic persona of

Father Frank was renowned throughout Jacobs Well, and not just among practicing Catholics.

Of course, that departure from the traditional homily frequently provoked his superior, Father Patricio, to lecture him on following the time-honored path of the past. In fact, the only feature of Father Frank's pursuits that raised any serious disapproval from the pastor was his open fascination with the paranormal—particularly with what Father Patricio saw as an unhealthy interest in the metaphysical manifestations of evil. Despite the younger priest's assurances of keeping his diversion confidential (often accompanied with a sarcastic promise to refrain from performing any exorcisms), whisperings among certain parishioners held that Father Frank was indeed something of a mystic, much to the consternation of his mentor.

Though he would never attribute that level of distinction to himself, he did experience periods of intuitive insight that ranged from clear and extraordinary to cloudy and confusing.

One such portentous inkling was the source of his distraction that night. The performance of the evening's particular homily seemed to make its mark as always, but the story had taken too long in the telling. He'd caught several of his followers checking their wristwatches. The show was over, and the audience had gone. Twilight was waning, and he thought of switching on the office light as he glanced at his own aging wristwatch.

"That's it!" Father exclaimed aloud. At the instant his eyes fell upon the blurred dial, he realized he'd left his reading glasses in the narthex, where he'd bid his parishioners a good evening only a half hour earlier. He remembered as he locked the office door and hurried across the darkening breezeway that he'd set them on the table where the weekly bulletins were stacked for distribution. That seemed to be it, and yet…the order of events was wrong. The creeping sense that something else was amiss came over him during the Mass, not after—that, and the notion that an absentminded misplacement of something so trivial would not feel quite so disquieting.

The narthex door was always left unlocked until Father Frank made a final sweep of the nave for possible stragglers and then turn out the lights. The priest entered, went directly to the table where his misplaced spectacles were waiting for their owner, and thrust them into his tunic pocket. He chuckled to himself as he pulled open the door to the nave to douse the lights, but the lighthearted self-jibing did not alleviate a growing sense of anxiety.

Saint Tim's church itself was a modest one—not even a poor attempt at replicating the magnificence of the cathedrals in the city centers. Its style was more rustic than Romanesque. There were none of the traditional fluted columns, no ornately carved capitals, corbels, or cornices. There were no high groin vault ceilings at the transepts, nor any elaborate stained glass panels depicting the stations of the cross. The founding construction endowment for the church, bestowed some twenty-five years prior, had to be shared equally with the adjoining parochial school, and so both buildings had escaped the blessing of a fabled Catholic opulence.

The cleric gazed down the gradual slope of the center aisle that divided two columns of thirty dark, empty wooden pews to the raised sanctuary. He took some pleasure in noting that the altar and tabernacle, at least, were given their due respect. The residence of the Host was, of course, a golden box, and the altar that it rested upon consisted of a large marble slab. Father Frank chided himself, as he often did, for his ambivalence on the importance of wealth with regard to these spiritual accoutrements—"props," as he irreverently referred to them lately in his more cynical moments.

He began to turn away, back toward the battery of light switches to the right of the double doors, when a slight movement near the front pew, just left of the center aisle, caught his eye and riveted his focus there. A dark-clad figure facing away from the priest bowed low toward the altar. Father Frank could barely make out the form in the subdued light, but it appeared from behind to be a rather large man nearly prostrating himself on the carpeted floor where the nave met the crossing of the transepts.

Ignoring an inexplicable wave of foreboding, the agile clergyman glided quickly down the aisle and hailed the figure in a booming but friendly voice. "Can I be of some assistance, my son?"

The figure rose abruptly, but continued to face the altar, crossing himself hurriedly. "Forgive me, Father," he exhorted loudly. Then, giggling childishly, the intruder strode quickly to a small, darkened adjoining chapel where he exited through a side door and plunged into the evening shadows, never having faced the priest.

Such strange behavior heightened the eerie sensation that had accosted the bold cleric from the first sight of the mysterious figure. Even so, Father Frank continued down the aisle to the crossing to see if the visitor had, in such a hurried exit, left behind some careless remnant of his calling. There was nothing but a darkened area about the size and shape of a human form soiling the azure carpet. The priest stepped closer to investigate, but was met by the blast of a powerful, acrid odor.

Acting on a stroke of combined logic and premonition, the father quickly secured all of the entries, raced back to the office, and dialed the telephone.

"José? This is Father Frank. Something is very wrong. Can you come to the parish office right away?"

———◆———

"Father, I'm trying to grasp what it is you're telling me, but, so far, it just doesn't add up to be a crime—or even an attempted crime, for that matter," said Joe Garcia, trying to conceal his impatience in a tone that only sounded patronizing to his friend the priest.

The priest furrowed a bushy brow, doing his best to ignore the officer's skepticism. Given other circumstances, Frank Cullen might have tweaked his parishioner's religious sensibility with a reference to doubting Thomas, but the cleric's mood was much too grave for jocularity.

"I know it doesn't sound plausible, and that's why I called you in particular instead of the JWPD dispatch."

Joe reconsidered in light of Father Frank's apparent conviction, and temporarily suspended his professional skepticism. "Of course, I don't doubt the facts as you have related them to me. I'm sure they unfolded just as you say. It's really just your conclusions that seem rather hasty. Forgive me, but I hope you understand my reluctance to make the same leap."

"I suppose I do." The cleric sighed and stared sullenly at the darkened spot on the nave carpet.

Sergeant Joe had known the priest for more than twelve years. For as long as the cleric could remember, they'd visited the same gym together twice a week. Joe often helped Father Frank with coaching activities during the schoolboys' football and track seasons. The two had developed a unique friendship that both men managed to reconcile with their religious relationship. Joe noted that the dark mood that his friend was in was way out of character. Perhaps another approach was in order.

"Okay," Joe rebounded, "let's go through the whole scenario again, and let me play the devil's advocate, if you'll pardon the term."

"Listen, Joe, I'm not asking you to humor me; I'm insisting that you believe me and understand the gravity of the situation. The safety of innocent people may be at stake."

"Father, with all due respect, cops aren't like priests or doctors. We don't practice much preventative police work."

Frank Cullen was losing his patience. "Then you should!" he admonished. "Look, José, I didn't call you instead of some random rookie on patrol simply because you're a parishioner. I called you because you're my friend, and because I know you're bright enough to figure this out."

Sergeant Joe pondered the priest's words for a moment and explored an avenue of thought he hadn't previously considered. "You've been reading the police reports on the back page of that wad of rubbish they call a newspaper, haven't you?"

The cleric nodded. "Yes, I have—I always do."

"You're trying to link this incident tonight to the false alarm you read about at the Seventh Ward last week, and to that small trash fire at the First Methodist six weeks ago, aren't you?"

Father Frank continued nodding and almost cracked a smile. "You see? You're making the same connections!"

"I wouldn't go so far as to say that, but I am willing to put your conclusions to the test and see if they hold up."

"Fair enough."

"How can you be certain that this man had not just come to kneel and pray in meditation, as I'm sure dozens of parishioners do every week?"

"Because, José, he was not kneeling. He was sprawled out on his hands and knees spreading something on the floor—something flammable, I think."

"But it just smells like cleaning fluid to me. And tell me this isn't the very spot where the little Valenzuela boy threw up at the nine o'clock Mass last Sunday. I'll bet the cleaning crew came in here and doused the carpet with some spot remover and…"

"The smell was much stronger over an hour ago when I called you. Most of whatever it was has evaporated."

The thinly veiled reproach for his slow response time was not lost on the officer, and he was becoming annoyed. "I came as quickly as I could under the circumstances. Let's not forget, I am off duty."

"A policeman and a priest are never off duty, are they, José?"

Sergeant Joe was at a loss for words, so the cleric continued.

"The cleaning crew has not been here yet, Joe. They usually come around nine. No one's been in the church since Mass ended except me…and…*him.*"

"But you said yourself that you left the sanctuary to put the offering in the office safe. Isn't it possible they came in while you were gone, and your visitor was just the last of the crew finishing up?"

"They've never come this early before, but I'll call and ask, just to dispense with your little hypothetical scenario." The priest was becoming weary of his friend's tireless skepticism.

"Look, Father, I want to help you, but I have to be honest. I am still doubtful. I mean, with only this to go on, I don't really understand how you can be so certain that this was an arson attempt."

The cleric rolled his eyes upward and threw up his hands in a gesture of surrender. "Okay, Joe, you've forced my hand with your doubting. There's more to this, I must confess."

"Now, there's a switch." The officer chuckled.

The priest kept still, barely breathing, for what seemed to be several minutes. He broke his silence as his reluctance to divulge what he had pent up was overwhelmed by his need for an ally. "I know who the perpetrator was, Joe. I haven't seen him for over a year, but he returned this evening."

The sergeant's eyes widened. "But you said you didn't see his face."

"That's right—he was very careful to keep his head turned away, but I would recognize that voice anywhere."

"Father, are we going to play *I've Got a Secret*, or are you going to tell me who it was?"

The priest spoke the name clearly, with just a hint of disdain in his voice.

"Scott Sizemore."

And, though the officer knew the name of the City Manager's son, his thoughts raced from a dismal acknowledgement of that name to the name of another character, connected if only by an unfortunate string of events. A wave of guilt rushed in as he spoke the other name aloud, as if it were part of some personal rite of reconciliation.

"Curtis Jefferson was innocent, then," he muttered grimly as he shook his head.

Father Frank gaped at his friend in wonderment. "Would you perhaps like to confess something to *me* now, Joe?"

Total Recall

etty Wood awakened just before midnight with a start, sensing another presence in her private hospital room. She held her breath, listening intently for a sound that might indicate an intruder. What she heard made her blood run like ice water in her veins. It was a faint sort of *snuffling* sound that permeated the darkened room, reminiscent of the sound of a dog sniffing the air. Panicking, Betty fumbled for the call-nurse buzzer that dangled over the side of her bed by a cord, but inadvertently bumped the control console that switched on the reading light perched above her bedside table. The weak illumination that the little gooseneck fixture put out barely cast a glow over the room, creating shadows rather than chasing them away. One dark shadow in the far corner of the room instantly caught Betty's eye, as it harbored a pair of smoldering red eyes that locked onto her own frozen stare! A soft gurgle like a muted drum roll replaced the prior sniffing—a growling sound that assailed her already terrified senses.

Nearly petrified, Betty continued to grope for the control that housed the call button. Flailing and groping, she inadvertently pulled the oxygen cannula from her nose before latching on to the call button's cord. As she reeled the handle in by the cord, the shadow rose and began to move slowly and silently across the room toward her bed. As it approached, the muted light projected the image as more solid in form and substance than just a shadow, and what she saw in those emerging details further filled her with dread. The *thing* had the immense shape of a man, yet the features of an animal in every other respect. Its furry trunk and distended canine snout resembled those of a huge dog. Its hands were outsized and clawed, not unlike the forepaws of a bear, and the creature's pointed ears pricked like those of a Doberman. The man-beast walked upright but stooped, and the ungainly steps that it took amounted to a stalking gait. Betty immediately recognized the thing as the fiend from her previous nightmare experience as she'd recovered from her coma the night before—a nightmare apparition that had somehow materialized.

At last, Betty's fingers grasped the call-button handle, and she held the button down. She could hear the buzzing nonstop outside her door in the nurses' station. She held it steady until the beast reached her bedside, then she buzzed it in staccato bursts to signify urgency.

The floor nurse crashed into Betty's door at a dead run and immediately flicked on the bright overhead light, which filled the room with a blinding glare. To Betty's amazement, her fiendish assailant vanished with the darkness, as if the illumination itself had vaporized it.

"Are you all right, Miss Wood?" The nurse was at her bedside in a trice. "My goodness, you're trembling!"

Indeed, the wide-eyed Betty was visibly quaking from her traumatic encounter. She tried to speak, but her mouth felt numb, unable to form words.

"Give me your hand," the nurse instructed. "I want to take your pulse." She grasped Betty's wrist and gazed at her watch. "It's elevated all right, but it's dropping toward normal. Can you tell me how you're feeling?"

"Rr…right here," Betty stammered. "It was right here where you're standing," she gasped.

"What was right here, dear?" The nurse smiled sympathetically as she replaced the nasal cannula.

Betty scowled. "Goddamn man-beast—that's what was here! Vanished the second you hit the lights. Goddamn werewolf—right here!"

"As you can see, there's nothing like that here now, Miss Wood," the nurse assured her. "This hospital is one of the safest places on earth. The place is crawling with security cops. I'll post one outside your door if you like. But what you experienced here was likely a hallucination—not unheard of in cases of head trauma."

"You think so?" Betty muttered meekly. "It seemed so real."

"Most psychiatrists say hallucinations seem hyperreal because they are products of a vulnerable state of mind. The images are enhanced by your own belief in them."

"I guess that makes some twisted sort of sense," said Betty.

"And a hallucination is the only thing that makes sense in this case," the nurse added, "unless you're given to believing in vanishing werewolves."

"Which I'm not. But I'm still shaking like an aspen leaf over what I thought I saw. And I'm sure not up for a repeat performance—hallucination or not."

"Tell you what, I'm gonna order you up a sedative for your IV drip that will put you into a dreamless sleep—far beyond the reach of any fiend your mind can conjure. How does that sound?"

"That suits me just fine," Betty replied. "Just one more thing, though."

"What's that?" the nurse asked.

"Can you leave the light on?"

———◆———

It was seven o'clock the next morning when Stephen Robson entered the room carrying a briefcase and a brown paper bag. Betty had called him an hour earlier to let him know she'd had an overnight epiphany.

"I brought coffee!" Stephen announced as he pulled two cardboard cups out of the paper bag. "As I recall, you like it black," he ventured.

"You recall correctly," Betty replied, accepting the steaming cup. Her bed was already raised to the sitting position, and she placed her coffee on the bedside table next to a hardbound book with a colorful dust jacket. "And so do I."

"And so do you what?" Stephen asked, somewhat puzzled at Betty's response.

"And so do I recall correctly," Betty declared proudly. "In fact, I recall quite clearly what happened on Friday evening—at least, right up to the time I was knocked unconscious."

"That's good news, Betty—exceptionally good news."

"What's more," she continued, "I remember the order of events that led up to that episode."

"And to what do we owe this sudden restoration of your memory?"

"There were a few things that I believe were triggers. First, your use of the term 'my dear' provided the tail to a sentence I thought was somehow significant."

"Thus the phrase you had me recite yesterday…'We'll have to take a rain check on our little date, my dear,' I presume."

"Yes, that's right. That phrase seemed to me connected to what happened that evening. And so I began to recite it to myself—chanting it like a mantra all day yesterday between chapters of this book I've been reading."

"Did that stimulate some memories?"

"Not at first—not that I could tell, anyway."

"Then what?"

"Apparently it wore down some emotional barriers that I was not aware of." Betty sipped her coffee. "Still a little hot, but good."

"Please continue," said Stephen a bit impatiently.

"The chanting had opened some doors for me. The first character to come through one of those doors was an unwelcome one for sure." Betty described the midnight incident with the man-beast in great detail.

"Sounds quite harrowing, my dear. But it was as the nurse said—a product of an overactive imagination. How does that shed any light on what happened on Friday?"

"I can't explain it, but I know the hallucination is connected, because it ushered in an epiphany."

"You used that term when you called me this morning. What do you mean by it?"

"Last night, before the nurse left, she gave me a sedative that was supposed to put me out beyond any nightmares. But what it did for me was to create a sort of cerebral vacuum where all the forgotten information flooded in to fill the void. Within the course of a few minutes, I'd regained total recall of the events of Friday evening. Voilà—an epiphany! And, when I woke up this morning, the forgotten material was still waiting at the surface for easy retrieval."

"Excellent!" Stephen boomed. "Because I've come prepared to preserve your every word as you recount your steps." He pulled a miniature tape recorder from his briefcase and placed it on the nightstand next to Betty's bed. "I hope you don't mind. My paralegal usually takes shorthand notes, but she seems to be indisposed right now."

"Not at all," said Betty, "but I'm going to back up and give you some background before I get to the actual incident, if that's okay."

"Take as long as you need. I brought extra tapes and batteries, just in case. And we've got until this evening before the tribal police darken your doorstep. Anyway, are you ready?"

Betty nodded as Stephen pressed the record button. "7:30 a.m., May 1, 1963," he said in his most professional voice. "Interviewing Betty Wood regarding the murder of Officer Eduardo Cruz." Stephen nodded to Betty.

Betty started her detailed account, beginning with Kenny's contributions to the story, through Cruz's encounter with the transformed devil-dog, Bingo, to the officer's intended meeting with the old Apache *brujo*, and on to the old man's brutal attack on her. Stephen let her narrate uninterrupted for nearly an hour until Betty's voice trailed off at the point in the story where she was bludgeoned and knocked unconscious.

"I don't suppose you have a name for this mysterious medicine man, do you?"

"Just a first name—Ezra."

"And a description?"

"It was dark, but I could see he was old. He had a craggy old wrinkled face and long silvery hair."

Stephen chuckled wryly. "Of course, you've described every old Indian on every reservation in Arizona."

"Maybe so, but Eduardo gave me the name of a seer who knows more about Ezra."

"A seer? What's his name?"

"Phillip Clah. He's a friend of Kenny's," she added. "And…one other thing: there is one unique identifying characteristic about Ezra."

"Which is?"

"He has only one arm. He carries the severed one with him. He clubbed me with it."

"That certainly narrows things down. Is there anything you would like to add?"

"No, I don't think so."

"End of interview, approximately 8:25 a.m."

"How was that?" Betty wondered aloud.

"It's an incredible story," said Stephen, shaking his head in wonder. "A little too supernatural for my personal liking, but just the thing for the reservation cops. They love this kind of mumbo jumbo. They'll eat it up with a spoon and then go snooping elsewhere. It couldn't be more perfect for our purposes."

"But it also happens to be the truth, Stephen."

"So much the better. They'll sense your conviction and, hence, your innocence. Just stick to this story, and I think we'll be home free."

"It will be nice to be believed," Betty muttered, a little peeved.

Stephen glanced at the book on Betty's overbed table. "So what's that you're reading that's so engrossing?"

"It's called *One Flew Over the Cuckoo's Nest*. It's by a new author named Ken Kesey."

"What's it about?"

"The inner sanctum of an insane asylum. Interestingly enough, one of the patients is an Indian."

"You know I'm much too busy to read an entire novel. Just tell me how it ends."

"The Indian escapes."

"Wow, that's certainly prescient!" Stephen exclaimed, missing Betty's attempted segue entirely.

"Why is that?"

"Harvey Huish has gone missing."

performances

Ray Cienfuegos muted the fading vibration of the final chord with his right palm, and, like the deadened strings, an eternal second of dead silence descended on the room. He *lived* inside of that second, wondering whether he had only dreamed that he was playing and singing before an audience of more than two hundred thirsty patrons that crowded into Freddy's cantina every Friday night. Where were the crude shouts at waitresses, the bawdy laughter, and pounding of beer mugs on tabletops that had prevailed at the beginning of his song? Had the crowd left, or was he really back in his attic room only practicing the Spanish-style guitar runs that punctuated the verses of "El Paso?"

In the next split second, a thunderous applause abruptly broke loose, a rolling wall of noise that nearly bowled Ray off the wooden barstool upon which he perched himself for his performances. He'd drawn some smattering applause at times for certain songs, but never such a deafening ovation. Overwhelmed by the apparent approval of the raucous crowd, a wide grin gradually stole across his features, as the boisterous acclaim continued to resound with a stamping of boot soles on wooden floorboards. Ray nodded politely to cowboy whoops as the dark lenses of his Ray-Bans glinted in the spotlight that Freddy had rigged for the performances.

"Thank you so much! I'm so glad you like that song as much as I do." Ray chuckled into the microphone as the din finally fell back to the usual level of cacophony. "Thanks to Marty Robbins for lending it to us tonight," he continued. "Now, *con sus permisos*, I think it's time to take a short break. You know, I get thirsty too?"

A feeble swell of smirking laughter rose and fell as the spotlight went dark, and Isabel rushed to her nephew's side to help stage his gear.

"Still wondering if the crowd here likes you, Raymie?" she hollered above the noise as she guided him by the arm to the bar. "I can tell you right now that there's a line at your tip glass." She was referring to the fishbowl snifter perched atop a small two-channel Fender amplifier. The oversized glass goblet was rapidly filling with a plethora of dollar-bill gratuities.

"I'll bet it's within five dollars of fifty again," said Ray.

"I'll bet you ten that it's at least seventy-five tonight," Isabel retorted.

"You're on, *Tía*," Ray laughed as they reached the bar where Freddy was already waiting with a frosty mug of cold beer.

"You knocked 'em dead with that last number, Ray," Freddy shouted as he guided the young man's grasping hand to the mug handle.

"They seemed to like it all right, but I think it was more the song choice than the performance," Ray observed between long draughts of the icy brew. "'El Paso' is the perfect song for this place and its mixed patronage."

"Oh, stop it, Raymie," Isabel broke in. "False modesty is unbecoming. You nailed that song, and you know it. I heard you practicing it for hours on end all week long. Freddy, tell him to cut the crap."

"It's like your *tía* says, Ray. You know you nailed it, so don't act so humble. It sounds a little bit phony, and that's just not you," said Freddy.

"All right, already," Ray replied. "I know when I'm outgunned, so let's just leave it at that."

"*Oye, joven,*" Freddy hissed in Ray's ear. "Heads up—you got a fan moving this way, and she's a real looker."

"Hello, Ray." The voice was pleasantly familiar. Ray turned his face toward the sound of it. The smell of cigarette smoke and liquor were suddenly eclipsed by the familiar fragrance of a certain cologne, and, despite his blindness, he recalled the strikingly alluring image of the dark-eyed beauty lingering before him.

"Hello, Rosa. Long time, *no see*," he replied, grinning.

Although he could not see her horrified expression, he sensed the uneasiness his quip had created by the silence that ensued.

Freddy turned away and spat a mouthful of beer onto the bar counter in a losing attempt to stifle a burst of laughter. Isabel aimed a glaring look that would have halted a runaway semi on a steep mountain grade—first at Freddy and then at Ray.

"Hello, Rosa," she said. "I think we met briefly once before," she added as she offered a friendly handshake. "Please, pay these two clowns no mind. Their juvenile sense of humor isn't meant to offend. It's just too silly for us sophisticated ladies to grasp."

"Good evening, señora," Rosa Moreno said, returning the gesture and sounding relieved. "It's always a pleasure."

"Hey, I'm sorry if that seemed rude," Ray offered. "Really, I just have a hard time passing up an opening for a good blind-man wisecrack. But, seriously, it's good to…uh…it's good to *hear* you, Rosa. Please, have a seat. Can I buy you a drink?"

"Sure, Ray. I'd like that," Rosa replied.

"Piña colada, right?" Ray countered.

"You remembered," she answered.

"Of course. I always teased you about your fruity rum drinks. Besides, it hasn't been all that long—just a couple of months, I think," Ray remarked.

"Seems longer, but I guess that's right."

"Manny!" Freddy shouted at a harried bartender. "Rustle up a nice piña colada for the young lady here. But, first, toss me a rag to wipe up this mess."

"*Aquí lo tienes!*" Manny returned as he threw a white dish towel to Freddy, who fielded it with a flourish.

"Please, miss, take my stool here," Freddy said to Rosa as he stepped behind the bar and began to sop up the expectorated beer. "Señora Cienfuegos and I were just about to adjourn to another room."

He turned toward Isabel, winked, and jerked his head toward the kitchen.

"I guess I'm being summoned." Isabel sighed as she eased herself off her stool. "It's good to see you again, Rosa. I hope to see more of you," she added, following Freddy's lead toward a pair of saloon doors that opened into the back of house.

"Likewise, señora," Rosa called out as the elder twosome withdrew.

"Man, those two are a real pair, aren't they?" Ray observed.

"I guess so; I mean, are they? A pair, that is," Rosa wondered aloud.

"Well, they seem to be hitting it off pretty good lately," Ray observed.

"He seems like a nice man, all right. It's just that…I don't know."

"No, please—speak your mind, Rosa. I'm curious about what you're thinking."

"I guess they just seem somehow mismatched," Rosa ventured.

"You mean like she's Sheena, Queen of the Jungle, and he's Mickey Rooney or something?" Ray quipped.

"No, not so much the physical differences, but there *is* something…something that I can't put my finger on," Rosa mused. "Just intuition, I guess."

"Hmm. I never dismiss a woman's intuition—not anymore, at least."

A thump at the bar counter signaled Ray that Rosa's cocktail was being served.

"Thanks, Manny. Keep my tab running, please.

"*Bueno, Ramón. Y otra cerveza?*"

"Sure, thanks. I've got time for another before the last set."

"Ray," said Rosa after taking several dainty sips of rum and pineapple juice through a pink straw, "you seem to have become something of a local celebrity in a short time."

"I'm not so sure I'd put it quite like that, but I will say that switching from my art to my music so quickly and smoothly probably saved my life. I owe this whole gig to Freddy. He opened a door for me when all others seemed to be slamming shut. After the blindness, he gave me a way to get busy with a form of expression that distracted me from my self-pity."

"You know, Ray, when I heard about what happened to you, I wanted to call," Rosa told him. "I even saw you a couple of times at church, but I was just at a loss as to what to say. I just couldn't get up the nerve to talk to you. I guess it took a couple of drinks tonight to finally give me the courage. Damnedest thing, though: I still really don't know what to say."

"Say about what, my blindness? There's really nothing to be said. People want to sympathize, but they really can't." Ray drained his mug.

"But it wasn't that I wanted to sympathize, Ray," Rosa broke in. "I just wanted—or *want*—to know why you suddenly stopped calling…stopped coming by. I mean, one week we were together for most of the day, every day, and the next, *nothing*. If it was something I said or did, then I think you at least owe me some explanation, don't you?"

Another bump at the bar top indicated the arrival of Ray's second beer.

"Thanks again, Manny," said Ray, grateful for the intrusion. "Hey, Manny, tell me, how much time have I got?"

"*Diez minutos, más o menos.*"

"*Muchas gracias,*" he returned before taking a long tug from the tall mug.

———————

"Those two are a pair if I ever saw one," Isabel remarked.

"Ray and that girl? I guess, if you say so," Freddy responded off-handedly.

"You don't know the whole story," Isabel continued. "They were quite an item a few months ago, but Ray got his usual case of cold feet and dropped her without a word as to why."

Freddy had guided Isabel to his private office and dining room off the kitchen, where the statuesque lady mixed them their customary Cuba Libras in a space removed from the din of the place and an atmosphere more conducive to conversation.

"Yeah, I gotta say when it comes to the ladies, that boy doesn't let any grass grow under his feet. Always movin' on to greener pastures," Freddy observed.

"Well, that was the old Ray. I can't wait to see how the new Ray responds to a young woman's feminine wiles."

"The *new Ray*?" You make it sound so sinister—like one of the victims from *Invasion of the Body Snatchers,* or something. By the way, this drink tastes a little *different,*" Freddy observed. "Did you change something?"

"Lemon instead of lime," Isabel answered, "and Pepsi instead of Coke," she added. "That's what you have behind the bar. It's okay, isn't it?"

"Sure—to be honest, I don't usually drink these things except with you, so I'm no judge on how they should taste. So, what's all this about the new Ray?"

"Surely you've noticed a change in him since the incident, haven't you?"

"Well, yes. Since you mention it, I have to say that his talent at the pool table has certainly gone downhill, and I doubt that I'll be taking him dove hunting any time soon. But other than that, no—he seems pretty much the same to me."

"You shouldn't joke, Alfredo," said Isabel coolly, fabricating some indignation.

"Please, he'd be the first one to laugh, and you know it. Besides, the outlook isn't as bleak as everyone seems to think. His condition is temporary, and he sees better every day. He's gone from full Ray Charles to Mister Magoo in just the past two weeks. I'll wager my entire hacienda on a full recovery inside of three months."

"I hope you're right. I just wish the doctors sounded as certain as you do."

"Ah, what the hell do doctors know, anyway? They're just a bunch of overeducated fortune-tellers, hedging their bets so you don't sue when it doesn't turn out like they said."

"My goodness! Where did that come from?"

"I'll tell you where. My own doctor, Dr. Mort, told me several years ago that if I didn't give up drinking, smoking, and eating spicy foods, I'd be dead within a year from bleeding stomach ulcers. I refused to give up any of those things, and, as you can see, I'm still very much alive and kickin'. Hell, if I'd listened to him, I would've hoped to die from a boring, dreary, and altogether miserable existence."

"Aha! So, now the truth comes out about the bland food here at the cantina. You're not catering to the *turistas* like you said. You're nursing a tender stomach."

"Isabel, does a day ever go by that you don't see me wolfing down one of your legendary brimstone breakfasts or lava lunches at La Cocina? Does that describe a man who's pampering his *estomago*?"

"*Pues entonces*, Freddy, maybe you should."

"What, and lose my excuse for feasting my unworthy eyes on your loveliness every day of the week? Not on your life. Besides," he continued, "I crave your food almost as much as I crave your constant company."

"Please." Isabel laughed in flattered embarrassment. "Why do I have the sneaking suspicion that this is leading up to another proposal?"

"No, I'm still healing from the last rejection. I won't do that again until the next time."

They both laughed heartily. Then Isabel muttered, almost inaudibly, "Don't give up yet."

"But listen," said Freddy in a more sober tone, "I do have a proposal of sorts that involves *El Tercero*.

"Oh, really?" said Isabel, shaking her dark tresses back behind her shoulders. "Well then, I'm all ears."

———◆———

"Listen, Rosa—I'm going to tell you something kind of personal—something that you might not understand and might not exactly like," Ray offered, sheepishly.

"Try me."

"Okay, it's like this: every now and then I get hooked on something—some idea about a project or plan—and everything else seems to fade into the background."

"And so?"

"I gotta tell you, when I get a notion, I really get obsessed, and when this happens, the thing I'm working on gets all my attention—I mean *all* of it."

"Really?"

"Yes, absolutely. Just ask my *tía*. She'll tell you—I can go for days without sleeping or eating or talking to anyone."

"Is that right?"

"Yeah…and see, that's what happened a couple of months ago. This sort of once-in-a-lifetime chance came along to create this huge metal art project, and right away that old tunnel vision I'm talking about just kinda kicked in. I must have gone at least a week without thinking about or doing anything else. I was totally absorbed in the initial work. When I finally realized an entire week had gotten behind me without calling you, I was too embarrassed to follow up. I put it off and put it off until I got fixated again. This just went on and on for over a month. You gotta understand—my art is a passion; it overwhelms me."

"I see. So you're saying that you got busy and just sort of forgot about me for weeks at a time? Not very flattering to me, Ray."

"That's not what I said."

"That's *exactly* what you said—you just wrapped it up in a little fancier package. But you can claim 'artistic passion' all day long, my friend. It's a really weak excuse, and I don't believe it for a minute."

"You don't?"

"Not a word of it. Face it, Ray, the fact is we were growing close—very seriously close. Too close, I think, for your comfort. I was becoming an important part of your life, and you got scared."

"Scared? Wow! Rosa, what's in that drink of yours, anyway? I'll have some of that!"

—◆—

"I said, I'm all ears," Isabel repeated, leaning in closer.

Freddy's eyes widened as the neckline on his date's peasant blouse scooped low enough to allow a clear shot at her generous bosom. "I'd have to disagree, my dear," he chuckled. "You're definitely not *all* ears, and I'm all too happy to say it!"

"You're a beast sometimes, Alfredo, I swear!" Isabel hissed in mock protest. She retracted a bit and pressed her hand to the drooping neckline, coyly. "But please, do tell me your idea."

"Well, I've been talking to this disc jockey friend of mine from Tucson who dabbles in the recording business on the side. Maybe you've heard of him—Dave Randall?"

"Sure, I have. I listen to that station whenever I can."

"Okay. Anyway, I was telling him about Ray and how his music has caught on up here, and he said he might be interested in doing some demo tapes. He's had a few records go regional, and he specializes in popular Tex-Mex types of performers, like Ray."

"That sounds encouraging," said Isabel.

"The best part is that Dave's in the audience tonight, and after that rousing ovation for Ray's rendition of 'El Paso,' I'd say he's a shoo-in for an audition."

"Really? That would be a great opportunity for Ray, even if it's just for the experience."

"I think so too," Freddy agreed. "You know, regional exposure like this is how Ritchie Valens and Buddy Holly got their start. With Ray's talent, who knows how far he could go? At the very least, he'll get some air play on Randall's radio show."

"So why are you proposing all of this to me and not to Ray?" Isabel wondered aloud.

"Are you kidding? I know better than to get the prince's hopes up before running it past the queen. The last thing I want to do is drive a wedge between my two favorite people."

"That's very considerate of you, Freddy."

"There's an element of self-interest here as well. I would want to manage Ray's business affairs—for the customary ten percent off the top, of course—that in exchange for some up-front investment on my part for promotion."

"Those details are for Ray's ears, but I'm all for it in principle, and I'm sure Ray will be more than grateful for your involvement. You've been so kind in getting him back on track."

"Speaking of which, it's almost time for him to get back on for the last set," Freddy commented, glancing at his watch. "Five more minutes."

"Just enough time to finish our drinks, Alfredo," said Isabel as she raised her glass. "*Salud!*" She leaned over the tiny table again and planted a quick kiss on Freddy's delighted lips.

"*La misma para ti,*" he returned, grinning. "That was a pleasant surprise."

"I don't know what came over me," Isabel giggled mischievously. "I guess I just got overwhelmed by your inescapable charm."

"Well, I'd say it's about time!"

"Don't get too smug, or that little peck will be your last."

"A warning duly noted." Freddy chuckled, raising his glass. "Now, let's drink up 'cause this crowd can get ugly without music." With that, he drained his cocktail in a couple of gulps. "By the way," he added, "have you heard about the escapee from Fort Grant?"

"No, what happened?"

"There was a fire that burned down one of the buildings a few nights ago, and now there are staff people missing. Damnedest thing, though—no bodies were found in the rubble. And just about the same time, a couple of the inmates slipped away."

"So what's the big deal? None of those kids are exactly dangerous criminals."

"One of them could be. He was in there for arson. The cops are tying him to the fire there at the fort. Once they find those bodies, he'll likely be facing a murder rap. They say to be on the lookout for him in this area. Colored kid, they say."

"I swear," Isabel muttered, "that place has got to be cursed."

———◆———

The buzz and murmur of the crowd filled an uncomfortable void in the conversation, with Ray finally breaking in. "I think it's probably time for me—"

"You've got five minutes," Rosa declared, interrupting. "I've been watching the time for you. So, where were we? Oh yeah, you were telling me that our budding romance just sort of slipped your mind for a couple of months."

"Actually, Rosa, I really did get pretty seriously distracted about that time."

"Well, maybe *conveniently* distracted."

"Jeez, you don't ever let up, do you? Sounds to me like you've already made up your mind about all the whys and wherefores. Makes me wonder why you even bothered to ask me about my take on it."

"I'm sorry, Ray," said Rosa, suddenly taking a softer tone. "I really have put you in a corner, haven't I? That wasn't my intention when I came here."

"This wasn't exactly a chance meeting, then?" Ray asked.

"Are you kidding? Do you really think I'd come to a dive like this by myself if I didn't have a purpose in mind?"

"And that purpose was…or, *is*?"

"I really don't know at this point. Now, I wonder." Rosa muttered.

"You're confusing me. Wonder what?"

"I'm not sure now. I just wonder."

"I really do have get back up there to perform now. Would you do me the courtesy of guiding me up to my perch? I seem to have lost my seeing-eye aunt."

"Sure, I'd be happy to. What do I do?"

"Just give me your arm and walk me slowly over to my stool," Ray instructed.

"Like this?"

"Yes, thanks."

The pair strolled arm-in-arm slowly toward the front of the room, halting and sidestepping oblivious patrons, making their way to the makeshift bandstand consisting of a solitary barstool and the afore-mentioned miniature amplifier flanked on either side by an open guitar case—one yielding a nylon-stringed classical and the other a steel-stringed folk guitar.

"Put my hand on the stool when we get close enough—that's it, thanks." He seated himself in the semidarkness. "Now, if you don't mind, could you hand me my guitar?"

"Sure, which one?"

"The classical—the one on the right with the nylon strings. I'm going to try something new."

"What do you mean—you're going to do something you haven't practiced?"

"Sure—it's an easy progression, I know all the lyrics, and it lends itself to some improvisation. Besides, it's a beautiful song."

"Why would you go out on a limb like that—why not stick to what you practiced?"

"Because I want to do something on impulse—something inspired by you."

"By me—but why...?"

"To get you to stick around through my last set, so maybe we could have another drink together?"

"You could have just asked."

"I think I just did. Please, now, just adjust the mikes—one up near the guitar strings and one mouth level to me. That's it. Now, flip the toggle switch on the amp and take a chair just outside the spotlight," Ray instructed.

Rosa did as directed. Ray purposely tapped each microphone to ensure that they were both live, then started to tap out a sweet bossa-nova rhythm with his fingers on the polished face of the guitar. The accented beats rang out from the hollow wooden body like a primitive drum and continued to reverberate for nearly a minute as the room quieted. When Ray added the chords for the intro—a familiar D-A-G-A Latin fill—the spotlight spewed its brilliance on his grinning face as if on cue, and Ray delivered the well-known first lines of "A Rose in Spanish Harlem" in a clear, sotto-voce tenor.

A murmur of approval for the Ben E. King selection swelled among the crowd. Ray had them right there, and her as well, he thought. Then, taking some artistic license, he plunged headlong into an extended instrumental break instead of the next verse—an improvised medley of classical riffs and flamenco flourishes that strained the limits of the simple progression but, nonetheless, teased spontaneous applause from the somewhat less than musically sophisticated throng. Taking another chance, he skipped repeating the initial lines and went directly from the break into the vocal bridge.

He repeated the last two lines a cappella, intoning sweetly as he imagined Rosa's comely face. The closing "la-la-las" with accompaniment were drowned out by a thunder of premature applause. Ray unstrapped his classical guitar and raised it aloft as if presenting it before the applauding crowd for its own share of the acclaim. But Isabel, having reentered the room, recognized it as his signal for assistance in switching instruments. She hesitated briefly as the ovation died away but, when Rosa failed to come forward, she strode across the room and wrested the guitar from her nephew.

"I've got it," Isabel assured him, making certain he recognized it was her.

"Where's Rosa?" Ray demanded.

"I'm not seeing her, *mijo*. Maybe she went to the ladies' room. Anyway, you want the folk guitar now, right?"

"Yes, please, *Tía*. And please turn up channel two a notch on my amp."

Isabel turned to comply and froze at what she saw there. She whirled and beckoned Freddy over who was at her side in a flash. Wordlessly, she motioned toward the miniature amplifier. There, atop that black box, in place of the fishbowl snifter was an upturned fedora—a familiar white fedora filled with the night's tips.

"Hey, what's with the hat?" shouted Freddy. "And what happened to my snifter?"

"You don't get it, Freddy," said Isabel, visibly shaken. "That's Ezra's hat."

"But I just—"

"But *nothing*. Ray and I need to clear out of here—*right now*!"

Friendly Persuasion

Stephen Robson waited just inside the threshold of Betty's hospital room until he heard the swishing sound of the elevator doors closing, then he peeked out into the corridor.

"All clear!" he announced before he resumed his place in the visitor's chair at Betty's bedside. "I'm very pleased at the way that all went, Betty. By God, those tribal cops nodded at your every word like you were reading straight out of the Gospel."

Betty frowned and plucked the nasal cannula from her nostrils. "Thank God I can get rid of this. I'm sure it looks hideous," she whined.

"Better to look sympathetic under these circumstances," Stephen observed. "But you said all the right things to divert their suspicion away from yourself and on to some old Apache witch doctor—that's the main thing."

"I guess the big question is whether the Feds will buy all that *mumbo jumbo,* as you call it, once they get involved."

"Oh, that whole mysterious medicine-man tale won't make it outside a small circle at the core of the tribe," Stephen said.

"It won't?"

"No, the official story is that Officer Cruz's death was accidental—that he stopped to help a stranded motorist, there was an engine fire, and the cop died from the extensive third-degree burns he sustained there. No one outside the tribe will pay the incident any mind."

"Then the tribal police won't pick up on Eduardo's investigation and pursue it?"

"Officer Cruz was well-liked among his colleagues. My sense is that his friends will follow up on what he uncovered."

"And what about Kenny Armenta?"

"What about him?" Stephen shot back coolly.

"After everything that Eduardo did—gave up his life trying to exonerate him—are they still going to let him rot in that godforsaken dungeon they call an asylum?"

"As we should expect," Stephen responded in a low voice, "the tribal council is deeply concerned about its public image. Consider what we have here, Betty: an Apache medicine man who converts docile pets into murderous beasts through black magic, burns tribal cops alive, and beats women half to death using his own severed arm as a club. If the press ever got wind of this, they'd have a field day with it. Every Indian in the state might just as well have 'savage' stamped on his forehead. No, with regard to the Kenny Armenta affair, the tribal elders would just as soon let sleeping dogs lie—no pun intended."

"You haven't seen the conditions that the old guy lives under in that place. They're downright medieval. They dole out electroshock therapy like it's baby aspirin." After a moment of silence, Betty switched to a more upbeat tone. "Listen, Stephen, I've been in contact with the administrator at Squaw Peak Psychiatric Retreat up in Paradise Valley. You recall that I did some research on them as an alternative to incarceration for Harvey a few years ago?" Betty said.

"I do—but what does this have to do with the issue at hand?" Stephen retorted impatiently.

"Yes, well, back then they weren't too interested in taking in a homicidal teenager. But in my recent talks with them, they say that they've had good success with treating patients in catatonic states. Kenny would be a good candidate for therapy there. I thought that since it's obviously true that Kenny had nothing to do with Primrose's murder, the tribe might be inclined to move him to a more humane facility."

"The tribe's position is this: Kenny is just this side of comatose—you said it yourself. He is not aware of his surroundings or his treatment. The tribal elders see no sense in incurring cost for someone who won't know the benefit. Can't say that I blame them for taking that position."

"But, Stephen, you have a great deal of influence over the way the council perceives things. Could you convince them to quietly move

Kenny to a better place? Surely they have the resources to provide for one of their own."

"You're right about the tribal elders trusting my judgment. That comes from years of cultivating that trust—by offering them advice that is sound in logic and fruitful in result. I am very careful about how I counsel them. I aim to continue to maintain that trust. Why would I now suggest they take a step that is neither logical nor fruitful—one that might even draw attention to a sensitive issue?"

Betty wanted to say *because it's the right and honorable thing to do,* but instead she said, "Because I've never asked you for a favor, but I'm asking for one now. Because Will Farnsworth and Eduardo Cruz would have wanted you to."

Stephen took advantage of a long silence to change the subject.

"You haven't asked about the strange disappearance of our own devil's disciple, Harvey Huish."

Betty sighed. "Didn't occur to me. What's to report?"

"Nothing conclusive. I suspect that Pinky provided some avenue of escape when our efforts to get Harvey off perished along with Will. Damnedest thing, though—Pinky usually confides in me when he goes rogue. This time, he swears up and down that Harvey's actually gone missing. I don't quite know how to read this, but I've got a couple of detectives working on the boy's whereabouts. I just hope he turns up soon. He's been a source of steady income for us."

"Yes, and he cost us two good lawyers," Betty observed.

"Harvey had nothing to do with those unfortunate fatalities," Stephen retorted.

"Maybe not directly, but they both died under mysterious circumstances—and now Eduardo Cruz—"

"What does Cruz have to do with Harvey Huish?" Stephen broke in, clearly annoyed.

"I don't know, but Cruz was convinced that Kenny's situation and Will's death were somehow linked."

"What kind of evidence did he have to support such a stretch?" Stephen asked.

"Nothing substantial that I know of, I admit. But Will *was* working on Kenny's case when he was killed. And Eduardo was so absolutely certain the cases were related. He said there is a standing Apache curse on Fort Grant. And, after all, the old shaman, Ezra, is an Apache," Betty's voice was becoming ever more emphatic.

"All superstition," Stephen grunted. "Will's death was an accident. It sounds to me like Officer Cruz was just playing on your sympathies to enlist your aid."

"Maybe so," Betty muttered. "Returning to Kenny Armenta, will you please just consider the favor I asked—just maybe think about it?"

"Listen, Betty, I'm well aware that the state hospital is no country club. But it makes no sense at all to waste resources on a cushy facility for somebody who isn't even aware of his own existence."

"So you're saying if that weren't the case, you'd consider my request?" Betty pressed.

"If, by some miracle, the old boy suddenly became sentient, I'd foot the bill for that upscale clinic myself."

"That's more than I could ask."

"No, actually, it's a pretty safe bet. That's because I happen to know that Kenny Armenta operates on about the same cognitive level as a turnip. That comes from an unimpeachable source."

"Who's that?" Betty asked.

"You."

Out Through the Back Door

"There's certainly no need to panic," said Freddy confidently. "There are plenty of folks around here who wear white fedoras. They're still pretty popular with the old fossils."

"This is no time to question it, Alfredo." Isabel was adamant. "Ezra is here somewhere, and that hat is his calling card. Here, take Ray's guitar."

"What's going on?" Ray demanded, having heard only the hushed urgency in Isabel's voice, muted by the rattle and rumble of the crowd.

"I'm sorry, Raymie, but we've got to clear out of here in a hurry. Just take my arm and leave your stuff. Freddy will pack it up for you."

"But what about Rosa?"

"You can call her tomorrow. Right now, you are in danger in this place."

"Isabel, you don't have to leave. I can protect you right here," Freddy insisted.

"Not with a pistol, you can't," Isabel returned, latching on to Ray's arm and pulling him from the stool. "You both need to trust my judgment here."

"If you won't stay, I'll come with you," offered Freddy.

"No, you stay here and make excuses to your patrons. The last thing we want is an angry audience. Take Raymie's tips and buy a round for the house," she called over her shoulder as she led a compliant Ray toward the kitchen. "Manny, watch our backs—*hay peligro aquí!*" she shouted to the puzzled bartender as they breezed past him.

The pair raced arm-in-arm through the kitchen, past gaping cooks and staring waitresses. Bursting out through double delivery doors onto the rear dock, Isabel halted to take stock of the gravel parking lot and the last hundred feet of their path to her car. She scanned the darkened lot with narrowed eyes. There were the usual few shadows of patrons hanging out in the lot—couples necking and scavengers searching for an unlocked car door. She could perceive nothing out of the ordinary—no F-100 pickup, and no menacing devil-dog.

"Okay, *mijo*," she breathed in hushed tones, "we're about fifteen seconds away from the car if we walk really fast. Hold tight to my arm, and I'll guide your hand to the passenger-side door handle when we get there. I'll let you in first. Then, you lock the door behind you while I step over to the driver's side. Sound like a plan?"

"I'm ready, *Tía*. Let's go for it."

With arms firmly locked together, aunt and nephew strode briskly across the gravel lot, closing the distance without incident. But a strong feeling of foreboding persisted as Isabel keyed the passenger door lock.

"Get in and lock the door," she barked as she strode quickly to the driver's side and popped inside.

As expected, the engine turned over on the first crank. Isabel switched on the headlights, spun out of her parking spot, and tore across the lot, peppering cars with salvos of gravel from slipping rear wheels as she headed for the exit driveway that emptied onto an adjacent side road.

Braking in an adjoining vacant lot, Isabel saw that a pair of suspicious headlights was moving slowly through the lot toward them.

"Hold tight, Raymie. I think we've got ourselves an unwanted tagalong."

She shifted into first, gunned the motor, and released the clutch, lurching and fishtailing headlong over clumps of creosote and tumbleweed, aiming the bouncing Beetle toward the main highway that fronted Freddy's establishment. Reaching that landmark, she jumped the curb, narrowly missing a semipickled pedestrian, and jerked the steering wheel to the left, raising the tiny car up onto two wheels briefly. It swerved dangerously, its right-side tires whining as the left-side pair slammed back down onto the blacktop.

"Holy shit, *Tía*," Ray shouted. "I mean it. If you don't ease up a little, we're going to have to make this getaway on foot! You're lucky I welded a skid plate to the bottom of this thing, or you'd be spewing an oil slick from here to eternity. I mean, you're really lucky."

Isabel ran up through the gears, glancing nervously in the mirror for headlights in pursuit.

"If I were *lucky*," she retorted, "I would, right now, be comfortably perched on a barstool sipping on a crystal flute filled with expensive champagne at the Whisky a Go Go, checkin' out the Johnny Rivers show. Instead, I'm stretching the blacktop between us and some blood-thirsty devil-dog bent on our death—me, unarmed, equipped with a feeble four-cylinder Volkswagen turtle, accompanied by a whiny nephew who happens to be blind as a bat. Good thing I don't rely much on luck. I might be rather dismayed at this point."

"Sorry, *Tía*. What can I do?" Ray asked.

"Well, you can pray to our Lord, Jesus, and all the saints in heaven that the headlights that I'm seeing about a hundred yards back aren't following us, and that they aren't Ezra, because his intentions for us are not the best, and the only thing that even seems to slow him down is a shotgun, something that I'm not packing right now—a serious oversight on my part, I admit."

"Okay. I've got that covered."

In fourth gear, a slow crescendo of momentum and pitch from the engine began to build. Forty-five. Fifty-five. Sixty-five. Approaching seventy, the build leveled off. On a level grade, it was the best speed that could be coaxed from the straining four-banger. At seventy miles per hour, it was another six minutes to La Cocina. Ray was silent.

"Raymie, you okay over there?" Isabel asked.

"Praying," he returned.

"Okay, good."

Gazing in the rearview, Isabel noted that the pair of headlights that had been some distance behind was gaining on them rapidly. As the lights drew within fifty feet, the acceleration dropped off. Isabel deliberately slowed to sixty, and the pursuing vehicle did likewise. She sped up, and so did the harrier, always maintaining a fifty-foot buffer and exhibiting no intention of passing.

"Well," Isabel said, "I hate to be the bearer of bad news, but it looks as if the first part of our prayer didn't quite make it upstairs in time. We are definitely being followed."

"How can you tell?"

"The headlights behind us are sticking to us like a goddamn tick."

"Headlights?" Ray turned around and faced the rear window. "Headlights are something I actually can *see*." He studied the two glowing orbs for a minute. "I think maybe our entire prayer wasn't ignored. Those headlights don't belong to Ezra's pickup—no way."

"How can *you* tell?"

"They're set too far apart and too low—that and they don't bounce with the bumps in the road, so it's not a truck suspension. Those lights belong to a good-sized, wide-bodied vehicle, probably a smooth-riding luxury car."

"Then maybe it's Freddy in his Imperial," said Isabel hopefully.

"That would be my guess," Ray returned, "although it could just as easily be a Lincoln."

"Now, he's flashing his high beams on and off."

"A sure sign that it's a friend," Ray stated confidently. "Maybe he wants us to pull over."

"There's no way that's happening in this lifetime. Not at least until we get to La Cocina, anyway. We're just speculating that it's Freddy. Just tell me this," Isabel continued, "is there any obvious difference between the headlights of a Chrysler Imperial and a Lincoln Continental?"

"I guess if you look hard when they flash the high beams, one will look like it has eyebrows, and the other will look like it has side blinders on."

"Which is which?" Isabel wondered aloud.

"The Imperial has the eyebrows."

"Oh."

"*Oh?* What is this *oh?* Are you gonna keep a blind man in the dark?"

"The car behind us doesn't seem to have any eyebrows."

"So who is our mystery tagalong—our *likely* tagalong, that is?" Ray asked.

"I don't have to cast my memory back too far to recall the last time a black Lincoln Continental pulled into my lot. And as I recall, you were riding in it."

"Hoo-*hoo*!" Ray hooted. "I believe you're onto something there, *Tía*. You think it's the headless hero, don't you?"

"We'll soon find out. La Cocina's parking lot is about thirty seconds ahead. But I'm less certain about my conscious conclusions than I am about my premonitions. So, let's follow a plan that assumes we're being dogged by the enemy," Isabel suggested.

"Sounds reasonable."

"Then take this key to the front door. I'll pull in and up to the porch with the passenger side facing the entrance. If you can, get out, get up the steps, find the door by yourself, and get it unlocked. That would be twice as quick as me getting out first and guiding you there. Do you think you can do that?"

"Are the porch lights turned on?" He knew well the twin coach lights situated on either side of the entrance door; he had fashioned and installed the black iron fixtures himself.

"Like always."

"Then, hell yes. I can get the front door open PDQ."

"Good. Then I'll follow right behind. Just give me a clear path to my shotgun in the kitchen, and we're home free. I've got that thunderstick loaded to the gills with buckshot, and if our tagalong happens to be Ezra after all, I'll blow his sorry head clear off of his shoulders."

"Calm down a little there, Annie Oakley. We're still pretty sure it's *el Jinete sin Cabeza* back there, so don't get too trigger happy."

The tenor hum of the highway gradually fell to a baritone as the little car decelerated. A sudden right-hand swerve and the familiar crunch of gravel under the tires told Ray that they were seconds from the front porch. His hand was already on the door handle when the Beetle skidded to a stop at the steps. He burst from the door and bounded up toward the dual carriage lights that defined the margins of the doorway.

Isabel stepped casually from the ladybug car as the funereal black Lincoln pulled alongside. She closed her eyes coolly as the slipstream of dust from both automobiles breezed past. The whir of a motorized window teased her into opening them again. It was a rear passenger-side window that was lowering eerily. The sweet sound of Mel Tormé's silken voice issued from the front compartment in soft tones. She could see Ray's image hesitating at the open door to the café reflected in the raised front window of the immaculate luxury car.

"Excuse me, ma'am," a scratchy adolescent voice hailed from the darkened rear compartment, "but you don't happen to have a glass of water to spare now, do you?"

"Pardon me?" Isabel gasped, suddenly awestruck.

"A tall glass of ice-cold water would do me just fine right now," the voice repeated its raspy request. "In fact, a whole pitcher would be even better."

"Who is asking?" Isabel demanded, approaching the open window and peering in. A pair of ebony eyes shone from within.

"Just a poor desert survivor who's dryer than a popcorn fart in a dust storm, ma'am. I already drank a canal nearly dry, and I'm still about as parched as a peanut butter sandwich." Though the wit was quick and confident, the words came slow and trembling. "Maybe a damn *barrel* of water and a really long straw would be best of all."

Isabel hesitated for a brief second.

"*Tía!*" Ray was somehow at her side. "What was the first thing I asked for when the headless driver brought *me* here?"

"Of course I remember, Raymie. It was for water."

"Then why do you hesitate now? How is this any different?"

"Only because I sense that this is some kind of momentous episode, a turning point in our lives. It gives me pause."

"I can only guess what that means, but I do know that we have one here who thirsts and asks us for water. Shall we discuss the meaning of his coming while he suffers?"

"No, of course not. I just…never mind—you're right. Stay here while I bring some water."

"Good, but let's not get too distracted, eh?"

"Huh?"

"Ezra is still out there somewhere. Did you forget the shotgun?"

"Not for a heartbeat."

The instant that she disappeared inside, Ray heard the driver's door clack and the gravelly sound of footfalls crunching back to the rear of the idling vehicle, around the trunk, and then coming up on the passenger side. The ghostly footfalls halted right next to Ray. Though he could not see the fearful apparition that stood before him, he sensed the terrible yet pitiable image that the specter presented.

"*El jinete*," Ray addressed the phantom knight, trembling, "I want to thank you for saving my life. You are the enemy of my enemy, and so we are allies in this way. I ask you, is there any courtesy that I can extend to you, my friend?"

A brief silence was broken by the clack of the rear door latch. There was a slight squeak as the rear-hinged door swung open.

"I think he wants you to get out here, young man," said Ray.

The boy, stricken dumb at the first unobstructed sight of his ghostly rescuer, managed to squeak out a voice, and it was a simple excuse for his reluctance: "I…I'm scared shitless of him!"

With that, the driver backstepped a few paces to the rear of the car. Ray extended his hand at the open door.

"He won't harm you. Pay no attention to his appearance. You'll never meet a kinder soul than this one," Ray assured.

The boy grasped the offered hand, emerged timidly from the back seat, and scrambled to Ray's back side, cowering behind him as Ray slammed the "suicide door" shut. Isabel suddenly appeared on the porch with a tumbler of ice water and a shotgun, watching in wonder as the spectral knight returned to the driver's-side door.

The young colored boy seized the water glass from Isabel's hand and began to guzzle. Ray raised his hand and waved, almost as if he could see the phantom driver pause before entering his car.

"We're forever in your debt," he called out.

The apparition bowed at the waist as he had once before, mounted his motorized steed, and sped off into the middle of the night.

"Out of the frying pan and into the fire," Isabel muttered. "Wait a minute. I almost forgot: we're not even out of the damn frying pan yet—not by a long shot."

"What do you mean by that?" Ray demanded.

"More water, please." The boy gasped.

"Let's all just get inside before somebody sees us," said Isabel.

"What's the problem, *Tía?*"

"Sorry, but sometimes I forget that you can't see, *mijo*," she returned, herding them both in through the open door. "The problem is that this little *huérfano* that Sir Headlessness left on our doorstep is an escapee from Fort Grant—wanted in three counties for arson and possibly murder."

"How do you know that?" Ray asked.

"Because he's a Negro, for God's sake, and the fugitive is a Negro boy about sixteen years of age. Not too many boys fitting that description running around Oracle Mesa."

"Just like Marcus always said," the boy muttered almost inaudibly. "Bad news rides a fast horse."

Ray whistled a low falling note. "*Dios mío*…that *is* an unexpected twist."

Once inside, Isabel turned to the boy. "So, just who *are* you, young man?"

"My name is Curtis Jefferson, and the truth is that I am the boy on the run from Fort Grant," he said.

"Well, Curtis Jefferson, what do you have to say for yourself?" Isabel demanded.

"Three things, ma'am," said Curtis.

"And they are?" Isabel asked.

"First, I never started no fire, and neither did I kill nobody. I went over the wall because there *was* a fire, and I knew the fuzz'd try to hang the rap on me. I may be a fugitive, but I'm completely innocent—kinda like Richard Kimball. Second, I have to say, ma'am—and don't take this wrong—you have to be the most beautiful woman that I have ever laid eyes on. I think you must be an angel of mercy," Curtis confessed.

"And third?" Isabel demanded coolly.

"Third, I'm still thirsty. Could I please have another glass of water?" he begged.

"Of course you can." Isabel handed the shotgun to Ray, took the glass of half-melted ice, refilled it from the kitchen sink, and returned it to the boy's hand.

"Now, tell me something, Curtis Jefferson: if the authorities caught up with you, could you tell them who started the fire?" Isabel asked.

"No, ma'am, I could not."

"Why not—don't you know who it was?"

"Yes, ma'am, I do."

"Then unless it was the one-armed man or Lieutenant Gerard, why couldn't you just tell them the truth?" Isabel entreated.

"Because the truth is even less believable than the one-armed man story; the one who started the fire has been dead for almost a hundred years!" he blurted between gulps of water.

"Sounds to me like Curtis Jefferson fits right in with this little family," Ray chuckled.

"Maybe so, but he can't stay here, Ray," Isabel returned sternly.

"But Sir Headlessness left him here in our care, *Tía*. We owe it to him to take Curtis in."

"It's okay, folks," said Curtis. "The water is all I ask for. I don't want to bring no trouble to you people. I know I'm in deep doo-doo. I can be on my way…"

"Listen to me, both of you. I didn't say we would turn you away, Curtis. I only said we can't keep you *here*. This is a café; there's too much traffic in and out of here. Someone would be bound to catch a glimpse of you, and that's all it would take. The police would be swarming all over this place," Isabel reasoned.

"Then what do you have in mind, *Tía?*" Ray pressed.

"We'll take him out to Hayseed Heights," she resolved.

"When?" Ray wondered.

"Now, right away. I'll call Freddy and tell him not to come, that everything's okay."

"That's perfect, *Tía*. I need to get back out there, anyway. Everything's going to hell without me there."

"Now, hold everything, folks," Curtis interrupted. "Do I get a say in this? I mean, what the hell is *Hayseed Heights*, anyway? Sounds like an Arizona version of Mayberry."

"You explain, *mijo*, while I make the call and pack up some food. But make it the abbreviated version. The cops may be checking on places around here as we speak."

"Okay, *Tía*. Now, listen, Curtis, Hayseed Heights is my home off the beaten path—just a little adobe shack, but there are no neighbors for miles in any direction and no traffic on my stretch of road. I'm not living there right now because I've temporarily lost my sight, and I need help getting around, so I live here with my aunt for now. But, anyway, Hayseed Heights is the perfect place to tuck you away out of sight until all of this shit blows over. Any questions?"

"Only one: how come you two just assume I'm telling the truth so easily—that I'm innocent, I mean?" Curtis inquired.

"Because the headless one brought you here, and, from what I can tell, he knows good from evil and performs only acts that are good and just," Ray stated.

"But he sure *looks* like a sinister character, I tell you no lie," Curtis observed.

"Maybe so, but you should look at his deeds, not his appearance. After all, he rescued you from the desert and brought you to us for refuge. He saved me, too, when I had my incident. He gave me this to remember him by." Ray pulled on his necklace chain and popped out the Saint Thomas More medal that his rescuer had bestowed upon him.

"Look here, no offense, but if you're as blind as you say you are, then you haven't really seen him face-to-no-face, so it's pretty easy for you to ignore his appearance. He may *act* like Dudley Do-Right, but he *looks* twice as spooky as the Headless Horseman of Sleepy Hollow, I'm here to tell ya," Curtis said.

"The Lord works His wonders in mysterious ways, young man," Isabel broke in as she returned with two large grocery bags. "And it's hardly beyond His power to animate a cadaver with the purified spirit of goodness from his former life. But I confess that I do often wonder about that former life, and who our headless friend was, and what his whole story is. All we know is that he seems to be a big Mel Tormé fan." Isabel sighed.

"I might be able to help you with a couple more clues on him, ma'am," Curtis offered.

"How so?" Isabel asked.

Curtis held up a small, white rectangular piece of poster board containing some script. "Because I've got his business card!" he exclaimed.

"Here, let me see that, son," Isabel demanded. She scrutinized the card closely, narrowing her dark eyes as she read. "I'll be damned," she muttered.

"It was just lying there on the floor board, so I picked it up," Curtis explained.

"We'll have to look into this when the present storm passes," she said, more thinking aloud than speaking. "Surely he must have family. They need to know that Will Farnsworth is a hero."

"Amen to that; he saved my life," said Ray.

"Mine too," Curtis added.

"All right, enough of the chatter," Isabel barked. "We need to get moving. Let's get in the car." She turned to Ray as she cranked the little engine to life. "Raymie, when was the last time we fed those hogs of yours?"

"I think it's been a couple of days since they would have run out. Good thing we're headed out there. They must be half starved."

"*Mijo*, listen to me. Don't feed them," Isabel directed as they rolled back onto the highway.

"What? Why?"

"Never mind, just do as I say. I want them hungry."

"Okay," Ray sighed. "At this point, I know better than to argue."

With a Kiss

"Who's there?" Freddy Hightower called downstairs to an empty and darkened barroom, a stark contrast to the revelry of only just a couple hours earlier.

He had stayed late to help close up and decided to settle into his loft apartment above the cantina as he often did after long hours at the tavern instead of driving the ten miles to his ranch house in the valley. He'd long since locked all the doors and turned out the lights, and had been lying awake atop a damp sheet, contemplating his circumstances and fighting down a churning stomach for a good half hour before the muffled groan of a loose floor joist issued up from behind the bar and rousted him from his restless reverie. There was no answer, save yet another whine from another aging timber.

"Is that you, Manny?" Freddy shouted into the black emptiness from his perch on the stair landing. "Hell, I thought you left an hour ago."

Still, there was no response. With a bubble of blood and digestive acid building in the pit of his stomach, Freddy stepped backward through the doorway to his room. He flicked the wall switch for the overhead light that blazed forth and illuminated the room. The revolver he kept waiting on the nightstand glinted and winked at his approach. The cold steel weight of it in his grasp lent him the reassurance he needed. He returned to the landing and noted that the light from his upstairs apartment added only a faint, lambent blush to the spaces below—just enough, though, to light his way down the stairs. Barefoot, he padded along the familiar route to the bar counter, clad only in a pair of boxer shorts. He settled onto a stool as the shadowy figure behind the bar filled two half-barrel shaped glasses with ice and bourbon.

"That didn't take near as long as I expected," Freddy croaked as the surreal figure slammed the two glasses down on the bar top. "Everything go as planned?"

"It took *forever*, and, no, it went badly or, I should say, not at all. They weren't there. I waited in the dark for them for a fucking hour." The voice was low and measured, but the anger came through notwithstanding. "Not a living soul within or without."

"You went inside, didn't you?" Freddy asked.

"Of course I did. I found that casement window in back—the one that you left open for me."

"That makes no sense," Freddy sputtered. "I spoke with her five minutes before you left here. They were locking up and turning in. It should have been a pretty soft target."

"Nevertheless, the place was about as empty as Christ's tomb, if you still believe any of that nonsense. You know, that woman is pretty bright for a Mexican. You don't suppose she's on to you, do you?"

"Not a chance. Ever since our little performance when I rescued her from your hairy clutches, I've been her knight in shining armor. Now, I'm practically part of the family. She even gave me a nice little kiss tonight."

"I should think you'd be getting something more than that by now."

"You gotta be delicate about these things. Can't go charging in like a bull in a china shop. Besides, if I get a yearning for some paid pussy, Tucson's less than an hour drive. Anyway, I've got her eating out of my hand, for Christ's sake. She doesn't suspect a thing," Freddy stated with certainty.

"Then, maybe you got a sudden case of remorse and tipped them off, eh?" the mystery guest suggested.

Freddy reached over and took the glass closest to his visitor. He hefted the drink in his left hand and continued to grasp the revolver in his right, forefinger tapping the trigger ring nervously.

Ezra chuckled wryly. "Still don't believe that I have no interest in killing you, do you little man?"

"I trust you about as far as I can throw you," Freddy retorted, tossing back the cold bourbon. "You've got the heart of a pit viper, *viejo*."

"No need to trust me, just use your common sense. You're the last dying leaf on your miserable family tree, and, judging from your last marriage, there's no threat of you procreating, even if you were so inclined," Ezra mused. "Much like that swindler down in Catalina. His line died with his son. I won't bother with him either. Besides, you're of vital use to me alive, my friend."

"Only until the kid is dead, then what use am I, *my friend*?" Freddy wondered aloud.

"As I've told you many times, I will let you use the woman for your pleasure for a while, but then she must pay for the injury she's done me," Ezra reaffirmed.

"Oh yeah—from what I hear, you'll be squatting to pee for the rest of your years, however many that is."

"You would be amazed at my powers of regeneration, little man—especially for the restoration of such a vital appendage for such dark purposes. And, speaking of which, you do realize that I'll have my turn with her exquisite body at least once before we dispose of her, don't you? I hope you're pretty well resigned to that. I'd hate to have her come between us, my friend."

"Why don't you just let us both live out our days, old man? She's beyond the childbearing years. She's no threat to your mission to extinguish the Cienfuegos line."

"No, her disrespect will not go unanswered. You wonder what use you will be to me once the boy is disposed of. You will be instrumental in her slow demise. I'll delight in your performance as the attentive husband, as short-lived as that will be. But, mark my words, you will tire of her in less than a year. All of her allure is contained in that myth that she is unattainable. Once that facade is dispensed with, you'll find yourself muttering the word *bitch* more often than not—just as you did with your dearly departed former spouse. As for you, I'm content to watch you burn a hole in your bleeding stomach with liquor and green chili. You'll be worms' meat before long without my intervention."

"That's such a comfort," Freddy remarked.

"I'm content with the natural progression of things as far as you're concerned…that is, unless you were to betray me."

"Why would I go along with things this far and then tip them off? That just doesn't make sense. Besides, you know I want to be rid of the kid as much as you do. As long as she has him around to dote on, I'd be forever playing second fiddle. That's not the kind of arrangement I've got in mind. But, once he's gone, I'll choke up and commiserate with her about 'our tragic loss,' and I'll be her 'trusted ally' in her unattainable quest to avenge the boy's death. She'll be putty in my hands."

"But back to the present situation: how do you explain their absence?" Ezra demanded.

"I really don't know, but that little gag you pulled tonight with the hat sure made them skittish. Maybe something else spooked them, and they just bolted."

"I suppose that's possible. Or maybe she discovered your tampering."

"Very doubtful. She was all loaded for bear. There'd be no reason for her to check her gun again. Why would she?"

"I don't guess she would. But their absence is still troubling me."

"For Christ's sake, these things happen. Maybe they got a middle-of-the-night craving for sherbet and drove down to the ice cream parlor in Oro Valley. How the hell should I know?"

"You *should* know. That's your first responsibility in this arrangement—to keep me apprised of their whereabouts," Ezra instructed. "For your information, the ice cream parlor closes at midnight. I get middle-of-the-night cravings as well."

Freddy bristled. "Freshen up my goddamn glass and hand me the fucking phone from under the bar. We'll get this straightened out right the fuck now!" His hand left the gun to dial the phone. "By the way, you're a shitty bartender, you miserable old gut eater," he hissed.

"You try tending bar with one arm and see how you do!" Ezra sneered.

"And what's up with that? Can't you *reconnect*, or something?"

"Yes, but I've come to find that this temporary separation has its advantages. I can reach a great many more things than before, and it makes a formidable bludgeon," Ezra boasted.

"Shhh!" Freddy admonished. "It's ringing."

"You see? They're not there," Ezra smirked after a half minute of unanswered rings.

"Isabel?" Freddy virtually shouted into the phone at length. "I'm so sorry if I woke you up, but I couldn't sleep from worrying about you and Ray. Is everything all right? Good, good. No, everything is fine here. I just couldn't sleep. Are you sure you don't want me to come over and keep watch? Okay, you go back to bed. All right, good night, my dear, and sleep tight."

"That was sweet," Ezra remarked sardonically.

"Cool it with the sarcasm. The point is they're there. Any reason why you can't continue with the plan now?"

"I don't see why not. There's still a good couple of hours or more before first light."

"Remember, don't hurt her too badly if you can help it. And snatch up the shotgun so she can't check it later."

"Don't worry—I won't disfigure her, at least. Now, the nephew?" he chuckled sinisterly. "That's quite another matter."

"One more thing, Ezra," Freddy concluded. "Leave the goddamn bottle on the bar counter. It's gonna be a long one."

Now, and at the Hour
of Our Death

Freddy's three o'clock phone call left Isabel in a troubled state of mind. She'd dropped Ray off at Hayseed Heights to spend the night with Curtis and to explain all the dos and don'ts of the place to their guest in the morning. Being alone in the café at night had never made her uneasy before. But that was before. So, rather than return to bed, Isabel paced into the kitchen, fixed herself a stiff Cuba Libra, plucked her shotgun from the wall, and settled herself down into a bench seat on the porch. With the twelve-gauge resting across her lap, she clutched her string of rosary beads and began to whisper the appropriate rote prayer. The aroma of the first hay cut was drifting on a predawn breeze, and she inhaled the sweetness deep into her chest as she gazed out beyond the light, where the road ran through the dark and empty gloom. It was technically Sunday, so the five glorious mysteries of the rosary applied. She had only gotten through the first mystery, that of the glorious resurrection of Christ, when Ezra stepped from the velvet blackness into the halo of light cast by the porch lamps.

"You are either a fool, old man, or a real glutton for punishment," Isabel called out with no small measure of false bravado as she pocketed the prayer beads.

Ezra kept silent and moved toward the porch with slow determination. Isabel could not be sure if it was the yellow artificial light that exaggerated and distorted his features, but his face seemed to be twisted in a grotesque canine grimace. He carried the severed arm high in his right hand, as though he were brandishing a club, a knobbed humerus bone at the business end looking anything but humorous. The terrifying image was more of a beast than a man.

Isabel rose, closed the breech, and shouldered her weapon with grim resolve. As the zombie-like Ezra closed the distance between them to thirty feet, she clicked off the safety and moved her long, slender forefinger into the trigger ring. At twenty feet, she let loose with the first blast, aimed directly at the torso. The report rang out in the night like a small explosion, and a bolt of flame spewed like lightning from the muzzle. But, despite her superb marksmanship, the old man continued his approach without faltering, seemingly unscathed—in fact, not fazed in the least. She quickly pumped another shell into the breech and fired another round as Ezra came within twelve feet of her.

Isabel's face went pale as she perceived that her target was again unaffected. Something was dreadfully wrong; she knew that her aim was dead-on, as the paper wadding actually popped the old man in the chest. She noted that the blasts seemed to lack the kick to her shoulder that she'd expected. Evidently, the shells were defective—blanks, in fact! A mask of abject horror froze her features as she seemed to weigh the terrifying prospect of facing her adversary, a fiend bent on double murder, virtually unarmed.

Ezra's contorted scowl morphed into a grin. His mouth gaped open, and drool trickled down his chin as a sinister chortle escaped him. He was feeding on Isabel's fear, and the sight of her terrified visage raised a delight in his body that was nearly erotic. Seeming paralyzed, she continued to hold the gun level, but the barrel was wavering as her arms began to tremble. To him, she was the perfect image of beauty, vulnerability, and horror. Despite what he had told Freddy, he would not spare her. He would beat her unconscious with his arm, then cut her throat with the Buck knife he had brought along. After that appetizer, he would let himself in to tease Ray to death with a cut here and a stab there. The mere thought of toying with a blind man in that way, with no one anywhere near within earshot to hear his screams—the pleasure of ending the life of the stubborn last-in-line would be most exquisite. He could take a good hour with him before the ecstasy of the act would bring on the transformation. Then, he would feed on both of their remains until daylight. The anticipation was physically exciting him. He was within ten feet of Isabel and that delightful mask of fear. And yet…the look was startlingly different.

The old shaman was incredulous: Isabel was *grinning.*

"You stupid son of a bitch," she hissed through clenched teeth. At a range of only six feet, she cut loose with a blast aimed point-blank at the old man's head.

Boom! The big gun thundered, spit fire, and knocked Isabel back onto her heels. The pattern of double-aught buckshot was tight at that range, about the same diameter as the old Indian *brujo's* skull. The nine .30-caliber pellets traveling at 1,200 feet per second put out a wicked level of murderous energy topping 1,500 foot-pounds at the muzzle's end. Ezra's craggy face was instantly liquefied before he could scream. His skull exploded with the force of the blast, and a cloud of nebulized brain tissue and blood rained over the gravel lot behind the headless cadaver. Glancing up from the top rail of the barrel, Isabel caught a glimpse of the rear portion of the skull, the parietal bone, which had separated intact, sailing backward through the air, scalp and hair still attached. The lower jawbone dropped to the ground in front of the wooden steps; the peeled mandible still retained most of the lower row of ivory teeth.

Isabel chambered yet another round and steeled herself, as she fully expected what came next, and yet was horrified by it nevertheless. Seeming to be fully animated despite its present loss, the remaining body—torso and three limbs—dropped to its knees and began to feel about the ground in an apparent blind search-and-recovery mission for stray body parts. Indeed, the hand came up with a few upper teeth and squirreled them into a bloody shirt pocket. Blindly seeking its fellow components, the hand managed to grasp the detached mandible before Isabel, out of pure revulsion, raised her lethal weapon and blew the remaining arm off at the shoulder.

"I knew you'd die hard, but this is completely absurd," she muttered as she began to step down from the porch. The spectral torso with only two limbs suddenly rose up on its feet in a menacing pose, and the lady responded by blowing the right leg off just above the knee. "I think I'd have better luck stompin' out a scorpion with my bare feet."

Finally, what was left of Ezra toppled at Isabel's feet, still writhing with energy, openly raging, but also aimlessly so. With the shotgun cradled in the crook of her left arm, she grasped the old cadaver's remaining ankle and began to drag the headless torso around the north side of the building where the Beetle was parked in the dark.

"Can't blame you for squirmin' old man. You must sense what I have in store for you." Her heart was hammering, but the bluster in her words helped keep her welling fear at bay. "But I hope it's at least slightly more merciful than what you had planned for me and for Ray, you bloodthirsty son of a bitch."

She paused from her laborious task of lugging the body as she reached the car. Releasing the flexing ankle, she propped the shotgun against the side of the building and wiped the sweat from her brow with her fingers. Her next vocal musing was punctuated with the still-labored breathing from the haul.

"Umm, then again, maybe not. But, hey, you should appreciate what I'm doing. After all, there is some ceremony to it, and you're supposed to be a very serious fan of the ritual stuff, or so I'm told," Isabel said aloud.

She opened the passenger-side door, folded the front seat forward, and pulled the weed burner out from the rear foot well. She then unfolded a reinforced plastic tarp she'd taken from Ray's shop and spread it meticulously over the back bench seat.

"C'mon, old man," Isabel puffed. "As you can see, I've been preparing for your visit. Don't fight it. You're goin' for a short ride, like it or not."

She was a strong woman, and, with the blood-soaked cadaver having been stripped of the added weight of a head, leg and both arms, she managed to wrestle the writhing torso into the back seat of the car with some effort.

Slamming the door shut on that chore, she hefted the weed burner, complete with propane tank, and marched her way back around to the illuminated field of carnage at the front of the café. As she rounded the corner and gazed upon the appalling scene there, her stomach churned at the loathsome image she beheld. The old man's severed limbs had somehow wormed toward each other and merged in a twisting and writing three-way embrace that reminded Isabel of one gigantic, wriggling nightcrawler, freshly pierced by a fishhook. The leathery hands were relentlessly grasping and releasing the leg and each other in a kneading fashion, as if each was confirming the tactile existence of the other, seeking the reintegration with the torso.

The morbid caper, the supernatural quickening of the limbs taking place before her, was more than Isabel could tolerate. She opened the valve on the propane tank and ignited the weed burner. *POOF.* The blue-orange flame bursting out of the iron cone at the end of the rod produced a deep, throaty roaring sound as the statuesque *dueña* advanced on the twisting appendages. She steeled herself as the pungent stench of burning flesh invaded her nostrils. An orange light, perhaps the reflection of the flaming wand burning human meat, arose in her dark eyes. Or perhaps it was something else.

Lazarus Moment

In the wee hours of a momentous morning, an abrupt disturbance in the order of all things rousted Kenny Armenta from his dark night of the soul. He opened both eyes and blinked. He unfurled himself from his usual fetal position and quickly rose to his feet as if a great suffocating weight had been lifted from his trunk. The once rotund Pima lapidary had indeed shed a great many pounds from the marginal nourishment offered by the state institution. But the relief he felt was more from a spiritual weight than a corporeal one, and Kenny was instantly aware of the source of his sudden emancipation.

"Ezra is dead!" he cried aloud. The padded walls and floor of his cell deadened the joyful announcement, but it echoed in the depths of his spirit nonetheless.

Kenny's excitement was heightened by all his senses—the musical sound of his own voice, the brilliant whiteness of the canvas wall lining bathed in a florescent glow, the cool, moist feel of perspiration evaporating from his skin, and even the acrid smell of his own urine—and he became overwhelmed with the regained sense of what it is to be human. His eyes welled with tears until they streamed down his dark cheeks.

Of course, his newfound sense of freedom was fated to be short-lived. He was already getting inklings, and he would soon recognize his circumstances and the place of his confinement. In the immediate presence of the moment, having shed the fetters of Ezra's spell, Kenny felt as free as a soaring hawk, internment notwithstanding.

"Ezra is dead!" he shouted again triumphantly.

The rattle of keys and a dull clunk at the cell door announced the entrance of Odie, the night orderly. Kenny's shouts of joy had obviously caught his attention as he made his rounds.

"Kenny? Is that really you, standin' up tall and speakin' English? Man, you are like a walkin' and talkin' miracle!" Odie cried at the sight of Kenny's resurrected self.

"All things are possible," Kenny observed, matter-of-factly. But then, "Ezra is dead!" he shouted once more.

"I don't know who this Ezra guy is, but it sounds like maybe his death brought you back to life. Is that it? Anyway, welcome back to the world, brother!" Odie chuckled and extended his hand. "My name's Theodus, but my friends call me Odie."

"Thank you, my friend," Kenny returned, shaking the orderly's hand vigorously. "I seem to sense that you are indeed my friend."

"Man, Kenny, the shrinks are gonna be absolutely amazed at this instant recovery. Of course, they'll try and say it was the shock therapy, but you haven't had one of those in a while. Still, them bein' men of science and all, they aren't given to believin' in miracles—but I do!"

"The cause is beyond their understanding," Kenny mumbled, glancing at his surroundings.

"Now don't go thinkin' maybe they'll change your digs. You're already in solitary confinement in the high-security ward, and that's likely where you'll stay, given the reasons for you bein' here and all."

A puzzled look stole across Kenny's face. He had experienced periods of partial awareness following each electroshock session. He was coming to the realization of his deplorable situation. Sensing the weighted effect that his words were having on Kenny, Odie quickly abandoned the topic.

"Listen, Kenny, my shift is almost over, but is there anything I can get you before I leave?" Odie asked.

"Perhaps I could get my dentures back?" Kenny wondered aloud.

Odie sighed. "That would be up to the shrinks, but I wouldn't count on it—not after that stunt you pulled with the bloody nose. C'mon, chief—is there something I can do that's within my grasp?"

"Yes, Odie. It seems to me that I don't belong in this place. I think maybe I need to get out of here."

"Well, that *is* a stretch, chief. After all, many things are beyond my ability."

"Oh, my friend," Kenny said with a toothless grin, "all things are possible."

All's Well ... (Interlude Two)

"**S**omethin' eatin' you again, brilliance?" Curtis asked abruptly.

"Sort of," I responded with some reluctance. "How'd you know?"

"I just know, that's all. Kinda like the way Santa Claus knows if you been bad or good."

That made just about as much sense as anything. I know my facial expressions can make me pretty transparent at times, but the darkness that night out by the canal was like an inky-black curtain. He would have needed infrared vision to see my hidden face. There was no better way to explain how Curtis could tell what I was thinking, other than he *just knew.*

"That's kind of creepy, the way you do that." In fact, it was downright clairvoyant.

Curtis sighed. "I don't know—it's like it's so quiet out here in the boonies, when you get a notion, Vince, your brain practically screams it out so I can hear it. Like, right now, you're wantin' me to jump ahead in the story, aren't you?"

"Not exactly," I returned smugly. "It's more like I already know the ending to this part."

"Oh, is that right?" My friend's tone conveyed his annoyance with me. "Maybe *you* should tell *me* how this story goes."

"Ah, don't be like that, Curtis. It's just that I have some insight that tells me where this ends up."

"Well then, please, by all means, enlighten me, O wise one," Curtis remarked sardonically.

"First thing is that I've read that book *Cuckoo's Nest*—the one Betty Wood was reading in her hospital bed," I informed him.

"And so?"

"So the Indian in the book escapes from the loony bin in the end."

"That's it—you're goin' on the ending of a *different* story?" Curtis sputtered incredulously.

"No, not just that. I was reading somewhere that escapes from the mental hospital are pretty common, and that the press doesn't even bother with them," I stated.

"That all you got?" Curtis pressed.

"Then there's the last thing that Kenny said to Odie about escaping: *All things are possible.* Seems like a pretty broad hint."

The unmistakable sound of a long, low chuckle floated across the darkness. My face burned. Curtis was laughing at me.

"So, am I right—Kenny escaped from Arizona State Hospital and was never heard from again?" I guessed.

"Man, you are off by a mile," Curtis answered when he was done laughing. "And you missed the biggest clue of all on how this would end up, and it was right under your nose, chump."

I was at a loss. "What's that supposed to mean?" That was the best I could come up with.

Curtis chuckled again. "Tell you what, I'm gonna tell you the end right now, just to show you how wrong you are…and to teach you not to try hijackin' my story again."

"Sorry," I said. "Maybe you shouldn't." But I was all ears.

"Don't you remember what Stephen Robson told Betty Wood about that fancy clinic up in Paradise Valley?"

"Don't tell me¬—"

"Of course it's true. Robson kept his promise—pulled a few strings and got Kenny transferred to the cushy nuthouse, all on his dime. Bought the old boy's silence in the bargain."

"But Kenny doesn't belong in a nuthouse at all," I protested. "He's got all his marbles."

"Yeah, but he doesn't like to make waves either. Besides, he's good with where he's at. He teaches a jewelry makin' class on Tuesdays and Thursdays, he got his dentures back, and I hear he even has a girlfriend—one of the lady shrinks up there. His friends from the rez visit and bring him fry bread. In fact, old Kenny is happier than a pig dipped in shit right now."

"And just how do you know all of this?" I probed suspiciously.

"A long chat with Betty Wood before I left Oracle Mesa, and a visit I paid to the old boy himself a couple of months back," he countered smugly. "That's how."

A devilish thought crossed my mind, and I began to chuckle myself.

"What's so amusing, brilliance?"

"Who's the chump now, Curtis?"

"Whatchoo talkin' 'bout, clown?"

"I got you to jump ahead and tell me an ending."

"Oh no—don't you pull that shit. You're just tryin' to cover up your mess, like a cat in a sandbox. But I know your game, and I'll go you one better. See, that endin' I just told you—I made it all up. It really ended the way you said, with Kenny escapin' and all. I created another endin' just so you wouldn't have the pleasure."

"You didn't…you wouldn't!" I stammered.

"All things are possible," he said. I could picture his face beaming with self-satisfaction, though it was really too dark to actually see it. "Fact is, it ended one of those ways, and only I know which one is real. Now, shall I continue the tale?" Curtis concluded, victorious.

"Please do," I grumbled, shaking my head.

Never on Sunday

It was after five when the wheels of Isabel's Beetle met the rise at the end of Ray's stony driveway. A barely discernible gleam, faint precursor of dawn, paled the eastern sky and cast a muted and surreal luminosity over the still-darkened homestead of Hayseed Heights. She doused the headlights and coasted up to the murky yard that separated the little adobe shack from Ray's garage. A couple of staccato toots on the horn announced her arrival as she switched off the ignition and rolled down the window. The dead silence was occasionally disturbed by a sinister writhing from behind her seat back. Secure in the knowledge that the arms and hands were sufficiently disabled, she dismissed any concern that the thrashing torso might cause her harm.

Isabel waited patiently for several moments, then tooted once more. Ray's seven remaining hogs stirred nearby in their pen, sent up a short-lived chorus of snuffling guffaws, and, under the spell of subdued darkness, fell silent once more. A smile bloomed across her face at the notion that her tiny honk had aroused them and gently reminded them of their prolonged deprivation. It was their hunger that brought her there, and she grinned at having teased out a brief awakening of their Pavlovian response.

Isabel released the seat back and reclined a bit. There was no real hurry for once, and she was suddenly seized with a weariness that overwhelmed. The long, eventful night with no sleep was catching up with her. Her head slumped, and her mouth fell open, taking in long draughts of the cool predawn air as a solitary mourning dove cooed her to sleep with its inquiring lullaby.

"*Tía,* wake up!" It was Ray reaching in the driver's-side window and prodding her shoulder. Isabel opened her eyes to a brighter picture, though the landscape was still bathed in the gray of predawn. Curtis was standing beside Ray, wide-eyed with a bashful sort of half grin. Both boys were clad in jeans and T-shirts, Curtis looking somewhat comical in Ray's outsized togs.

"*Mijo!*" Isabel grinned. "I've got the best news you'll ever hear."

"What is it?" Ray asked. "And what the hell is that horrible stench?"

"That's the news, *mijo*. Ezra *es muerte*—he's dead!"

"Dead? Are you sure? I thought he was impossible to kill," Ray said doubtfully.

"He's as dead as I can make him for now. That's why I brought him here—to finish him off," Isabel stated.

"You brought him *here*?" Ray asked incredulously.

Spellbound by the woman's statements, Curtis's curiosity lured him to peer into the back window. He recoiled in revulsion at what he beheld there. "Oh my God!" Curtis exclaimed. "That can't be real. It…it's a body!"

"A dead body," Isabel clarified. "Or, at least, pretty well dead."

"You're not making sense, *Tía*," said Ray. "Is he dead or not?"

"He's…he's…*sort of* dead," Isabel stammered. "No, he's *mostly* dead."

"What, exactly, do you mean by that?" Ray pressed.

Isabel sighed, exasperated. "Some things you just need to accept because I say so, Raymie. But since you haven't fully regained your sight, I'll cut you some slack in this case. Curtis, describe to Ray what you see in the back seat."

"Ma'am, I see a headless corpse back there," Curtis stated as deadpan as Joe Friday.

"Good. And, by corpse, you mean a dead body, right?" Isabel quizzed.

"Dead by the fact that it doesn't have a head…but…" Curtis's voice trailed off.

"But what?" Isabel prodded.

"Judging by the way it's all squirmin' around back there, I'd say it isn't quite dead, ma'am," Curtis answered

"*Exactamente, chico!* I couldn't have said it better myself." Isabel exclaimed.

"Not to be rude, ma'am," Curtis interjected in a hushed tone, as if someone might overhear, "but would it be too much to ask *why* you've got a body in your car?"

"Because he wouldn't come here on his own, *chico*," Isabel quipped. "He needed a ride."

"He sure as hell *smells* dead, I'll say that," Ray observed, crinkling his nose, "but if both of you insist that he's still movin', I'll have to go along with you. So, what now, *Tía*?"

Isabel popped open the driver's-side door, stepped out and stretched her full statuesque form against the glowing steel blue of the eastern sky. "You know, I don't have any supernatural notions on how to dispose of a body animated by the Evil One," she confessed. "Despite all the rumors about me, my abilities don't measure up to those of a true mystic. But I do know of one metaphysical method that I learned from a trusted source. I believe it will serve our purpose here, and it involves your pigs."

"My pigs?" Ray muttered.

"I'm afraid so, *mijo*. By the time we're through with them, they won't be fit for human consumption anymore. I'll have to reimburse you," Isabel stated.

"What the he—" Ray cut himself short

"I'm going to remind you to walk by faith, not by sight, Raymie. Just do as I say, and don't ask questions. Can you make it over to the garage door without help?"

"Yeah, I could do it blindfolded," Ray retorted.

"Good. Head over there, roll up the door, get in your truck, and give us a healthy blast on that air horn of yours," Isabel instructed.

"Oh my God, *Tía*! You're not going to—" Ray started

"It's the only way I know, *mijo*," Isabel confirmed. "And you have to admit, it seems fitting. We need to be certain that he can't resume another shape and return to his murdering vendetta, or we'll never feel truly safe again."

"I hope you're right about this," said Ray, still doubtful.

"One can never be completely certain about these things, *mijo*," Isabel explained. "Lord knows, I'm not Jesus of Nazareth, nor even one of His apostles or priests. But if we do as He did, I don't see how we can go wrong. He may even lend us some of His authority for this particular mission. Now, Raymie, go and blow that horn like you're Gabriel himself."

"Yes, ma'am!" Ray turned on his heel and, counting steps, strode gingerly over to the looming garage building.

Isabel turned to their incredulous guest. "Curtis?"

"Yes, ma'am?"

"You, my young friend, are about to start earning your keep here," Isabel stated.

"Ready and able, ma'am." Curtis almost saluted.

The clatter of the garage door rolling up briefly stole his attention.

"Get ready for it!" she hissed, heightening the boy's anticipation.

The long and loud blast from the air horn split the silence of the morning and, although expected, caused Curtis's heart to race. As the reverberation of the blare died away, the boy's ears pricked up at a sudden commotion.

"Watch the pigpen, son," Isabel told him.

As he did so, his eyes widened. Even in dim light, he could see the seven mature hogs break into a run, forming a herd and galloping in a counterclockwise motion around the perimeter of the swineyard like a field of quarter horses. The squealing and grunting cacophony that broke the stillness of the dawn sounded like a chorus of chaos.

"What makes them do that?" Curtis wondered aloud.

"Hunger," Ray answered, rejoining the two. "They're half-starved, by design."

"What do you mean, *by design*?" the boy demanded.

"I mean my aunt has deliberately kept them hungry."

"What for?" Curtis wondered.

"All right, enough idle chatter," Isabel declared. "Let's get this over with—it's gonna take all three of us, because I doubt that he'll go without putting up a fuss."

She methodically opened the passenger door, pushed the seat forward, and, with a heave, pulled the plastic tarp, cadaver and all, out onto the ground before them.

Curtis's eyes went from poker chips to saucers. "Holy shit—he's still kickin' without a head! This is the spookiest stuff I've ever seen, and I've seen some pretty spooky stuff—'specially lately."

"Curtis, have you ever seen chickens get slaughtered?" Isabel inquired calmly.

"Yes, ma'am—I have seen that. I've seen them flap their wings and go runnin' 'round without their heads until the blood runs out. Yes, ma'am, I have seen that."

"It's the same principle. It's what they call *postmortem reflex.*"

"No, ma'am. With all due respect, this is not the same principle at all, ma'am. Just look at him. This is entirely different from a chicken— not the slimmest connection at all. A chicken runs 'round without a head for about thirty seconds, tops, because its body is *confused* about bein' dead. This is a human that's been dead for hours, and he's still movin' like he's got a few more dances left in him. He's resistin' bein' dead. You can hang whatever fancy scientific name on it you want, but what I'm lookin' at has no resemblance to a chicken at all…ma'am, no offense intended." He forced a grin, even as shining beads of sweat popped out on his brow.

Isabel stared at the young man without comment for a moment. "Okay," she responded at length, "that was just a *symbolic* comparison, Curtis. I thought it might help you deal with your apparent queasiness. Regardless, it's fifty feet to the pen, and I can't lift this bag of filth over the fence by myself. Are you with us, Curtis—like we were with you?"

The boy swallowed and steeled himself. "Yes, of course, ma'am, I am. Sorry if I gave any different notion."

"All right, then, I'll take what's left of his shoulders and do the backwards stepping, because Ray needs to just lift and follow along," Isabel reasoned. "Curtis, you take the leg, and Ray—you take the…um…stump. Everybody ready to do this?" Isabel scooped her hands under the cadaver's armpits. "Curtis, guide Ray's hands to the stump, then you get hold of its ankle. Everybody ready? On three— one…two…three!"

The second that the trio hefted the body, it began to thrash violently, kicking at Curtis with its remaining leg and pumping its hips, the entire form undulating with a forceful electric energy that defied all reason. Curtis lost his grip on the ankle twice during the short traverse, but was able to regain it without breaking the steady movement to the pen. Once there, the three immediately hoisted the quickened cadaver high, over the top rail, and into the feeding trough.

Whump!

It was as if the hollow sound of Ezra's body hitting the trough was a secondary cue to the prior blare of the horn. The pigs fell as silent as a tomb for only an instant, then screamed with starvation and dashed for the feeding end of the pen, squealing and wailing with twice the volume as before. The seven three-hundred-pound barrows approached the near rail at a dead run, and the three humans backed away from the fence for fear the hogs' braking mechanisms might fail, and the wooden wall might give way at the onslaught. Despite its vigorous undulations, the pigs had no trouble whatsoever identifying the torso as food, and, upon reaching the generous offering, wasted no time in seizing the wriggling prize in their devouring jaws.

The initial quandary of having a single piece of meat to be shared among seven diners was quickly resolved. There was no semblance of cooperation, but each ravenous beast took a position opposite its adversarial contender and began to pull for its own piece of the tasty trophy, tearing it to pieces in a trice. The spillage from the trisected torso made Curtis turn away in revulsion but captured Isabel's intensely focused attention.

"Oh, Ray!" Isabel exclaimed. "I wish you could see this, *mijo*. It's a sight for sore eyes, if you'll excuse my impertinence."

"Why don't you give me a play-by-play, *Tía*. The feeding sounds are already teasing my imagination, but a little visual detail would be a nice touch."

"First of all, the blood isn't quite like blood at all. It's brown and thick like mud, and the pigs are sucking it up off the ground like it was roast beef gravy. And the entrails are black—as black as coal," Isabel said, her voice dramatically rising and falling with the vivid description.

"Black entrails—sounds delicious," said Ray with an eager grin. "Are they moving at all?"

"You got that right—like snakes and worms, but that just seems to excite the pigs all the more. You hear that ruckus? Two of the bigger barrows are fighting over the entrails, like they're some kind of delicacy." Isabel hooted, apparently thrilling to what was happening.

"Now I know what they mean when they say *hog wild*," Ray quipped.

"Listen, *mijo*, do you hear that loud crunching sound? One of the boars is tearing meat-covered bones from the ribcage and gnawing them to bits—devouring them completely!"

"Music to my ears," Ray remarked.

"A ravenous rhapsody!" Isabel exclaimed. "This is better than I'd hoped for; the pigs are devouring everything—the flesh, the blood, the bones, the entrails, even the blood-soaked clothes. There won't be a single stinking scrap of the old bastard left when they're finished."

"Ma'am?" Curtis piped up weakly. "May I be excused for just a minute? I think I'm about to toss my cookies."

"I can't say as I blame you, *chico*," Isabel allowed. "The stink alone is nauseating enough. You don't have a stake in this, and you must think Ray and I are monsters, carrying on like this. But you need to understand that we have been stalked and threatened and nearly killed by this lowlife devil for over a month now. The relief we feel this morning is hard to describe. We're… we're… *elated*. We've gotten our lives back, and life is good," she concluded a little tearfully.

"Are you finished, ma'am? 'Cause I'm tryin' real hard not to puke, but I'm losin' the battle," Curtis whined.

"Sure, sorry. You go on over by that oleander hedge if you need to upchuck. Then go to my car and get the package that's in the front hood compartment."

"He's a good kid, *Tía*," Ray observed as Curtis staggered toward a hedge, "and he's had a pretty tough last couple of months himself to hear him tell it."

"I'd like to hear him tell it, but there're more loose ends to tie up before this is all through. Speaking of which, I'm gonna need your truck and the name and number of the place where you rent the stock trailers," Isabel stated matter-of-factly.

"Okay, *Tía*. Anything else?" Ray asked.

"No, just stay here with Curtis for a while," Isabel instructed. "And when the pigs get finished, show him how to sequester them and have him burn any leftover morsels of our dearly departed Ezzy that they might have left behind. And have him rake up and burn any manure they produce before I get back. The weed burner is in the front seat of my car." She rattled these directions off as he handed her the keys to his truck. "Most importantly," she added, "be sure and have him save the ashes."

Lifeline

Three dazzling shafts of first daylight streamed in through a trio of clerestory windows and met the darkened barroom floor with a warming kiss just where Freddy Hightower lay collapsed, bellydown, head turned sideways so the face received the full illuminating effect. The brilliant white beams teased him up from a near-coma state, through multiple levels of narcotic visions, to the rude awakening of his very real and very dismal circumstances. He deduced that he'd been poisoned. He recalled thinking that he would surely die when he'd slumped on the floor in that very spot a couple of hours before. The way he felt as he regained consciousness, he almost wished he had.

His eyelids fluttered briefly, then closed again, tightly, in a futile effort to keep out the stabbing glare. His entire head throbbed as if an internal trip-hammer had invaded his skull. The excruciating cranial pulses precisely matched the rise and fall of an intense ringing in his ears.

It was only when that infernal ringing suddenly and miraculously ceased that Freddy was able to bring some semblance of order to his thoughts and take stock of his situation.

Poisoned! That wily old bastard Ezra had somehow slipped some sort of deadly potion into the bourbon bottle they'd shared. Never had Jim Beam's good name been desecrated in such a vile manner! How Ezra managed to taint the whiskey that Freddy drank without poisoning himself was beyond the victim's reckoning. Perhaps it was some sleight-of-hand maneuver—something that would certainly fall within a shaman's repertoire. A more likely scenario would have had the old *brujo* drinking the poison as well. A toxic concoction proving fatal to a mortal might well be a mere liqueur to a demon—an aperitif, in fact, to a feast of blood.

Then, as suddenly as it had ceased, the ringing in Freddy's head resumed, reprising the same painful pulses as before. He instinctively raised his hands to his ears as if he could shut off the wicked blasts from the outside. To his amazement, it worked. With hands cupped over the ears, he actually muted the ringing effect. The pulses were reduced to a mild intermittent buzzing. It wasn't inside his head after all; it came from some external source. Absent the amplified attack on his brain, he was able to get a fix on the origin of the horrible noise: it was the telephone. Someone was calling the bar phone, and quite persistently so.

Steeling himself for another salvo of auditory assaults, Freddy removed his hands from his ears. With an immense effort, he pushed down on the floor and raised his torso, but several attempts to get to his feet failed. Again, the ringing ceased, and the only remaining sound was that of his own pathetic whimpering.

It was probably Manny, his faithful servant, calling so frequently. He'd be concerned that Freddy had stayed at the restaurant digs without calling to let him know, as was his habit in such cases. Good old Manny's loyal concern just might be Freddy's saving grace. If he could make it to the bar and grasp the receiver on his faithful attendant's next call, he would get the old man to roust Dr. J. P. Morton, Freddy's close friend and physician. He'd survived the initial onslaught of symptoms; there was good reason to believe that, given some medical care, he might win yet another reprieve from death.

Believing the phone to be a lifeline, Freddy somehow mustered the energy to raise himself up on hands and knees. At a turtle's pace, and stopping to rest three times, he closed the distance between the site his of collapse and the bar inside of five minutes. It was a ponderous journey, albeit short in terms of distance, and it sapped what little strength he'd regained with his awakening. Nevertheless, he grasped the frame of a barstool and pulled his chin level with the bar. The telephone sat inches from his face when it began to ring again.

The roaring blasts from the phone at that close range proved overwhelming to Freddy's raw senses. He stifled an urge to scream from the cranial pain that the ringing invoked. A new wave of nausea swept over the diminutive restaurateur, and the inches of distance to the phone suddenly became miles. He reached out with a swiping paw as his knees buckled, and he managed to bat the receiver off the hook in a valiant but failed attempt to grasp it.

An eternity and several hundred feet of dizzying descent seemed to pass before him until his limp body finally met the floor again. The retching began anew. The flow of blood streaming from his parted lips was alarming. The floor began to rock like a pendulum, and Freddy fought to retain his consciousness. Opening his eyes, his blurred vision landed on a strange black object, about the size and shape of a small shoe, seeming to dangle before him, suspended from some unseen tether.

"Hello, Freddy—are you there?"

Despite the exaggerated tinny quality of the sound, Freddy recognized the voice emitting from the object to be Isabel's—a tiny Tinker Bell version of Isabel, calling from the depths of a coffee-can prison— but Isabel's distinctive voice nevertheless. Miraculously, it was the telephone receiver that danced before his face, strung up by its own cord. He mustered all of his waning vitality to utter a response.

"Isabel!" he croaked, but could only manage that much.

"Alfredo, are you okay? I have some wonderful news...are you okay? I can't hear you. Are you okay?"

With an enormous effort, he drew in a deep breath and ejaculated the single word that summed it all up: "No!" Freddy cried out loudly, and then passed immediately into oblivion.

The Doctor Came In...

Isabel had already been at Freddy's bedside for almost an hour when James Patrick "Dr. Mort" Morton arrived at the cantina just a few minutes shy of eight o'clock. After all the years of being the sole general practitioner in the sleepy Santa Rita Valley, he rarely, if ever, had any inclination to shift into emergency mode. Even if he had possessed a higher gear to shift into, which he didn't, it certainly would not be applied to attending another one of his friend's regular episodes. He might have even skipped the visit altogether had it not been for Isabel's frantic plea on the phone. Of course, Freddy was not dying, as Isabel had raved. By Dr. Mort's reckoning, it would be more accurate to say that the event was neither more nor less likely to be his last. Nevertheless, Morton eventually caved to the obvious distress in the lovely *dueña's* voice and agreed to administer to his long-suffering patient-compatriot, if only to assuage Isabel's heartfelt concerns.

"Good morning, señora." He nodded toward Isabel, sort of slightly bowing in a debonair fashion. Isabel nodded in response. "Hello, Freddy." The doctor sighed with markedly less enthusiasm as he turned toward the patient.

Upon their few encounters, Isabel had noted Dr. Morton's suave manner and his distinguished use of language. She also considered him quite handsome with his thick, coal-black hair, dark, flashing eyes, and neatly trimmed mustache. She thought he was a dead ringer for comedian Ernie Kovacs, and the resemblance made it hard for her to hold Dr. Mort in any serious regard. She also wondered why he'd never married.

"*Bienvenido*, Jay Pee," Freddy croaked, his throat raw from vomiting. "Thank you for coming, compadre."

Alfredo Hightower and J. P. Morton had been classmates and close friends even long before their freshman year at Seton High Academy, a Catholic prep school in nearby Catalina. They had been classmates again through their sophomore year at the UofA in Tucson, when Freddy quit school to take over his dying father's restaurant and cattle ranch, while J. P. stayed on and eventually graduated from the med school there. And it was their mutual familiarity that allowed Freddy to address his friend as "Jay Pee," which stuck for dual reasons: apparently due to his first and middle initials, but also because Morton had, out of sheer boredom with his slow provincial practice, gotten himself elected as the local justice of the peace to occupy his days more fully. Even so, only Freddy addressed him that way as an alternative, mostly because ninety-nine percent of his fellow Oracle Mesans took a twisted delight in the moniker *Dr. Mort* they'd bestowed upon him which, just subliminally known to the good physician, loosely translated from the Spanish as "Dr. Death."

"Here we are again, it seems." The doctor sighed. "At least the scenery is better than usual," he added as an acknowledgement of Isabel's presence. "So tell me, Freddy, was there blood in the vomit?" he inquired as he rolled back the thin cotton sheet and began to poke and prod in the usual doctor's manner.

"Yes." Freddy groaned.

"More or less than usual?"

"More."

"Really? How much more?"

Freddy longed to confide in his friend about the copious amounts of blood he had expectorated. He wanted to tell him that it wasn't just another bout with the bleeding ulcers. He wanted to speak up and say that he'd been poisoned. He was hoping beyond hope that he could simply describe the symptoms and his friend would immediately identify the offending toxin and prescribe an antidote on the spot, as unlikely as that was.

With Isabel present, Freddy dared not convey any such scenario. Clearly, she had not discerned his alliance with Ezra and their conspiracy to dispense with Ray. Any mention of poison could lead her into wondering about some connection with the old demonic Indian, and, at that point, keeping her oblivious to that notion was more important than any wishful thinking about an antidote. Besides, the worst of the symptoms seemed to be passing. He was beginning to put some stock into the notion that his indomitable liver was winning the battle for his survival.

"More, but not much more," Freddy stoically answered after a long silence.

"Well then, *mi viejo amigo*," the doctor responded, "do you think this episode merits another trip to the ER in Tucson? I'm leaving it up to you to judge the severity of this one. No doubt you can tell better than I can."

"No, Jay Pee, that's definitely not what I want right now. I think I'm starting to feel better. Still nauseated, but the pain is dying down."

"Good, and we both know what the ultimate cure for your ailment is. Pity you refuse to take it," Dr. Morton implored.

"You mean Mylanta?" Freddy quipped.

"Very funny. I'm relieved that this present attack hasn't dulled your droll wit." He looked up and spoke directly to Isabel. "Your friend and mine here is slowly but surely dying from a common malady that can easily be reversed with a simple adjustment to his lifestyle."

"We're all dying, Jay Pee, one way or another," Freddy mumbled.

"I'm sorry, Dr. Morton," said Isabel, "I don't quite understand."

"He does, and that's what is so frustrating." Isabel stared blankly, so the doctor addressed Freddy. "Do you mind if I divulge your condition to your companion?"

Freddy shook his head.

"You see, my dear, the drinking and smoking and consumption of foods that would burn a hole in a stainless steel holding tank have all compromised his stomach lining. He has a set of peptic ulcers that look like the craters of the moon on an endoscopy," the doctor explained.

"Lots of people have ulcers, and not all of them are dying, right?" said Isabel.

"True, but those people manage their condition by restraining their habits. Freddy's condition continues to deteriorate because of his indulgence in his appetites. If he keeps trying to keep up with Dean

Martin, he'll develop a perforation—that is, if he hasn't already," the doctor divulged.

"I see," said Isabel.

"And this vomiting of blood is a very disturbing sign," Dr. Morton continued. "One of these times, he's liable to hemorrhage to death. If I were less a friend and more a doctor, I'd call for an ambulance right now, his opinion be damned. Perforations require surgery."

"All right, that's enough." Freddy growled. "He always exaggerates, Isabel. Besides, he's pretty lubricated himself most of the time. Gets the drama going."

"A nightcap or two to unwind before bedtime is nobody's business but my own," the doctor retorted.

"Hah! Nightcap or two? Truth be known, you're probably half twisted right now."

"I see that your strength is returning along with your belligerence, my friend," the doctor observed. "But it seems to me that you are the one given to hyperbole. Besides, my habits are irrelevant and not immediately harmful to my health, as yours are."

"Now that you mention it, I am sensing another reprieve from the reaper—uplifted, no doubt, by the fabulous and long-awaited message that I just received," Freddy hinted, casting a knowing glance at Isabel.

"Which would you prefer, Freddy, a serious warning or an early-morning celebration?" Dr. Morton retorted, sardonically.

"Actually, if I continue to recover like this, a celebration is exactly what I would prefer," Freddy added.

"What? You're not making much sense," the doctor responded, puzzled. "First you're at death's door and then you want to celebrate. I think maybe you're delirious. A celebration? Indeed!"

"Yeah. In fact, given the circumstances, I'd prefer a ceremony *and* a celebration!" Freddy continued.

"Hmm…misery punctuated by sudden outbursts of euphoria. I believe you *do* need some compulsory treatment, my friend. Maybe we should call the ambulance after all," Dr. Morton declared, half-serious.

"To *hell* with all this bickering, Jay Pee!" Freddy suddenly cried out. "It's true, I *am* feeling really happy and really sick at the same time, but, in light of my good fortune, an ambulance ride to the ER in Tucson is the last thing I want to be doing right now."

"What good fortune might that be, Freddy?"

"The great news, my friend, is this…" He gestured weakly toward Isabel. "The lovely señora has at last consented to be my bride!"

Isabel cast her eyes downward demurely as Dr. Morton's widened. "My—that is stunning news! Congratulations to you both. I hope you don't mind if I act somewhat surprised, Freddy. I know you've been pursuing the lady's affections for quite some time, and with very

little encouragement. May I be so bold as to ask what brought about this turn of events?"

"I'd say Alfredo's perseverance wore me down, all right, but his loyalty to me and Ray is what won me over," Isabel cooed. "A great darkness has just been lifted from our lives, and I feel free now to give myself over to him."

"Well, that *is* cause for celebration," the doctor declared, grinning widely, "Freddy's poor condition notwithstanding."

"Jay Pee, I said a *ceremony* and a celebration," said Freddy, "and I'd like you to perform the ceremony."

The doctor shifted his gaze toward Isabel and responded tentatively. "Of course, I'd be honored," he stated reservedly, "but I assume the lady would prefer a priest. And, of course, while my authority as justice of the peace extends—"

"You don't get it, Jay Pee," Freddy interrupted with a subtle smile. "We want you to marry us *now*—right now, in fact."

"But…but that…that's impossible!" Dr. Morton stammered. "And, if you're serious, I'd say you're being much too impulsive about this."

"Let me explain, Doctor," Isabel interjected calmly. "When I got here about an hour ago, Freddy thought he was dying. He asked me one more time if I would marry him. The irony is that I've been waiting for him to ask me again for several days because I wanted to say yes. Anyway, you were already on your way here, and Freddy reminded me that you have the authority as justice of the peace to tie the knot this morning, so I agreed to let it happen here and now. Now that he seems to be recovering, I don't want to disappoint him if he's still game."

"Of course I am," Freddy agreed.

"There, Doctor, can you see that the last thing I want him to think is that I only wanted to be his widow, but not his wife. Please do this one thing for us now—it's what we both want," Isabel implored.

"I'd do almost anything for my old friend here," the doctor acquiesced, "but it's just not possible. First of all, there's that annoying little technicality of a marriage license, and…

"Technicalities can be overcome," Freddy stated flatly. "You forget that I am the former mayor. The county clerk still owes me a couple of favors. Paper dates can be quite flexible if need be."

"Then there's…"

"You're stalling, Jay Pee. What's the problem?"

"This is just so impetuous. I just want you both to be certain."

"Don't patronize us," Freddy snapped. "We're both adults."

"We're both very certain, Doctor," Isabel assured. "Please."

"Okay, let me get this straight. Freddy is no longer at the threshold of his demise, and instead of a medical opinion, you want me to perform a spontaneous wedding ceremony."

"Yes," said Freddy with certainty.

"Yes," Isabel stated flatly.

"If you both insist," Dr. Morton conceded reluctantly. "But I must advise you both that this contract is not legally binding until Freddy files the papers retroactively."

"So, if I die this afternoon, Isabel won't inherit the cantina and the ranch?"

"I'm not after your property, Freddy," Isabel protested with mock indignation. "More likely you're out to get mine—it's more profitable." She chuckled.

"It's a good thing that neither of you is terribly concerned about the inheritance process in this state, because your legal state of matrimony will be seriously exposed to contest until you tie up the loose ends."

"We take your warning under advisement, Jay Pee," Freddy conceded. "Now, let's get on with the ceremony!"

Bedside Bride

"Don't forget the lime, my dear," Freddy shouted from his bed to Isabel who was downstairs behind the bar. "A Bloody Maria is nothing without the lime."

"Do you think I don't know how to fix *una María Sangrienta*, Freddy?" his new bride called back up to him. "How many times have you repeated the story and recited the recipe behind the famous drink that killed Tom Mix?"

"Don't forget the dash of hot sauce," Freddy added a little sheepishly.

"Already in there," Isabel retorted as she hefted the serving tray with the two tall "morning after" cocktails and a couple of cloth napkins.

"I can't wait to celebrate our nuptials, Isabel. I thought Jay Pee would never leave."

As requested, Freddy's old friend had performed a simple wedding ceremony there in Freddy's bedroom. Dr. Morton had scribbled an improvised marriage license on a prescription pad, and Isabel had stepped outside to pick some flowers from the front porch for her bouquet while Freddy, still bedridden, dug through his nightstand drawer and came up with an old high school class ring to slip on his bride's finger. The whole procedure took less than ten minutes. The doctor, feeling a bit awkward as the sole attendee, made his excuses and left no more than five minutes after the nuptial pronouncement.

"If he knew I was making you *una María Sangrienta*," Isabel said, mounting the top of the stairs, "he would probably have me arrested."

"For what?"

"For attempted murder of my newlywed husband, Freddy," she returned as she entered the room. "Are you sure this is a good idea? I mean, with your being sick and all, maybe we should hold off."

"Nonsense, my dear. I'm feeling much better, and a celebratory libation is just what the doctor ordered, so to speak."

Freddy was apparently more than ready to bury his shameful treachery in the back pages of his mind and live a life of blissful dishonesty with his long sought-after jewel. The sudden and favorable turn of events—Ezra's death and Isabel's obliviousness to Freddy's participation in the conspiracy to murder Ray—buoyed his spirits immeasurably, and his previously debilitating infirmity had all but dissipated.

"I'm pretty sure the doctor would not approve of this remedy." Isabel giggled. "Now, can you sit up?"

Freddy groaned as he leaned forward while Isabel propped two pillows and handed him one of the frosty tumblers. He raised it up for a toast, and she did likewise.

"To a long life together, full of love," Freddy pronounced.

"Hear! Hear!" Isabel exclaimed in agreement as she clinked her glass with his.

Freddy took a long pull from the drink before coming up for air. "What's this?" he demanded suspiciously. "A lemon instead of a lime?"

"I told you last night that the bar is out of limes, Alfredo. I didn't think you would notice."

"Notice? The whole thing tastes like lemonade. This is not a proper Bloody Maria."

"I'm sorry, Freddy. Would you like me to take it away?"

"Not on your life, dear. First of all, it's our wedding toast, and, secondly, I never waste good tequila. You used the top-shelf tequila, didn't you?"

"I did."

"Good, because it's not really a Bloody Maria without the best tequila, you know." He took another long drink and exhaled loudly. "Drink up, my dear, and I'll have you fetch another round." He grinned. "It really tastes okay. It was just that initial flavor surprise that threw me off."

But instead of "drinking up," Isabel seated herself on a wicker chair next to Freddy's bed, gripped his hand, and sipped her own drink demurely while her husband continued to gulp his.

"Maybe you should slow down a little, Alfredo," she warned at length. "This can't be too good for your stomach."

"Perhaps not in the long run, but it's doing wonders for my general outlook on things right now," Freddy observed.

"For a while—until you get sick again and maybe die this time like the doctor said," Isabel retorted.

"Don't let old 'Dr. Doom' put such dark thoughts in your pretty head. I have no intention of dying, Isabel. I have everything to live for now."

"If that's true, then you should start living your life like you want to keep on living," Isabel suggested.

"And I'll probably do just that, now that things have changed for the better," Freddy returned. "But right now, given the circumstances, you wouldn't begrudge your new husband a little celebration cocktail, would you?"

"Since you put it that way, no, of course not. Go ahead and drink your drink," Isabel allowed.

Freddy took another long pull, almost draining the glass.

"Aahh….that sure hits the spot."

"I hope it does."

"What's that?"

"I said I hope that hits the spot," Isabel repeated.

"Don't worry, dear. I'm fine for now. You know, Isabel," Freddy continued softly as he squeezed her hand, "I think that even if I were to die this morning, I'd be content in just knowing that everyone in this backward little pueblo, *everyone* would have to admit that I finally captured that elusive prize. They'd have to say, 'Freddy Hightower finally won that unreachable, raven-haired beauty.'"

"That is *so* romantic, Freddy." Isabel feigned a swoon.

"I know." Freddy sighed, missing the sarcastic inflexion entirely.

"That's what I am to you?" Isabel burst out after brooding a moment, releasing his hand and standing. "Just a conquest—a trophy that you can brag about to your friends?"

"Please, Isabel," said Freddy, a little surprised at the offense he had caused. "Let's not put it that way. Still, you have to concede, after all these months and years of pursuing you, I should think I'd be entitled to a little gloating."

He abruptly choked on the word "gloating" and began to gasp intermittently.

"What's the matter, Alfredo?" Isabel wondered aloud, sounding moderately concerned.

He continued to wheeze sporadically, making it hard for him to form a phrase. His eyes bulged as he forced out a few words between gasps.

"Something wrong…suddenly feeling dizzy…nauseated."

"Not surprising, the way you sucked down that drink. What do you expect?" Isabel scanned the room and spotted an enamelware bowl that Freddy sometimes used as a stopgap chamber pot tucked halfway under the bed. She dutifully exchanged the bowl for the empty tumbler and instructed him to lean forward.

"If you're going to be sick, and you are, then use this for a catch basin," Isabel instructed.

"How would you—"

"You know me. I just know these things—much more, in fact than you would suspect. Actually, I can tell you that you're about to vomit your guts out right about now," Isabel stated matter-of-factly.

As if on cue, Freddy regurgitated the better half of his drink into the bowl in one violent heave, and the wheezing immediately subsided.

"Good job, Alfredo!" Isabel exclaimed cheerily. "You kept it all in the bowl. You wouldn't want to mess those nice clean sheets." She took the bowl away and handed him one of the white cloth napkins from the serving tray.

Freddy wiped his mouth and held the napkin out with a trembling hand. "It's blood again, Isabel," he said between gasps. "Just look."

"I can't tell for sure," she muttered, inspecting the crimson stain on the otherwise pristine cloth, "but it looks more like Bloody Maria to me."

"It's blood, believe you me. I know it when I see it." His speech was slightly slurred and airy. He lay back on his bed and gazed at his new bride. Her tender lips were upturned slightly in a Mona Lisa half smile. He silently wished that he could hold that image in his sight, his mind, and his heart forever. But then it dissolved into the swimming blur that obscured his picture of the rest of the room. An annoying ring commenced in his ears again, but not the blasts from before but a steady whine that invited madness.

"You seem alarmed, Freddy. Isn't this a fairly common thing with your condition?" Isabel asked, feigning innocence.

"No. These symptoms…they're like…before. Better call Jay Pee to come back."

"It will be twenty minutes before he gets home, Alfredo. And that's if he doesn't stop off somewhere on the way."

"He's got… a pager."

"Of course he does, and a lot of good it will do him out on County Road 234, where the nearest phone is half a world away. I'll just stay here with you until he's able to be reached." Isabel settled back into the wicker chair and grasped his hand again. "Now, tell me about your symptoms so I can repeat them to the doctor when…I mean, *if* you lose consciousness."

"Stomach pain, nausea," Freddy stated.

"Uh-huh. Go on."

"Blurred vision, ears ringing," he continued.

"Interesting—anything else?"

"I'm feeling kind of drowsy," Freddy croaked at length. "My head is starting to ache," he complained.

"There goes the honeymoon," Isabel quipped.

"This isn't funny," Freddy shot back, annoyed.

"Of course not, dear," Isabel agreed in a consoling tone. "I know you're seriously ill. I'm just trying to lift your spirits a little."

"Not working." He groaned.

"Apparently not. Now, any other symptoms?"

"I'm starting to tremble all over—like before."

"Poor dear," Isabel purred. Freddy thought he detected a note of condescension. "Tell me this," she continued to inquire. "Can you raise yourself up and get out of bed?"

He grunted with effort. His whole body shuddered, then went slack. "No," he whimpered, "I can't."

"That's not good, Freddy, because one of the possible symptoms is diarrhea. I won't know what to do if you mess yourself in the bed."

"My God!" he hissed. "Call me an ambulance!"

"Now, let's not get carried away, dear." Isabel chuckled facetiously. "No pun intended, of course."

Freddy's eyes widened. "Isabel," he panted. "Why…so…strange?"

"Acting strangely? I don't think so, my love. In fact, I believe I'm behaving quite naturally for a woman so despicably *betrayed*." She leaned in and whispered the final word into his ear.

"Then you *know*!" Freddy sobbed at length.

"I'll bet you thought it was your pal Ezra who poisoned you last night," Isabel asserted coolly. "I suppose it could just as well have been. You know, Alfredo, you should be much more particular about choosing your playmates." She was speaking to him from a shimmering haze, in a voice that reverberated like it was coming from the bottom of a well.

"How long?" he groaned.

"How long have I known? Now, that's the frustrating part. For someone who has a sixth sense about such things, I was a real patsy right up until yesterday afternoon, when I decided to take the shotgun back behind the café. One of the patrons told me that double-aught buckshot kicked like a mule, so I figured I should test it out to see if I could handle it without sacrificing accuracy. When it didn't kick at all, I ejected the cartridges and discovered the blanks you planted. That's when I started to think about that bottle of champagne in the cooler, so I cornered Maria."

"Isabel…you must—"

"Oh, Freddy!" She snickered. "You should have seen the look on Ezra's face when he realized that only the first two shots in the magazine were blanks after I reloaded. It was a priceless face for that one split second before I blew it into tiny smithereens. In fact, that shocked expression was almost as precious as the look of horror and amazement on your own face right now."

"Isabel, please," Freddy whimpered, "I didn't—"

"Save your breath, little man," Isabel sneered. "Don't be a liar to the last. After all your treachery, nothing you could say would deter me from the enjoyment of watching you die in agony. Once I concluded that you were the only one with access to my gun, everything fell into place: the way you were always there just as Ezra was leaving the scene, the way you failed to make it to Ray's place on time to prevent the abduction, the way you came back in the nick of time to 'rescue me' from being raped by that thing that you conspired with. Then, some other details came home. I recalled two of the many things that my *abuelita* told me on her deathbed: that there were *two* cursed family names in Oracle Mesa, Cienfuegos and Mendoza. You are a Hightower on your father's side, but your mother's maiden name was Mendoza. You fell into league with the old *brujo* so he would spare you while he killed off the rest of your family, including your wife. And something else—my *abuelita's* last words were, 'Beware all I…' At least, I thought so. Now, I'm certain she was saying, 'Beware *ally*.' Yeah, Freddy, every finger pointed at you once the veil of the ruse was stripped away. You continued your unholy alliance with that demon in his quest to get to Ray and me, right to the end. And you might have succeeded if Providence had not intervened and told me to check my ammunition."

"Whu…what…?"

"Don't waste your strength, my love. You're going to need it to fight for your life. Make no mistake—you'll lose in the end, but it will be great entertainment while it lasts."

Freddy sobbed loudly, and his body began to shudder.

"You're losing the ability to talk now, so let's do this: when you have a question, just think about it really hard, and squeeze my hand, and I'll know and explain. Because really, my dear, I want you to take all the knowledge of this to your grave. Now, you were about to ask what it was I gave you that's bringing a close to your miserable, bottom-dwelling life as we speak—right? Let's just say that my choice of the oleander flowers that I picked just now for my wedding bouquet was quite apropos. Last night, the dose I put in your Cuba Libra was too weak. I was afraid you would become suspicious of the telltale lemon flavor. This morning, the overwhelming *sabor* of the Bloody Maria masked the taste better, and I was able to slip you a dose of tea that would kill a horse, even after you retched half of it up."

Freddy pressed her palm and gazed imploringly at the shadowy form of the woman he loved—or thought he loved. He tried to speak but was unable. The paralysis she was counting on had set in quickly.

"Call the doctor? No, not quite yet, *querido*—not until I'm fairly certain that you've reached the point of no return."

Freddy sobbed again; salty streams welled from his bulging eyes.

"Tears of remorse? *Pobrecito*—I am *so* sorry for you. Shall I forgive you—hmm? You, who introduced that devil's henchman into our lives? You, who allowed him stealthy passage into our home? You, who pretended to be an ally when all the time you were distracting me from protecting Ray from torture and death? You, who allowed that filthy animal to lay its paws on me so that you could play the hero? You, who disarmed me so that I would be defenseless when he confronted me? Now you are feeling contrite?" Isabel spat on the floor. "*No me haces reír*, Alfredo. Don't make me laugh. I'll forgive you when the devil shits snowballs." She growled through clenched teeth. "However," she added, almost in the same breath but softly, "if you want me to call you a priest, I'd be willing to do that. The mercy of Christ extends far beyond my exhausted capacity to forgive."

Freddy closed his eyes and twisted his head to indicate in the negative.

"No?" Isabel reflected. "I didn't think so, but you never know what goes on in hearts and minds at the end. There have been many deathbed conversions, or so I am told. You never were a believer in anything but yourself—isn't that right?"

Freddy squeezed her hand again, and an expression of intense concentration stole across Isabel's face—a look that slowly morphed into a smile.

"Why did I give consent to marry you with full knowledge of your cowardly intent? *Querido*, that little charade of a ceremony will be annulled right after I use whatever scarce legitimacy it provides for my own designs. I did not do it to take your property, Freddy. I meant what I said about not wanting the cantina and the hacienda. They are tainted with the ghost of your foul ownership. No, my husband, what I really want is a widow's prerogative: *el poder sobre el cadáver*—guardianship over the corpse. That's right, little man, I just want your ashes!

Freddy opened his mouth and let out a mournful wail that rose in pitch, then deteriorated into a loathsome gurgling sound.

"What's that, my dear? Didn't quite catch the meaning of that."

He hissed and gnashed his teeth like a wounded beast.

"Time to call the doctor? *Gracias, querido.* I almost forgot. Yes, I believe you're right. I think it is about time. I'll just go quickly downstairs to the bar and call his service. *Pero, por favor,* try to hold on until I get back. I'd hate to miss any of the drama. You know, final throes and all."

She rose and released his weakening clutch. The dying man's face twisted into a horrible mask of pain and anger. He hissed again, that time more like a serpent.

"*Por qué,* Freddy?" Did you really ask why?" Isabel chuckled in astonishment. "Why, I think you've heard me say it maybe a dozen times or more, my dear: *We do what we have to.*"

In the First Degree
(Interlude Three)

"Holy shit, Curtis!" I exclaimed, once again letting my reflexes get the better of me. "She killed him, man."

"Yeah, I know," my friend muttered wryly. "I had a hard time chewin' on that one myself. But hey, don't you think that son of a bitch had it comin'? I mean, the way he set up my friends for a slashin'—hell, if anybody deserved that medicine, it was him."

"Maybe so, but that's not the point," I replied, quite agitated. "Isabel murdered Freddy in cold blood. You know that, and now I know it. That makes us both accessories after the fact if we don't tell the authorities. I saw it all on *Perry Mason*."

"Well, I'm glad that you've come to be such a true believer in my tale, Vince, but all this happened in another time and another place. You and me jus' *talkin'* about it in the dark out here in the boonies doesn't really involve us in the crime. You know, you're not the only one who watches *Perry Mason*."

"It was only a year ago and a couple of counties over. You gotta understand—time never runs out on murder. What you're talking about is called the statute of limitations, but it does not apply to homicide. Curtis, this is serious shit!"

"Of course it is—this is all serious shit, but that don't mean you need to go blabbin' it all over town, least of all to the fuzz. I never meant anybody else to hear the tale but you. Don't you know that?"

"So you're telling me all of this in confidence? I didn't know that when we started."

"I thought it was *understood.* I told you there are parts that are hard to believe, and some parts are hard for me 'fess up to. You remember?"

"Yeah, but…"

"Yeah but *nothin'*! Now, listen up: there's two roads we can take from here, Vince. One, I can tell you right now that I made all this shit up and pack it in for the night."

"And the other?"

"You can put on a different pair of ears from here on out, listen to the rest with an open mind and a closed mouth. 'Cause there's more incidents up ahead that might strain your belief and bruise your candy-ass sense of justice."

"Well…well, of course I want you to continue, Curtis. It's just that it gets to be too much in some places. And you threatening to say it's all a fiction makes me wonder if all of it—or any of it—is really true."

"It's all true—that is, what happened is all true. How it happened and why it happened, well, that's the story tellin' itself. Let's say you go tell Sergeant Joe that Isabel murdered Freddy. First thing he'll ask is how you know that. Then you get to tell him that *the fuckin' story* told you. How lame is that?"

"Pretty lame," I admitted.

"There. Like I told you before, this story wants to be told—*needs* to be told. It's got a life of its own. You just gotta listen with less judgment and more wonder. Think you can do that?"

"I'll sure try. But, Curtis," I blurted, "I've got to say something before you start again."

"Go ahead, get it out of your system." He sighed, clearly exasperated with my persistent uncertainty.

"I had no idea that oleander was so toxic."

"Me neither…but the story knew. Shall I go on now?"

"Yes, please do," I implored.

When Pigs Fly

The phrase *we do what we have to* came back to haunt Isabel in spades. The myriad tasks and responsibilities that immediately befell a newly wedded, newly widowed perpetrator of a double murder were unexpectedly staggering in number and complexity. Even so, having been relieved of the death sentence that had dogged both her and her only kin of late, the adversity was painless in comparison, and she took it on with the bulldog tenacity so characteristic of the Cienfuegos *familia*.

The first hurdle, of course, was explaining Freddy's sudden demise to Dr. Morton without arousing any undue suspicion. That proved to be less difficult than anticipated. He was half expecting it.

"For as long as I've been a friend to that man," he choked when he arrived at the cantina, "I've always known when he's hiding something." Isabel fought with an overwhelming urge to roll her eyes at that, but she managed to twist her face into a withering smile as the doctor continued. "He knew this was his last day on earth. I could tell by his evasive way of speaking to me. And bless you, dear lady, for granting his last request by marrying him."

In fact, Jay Pee was so certain that Freddy had died from a perforated stomach as a consequence of his ulcers that he deemed the indignity of an autopsy or toxicology report totally unnecessary. As the attending physician, he would recommend against it. As justice of the peace, he would see to it that his recommendation was honored.

A surprise bonus dropped in Isabel's lap when she learned that the good doctor was also executor of the deceased's estate. Once he was convinced that Isabel was not the least bit interested in inheriting, but only wanted some administrative rights, Jay Pee was amenable to helping to legitimize the marriage ceremony he had performed, if only to have an assist with all the many duties that would otherwise fall solely incumbent upon him.

"You know," he confided, "Freddy died intestate, but there is a very distant next of kin, a great-uncle who must be contacted, but who I would guess will probably decline any claim because of his advanced age."

Isabel was surprised at that, as Freddy had always maintained that he had no living relatives. But it fascinated her when Jay Pee disclosed that the relative was 102 years old and lived at the same facility where her *abuelita* Veronica spent the final phase of her life.

"I know the resident physician there, a Dr. Gilbert; I can make that contact," she offered.

It was late afternoon when she finally rumbled into the gravel lot in front of La Cocina in the cumbersome truck she'd borrowed from Ray. She felt pleased with herself that she'd gotten over the first set of hurdles without a hitch. Jay Pee had stayed with her at the cantina to help handle the inquiries of the sheriff's deputy, the coroner, the mortician, and Freddy's trusted manservant Manny—an ordeal that lasted several hours. She struggled with the proposition of driving out to Hayseed Heights to tell Ray of Freddy's demise, but emotional exhaustion advised her to postpone that chore until after she'd had some sleep. She set the parking brake on the C10, killed the motor, leaned back, and breathed a sigh, waiting for the wake dust to pass before getting out.

Once inside, Isabel made several phone calls. She had missed Mass, something she hadn't done in years, but for good reason: she would not compound her offense to God by taking Holy Communion without first confessing a mortal sin. Her absence, however, was bound to raise an abundance of eyebrows so she called a few key parishioners, including the deacon, to share the news of her loss. She inquired and got the name of a priest up in Jacobs Well, explaining that she had business up there in a couple of days and would like to attend a midweek confession to compensate for her failure to attend Mass that day. Next, she called Maria and explained the situation. She said that she would be closing

La Cocina for a few days to tie up loose ends and asked whether she, Maria, would sit out on the waiting porch the next morning to inform her regular patrons of the reason for the sudden closure. She then called Jay Pee and made some preliminary arrangements concerning a funeral. They agreed on several details: they picked Wednesday afternoon for a nonreligious, open-casket memorial service at the cantina—more of a wake than anything. The body would be cremated shortly thereafter. Finally, she phoned Desert Shadows Nursing Home and managed to raise Dr. Gilbert. Yes, he would inform Señor Mendoza of his grandnephew's passing and of the funeral service, although he had his doubts about the old man's ability to attend. Isabel hung up the phone after exchanging a few pleasantries with the doctor and breathed another sigh of relief.

It was nearly sundown when the weary lady toweled herself off from a long-overdue shower, slipped on a loose-fitting housedress, and padded barefoot down to the kitchen to nibble a few bites of a cold burrito washed down with a glass of tummy-warming merlot. She strode over to the casement window and watched the waning sun lower itself behind the rugged Catalina Mountains. It was too nice an evening to spend indoors. She refilled her glass and stepped out onto the porch, where a warm evening breeze, herald of a coming summer, caressed her bare legs. It occurred to Isabel that so much of the previous month's story had come to pass right in that place. The peace she felt was so inconsistent with past events, she half expected Ezra to pull up in his tan pickup, or the headless knight to go speeding past in his jet-black Lincoln. Yet nothing more startling than the plaintive cooing of a mourning dove visited her porch that evening. And that solitary bird's sad song slowly faded to silence as the stars came stealing onto the black velvet drapery of night.

———

Isabel awakened well before dawn, clearheaded and determined to confront the day's events with her usual vigor. She quickly dressed herself in jeans, a denim work shirt, and an old pair of western boots. She then packed up a bundle of food and scrawled a short message in black felt-tipped pen on the back of a paper menu announcing the temporary closure of the café in both English and Spanish, which she pinned to the front door as she walked out into the cool air of the dawning day. Maria was just arriving as Isabel idled Ray's truck across the gravel lot. She rolled down the window, shouted a few last-minute instructions to the girl, and eased the lumbering vehicle onto the highway, determined to arrive at the rental yard's opening at six to hitch up the stock trailer before the Monday morning crunch.

That errand was completed as planned inside of twenty minutes. It would have taken only ten if not for the profuse condolences from the proprietor and everyone who walked into the store, all of whom had apparently heard of Freddy's untimely death. "Bad news rides a fast horse," she muttered to herself, trying to recall where she'd heard that line as she throttled the truck back onto the highway.

The next task was less perilous than those of the prior afternoon, but it presented no less difficulty. Isabel would have to drive out to Hayseed Heights and break the news of Freddy's death to Ray. She thought about how she would present the situation as the C10 rumbled north on Highway 77, but she kept coming back to the certainty that it would at least be easier by far than telling him that his friend—his big brother of more than ten years—had been coconspirator in Ray's intended torture and ultimate murder. The lady clenched her teeth and gripped the steering wheel hard at the very thought of Freddy—that Judas Iscariot—and his dark collusion with the demon Ezra.

It was nearly seven, and the sun was shining brightly when Isabel roared up the drive to Hayseed Heights tooting the air horn. Curtis was already out at the hog pen with hammer and nails, apparently doing some patch and repair while Ray kicked open the screen door and stepped out of the little adobe shack carrying two tin cups of coffee. Curtis jumped up and strode toward the truck as Isabel got out.

"Good morning, *mijo*! Good morning, *chico*!" she sang out as the two approached. Even the hogs seemed excited at her entrance, although it was really the tooting of the air horn that sent them into their usual stampede.

"*Mucho gusto en verla, señora!*" Curtis called to her confidently.

"My goodness, Ray is making you into a little *chistoso* already." Isabel laughed. "And you, *mijo*—what are you, a blind man, doing walking around with hot coffee?"

"As for the coffee, I've got to tell you that I can see at least twice as well as I did yesterday. Still a little blurred, but getting close to normal vision," Ray stated proudly.

"That's wonderful news, Raymie! You have no idea how happy that makes me."

"I hope you brought food, 'cause this boy here has been eating me out of house and home."

"Yes, Ray, I brought food." She hesitated. "I also bring bad news, I'm afraid."

"What bad news, *Tía?*"

"Actually, *terrible* news, Ray—really horrible news." Isabel choked, her eyes tearing.

"Aw, shit! Okay, out with it," Ray demanded.

"I don't know how to say it. Yesterday, Freddy suddenly became very ill. I'm sorry…he died, Ray."

"What do you mean, *died*?" Ray muttered in disbelief. "We just saw him Saturday night. He was fine. How could he just *die*?"

"*Mijo*, I'm not sure if you knew, but Freddy had a very serious stomach condition."

"He had chronic heartburn, for Christ's sake. People don't die from *chronic fucking heartburn!*" He threw the tin cups of coffee onto the gravel driveway.

"No, *mijo*. It was more than that. The doctor said his stomach lining had holes in it. It was that way for years. He died from internal bleeding."

"Who said that, Dr. Mort? 'Dr. Death' said that? I'm not surprised. He should be an undertaker instead of a doctor."

"I don't blame you for being angry, Ray, but that's not fair. Dr. Morton was his good friend. He loved Freddy, just like you did." Isabel approached Ray, arms opened for a sympathy embrace. He turned away.

"Why didn't you come and tell me yesterday?" Ray growled angrily. "Why did you wait until now? He was my friend—you should have told me sooner. You should have come right away."

"I don't know—maybe I…maybe I should have," Isabel stammered. "But after all the hours and hours of questions from doctors, coroners, police…I was just too exhausted to drive clear out here just to ruin your night's sleep. It was a choice. I waited. I slept. Maybe that was wrong."

Ray began to stumble back toward the shack, eyes welling.

"Ray—wait up!" Curtis called and raced to his side. "Listen, man, I know how you feel, but from what I've heard, this guy was your aunt's friend as much as he was yours. Don't you think she needs you in her corner right now?"

"What the hell are you talking about, *you know how I feel*? You don't have the slightest fucking idea how I feel," Ray snapped.

"Yes, I do," Curtis retorted. "Right now, you're so fuckin' angry you don't know whether to cry or whip somebody's ass. You're even pissed at the dead person for leaving you. That'll all pass—the sooner the better, that part's up to you. After that, you'll just be sad for a while, and then you'll just start to remember all the good things about that person, and you wind up feelin' kinda sweet and sad at the same time. But I can tell you one thing for sure. Your aunt is the absolute *wrongest* person to take it out on right now. She doesn't deserve it, not one bit. She's hurtin' too, y'know."

"Since when are you such an authority on grief, kid?"

"You think you're the only one to suffer over a dead friend? I lost two of them back at that godforsaken lockup."

"Listen, Curtis, just leave me alone for a minute or two, okay?" Ray implored.

"Sure, no sweat."

Curtis ambled back over to Isabel, who was leaning on the truck hood and gazing at the hog pen. "He's not really mad at you, y'know. He's just mad right now."

"I know. I just hoped he wouldn't take it quite so hard."

"Why?"

"What do you mean, *why*?"

"Why would you hope he wouldn't take it so hard? Takin' it hard just means he cared a lot. Nothin' wrong with carin' a lot."

"I guess you're right about that, Curtis." Isabel sniffed.

"You know, ma'am, I sure am glad you came this mornin' with this stock trailer, 'cause whatever you plan on doin' with these hogs, it ain't comin' a minute too soon. They are really startin' to give me the creeps."

"How's that, Curtis?" Isabel felt some relief that he was steering the conversation to other matters.

"Ever since they gobbled up that spooky old corpse, they've been actin' awfully ornery."

"Ornery—how?" Isabel inquired.

"Let's put it this way: I worked all day yesterday and into the evenin' fixin' rails they busted off the fence. Ray says they'd never done that before, but by the blisters on my hammer hand I can tell you they're sure as hell doin' it now."

"Is that so?"

"It is, ma'am—that and they've been fightin' amongst themselves, and some of 'em are getting' pretty tore up. Truth is, they make me about as nervous as a long-tailed cat in a roomful of rockin' chairs."

Isabel gazed over at the herd anxiously. "You burned any scraps left over from their little feast, didn't you, Curtis?"

"Yes, ma'am, just like you said."

"The manure?"

"That too, for a while—up until they broke down the holding pen. Now that they've got the run of the bigger yard, I'm scared to death to go in there with 'em. I'm tellin' ya—those critters have got me spooked. I slept with one eye open last night."

"I don't blame you, *chico,*" Isabel muttered. "And you saved the ashes, I hope?"

"Yep. Got 'em sealed up in a coffee can settin' on the work bench over in the garage."

"Thank you, Curtis. You've done a real good job of it."

"My pleasure, ma'am." Curtis beamed. "I'll get the rest of that manure as soon as you load 'em up and haul 'em off."

"As soon as *we* haul 'em off, you mean." Isabel grinned. "Now, don't you worry. I won't let them get to you. Just stand over there by the loading chute and guide me in while I back up the trailer."

"*I* better do that," Ray asserted, suddenly reappearing. "I'll guide you in, *Tia*. Curtis, you run over to the garage and bring a half bucket of grain to bait the trailer."

"I'll have to get used to the fact that you can see again." Isabel smiled.

"Maybe not well enough yet to back up the trailer, but well enough to direct you."

"Have the hogs been fed, Ray?"

"Not since they dined on old Ezra's bones, they haven't."

"Good, it should be pretty easy to play them, then."

The ride out to Aravaipa Canyon on the two-lane highway was relatively quiet in the cab, the three occupants taking turns rolling their eyes at the cacophony coming from the weaving stock trailer that they watched in the rearview mirror. The squealing, snarling, grunting, and bellowing chorus sent up by their live cargo seemed to build in volume and intensity with each passing mile. It was as if the cloven-hooved beasts possessed some uncanny sense about their ultimate destination and were noisily trumpeting in protest. And, just when the reticent human trio believed that the discordance could not possibly get any louder, the thrumming of hooves against the bottom of the stock trailer intensified.

Curtis, seated in the center of the tuck-and-roll bench seat with the spindly floor shifter situated between his knees was the first to comment. "Man, those ham-heads back there are sure puttin' up a serious racket, y'know? Noisier than a four-alarm fire in a popcorn packing plant, I swear."

"If I thought they had enough room, I'd say they were staging a full-blown stampede, given the way they're thrashing around back there," Ray observed. "But, hell, we packed 'em in there tight as a can of sardines. I just can't imagine."

"I can say it sure *feels* like a stampede," Isabel complained. "They've got that damn trailer rocking so bad, I can barely keep us on the road."

"One thing I know," Ray returned, "I've never seen a tandem-axle stock trailer fishtail like that. I personally torqued the tensioner down on the sway bar as tight as it would go. But the fact is, *Tía,* you've got about two thousand pounds of lively bacon in tow, and they're not about to take this unwanted ride without kickin' up a fuss."

"Doin' that and then some, I'd say," Curtis piped. "Excuse me for sayin' so, señora, but you are weaving all over the place, only I thought it was just because you aren't such a great driver."

"You think so?" Isabel countered. "Well, *chistoso,* if I didn't value our lives so much, I'd turn the wheel over to you to see if you could do any better on this climb up ahead."

As predicted, the grade got steeper, and, as the surrounding flora quickly morphed from clumps of cholla and prickly pear to scattered copses of piñon and juniper, the undulating curves in the road gradually developed into a series of sharp switchbacks. The big motor whined, drowning out the pigs' squealing parade anthem as Isabel negotiated the turns in the lower gears, steadily climbing. She could sense the load behind her shifting restlessly, but not as violently as before. No more near-miss episodes ensued before the road finally leveled off at the southern approach to a narrow bridge.

Curtis peered left and right, trying to get some sense of the height as they rumbled over the through-arch span. As they neared the opposite side, he could see that the road rose again beyond the northern approach, which consisted of two rocky shelves, each about fifty feet deep and wide, situated on either side of the steel bridge abutment. Each of the ledges was hemmed with a low steel guardrail at its outermost margin that made for a questionably adequate barrier at the edge of a sheer cliff. The boy's heart quickened as Isabel slowed at the end of the bridge, aimed the truck and trailer onto the right-hand pullout, and braked to a stop at the far end of the gravel shelf. She set the parking brake and left the motor idling.

"What's this place?" Curtis demanded suspiciously.

"It's where my *tía's tres primos*—her three cousins—left the road almost twenty years ago and took the late-morning flight to heaven. We still come here once a year and bring flowers to toss over the edge."

"It happened right here?"

"Over there on the southbound side," Isabel interjected, gesturing across the highway where three small white wooden crosses adorned the guardrail.

"We didn't bring any flowers," Curtis mused.

"Because it's not *that* time of year," Isabel returned. "Now, you two get out and guide me."

"Guide you where?" Curtis wondered aloud.

"C'mon, Curtis," said Ray. "Don't play dumb. She's going to back the trailer up to the guardrail." He jerked the door handle, slid off the bench seat and stretched himself out tall in the cool morning air.

Curtis's eyes widened. "Oh my God! You're not..."

"That's why we're here, *chico*," said Isabel. "To dispose of those hell-hogs the same way Christ dispensed with the demons that he cast into the swine. The Word tells us to do as He would do. It seems to me like the proper way to rid ourselves of our own demon once and for all. I know I'm not Jesus, and maybe I don't have the authority, but I kind of doubt that I could find us a priest who would do this peculiar kind of exorcism."

Curtis mulled it over for a couple of seconds. "I don't guess I could argue with that even if I wanted to," he muttered.

"Get out and help Ray direct me. Let's get this over with."

"Wait a minute, *Tía*," Ray called from behind the truck as Curtis exited the cab. "I've figured out why you were having so much trouble with this trailer." He stuck his head in the open door. "The electric brake hookup was unplugged."

"*Mijo*, that's not like you to miss such an important detail."

"That's just it. I didn't forget. I checked it back at the house when I tightened up the sway bar, which, by the way, is now as loose as a goose."

"*Dios mío!*" Isabel exclaimed. "The old coot's evil doesn't die easy. It's a wonder that the hitch didn't fail somehow."

"Let's do this, Curtis," Ray barked as he slammed the door, "before something else happens."

But Curtis had already trodden the distance to the guardrail and was taking his first dizzying gaze over the edge of the precipice. What he took in was a straight drop of several hundred feet to the creek bed below, interrupted only by a single sedimentary outcropping about a third of the way down.

Aravaipa Creek, a mere trickle for most of the year, was presently swollen with the spring runoff from the White Mountains that lay to the northeast. A raging torrent of muddy water coursed and crashed through the narrow channel it had carved for itself with similar floods over the eons. The unfathomable depth of the gorge and the motion of the rushing water beguiled Curtis's equilibrium, and he began to teeter somewhat.

"Hey, buddy, look away if it makes you dizzy," Ray admonished as he gripped the boy's forearm. "The last thing I want to do is spend the rest of my day fishing what's left of you out of the creek. Now, stand right here facing the trailer and give my *tía* hand signals, and I'll do the same. Got it?"

Curtis nodded dumbly as Ray strode along the guardrail and planted himself about twenty-five feet away. The trailer's back-up lights shone white as Isabel was already backing the rig slowly toward them. The two beckoned her to keep coming, and pointed one way or the other to indicate any deviation from a straight rearward approach. The pork chops on board were uncharacteristically quiet as the big stock trailer rattled near. Ray held up one palm to stop Isabel, and the brake lights blazed just as the rear bumper aligned with the top of the guardrail.

"We've got a problem," Ray announced, glancing over at Curtis.

"Yeah, I know. How're we gonna get 'em outta there? It's a serious pickle."

"I know just how to get them out, and so does *Tía*. My dilemma has more to do with the doors—as in who's going to open them. We usually unlatch them just before we get to the loading platform. But, in this case, given the temperament of the passengers, I don't think that would have been a wise move."

Curtis surveyed the situation. In order to reach the center latch and cane bolts one would have to step up onto the rear bumper and precariously inch his way to the joint between the swinging doors to release them. Walking a narrow ribbon of steel with the edge of doom at one's heels would be a perilous feat in itself, even without the added likelihood that the pigs would assault the gates before the novice tight-rope performer regained the security of terra firma.

"Don't look at me," Curtis declared, almost squeaking. "I'm still gettin' over my glimpse down that crack of the devil's ass. You just said you wouldn't want me to fall, didn't you? Didn't you just say that?"

"I'm legally *blind*, Curtis. Would you really expect me to get out there and fumble around?" Ray argued.

"Seems to me your vision has suddenly taken a convenient turn for the worse," Curtis retorted.

At that point, an impatient Isabel rolled down her window. "Any time now, boys. Just give me the signal," she sang out impatiently.

"You were bragging just yesterday about how great your balance was from all those agility drills you did back at the fort." Ray sniffed indignantly.

"What if I did step out there and couldn't get the damn doors open? I don't know how they work. Then again, you seem to have firsthand experience with them," Curtis reasoned.

"It's not complicated. Any moron could figure it out at a glance."

"What is taking so long?" Isabel shouted, emerging from the truck. "I've got other errands to run today."

"This one is scared to get out there and open the gates," Ray stated, pointing an accusing finger at Curtis.

"I'm not scared, just dizzy from looking down," Curtis retorted in defense. "Just give me a minute, and I'll do it."

Surmising the situation, Isabel immediately resolved the impasse. "Ray, go get in the cab and wait for my signal. Curtis, step aside. This was all my idea in the first place; I'll take the risk."

Grabbing a handle at the hinge side of the left gate, Isabel vaulted onto the narrow ledge of the steel bumper. The gate itself was riddled with numerous ventilation openings wide enough to serve as handholds, which she utilized as she inched her way to the joining of the hinged panels. Spotting the movement of her grasping hands through the vent holes, the hogs suddenly reversed their reticence and sent up a heart-stopping chorus of screams that surely resonated in the halls of the house of their master below. Startled, Isabel nearly lost her grip, but recovered in a trice. Keeping a grip on the gate with her left hand, she skillfully disengaged a latch, a slide bolt, and two cane bolts to free up both gates.

"See, Curtis? The trick is to resist the urge to look down." Just as she began to inch her way back, one of the biggest boars took a run at the door to which Isabel clung, slamming into it with all of his weight, forcing it outward. The door swung slowly out, stopping over the gaping gorge, Isabel clutching the vent holes for dear life as her feet dangled over the abyss. She glanced downward, and the unimaginable depth of the drop made her heart rush. Curtis instinctively grasped the bottom edge of the door panel at the hinged side and heaved with all his considerable strength until the gate swung the rest of the way open, bringing Isabel back over the shelf, inside the guardrail where she released her grip and dropped safely to solid ground.

"Thank you, *chico,* for your quick thinking!" she exclaimed with relief. "You were a real lifesaver." She planted a friendly kiss his forehead, and teased that she could see him blushing. "Okay, Ray," she shouted quickly. "Hit it!"

The blare of the air horn once again startled Curtis as the reason for it finally connected. All seven pigs screamed, almost in unison, and exploded from the back of the trailer like they'd been shot out of a gun. The boy's eyes widened like saucers as he gazed over the guardrail at the beasts' surreal, almost animated, descent into the chasm. The airborne hogs continued to squeal and to pump their legs while they plummeted, as the futile instinct to run from their fate overwhelmed them. Some of the pigs collided with the outcropping on the long journey down; some hit the craggy walls of the canyon as it narrowed to a slim crevasse. None escaped some sort of death-dealing impact before plunging into the icy waters of the surging stream.

"Plop-plop-plop," said Ray, who had rejoined them just in time to catch the final splash-down. "Just like seven turds in a toilet."

"That's a crude eulogy for our cloven-hooved companions, Ray," said Isabel.

"Would you like to say a few words instead, señora?" Curtis offered, half expecting a quote from chapter five of St. Mark's Gospel.

"Yes, I would, thank you." She gazed down at the water reverently, silent for a moment. "And they all cried *waa-waa-waa*, all the way home," quoth she.

An Incident at
Hayseed Heights

Judging by how long it seemed to have been since the sun set, Curtis put the time of night at about ten when he finished the last of the *sopapillas* that Isabel had included in his provisions. Licking his lips, he noted that the big honey tin was still more than half full, and it seemed a travesty to him that the supply of the fried Mexican flat breads had dwindled more quickly than the sweet goo. Facing up to the minor culinary crisis, he decided to stop procrastinating and finally turn in. He would have to turn off the generator the way Ray had shown him. It was his first night alone at Hayseed Heights, and the boy had been busy talking himself out of any undue trepidation.

"Hell, I'm not scared of the dark out here, anyway," he muttered to himself as he wandered outside to silence the purring motor. "Beats sleepin' at Fort Grant or out in the desert any day of the week, no question about it."

It was a moonless night, and he located the nearby generator by its sound. He fumbled in the dark for the toggle that choked off the gas, but his fingers found the hot muffler first.

"Ahh—son of a bitch!" he cried aloud. "That's fuckin' hot!"

He instantly remembered a stock tank that was only a few steps away. He plunged his hand into the watering trough, and the cold liquid quickly muted the pain. He tarried there for a few moments as the throbbing subsided, watching the depth of the nighttime sky with its dizzying array of stars.

It's not so bad out here, he thought to himself. *It's really nice and peaceful—the perfect hideaway. I could live out here for a spell, no sweat—just until the heat blows over.*

Buoyed by the notion of living at the Heights for a couple of months with Ray for a companion and Isabel for a guardian angel, Curtis ambled back over to the generator, located the gas valve, and shut it down. The engine sputtered and died, and the lights in the house flickered and went out. As he reached the doorway of the darkened shack, he turned and surveyed the adjoining yard to assure himself that nothing was amiss. His eyes had adjusted to the darkness, and he marveled at all he could see by starlight alone. He listened to the metallic song of insects. A screech owl hooted from a distant ironwood tree.

But then, *something else.* Curtis discerned the unmistakable crunch of tires rolling up the driveway. He glanced in the direction of the sound and noted the telltale halo of quivering light at the crest of the hill. *Strange,* he thought, *but I don't have a clue why Señora Cienfuegos would be coming out here at this hour.*

It was almost too late for concealment when the headlights crested the rise, and it was immediately apparent from their wide configuration that they did not belong to a Volkswagen Beetle. Cornered by the beams that had not yet fallen on the house, Curtis retreated inside, fastened the hook-and-eye screen door latch, and closed the inner door. He stepped to the kitchen and peered over the sill of a double-hung window that faced the drive. The vehicle pulled abreast of the house and stopped. The boy's heart fell to his feet. By the rack of lights on the roof, it was clearly a police cruiser. *The fuckin' fuzz!*

He dropped to the floor as a spotlight beam shone forth and lit up the western exposure of the shack. For a moment, the complete interior of the little two-room bungalow was lit up like it was broad daylight. Curtis squirmed on the floor, pinned down by the blazing light that streamed through the windows.

Then, in a heartbeat, the little house went dark once more. Curtis cautiously raised himself up from the floor and gazed out the window again. The headlights of the patrol car were turned off, but the spotlight swept over the outside premises like a brilliant probing eye. After several passes over the outbuildings and pens, the beam came to rest on the generator, then went dark. The door on the cruiser opened up, and Curtis could see from the overhead dome light that it contained a single occupant clad in the tan shirt of a sheriff's deputy. The officer stepped out, closed the door, lit up a bright flashlight, and made a beeline for the generator. The boy could see by the flashlight beam that the officer was feeling the machine with his hand.

Dammit! He's checking to see if it's still warm, and, without a doubt, it is. Now, he'll come and check the house, sure as shit.

The flashlight beam hit the house next. Fortunately, it was trained upon the door and not the window. Curtis tiptoed over to the door, slid a flimsy barrel bolt to the locked position, and resumed his place at the window. As expected, the flashlight beam was looming closer to the entry. Curtis backpedaled to the bedroom doorway and held his breath as he watched the door. Surely, the cop would not just break in. The boy-fugitive had watched enough *Perry Mason* episodes on TV to know that entry to a residence required a warrant.

Nevertheless, a rattling at the screen door turned into a violent tear, as the hook-and-eye latch was ripped from its anchoring in the soft wooden jamb. Curtis listened, terrified, as the knob to the inner door began to twist. He retreated farther into the bedroom as the weak barrel bolt blew off the face of the jamb, and the solid-core door swung open wide. In desperation, he backed into a tiny closet and closed the door quietly as the intruder made his entrance. It was a hiding place that offered hardly any refuge at all. The clomping of boot heels on the wooden floorboards told Curtis that the intruder was in the kitchen.

"Come on out, boy," the officer shouted with some wavering in his voice. "Let's make this easy on both of us."

Realizing the futility in his situation, the logic in immediate surrender momentarily appealed to Curtis. The little two-room shack offered precious few opportunities for concealment, the closet being the most obvious. He was, after all, only delaying the inevitable. But his intuition told him to hold tight, and so he did. The heavy footfalls tracked toward the little sleeping room.

"You best not make me flush you out," the deputy warned, voice still quavering. "I tend to get a little trigger-happy when rabbits bolt."

Curtis's blood coursed cold in his veins at the deadly threat. He saw the light from the flashlight under the threshold pan back and forth like a searchlight beacon as the deputy's rant got crazier. By the sound of his voice and weighty steps, he was nearing the boy's sanctuary.

"Come out, come out, wherever the fuck you are, nigger. I know you're in here."

Curtis bristled at the epithet, and a flickering orange flame sprang up in his chest, but he still sat tight in his hole. Beads of sweat popped out all over his brow, and he thought that the hurricane rattle of his loud breathing and the trip-hammer of his heartbeat were certain to give away his hiding place, such as it was.

"Eeny, meeny, miny, moe. Catch a nigger by the toe!" the deputy taunted maniacally.

The flame in the boy's chest leapt, and the urge to burst from his place of concealment was barely outmatched by his sheer will and self-restraint. He held his breath as the light panning under the door suddenly held still.

"You know how I know you're in here, boy?" The tormentor paused as if he were waiting for an answer. "Because you latched both doors *from the inside!*" The voice was so near the door that Curtis could hear the deputy's labored breathing. "And you know how I know that you're my runaway nigger? *Because only a nigger would be stupid enough to do that!*"

With that, the orange flame exploded into a full-blown conflagration, and Curtis swung the door open with all his might. Whether fate or Providence, the trajectory of the solid-core door panel struck the deputy's flashlight hand, as the electric torch was knocked from his grasp and went skittering off under the bed. The deputy, a tall drink of water indeed, stood blocking Curtis's flight path, trying to orient himself in the sudden darkness. Curtis, whose pupils were dilated from his stint in the closet, saw that he only had one shot at escape. He aimed a right-fisted haymaker at the darkened shape that resembled a head and landed a solid blow to the lawman's brow. The deputy folded like a deck chair, but, as his knees buckled, he instinctively reached out with his left hand and caught the waistband of the boy's jeans. Curtis struggled to free himself, but the kneeling officer held fast. Peering through the murk, he vaguely perceived motions that the deputy was reaching for his holster with his free right hand. The panicking boy brought a knee up and struck the lawman's mouth, but still he held fast. Another knee to the face, and Curtis heard the crunch of nose cartilage, but the hand that held him only gripped tighter. Upon hearing the snap of the holster strap, Curtis desperately unleashed a salvo of savage, bare-fisted blows downward onto the forehead of his would-be executioner. At last, the deputy's grip went slack.

The thump of the service revolver hitting the floorboards signaled to Curtis that the threat of being shot and killed had been narrowly averted, and the boy consoled himself as his attacker slumped from kneeling to prone like a gelatinous mass. The fugitive was left to live another day, or so it seemed.

With his mind racing over his precarious circumstances, the young pugilist kneeled beside his vanquished foe and cradled his head. He wet his fingers with his own mouth and placed them under the deputy's nose. The digits went immediately cold from the coursing of air. The breathing was shallow but steady. Relieved that the beating he doled out had not been fatal, he was confronted with the fact that his attacker would not likely be indisposed for long. *And man, when he comes to, will he ever be pissed.*

Curtis released the lawman's head, not too carefully, and it clonked against the wooden floor. He then scooped up the pistol and made for the short path of egress double time. He had disarmed his assailant, and his next thought was to disable his vehicle to eliminate any chance of pursuit. To that end, he tarried at the kitchen for an instant to snag a stout paring knife, and then continued to fly out the wide-open doors. Kneeling at the driver's-side front wheel well, Curtis plunged the knife into the sidewall of the patrol car tire. The *kwoosh* sound of compressed air escaping from the puncture and the smell of latex elevated his mood, and he toyed with the idea of slashing all four of the rubber doughnuts. There was plenty of time—even if the deputy came to, he was no match for Curtis on foot, and having the gun in hand certainly turned the tables in favor of the boy.

Plenty of time—yeah, plenty of time to think this all out. No reason to panic. The boy's entire mindset shifted from "fight or flight" to a reasoned analysis of the situation. *Slashin' all four tires would be gloatin'—and what would the upshot be? Chester in there would be forced to radio in for help. He'd be a laughingstock for comin' out on the losin' end of a tangle with a fifteen-year-old boy, but all that would only increase the hound count from one to a pack of a dozen or more. Chances are, the deputy would cover up this whole mess if at all possible, and it would favor me if he did. Scratch the whole slashin' of other tires notion. Let old Chester change the one and be on his way. Now, about this pistol: I don't need it—wouldn't ever use it—so best to ditch it, but where? The waterin' trough sounds good, but if he found it, would he still be able to use it? Need to figure out how to unload it. Not a clue. Best way to unload it would be to shoot it, but that would make too much noise. But there's the stock tank again.*

He carried the Smith & Wesson .38 Special over to the watering trough, held it below the surface, and fired off all six rounds completely submerged. The water muted the reports like a silencer. Trouble was, the stock tank was suddenly leaking like a sieve—not much good anymore for a place to conceal the weapon.

Wait a minute. Why exactly do I want to hide it? To keep him from usin' it on me if by some miracle he would ever catch up to me on foot. But, if it's missin', he's gonna believe that I'm carryin' it. Armed—that's what they'll say—armed and dangerous. Shoot to kill. Those will be the orders. Man, this is serious shit. I've got to do things just right, or I'm gonna wind up feedin' the fuckin' worms. I need to let him get his gun back so he knows I don't have it, but make sure he can't use it. Unloadin' it was just for the moment. He probably has more cartridges in his car. Another problem—my prints are all over the damn thing now. Without my prints, he can't be sure it was even me that was here. It was too dark back there in the sleepin' room, and it happened so fast, he could never ID me. I need to disable this goddamn gun somehow and get rid of my prints—but how? Sweet Jesus, this is serious shit! Sweet Jesus!

The *sweet* part of *sweet Jesus* somehow lodged in the boy's mind, and the perfect solution surfaced instantly. He walked back to the shack, strode into the kitchen, and dunked the firearm into the tin of honey, lock, stock, and barrel. With the inoperative pistol dangling by a forefinger thrust through the trigger ring—more goo than gun—he ventured back into the room where the deputy was still sleeping and dropped it on the floor beside him.

"Okay, Chester." Curtis chuckled. "You got your damn sidearm back. You best rouse yourself and get back on the case before the ants get wind of it." He strode once more toward the exit but hesitated at the door, unable to resist a final comment before making a starlit beeline for the river: "Not too bad for a stupid nigger, huh?"

Glances at the Rearview

The drive from Oracle Mesa to the east side of Jacobs Well was long, a little less than two hours, but not unpleasant. The Tuesday evening jaunt up Highway 75 provided a welcome respite from all the many chores, errands, incidents, and episodes that had befallen Isabel over the past three days, and it allowed for some objective distance to assess how well each piece of the jigsaw puzzle that her life had become had fallen into its own place. Her mind traveled easily on a backward path to the aftermath of the plummeting pigs episode.

Monday afternoon had been consumed with chores at Hayseed Heights, like cleaning up the stock trailer for its return to the rental yard. The task of scouring out and burning the putrid dung was largely delegated to Curtis, which he accepted good-naturedly, but commented that it would undoubtedly "gag a maggot on a gut wagon." In the meantime, Isabel cooked up some of the food she'd brought for the two young men to subsist on while she chatted with Ray and tried to soothe some of the anger and grief aroused by Freddy's passing. She shared the story of the impromptu wedding ceremony, being careful, of course, to omit the essential part where she murdered him in a particularly heinous way, and that seemed to buoy Ray's spirits some.

"I'm sure you gave him a lot of joy in his last hours, *Tía*," Ray surmised.

"You have no idea," said Isabel. "But you know how much he loved my spicy food. With his condition, I wonder if I wasn't partly to blame—killing him with kindness, sort of."

"You should never fault yourself, *Tía*. Freddy was a grown man, and he made his own choices. He was responsible for his own end."

"I couldn't have said it better." Isabel smiled a little tearfully.

Her *sobrino* confided in passing that sometime during the trip out to the canyon, his visual improvement had seemed to reverse itself. That was troubling, and she vowed that she would get him an appointment with Dr. Morton for the day after the funeral. Afterward, she spent an hour cleaning up after a fifteen-year-old fugitive and an over-aged sightless juvenile.

Ray insisted on riding back to town with Isabel to make some phone calls, most especially to touch base with Rosa to quash any mistaken impression that he was ignoring her as he had before. Hoping for an evening rendezvous with the fetching Señorita Moreno, he assured Curtis that he would be back by morning. Later, upon overhearing the phone conversation that confirmed Ray's high expectation of landing a date, Isabel became an early-evening shuttle service for her nephew.

The weary *dueña* arrived back at La Cocina in her beloved Beetle at around seven, and halfway through the first sip of her final glass of three merlots, she received a surprise phone call from Dr. Gilbert from Tucson, who informed her that, contrary to all expectations, Señor Mendoza was indeed looking forward to attending the funeral, and asking whether she, Isabel, would arrange for some accommodations where he could comfortably spend the night. She informed the doctor of a tidy little motel on the south side of town that would have vacancies for the old gentleman, his personal physician, and a couple of orderlies. And, yes, she would make the reservations, not that the place was ever fully booked.

After confirming the Wednesday accommodations with the motel, she once again stepped out onto the porch to unwind and take pleasure in the simple delights of the encroaching evening. She noted to herself the relief she felt at not having the need to carry the security of a shot-gun just to come out and enjoy the spectacular purple-and-orange sunset. She set her wine glass on a table close at hand, closed her eyes, and remembered times from years gone past when she would sit there with little Ray and *abuelita* Veronica, hardly speaking, just taking in the cool evening air. The welcome closure of a whirlwind Monday was settling into her mind as her signature half smile relaxed the tensed muscles in her face.

The darkening ambience of the veranda had Isabel nodding when the annoyance of a pair of headlights pierced the shields of her drooping eyelids. She sat up tall from a slouch and observed a car coming her way from across the parking lot. She noted that its approach was just a little too fast for her liking. The vehicle's last-second braking at the front of the porch caused a short skid on the gravel and kicked up a puff of dust. Isabel turned her head and held her breath for a few seconds while the cloud settled. She then faced the glare, shielding her eyes with her palm until the lights doused. She recognized the car and whose it was. It was a typical law-enforcement vehicle, and she pegged the driver right away as the same deputy sheriff who had attended Freddy's ad hoc inquest. The hulking shadow that eased its way out of the driver's-side door confirmed Isabel's presumption. He had seemed just a little too probing at their last encounter—probing questions and probing eyes. He sauntered up to the steps, stopped, and planted one square-toed boot on the second tread, resting his left elbow on his knee, as if he were taking half a load off. His right hand went up to just touch the rim of his signature white Stetson, the lethargic western version of doffing the hat to a lady.

"Good evening, ma'am," he intoned in his best John Wayne. Wherever he was from, he was reaching for a West Texas drawl but came up with an Oklahoma twang instead.

"It was." Isabel sniffed, visibly irritated from the unnecessary dusting.

The yellow porch lights exaggerated the man's birdlike features—his aquiline nose, closely set eyes, and small parakeet mouth. "I'm Myron Aycock, ma'am, deputy sheriff of San Pedro County. Perhaps you remember: I was there for the mayor's inquest on Sunday, and I…"

"I recall, Deputy."

"I am flattered that you do, ma'am."

"Please don't be. I remember the names of all casual acquaintances, all of their children, grandchildren, and all of their pets. Even so, having a photographic but very selective memory, I don't believe your name would ever have come to mind if not for your uncharitable behavior at my time of grief yesterday."

"I do apologize, ma'am, if it seemed that way to you. But we have to be very thorough in our investigations. It's just my job."

"Speaking of which, Deputy—why don't you please tell me what your business is here tonight?"

"Yes, ma'am. Let me begin by extending my sincere—"

"Oh, *please*, Deputy. Would you drop the formulaic pleasantries and get to the heart of the matter? I'm very tired, and I have a lot of early arrangements to make tomorrow."

"No need to be testy, ma'am. Actually, I'm out here to check on your well-being—why, since you're all alone out here, and with a fugitive at large and all, I just thought…"

"Thank you very much for your concern, deputy, but my nephew and I have gotten along just fine by ourselves for many years. Many years, I think, before you ever came to San Pedro County, if I'm not mistaken. In fact, I wonder…how many years have you lived around here, Deputy?"

"I'm sure it's been more than two years—closer to three, I think."

"Then I'd say that you have a thing or two yet to learn about the self-reliance of the people of this river valley."

"Maybe so," Deputy Aycock retorted, still trying in vain to establish the upper hand in the conversation, "but I do know that a blind boy—er, man—can't offer much protection to a woman who may be in some jeopardy."

"What sort of jeopardy might you be referring to, Deputy?" Isabel examined the unwelcome visitor with a jaundiced eye. "Maybe you'd like to tell me what I might expect—aside from the petrifying threat of a fifteen-year-old boy presumed to be unarmed."

"Let's just say that a deathbed wedding brings about all sorts of questions, and it occurs to me that a friend inside the county sheriff's department might be quite helpful at this point in time…if you please, ma'am. Besides, there remains the issue of that escaped black boy who is still at large. I think it might be a good idea for me to investigate the premises while I'm here, just to be certain that you don't have any unwanted visitors."

"Too late for that."

"What's that you said, ma'am?"

"I think you heard me just fine, Deputy. I was referring to unwanted visitors, as in *I've already got one, but he was just leaving.* I know—it loses something in the explanation, doesn't it? Truth is, I've already made my rounds and secured the place for the night, so let me be as clear as I can be: your offer to look around and your continued presence are both unwanted and unneeded. Good evening, sir."

"Have it your way, *Isabel*," the deputy sneered as he withdrew. "But you might want to reconsider my offer of friendship when you've had a chance to think about it. You know, there were a few rough spots in your story about Mayor Hightower's death that might flare up with just a little pokin' and pryin'." He opened the cruiser door but lingered there, speaking in a louder tone. "When folks start talkin', it's hard tellin' where or how far it will go."

"People will talk and go on and on until there's something better to talk about. I've never let talk bother me much," Isabel droned, tiring of the banter.

"No, I guess you've had plenty of practice—what with the way folks talk about how unnatural it seems for a grown man and his aunt to live together, neither one ever takin' a mate."

"Now, mister, you *have* crossed a line." Her eyes flashed with an obsidian fire, and she rose from her chair. "People who dream up such filth are fed up with their own dull lives—they're pathetic. Those who put stock in that sort of dirt and pass it on are equally despicable, only less creative. And, for the record, let's get this straight: Alfredo Hightower may be dead, God rest his soul, but I still have friends in high places whose fondest dream is that I might call for a favor. Do you follow my drift, señor, or are you really so dense that I have to spell it out?"

"No, no. I know what you're saying."

"My advice to you would be to close that troublemaking yap of yours and turn tail now, before you dig a deeper hole for yourself. You really are barking up the wrong tree."

"Clearly, ma'am, I've given you the wrong impression."

"No, sir. I read your fowl message loud and clear. Subtlety, apparently, is not your strong suit—although I can't even imagine what is. Now, for the last time, *good night, Deputy!*"

"Yes, ma'am," Aycock muttered sheepishly as he boarded his Detroit-bred steed and mounted a hasty retreat.

"*Mind like a steel trap,*" Isabel mused silently on her assessment of the unwanted visitor as she applauded herself on the efficacy of her bluff, "*rusted shut.*"

———

Looking back on that previous night's exchange from a viewpoint more removed, Isabel did not feel quite so smug. "That man is going to be trouble," she said out loud to no one but herself. "He won't be brushed off just like that," the lady muttered uneasily.

She let up on the accelerator and coasted as the highway dropped down into the rural hamlet of Florence. The pastoral farming village once deserved its name as the flower of Arizona. That was before the state determined that Florence's remote location could serve a higher public purpose.

Isabel shifted into third gear to observe the thirty-five mile per hour speed limit. In the distance to her right, a phalanx of mercury-vapor lamps perched upon high block walls illuminated the inside grounds of the state penitentiary. The dark ramparts obscured any view of the housing units, but a single cylindrical water tower, its sheet-metal cap threaded with a string of glowing bulbs, soared on spindly steel legs high above the yard lights and concertina wire. The tower, standing like some colossal sentinel, glowered down from on high at the inmates below.

The *dueña* turned her face away from the dismal view, accelerated, and shifted back into high, leaving Florence and its attendant penal colony behind in the gathering gloom. Her thoughts drifted backward again, to the beginning of the day.

———

She had awakened before dawn and showered as usual. Despite a dozen more chores that lay ahead before the funeral, she marveled at the freedom she was experiencing in not having to get ready for the opening of the café. She had volunteered to prepare most of the food for the wake buffet; it was the least she could do for her dearly departed spouse. She began the first portion of her day's effort by lovingly placing a large pork roast in a Dutch oven along with a chopped onion and a clove of garlic to slow cook. It was the first step in the process of creating a batch of tamales.

Next in order of importance was breakfast. After putting a pot of coffee on the boil, she called upstairs to her sleeping nephew.

"Hey, Romeo! Get your *nalgas* out of bed and come down here for some breakfast." Silence.

"Do you hear me?"

Silence.

"If you don't answer, I'm coming up there!"

A faint groan issued forth from the attic door.

"You better have your clothes on, because here I come!" Isabel stomped a few times on the floor to simulate climbing the stairs.

"All right…all right. I'll be down in a minute." Ray growled from upstairs.

They were soon discussing the day's plans over steaming plates of chilaquiles and hot cups of dark coffee. Ray was eager to get out to Hayseed Heights to check on Curtis as he had promised, but Isabel informed him that there were several loose ends she had to tie up before running him out there. The first words of a dispute were cut off by a phone call from Rosa Moreno: an invitation to coffee at her place. She would pick him up in ten minutes.

"Ha!" Isabel gloated. "See how quickly your concern for your friend vaporizes at the mere suggestion of romance. Men—you're all pigs."

Mock indignation notwithstanding, that unanticipated stall gave Isabel the opportunity to make some phone calls of her own while the pork for the tamales continued to cook. She took the card she had saved from their first encounter with Curtis and dialed up the offices of McBride, Matthews, and Robson. Her inquiry netted an eerie but not wholly unanticipated story: Will Farnsworth, an associate with the firm, had lost his life several weeks earlier in a tragic one-car mishap at a bridge on the return trip from an appointment at Fort Grant. A rather forthcoming paralegal named Betty Wood disclosed that, yes, he was survived by a grieving widow, and that, while she was not at liberty to give out personal contact information, she was certain that his home phone number was listed in the Catalina directory.

A second call raised Carol Farnsworth on the third ring, and, after an awkward introduction, Isabel assured the recently widowed Mrs. Farnsworth that she and her nephew had been the recipients of a particularly courageous deed that her late husband had performed, and that she wanted her to know what a heroic person Will Farnsworth was.

"A deed? Oh, did he perform some sort of pro bono property work for you?" Carol Farnsworth inquired, quite bewildered.

"Something like that," Isabel responded evasively.

After a rather perfunctory exchange of pleasantries, Carol informed Isabel that she and the paralegal, Miss Wood, were planning a day trip to the crash site on Thursday to erect a cairn—a little roadside shrine— and asked whether she, Isabel, would like to accompany them. Although that unanticipated twist would add to her growing list of activities and would extend the closing of the café by another day, it was nevertheless an invitation that the *dueña* accepted with much appreciation. The chivalrous Mr. Farnsworth had, after all, snatched her beloved nephew from the jaws of death. The sacrifice of a couple of hours dedicated to his memory was precious little recompense for his heroic endeavor.

Next, she called Maria to remind her that she was needed at the café at noon to help with the food preparation for the wake. No sooner had she hung up when the phone rang, practically in her hand. It was Jay Pee Morton, asking whether there was anything he could do to help.

"Yes," Isabel responded breathlessly. "I can use all the help I can get. Can you come to the café a little after noon to lend a hand with the food?"

"Of course, and shall I bring anything?"

"Clean hands and a good work attitude."

"I'm a doctor; I've got both covered."

After the pork was cooled and shredded and returned to the Dutch oven to steep in red chili sauce, Isabel packed some of the leftover chilaquiles into a container to take out to Curtis, who she imagined was probably half-starved by then. It was nearly ten before Ray returned with Rosa. It took a half dozen lame excuses to convince Señorita Moreno that it was not a good time for her to visit Hayseed Heights, but Ray assured her that he would call as soon as he got back to plan their evening together. She departed, but reluctantly.

The drive out to Ray's place was mostly silent, Isabel intermittently chattering, almost to herself, about the dishes she might prepare for the wake. Ray mentioned again in passing that his vision was waning and that he was beginning to fear the worst: that total blindness was returning. Isabel informed him that Dr. Morton would be coming around the café at noon, and she would impose upon him to at least comment on the regression.

They were both feeling a little guilty that it was late morning before the Beetle made the climb up Ray's driveway. Isabel was hoping that the chilaquiles would help to offset any hurt feelings that Curtis might have at their unintentional neglect. She brought the little four-banger bug to a stop in front of the modest shack that Ray called home and killed the engine.

"Something's wrong." Isabel hissed unexpectedly. "Don't get out."

"I feel it too," Ray whispered.

She rolled down her window, leaned back in the seat, inhaled deeply through her nasal passages and exhaled long and loud through pursed lips.

"A vision, *Tía?*"

"Mostly *jalapeños, mijo*. But, *sí*, I get a strong sense that Curtis is not here," she announced quite certainly.

"Yes, I can tell he's not," Ray agreed. "The air is as still as death—the generator is not running. Goddamn it, I wish we'd come sooner."

"No, it wouldn't have made any difference, Ray. Something happened here last night. There was some sort of incident. I don't know what the outcome was, but I'm having a premonition that trouble is returning. We need to get out of here now!"

Before Ray could mount a protest, Isabel had fired up the motor, turned 180 degrees, and was flying down the drive as he started in with his predictable string of hypotheticals: What if they were wrong, and he was just inside napping? What if he'd run off just momentarily, and would return to Hayseed Heights because it was the only refuge he had? What if he was just down at the river exploring?

"No, no, and no," Isabel retorted. "I know that none of those guesses fits the true situation, although I can't say what the true situation is— at least, not yet. But, trust me, my intuition is warning me about this very strongly. We need to get out of the way and let it play out."

She raced the yellow Beetle up the two miles of gravel road and made it to the blacktop of Highway 75 in less than five minutes. With five miles of southbound pavement behind them, they met a northbound sheriff's cruiser that whizzed past at a speed only legal for law-enforcement vehicles, but the car's flashing lights were not on.

"That was the returning trouble I was talking about, Ray," said Isabel, as she zeroed in on the rearview mirror to confirm that Deputy Aycock was not making a U-turn to pursue them. "Barney Fife is hot on the trail of a certain teenage desperado."

"What does that mean, *Tía?*"

She spent the next ten minutes filling him in on the nosey deputy's visit on the previous night, and told him what she suspected his role was in the latest disappearance of Curtis Jefferson.

Ray brooded in silence for a moment. "Why in the hell didn't you tell me about this jerk sooner?" he blurted.

"Partly because I thought it was an isolated incident and not worth mentioning, and partly because, lately, you've had your mind so set on how to get past Señorita Moreno's panties with some finesse, that you haven't had your ears turned on."

"Good. Blame it on me." Ray sniffed. "Makes me wonder what else you've kept from me."

"What's *that* supposed to mean?"

"I don't know—I guess when my best friend dies right after he marries my aunt, and I don't hear about it until a day later, that's a delay worth noting."

Silence ensued between them then, save the droning of the motor at highway speed.

———

As promised, Jay Pee had appeared at the café early in the afternoon to assist Isabel and Maria with the preparation of the food for the next day's wake. Isabel knew that he had merely given himself an opportunity to discuss the potential ways to dispense of Freddy's considerable estate, but, true to his word, he did plow into the kneading and rolling and shredding chores with surprising enthusiasm.

"You should have been a cook instead of a doctor," Isabel commented. "The hours are better and complaints are fewer."

"I do enjoy cooking for myself, when I get the time," Jay Pee grinned. "I was a chef at the Waldorf in a former life, you know."

"*Pues*, you didn't learn anything about making *empañadas* at the Waldorf, but pay close attention, and I'll have you cooking like a *cocinero* in no time at all. Just listen to the *maestra*!"

As the small talk developed into a more serious discussion, Jay Pee mentioned that he had serious doubts that the ancient Señor Mendoza would contest Isabel's legitimate spousal claim to Freddy's holdings, and that they should proceed under that assumption. He then informed her of several pending lawsuits that Freddy had incurred and suggested that they be settled amicably first and foremost. Those liabilities aside, Jay Pee inquired as to what Isabel's thoughts were on the distribution. She suggested that all property holdings excepting the cantina be liquidated for debts to be satisfied, the remaining sum going to charity, save a small consideration for Jay Pee's efforts as executor. She then surprised and delighted the doctor by insisting that the cantina be given over lock, stock, and barrel to Manny, Freddy's loyal, longtime, and long-suffering manservant.

"What a generous and thoughtful gesture!" Jay Pee exclaimed.

"I don't know about the generous part," Isabel responded modestly. "We both agreed that none of it should come to me anyway. But Manny deserves it, and, besides, if I fix his menu for him, and Ray continues to perform in the barroom, he might actually be able to support himself with that money-sucking dive."

"Yes, I must admit that Freddy's skills as a restaurateur had degenerated over the past few years. But, speaking of Ray, how is he doing these days?"

"I'm so glad you asked. He had almost completely recovered his vision until yesterday, when it took a turn for the worse again. The backsliding has taken a serious toll on his attitude," Isabel confided.

"I'm not a specialist, as you know, but I've read about similar cases—instances of people who have stared at the sun, viewing solar eclipses and such—and virtually none have lost their sight permanently. Tell Ray that regression is common with progress, and it's usually two steps forward, one step back, and so on. I'll be happy to examine him myself on Thursday. Just call my service later; I'll tell them to work you in."

"Thank you—that's very kind of you."

"Nonsense, it's my pleasure. Gives me an excuse to see you again— I assume you'll be driving him to the office?"

Isabel felt her heart flutter, and was stricken with a momentary loss for words. She stared at him, dumbstruck by his tousled good looks and Ernie Kovacs mustache. "Do you smoke cigars?" she finally blurted, the question seeming to come from nowhere.

"Yes—as a matter of fact I do enjoy a good cigar once or twice a week." He chuckled. "Strange that you should ask, though."

"I don't know." Isabel stumbled and glanced downward demurely. "I guess I can just picture you with a cigar, that's all."

The awkward moment was broken by the sound of tires crunching on the gravel driveway followed by heavy boot-heeled footfalls on the wooden porch.

"Expecting anyone?" Dr. Morton wondered aloud.

"Maybe Ray and his girlfriend," Isabel guessed.

A loud knock at the heavy wooden door shattered that speculation.

"Maria!" Isabel barked. "See who it is. My hands are dripping with grease."

Maria wiped her own greasy hands on her apron and went to the door. She cracked it open and a deep, all-too-familiar voice asked to see the *dueña*.

"Go ahead, open it wide, Maria," Isabel commanded.

As Isabel expected, the sunny portal revealed the hulking presence of Deputy Aycock, hat in hand.

"Afternoon, ma'am. Afternoon, Justice Morton," he called out. "I must say that the smells coming from this kitchen are absolutely heavenly. Would you all mind if I came in for a moment?"

"This is a pretty congested workplace right now, Deputy," Isabel stated coolly, "and I can hear you just fine from there, so please state your business."

The doctor was taken aback at Isabel's deliberate brusqueness, but, respecting her renowned defensive nature, kept his silence.

"Ma'am, it has to do with your property outside of town."

"My nephew's property, you mean," Isabel corrected.

"Yes, ma'am. Fact is, I believe that someone has broken into your place out there. I know your nephew stopped staying out there since his unfortunate accident, but there are definite signs of activity on the premises over the past couple of days."

"What signs are those, Deputy?" Isabel asked with a tinge of skepticism in her voice.

"The generator was warm when I checked the place last night. Then, for another thing, the locks to the house looked like they were tampered with."

"Did you go inside?" Isabel inquired, having a strong prescient sense that he did.

"No, ma'am—of course I did not. I would need a search warrant to do that."

"Yes, that's right, Deputy—you would," she taunted. "And you would never violate that principle of law, would you?"

"No, ma'am. I never would—only if I had good justification to believe that there was criminal activity going on inside. In that case, I could legally enter without a warrant."

"The only activity going on down there yesterday was me and my nephew loading up some stock to sell. We came back and did a few chores around the place until almost sundown. We even had a bite to eat there afterward, so I wouldn't be surprised if the generator was still warm. And, as far as the locks being tampered with, you must be mistaken: we haven't locked that place up since we've owned it, and that goes way back."

"Yes, ma'am. I'm sure it's just as you say it was. Just the same, I'd like to have your permission to enter the premises, just to be certain that our fugitive has not taken up residence."

"As I said, Deputy, the place belongs to my nephew, so permission would have to come from him. Besides, one or both of us would have to be present, and neither of us has the time or energy to go back down there today—what with all the preparation for the funeral."

"With all due respect, señora, since you're part owner of the property—"

"Look here, Myron," Jay Pee jumped in, "have some respect for a lady in mourning. It seems to me you're getting a bit too persistent." He wiped his hands and started toward the door. "Now, we all appreciate your dedication to your—*good God, man! What the hell happened to your face?*"

The doctor, up to that point, had been staring at a backlit shadow, but, upon his approach, observed a plethora of cuts and bruises that dotted the deputy's visage.

"That's no big deal," the deputy insisted. "I took a fall chasing a false lead at the bluffs down by the river. It's an embarrassment more than anything."

"Step inside, Deputy," Jay Pee insisted. "Let me have a look at you."

"No, it's okay, really, Doc," the deputy protested. "My wife already patched me up pretty good, I think."

"No, it's not okay. From the looks of the swelling, your nose is broken, and there are possibly some facial fractures as well. And that cut over your eye is going to break open again without some stitches. Isabel, look at this poor man's face."

Isabel muttered just under earshot that she thought it was a remarkable improvement.

"Maria, please fetch my bag from the back seat of my car," the doctor requested. "And, Isabel, can you bring us a chair?"

Reluctant, but not wanting to appear too uncharitable to Jay Pee, she silently complied and noted as she did that the deputy's face was indeed a pitiful sight. Both eyes were black and blue, swollen nearly shut. The straight aquiline nose took a decided turn to the left, and his upper lip looked as though it had recently been host to a swarm of bees. That, in addition to whatever superficial cuts were concealed by a half dozen square adhesive bandages, most of them arrayed upon his forehead like the patchwork on a tattered quilt.

Jay Pee cleaned up the battered deputy's face with alcohol swabs, replaced the old bandages with fresh adhesive patches, and stuffed two cotton balls into his nostrils. He even installed a couple of sutures on the cut eyebrow before sending Aycock on his way with some sage advice: "Call in sick, Myron. Go home, have a stiff drink, and get some rest. Then, come over to my office early tomorrow morning, and we'll check you out more thoroughly."

Although he seemed deferential to the doctor's orders, he turned toward Isabel on his way out the door and made one last stab at it: "Ma'am, I don't suppose you would reconsider—"

"Go home, Myron!" Jay Pee commanded in a loud voice. And, with that, the deputy donned his white Stetson and made for his cruiser.

Isabel closed the door and recounted to the doctor the tale of the deputy's attempt to intimidate her on his previous night's visit as an explanation for her terse demeanor. She also commented that the explanation for the nature of his injuries was questionable.

"He looked like he'd tried to stop a truck with his face, at least to me," Isabel quipped.

"I wouldn't jump to that specific conclusion, but I agree that those injuries were not consistent with a fall," said Dr. Morton.

"Unless it was a nosedive from Apache Leap," Isabel observed.

"I'll take all of this into account in any further dealings with Deputy Aycock," said Jay Pee. "He strikes me as something of a bumpkin, but a harmless one, I think."

"A hayseed, yes," Isabel agreed. "But harmless? I wonder about that one."

"You seem seriously troubled by him," Jay Pee commented.

"Let's just say that it's been hard getting to sleep since he crossed my path."

"The doctor can fix that." He opened his bag back up. "Here, I have a few Seconal Sodium samples with me. One of these little orange capsules will bring the sandman coming on the run." He handed her a little cardboard sleeve which displayed a long dissertation of instructions and warnings on the front, and contained three capsules. "Just don't take more than one," Jay Pee admonished. "Whatever you do, don't take one if you've had any alcohol to drink."

"That makes it less likely that I'll use them," said Isabel. "Still, I can't help thinking that one of these may somehow drive that pest out of my cares."

———

It was 7:40 p.m. when Isabel's backward-looking reverie gave way to the citrus groves that hemmed the eastern portion of Jacobs Well appearing on either side of Highway 60. Isabel rolled down the driver's-side window and breathed in the sweet fragrance of the orange blossoms that floated on the evening air. She would be a few minutes late for her appointment with Father Frank Cullen, but he would forgive her tardiness. She wondered what else he might forgive.

Woman at the Well

"Welcome to *Jacobs Well*—NO APOSTROPHE!" Thus reads the sign planted on the incoming side of Apache Trail at the eastern edge of town. Other satellites of the state capital sported catchy mottos that appealed to tourists, such as "The West's Most Western Town" or "The Sunshine Capital of the World." Nevertheless, the direct descendants of the town's founders remained adamant that the origins of the municipal motto provided not only something of a riddle for newcomers, but invited a history lesson in the bargain.

Jacobs Well was not named for the biblical patriarch, who also discovered a legendary well, but rather for the sole survivor of an ill-fated Mormon expedition whose aim was to find and develop a new promised land in the great Sonoran Desert. Leon Jacobs had volunteered to break with that party and scout for water when their small caravan ran too low on sustenance. It was too far into the late spring of 1875 to press on farther as a group. In his quest, Jacobs became disoriented, but eventually found water—an artesian well, in fact—on the east side of the Valley of the Sun. His triumph was short-lived, however, when he discovered that his party had disappeared without a trace upon his return to their campsite.

That debatable version of the town's origin was zealously defended by the controlling Mormon majority, who preferred to ignore the fact that Hohokams, Maricopa-Pimas, conquistadors, Jesuits, Apaches, and nineteenth-century Mexican gold-mining magnates like Don Miguel Peralta had previously established history there and partaken of the life-giving waters of the East Valley well years before any of the Latter-day Saints arrived.

Isabel smiled wryly as she sped across the concrete bridge over the Consolidated Canal that formed the eastern city limit. She was well acquainted with the small-town dynamic that constituted the true identity of Jacobs Well. Descended remnants of the early Mexican inhabitants, mostly Catholic, and the descendants of the Mormon settlers had been competing for social dominance of the little oasis since the beginning of the twentieth century in a mostly good-natured but hotly contested rivalry. By 1963, the trenches were deep and the battle lines well-defined. The Mormons ran city hall, but the Mexican Catholics controlled the police department. Old established Mormon families owned clothing, furniture, and grocery stores, while the Mexicans owned the majority of restaurants, liquor stores, and mercantile outlets. Mormons monopolized the public education system, but the Catholics preemptively evaded that power play by establishing two quite superior and well-attended parochial schools—one on the east side of town, at Saint Timothy's Church, where Isabel was just arriving.

The parking lot was abandoned, as she expected at that hour. The appointment she'd made with Father Frank Cullen to hear her confession was for 7:30. It was a quarter to eight. She hurriedly exited the little car and strode quickly to the office door, just to the west of the main entrance to the narthex. A bright coach light hanging at either jamb of the big wooden entry door illuminated a covered breezeway. She was surprised, and even startled, when the smaller office door opened before she reached it.

"There you are, señora," the priest declared as he emerged from the dimly lit room into the lambent exterior light. "I was beginning to get a little worried about you."

The two had never met face-to-face, and Isabel was somewhat surprised by Father Frank's physical presence. From the tenor of his voice over the phone, she had imagined a much older man, but the priest who stood before her looked to be perhaps in his mid-to-late thirties. A pair of wire-rimmed glasses gave him a professorial air, but his tunic and collar did nothing to conceal a pair of broad shoulders and a barrel chest that tapered to a trim waist. Isabel hoped that Father Frank's athletic good looks would not distract her from maintaining her purpose.

All of her previous confessions had been made with her own familiar, septuagenarian parish priest. Confessing to a stranger a bit younger than herself seemed alien and somewhat intimidating.

"I apologize, Father. The trip took a little longer than I remembered."

The priest looked puzzled. "I thought you were already up here on business, but perhaps I misunderstood."

"No, you didn't misunderstand. You see, I've been playing it pretty fast and loose with the truth lately, Father. But I'm sorry to say that the lies are the least of my sins at this point."

"This sounds very grave, my dear," said the priest with a tone of sincere concern. "Let us go to the confessional right away. Are you in mourning?" he asked as they walked. He referred to her outfit. She wore a long midnight-blue skirt and matching blouse, but the piece of her ensemble that caught his attention was the black lace prayer mantilla that she had draped over her raven hair.

"Yes, in a sense I am. But that, too, is something of a lie."

He pulled a set of keys from his trouser pocket and unlocked the main door. "We used to keep this open for most of the night for parishioners to come and pray, but we had a troubling incident a while back, and now we must be more vigilant."

He switched on the lights to the narthex, and Isabel instinctively strode across the reception chamber to the basin of holy water customarily perched on a stand next to the entry to the nave. She dipped her fingers and dutifully crossed herself. The priest gestured toward a side door, and they both entered a closet-sized compartment that served as the confessional. A lamp was already burning, and a votive candle in a red holder flickered from a high shelf. Father Frank folded back the wooden screen that might normally separate priest and confessor, and sat down on a high-backed wooden chair. Isabel knelt before him on a hard wooden kneeler, and she crossed herself again, as did the priest.

"In the name of the Father, the Son, and the Holy Spirit—may the Lord be in your heart and help you confess your sins with true sorrow," Father Frank intoned softly.

"Forgive me, Father, for I have sinned," Isabel chanted from rote memory. "It has been one month since my last confession."

A prolonged silence ensued until it was finally broken by the priest.

"Don't be afraid, my dear," Father Frank coaxed. "Our Lord listens with the spirit of forgiveness."

"I'm not afraid, Father. I just don't know where to start."

"Start at the beginning, as they say."

"Then this could take some time," she warned.

"I have all night."

"All right." Isabel sighed. "Let me start by saying that, up until Saturday night, I'd never killed any living thing that wasn't intended for food. But, over this past weekend, I killed two men."

The priest's eyes widened, and he sat up tall. "I see."

"No, you don't—at least, not yet. You see, one wasn't really what you could call a man at all. And the other was really less than half the man he seemed to be."

Another silence, and then the priest gestured to a chair opposite his own. "I see what you mean about taking some time. Why don't you have a seat and start over?" His tone was kindly, and Isabel felt strangely at ease in his company. "The kneeler is fine for a five-minute confession," he explained through a broad smile. "Beyond that, it starts to feel more like the Inquisition."

"Thank you, Father." Isabel smiled back. "You are very kind."

She settled into the chair, crossed her legs, and, according to his instructions, began at the beginning. "It started for me," she said, "about a month ago…although it really started more like eighty-something years ago…I think."

Father Frank peered at her with an intensity that was nearly palpable, but he kept his silence.

"I'm sorry," Isabel blurted, "It's all so complicated and so unbelievable, I'm finding it hard to be clear."

"Clarity comes with peace," the priest reminded her, "and you are in the presence of the Lord's peace. *Todo es pacífico en este lugar.*"

"You speak Spanish?" Isabel asked in surprise, as, by his name and the blue of his eyes, she had deemed him to be Irish.

"French as well, but I find Spanish to be much more useful for a priest in Arizona—unless and until, that is, the diocese finds a reason to send me off to Quebec." He chuckled. "But I should ask you, would you be more comfortable confessing to me in Spanish?"

"No, not at all. I am much more proficient in English. It's just that your phrase, *todo es pacífico,* is something that my *abuela* used to say to me as a child whenever I was restless or fearful."

"By all means, say it with me, and we will dispel your inhibitions. *Todo es pacífico.*"

Isabel repeated the phrase several times in Spanish in unison with the priest. The meter and phonetic pleasance of that specific string of words lulled the lady into a calm state of mind that allowed her a certain grasp on the accumulation of the past month's events—an objective distance that she hadn't previously had. She started again, beginning with Ray's announcement of his new relationship with Ezra and Freddy's reestablished courtship of herself. She left out very little detail, as every one seemed critical to a complete understanding of the story, and what started as a confession soon developed into a screed. She freely included the supernatural aspects of the tale, including her premonition of Ray's near-demise, her after-death dialogue with her *abuelita* Veronica, the Fort Grant curse, her encounter with the headless driver, and Ezra's very real shamanism…because it was all true. Accordingly, Isabel felt in her heart that God knew it to be true and only the whole truth would suffice for her confession, as incredible as it all might seem to her confessor.

After forty-five minutes, just at the point where Isabel was building to the episode of Ezra's final assault, it was the priest who was the first to declare an intermission. "I hate to disrupt your momentum, but would you mind if we took a short break? I assure you, I am riveted by your account, but there's a brief urgency that I really must attend to."

"Not at all," Isabel agreed. "It would take more than a *descanso* to break my stride now that I've gotten started."

After that break, Isabel resumed the story as if it had never been interrupted. She described her discovery of Freddy's treachery and how she lured Ezra into fatal range of her gun. She included a detailed account of her Christ-inspired disposal of the animated body. But, as her story progressed to her well-planned murder of Freddy and the following cover-up, the cleric's facial expression slowly went from one of fascination to one of grave concern. She finished by confessing her contrived marriage to Freddy and her feigned mourning of his death.

Father Frank sighed deeply, removed his glasses, placed them in his lap, and rubbed his closed eyelids. He did not speak for over a minute. Isabel began to feel uncomfortable.

"Are you going to impose a penance now, Father?" Isabel finally inquired.

"If only it were that simple," the cleric murmured solemnly. "But no, señora. I feel I must offer you some serious counsel first."

"Is it that you don't believe my story?" Isabel asked. "I know it seems unbelievable in part, but, I assure you, it's all true—as God is my witness."

"To me, your account, extraordinary as it may be, is by no means inconceivable at all. I don't question one detail regarding the veracity of your story. You see, my dear, you avoided going to your own priest, preferring instead a rite that was more or less anonymous by confessing to a priest outside of your acquaintance. But I believe it was not by chance at all that you wound up coming to me in particular. As it happens, I am something of an authority on such mystical phenomena. As a graduate seminarian, I did my theological dissertation on the manifestations of pure evil in human form. Your shaman lycanthrope, Ezra, is as real to me as you are. I have no trouble at all accepting every detail as you told it. So, you see, you couldn't have picked a better confessor for your story than if you'd looked up 'mystic priests' in the Yellow Pages. No, it is not the astounding nature of your confession that gives me pause."

"What, then?" Isabel asked.

"Let's begin with the first killing. I wholeheartedly agree with your assessment that, at some point, Ezra ceased to be a human being entirely—that is, if he ever was human at all. No, what you destroyed that night with your shotgun was the physical coil of an evil spirit—a devoted disciple of Lucifer—and not a fellow human being. But, even if that weren't the case, it is clear that you acted in self-defense and in defense of your nephew in the face of what was clearly an immediate and deadly threat. Use of deadly force under such circumstances does not constitute a sin and, as such, requires neither penance nor absolution. Quite the contrary, your actions that night demonstrated a full measure of fortitude, one of the cardinal virtues, and I'm certain our Lord commends you for the valor you brought to bear in your battle with, and conquest of, that disciple of Satan."

"I can only hope so, Father," Isabel choked out, suppressing a welling of forbidden pride, "but we both know that I am in need of absolution for my sin of killing Freddy."

"Yes, I dare say that you committed the mortal sin of murder quite clearly in that instance. You plotted and planned that killing by your own admission. And, although he deceived you and assisted the demon Ezra with his attempts on the lives you and your nephew, I doubt that Freddy Hightower posed any immediate threat to either of you once Ezra was dead. His treachery was driven solely by fear of the demon's threat to his own life. Before our Lord, you admit that to be true, don't you?"

"I can't deny that before our Lord," Isabel confessed, her eyes downcast in shame.

"You knew that to be true when you poisoned him, didn't you?"

"I suppose so," Isabel admitted reluctantly, "yes."

"The truth is, you killed him in anger and for retribution because he deceived you and betrayed you. It was a revenge killing, isn't that so?" the priest prompted.

"Yes, Father. I confess that to be true, but there was another reason."

"What reason was that?"

"Because I didn't want my *sobrino*, Ray, to learn that his best friend had plotted his murder. Given all that had happened to him, I thought that it might be more than he'd be able to endure. Killing Freddy preserved Ray's memory of him as a friend, a big brother, so to speak."

"Protecting a loved one from an awful truth—a noble notion indeed, but justification for murder? I hardly think so. In retrospect, I doubt that you think so either. I wonder whether you weighed the trauma he might have to endure if he finds out that he was not only betrayed by his friend but also lied to about his friend's death by his murdering aunt, someone to whom he always looked for guidance?"

"Of course I worry about that now, but that possibility took a back seat to my anger at the time," Isabel retorted. "Besides, I took great pains to ensure that Freddy's death would appear to be a medical issue. No one would or will ever suspect." She immediately dismissed a fleeting image of Deputy Aycock.

"I see. So you reinforced what you deemed to be a grand and noble lie by manufacturing a delicate structure of many lies. Hmm. Quite convenient that your noble cover-up to protect your nephew also happens to protect you from a grand jury investigation."

Isabel bristled. "This is beginning to feel like an inquisition. I admit that I murdered Freddy Hightower, and I confess my sin before the Lord. Now, I repent and ask for absolution."

"Señora, I hope that you recognize that I am only helping you to face the true nature of your sin. There is no justification whatsoever for what you did to that man. You ask for mercy, but temper your petition with a false justification. It is an imperfect contrition indeed, and there can be no absolution until you come to terms with that. You must be sorry, unconditionally, to receive what you ask for—the Lord's forgiveness."

"Of course, I am sorry…I—"

"No, please don't compound your sin with dishonesty. I don't believe for a single moment that you are the least bit sorry for what you did."

"How can you judge me like that? How can you withhold absolution?" Isabel implored.

"Because I am required by the Gospel to make that judgment, as unpalatable as that sometimes may be. I refer to the twentieth chapter of John, verse twenty-three: 'Whose sins you forgive shall be forgiven. Whose sins you retain shall be retained.' You know, St. Thomas Aquinas said quite famously, 'Mercy without justice is the mother of dissolution.' But he wisely added: 'Justice without mercy is cruelty.' Now, surely you aren't under the mistaken belief that you are *entitled* to mercy, are you?"

"No, but—"

"Good, because if you *deserved* it, it would not be mercy, would it?"

"No, I suppose not. But do I swear before God that I will never kill another man."

"I accept that, señora. I doubt that you will ever commit another murder in your lifetime. But that is not the whole of contrition, and complete contrition is what is required for absolution. Can you say before the Lord that if Freddy Hightower were alive today, you would not be angling for his demise?"

"Since you put it that way…"

"Thank you for your honesty. I'm sure it will ultimately be your saving grace. In the meantime, I warn you that contrition is not so easy. But, what's more, absolution requires not only contrition, but forgiveness, which is even harder. There it is, as plain as day in the Lord's Prayer: 'Forgive us our trespasses, as we forgive those who trespass against us.' Our Lord's forgiveness absolves every sin, even murder, but it has conditions, and the most difficult one for us humans, it seems, is the forgiveness of others. Nevertheless, it is what is required, and we must defer to the Lord our God, who was quite resolute in this matter."

"Forgive that wicked little man? Father, maybe I wasn't clear about what he did. He aided in the torture and blinding of my nephew. He sabotaged my efforts to rescue the boy. He set us up to be murdered— he might as well have been the one plunging the knife. Forgive him— that wretched bastard who faked his way into our hearts and then betrayed us? If that's what's required, then I'm afraid I am condemned."

At that point, Isabel hung her head and began to tremble.

"Señora," the priest admonished, "I'm a pretty good judge of character, and I don't have you figured for a quitter. Listen to me. Our Lord does not ask the impossible of us. Nor does he ask us to manufacture fond feelings where there are none. But it is possible to hate the sin and not the sinner."

"I can't even imagine how to separate the two," Isabel sobbed.

"I think you can, but it will take some effort on your part and a lot of prayer. Try to think of it this way: Christ told us, 'Love thy neighbor as thy self.' In this case, your neighbor includes your enemy. Now, try to see it this way: you apparently still love yourself even though you committed something thoroughly despicable—cold-blooded murder.

Clearly, you love and forgive yourself or you wouldn't have come to ask for God's forgiveness. Now, try applying that to Freddy. You can hate and despise everything he did—period. Then try leaving it there. I'm sure the man had some redeeming qualities. You know, many wretched souls ally themselves with evil, not by cunning or design, but by weakness and fear, and I'm sure if he were still alive, he would try to justify his actions in that way, just as you are trying to justify yours. But leave the judgment of him to God—that's His business, not yours. *Act* as if you are forgiving the man; that's a good beginning. Don't think of the funeral as a pretense. Focus on friends who sincerely mourn his death. Are you getting any of this?"

Isabel looked up with a tear-stained face. "Yes, Father, but it is just so difficult."

"I know. It will take time and prayer. I am going to give you some scriptures to read and to think about and to pray about. And, when you are ready—and you'll know when that is—come back to me for penance and absolution. Now, let's go over to my office so I can write those scriptures down for you, beginning with the fourteenth verse of the eighty-ninth psalm. I believe it is quite pertinent."

They rose to leave, but the priest hesitated. "You know," he said, "I got so caught up in our dialogue that I forgot to ask whether there are any other sins you'd like to confess while we are here."

"I do tend to swear a lot."

"I gathered that," the priest said with a grin. "You can say ten Hail Marys for that. Anything else?"

"I don't really know if it's a sin, but I was harboring a fugitive for a while."

Father Frank got a puzzled look on his face. Then, as he recalled where Isabel had come from, it struck him. "Your fugitive!" He gasped. "He was a young black boy?"

"Yes," Isabel replied, astonished. "How did you know?"

"Curtis Jefferson!" the cleric exclaimed. "It was most certainly not by chance that you came here tonight. Please, sit back down. I'm afraid we have much more to discuss."

Prelude to a Dirge

Ray and his beloved guitar arrived at the cantina at half past eleven, both of them chauffeured by Rosa Moreno. That was a full hour later than he had promised his *tía* that he'd be there, and he couldn't wait to tell her the reason.

Isabel, however, was in no mood for teasing. A rooster crowing at midnight had awakened her the night before, an omen that always cast a pall over the following day. And just that morning, the enchiladas she'd prepared as a main dish for the memorial buffet had not turned out as planned, which she knew to be a precursor of things going awry. With all the turmoil of the previous few days, she'd had no time to make her regular produce purchases and was forced to turn out a batch of red sauce without tomatillos. And, while she conceded that the subtle tang that the dish was lacking would scarcely be noticed by the funeral guests, she considered the unavoidable omission portentous, nonetheless.

Ray and Rosa were late, and preparations for the wake were falling perilously behind. As he expected, his beloved aunt greeted Ray with a tirade of half-meant aspersions.

"Where the hell have you been? As if I didn't know." She shot a quick but icy glance at Rosa. "It seems like I can't depend on you for anything these days, *mijo*. You stay up past midnight. You sleep till noon. You don't pick up after yourself. You let your hair grow long and shaggy, and you only shave when the mood hits you. Now this. You say that Freddy was your best friend, but then you're too distracted to help with the preparations for his memorial. And your suit jacket is wrinkled. What is that about? I raised you better than this, Raymie. At least you remembered to bring your guitar. And why are you grinning like an idiot? You look like Ray Charles, grinning with those dark glasses on."

"Because, *Tía,* I am going to make you take back all your angry words with one sentence." Rosa turned her eyes to Ray and gave a knowing look that he could not catch, although he stuck by her side and clutched her arm for guidance. "We were busy."

"I'm sure you were. Is that the magic sentence? Because if it is, it didn't cut it."

"I didn't finish. We were busy taking care of our lost refugee."

Isabel gaped. "You found Curtis?" she whispered, trying to contain her excitement. "Where was he? No, I mean, where is he *now*?"

"He found us. He showed up at the café right after you left, and, oh my, what a sight he was—or so Rosa told me. She said the little *chistoso* looked like he'd just taken the long way through a war zone, so we took the time to clean him up for the occasion. There now," he stated smugly, "*that's* why we're late."

"What the hell are you talking about, *mijo?*" Isabel demanded. "Just where *is* the boy?"

Ray cast a thumb backwards over his shoulder. "Back of Rosa's car, *Tía.* Considering the story he told us about that lowlife hound Deputy Aycock, we didn't think it was a good idea to leave him alone at the café."

"All things considered, I suppose I might have done the same," Isabel admitted reluctantly.

"Great minds think alike, *Tía.* So come and say hello; it'll lift his spirits. He's really fond of you. You know that, don't you?" Ray told her.

"That's just because he misses his mother, poor thing," Isabel observed as they strode across the lot toward Rosa's blue Fairlane. "That's okay, though, because I have a strong feeling he's going to be seeing her again real soon."

The rear window rolled down as they approached, and a familiar voice rang out.

"*Hola, señora! Me gusta en verla,*" called Curtis.

Isabel peered into the back seat. There sat Curtis, looking rather dapper, dressed up in a clean white oxford cloth shirt, black bow tie, and neatly pressed black slacks.

"I am pleased to see you as well, *chico*." She chuckled. "But where have you been? We were worried sick about you! And, *Dios mío*, what happened to your hair?" She suddenly noticed that his crown was as hairless as a billiard ball.

"I had a little run-in with the law again. Sorry I left the place a mess, but I had to leave in a hurry. And, as for my bald bean, just ask them," Curtis replied, gesturing with his chin toward the grinning pair standing nearby.

"We couldn't think of any way to change his appearance other than to shave his head," Ray offered. "And we dug out some of my old clothes from when I used to bus tables at the café when I was a kid."

"This is his disguise—Yul Brynner in a busboy's uniform?"

"Hey!" Curtis protested.

"Don't be offended, *chico*," Isabel assured him. "Yul Brynner is a handsome man—very macho, in fact."

"Okay, but I was thinking more like Woody Strode, maybe." Curtis struck an exaggerated Charles Atlas pose.

"*Por supuesto!* Him too, of course. How could I have missed the obvious resemblance? Woody Strode is a wonderful actor and a fine figure of a man."

Curtis's face lit up.

"Anyway, back to the point," Ray broke in. "We figured we could make him blend in with the kitchen help," he explained. "That way we can keep a close watch on our little friend and protect him, if need be. That deputy's got it in for Curtis, *Tía*. I hope he doesn't show up here."

"Anything is possible today, Raymie." Isabel sighed as she rolled her dark eyes upward. "I have a bad feeling about this whole event, and hiding in plain sight is always risky. Still, at this point, I don't see that we have any other choice." She opened the car door and beckoned Curtis out. "C'mon, *chico*. Sounds like you're the new dishwasher. And, when we get a minute," she half whispered so only he could hear, "I need to have a word with you in private."

"Yes, ma'am," he responded with an easily detectable note of eagerness in his voice.

Once inside, Isabel introduced Curtis as a kitchen helper hired out of a Tucson temporary service. Manny and Maria accepted the story without question. Manny handed the boy a clean white apron and directed him to the dishwashing operation. Rosa noted that the pass-through order window from the kitchen enabled them to monitor the boy's presence. Isabel added that other guests could notice him as well.

"I guess we can't have it both ways," she observed. "But, oh well, I've got to leave this all up to the Lord now, 'cause *I* sure can't keep a handle on it anymore." She literally threw up her hands and cast her face downwards. "It's all too much—even for me."

"I rather doubt that," Dr. Morton interjected as he entered through the open front door.

"Where have you been, Jay Pee?" Isabel snapped as she whirled around, surprising even herself at her sudden familiarity with the doctor. "I expected you back here an hour ago. We still have a lot of setup to do."

"I've been arguing with the undertaker here," Jay Pee replied, taking the lady's affectionate terseness right in stride. He gestured to a tall, gaunt figure in a rumpled black suit that he seemed to have in tow. "This is Harold Hackett, owner and operator of Peaceful Passage Mortuary. Hal, this is Señora Hightower, Freddy's widow."

Exuding a dreadful unguent of morbidity from head to toe, the mortician oiled his way across the floor and offered a limp-fish handshake to Isabel. "My sincerest condolences to the bereaved, señora," he chanted mechanically in a raspy baritone voice. The unmistakable odor of formaldehyde hovered like a cloud about his presence. "We've spoken only by telephone, so now I know the pleasure I missed at not having had the enchanting experience of meeting with you in person. I only wish these terribly unfortunate circumstances were more favorable." The dim lighting in the dining area created a certain dreadful shading effect that underscored the cavernous hollow beneath the mortician's prominent cheek bones while somehow accentuating his rather appalling, almost luminous pallor. "Now, I must apologize for the unfortunate confusion I seem to have caused," he croaked.

"What confusion?" Isabel demanded as she withdrew her hand from his clammy grasp. "What did you do with the body?"

"You needn't worry about that." He snickered nervously. "You will be pleased to know that the, um…that Mr. Hightower is resting peacefully parked out front in the rear compartment of my hearse—quite available, in fact."

"In this heat? What are you thinking?"

"I left the motor running with the AC on, of course," Hackett retorted. "No, the confusion I speak of involves the accessorizing of this solemn occasion."

Isabel turned to Jay Pee. "What is he saying?"

"It seems that Hal couldn't come up with the pine casket that you ordered over the phone for the viewing," the doctor explained.

"The Peaceful Pathfinder model was a very tasteful choice," Mr. Hackett chimed in, "but you must understand, señora, the combustible wooden casket line has enjoyed a phenomenal demand since the Church lifted its prohibition on cremation." The mortician clasped his greasy hands as if he were beseeching forgiveness. "With such short notice, I'm afraid that a premium quality wooden casket will not be an option."

"Why didn't you tell me this on the phone on Monday, Mr. *Hackett*?" She rolled the *h* in her exaggerated Mexican accent, making a sound like the clearing of a larynx.

"I was certain that I could procure your choice at the time, but, as you can see, unforeseeable circumstances intervened. I am truly sorry for this lapse in service." His voice broke on the end of the phrase.

"The short version of the story is this," Jay Pee offered. "Hal here wanted to sell us a high-end replacement box for a mere twenty-five hundred. The hitch is that it can't be used in the crematorium because it has metal components in its construction."

"Ours is a highly regulated profession, señora," the slender man rasped, wringing his sweaty hands.

"The gist is," the doctor continued, "that we would be paying top dollar for a box that would be used as a prop for six hours tops. I couldn't see doing that—even with someone else's money. I suppose I should have let you decide, Isabel, but as a responsible executor, I had to say no way."

"What choices are we left with in this mess?" Isabel sighed in exasperation.

"None, really," Jay Pee answered. "Freddy's out there in the cremation container."

"In a cardboard box?" Isabel shrieked, horrified.

"Actually, it's heavy-duty, multilayered, corrugated fiberboard with reinforced corners—quite durable and one hundred percent combustible," the undertaker stated a little boastfully. "It is a simple but very tasteful vessel of departure, I assure you."

"At this point, I suppose I should be thankful it's not a fruit-packing crate," the lady muttered. "No time for other options. Bring him in. Rosa, go get Manny and C…er, the Negro boy to help. We'll see what we can do with this latest nightmare."

"First," the mortician declared, "there is the unpalatable but essential detail of payment for services."

"Jay Pee, you didn't pay the man yet?"

"Sorry," Jay Pee responded, "I couldn't make the call, and, technically, it requires a joint check with each of our signatures."

Isabel quickly executed the check that Jay Pee produced and extended it to the undertaker.

"Here, Mr. *Hackett*. And…are you serious? Do you really hold corpses hostage until you're paid?"

"You have no idea the kind of larceny I am subjected to in this business, dear señora. After all, when the remains have been converted, there is not much collateral to collect on. I am only following a policy that is standard in our industry, good credit status notwithstanding," Hackett stated.

Isabel gaped at the undertaker but said nothing.

"I want to assure you, dear lady," Hackett continued, "that your departed husband received the most thorough and painstaking restoration that my talents could provide. I administer to each of my subjects according to his or her individual needs. Did I mention that I mix my own preserving fluids? I find that the premixed fluids that are commercially available do not always address a subject's distinctive rate of decomposition. Your husband, for example…"

"Please, spare me the grisly details, señor!" Isabel cried. "Have some respect for the grieving widow."

"As you wish." The undertaker sighed.

When the bearers brought the deceased into the cantina in his "vessel of departure," it was worse than Isabel expected. "It looks like an oversized shoebox!" she cried. "And where is the pedestal? There was supposed to be a pedestal and a skirt."

"The bier was part of the Peaceful Pathfinder package," Hackett explained. "The judge here decided on the economy option—no appurtenances included."

"Put it on the table over here," Isabel directed. "Take that dreadful top off the thing. I swear, I expect there to be a giant pair of tennis shoes inside instead of a corpse!"

Hackett, the only one of the group not helping with the heft, shot forward and removed the cardboard box top the instant that the container was settled. The odor of embalming fluid wafted up, and there lay Freddy in the bare box, wearing a fine-looking, charcoal-gray, three-piece suit and a frozen Mona Lisa smile. The mortician flashed a similarly morbid smile at the first unveiling of his workmanship, then silently withdrew.

Isabel was momentarily mesmerized by the sight of him. The sutures on his eyelids were visibly apparent, the chin was outthrust—the result of his jaws being wired shut with a grotesque underbite—the thinning hair was slicked back with some cheap pomade, and the face makeup was overdone, with too much rouge on the cheeks. Indeed, he looked the very epitome of a cinematic, Universal Studios corpse, and yet Isabel sensed, too, a certain real animation that the man had demonstrated in life, ghoulish appearance notwithstanding.

Isabel turned away briefly and barked some more orders. "Manny, take the boy back to the kitchen. Jay Pee, please stow that awful box top in the back room. Ray, go and get set up next to the podium; your audio is already hooked up. Rosa, please go upstairs to the apartment and get a top sheet and a pillow from Freddy's bed." She turned back toward the corpse. "I want to be alone with him for a few moments."

"May I be of any further assistance, señora?" inquired the undertaker, suddenly reappearing.

"No, you've done quite enough, thank you, Mr. *Hackett*." Isabel growled.

"I hope you don't mind if I stay for the fest…for the memorial, that is. The aroma from the kitchen smells heavenly."

Isabel shot the mortician a look that could curdle milk.

"Of course, I was very fond of Mayor Hightower," he added in thinly veiled recovery.

"You can stay and pay your respects," Isabel conceded. "Besides, just in case some of your handiwork fails, I may need you to fix him—like if something breaks open or falls off. Just try to make yourself scarce. Some of the guests will probably bring children."

"Excuse me?" Hackett wondered.

"We wouldn't want them to have nightmares," Isabel affirmed.

Hackett wandered off, shaking his head in wonder at her comment, and once the others had directed themselves to their appointed tasks, Isabel turned and began to gaze upon Alfredo Hightower lying in repose. It was his ghastly countenance that riveted her. The paralyzed facial muscles distorted his expression into an eerie rictus grin that seemed to be mocking her. Isabel shuddered briefly but regained her composure quickly.

"Freddy." She smiled wryly and bent closer as if he could hear. "I see you're doing your best to get some last-minute revenge on me. You should know that it will take more than a rooster crowing at midnight, a bad box, an evil smile, and a creepy mortician to vex me. So go ahead—do your damnedest. Anything short of you sitting up and pointing an accusing finger at me, I can take in stride—and you're in no shape to do that. Besides, you have no righteous grievance with me, anyway. I only gave you what you deserved. You made an attempt on my *mijo's* life; I took yours in return. It seems fair to me. When you think about it, the only difference between what I did and what you did is that I was successful. Why don't you just relax and call it even? Enjoy this memorial service that I've arranged for you. People will come to celebrate your life, completely unaware of your dark side. All of your wealth will go to good causes in your name. I did this for you— for your memory. Okay—I get the side benefit of appearing saintly, the perfect grieving widow—which should dispel anyone's suspicion of foul play on my part. As for you, you can rest peacefully knowing that your good name will never be tainted with the knowledge of your own murderous intent. Now, sleep well, little man. I have lots more work to do."

———◆———

With Rosa's guidance, Ray had settled onto his stool beside the raised platform that served as a podium of sorts. Jay Pee caught sight of him from across the room, sitting by himself, tuning his guitar. The doctor took the opportunity to have a word with him alone.

"Hello, Ray. Mind if I pull up a chair?"

"Not at all, Dr. Mort—as long as you don't mind if I keep tuning. This is a fairly new set of strings, and I have to keep working them," Ray said.

"Don't mind at all; pluck away," Jay Pee said. "By the way, that's a truly fine guitar you've got there."

"Thanks—it is that." Ray flashed his toothy Ray Charles grin. "It's a Manual Rodriguez Junior—custom made. My *tía* bought it for me several years ago. Freddy used to call it my Man-Rod."

"Very clever, that Freddy." Jay Pee chuckled. "Speaking of which," he continued, spotting the segue, "how are you holding up? I know you two were fast friends. He spoke of you often, and very fondly so."

"I'm okay, I guess. Still pretty sad, really, but nothing like I was when I first heard. I was mad as hell." He plucked a B string and adjusted the tension, twisting the tuning peg, modulating the pitch until it was a perfect third to the G string above it.

"Angry, huh? At whom?" Jay Pee asked.

"Sounds stupid, but at him."

"At Freddy?"

"Yeah, him most of all—and at God, and at *Tía,* and even at Curtis."

"Who's Curtis?" Jay Pee wondered.

"Just a friend—you wouldn't know him," said Ray.

"Just to let you know, I've heard that it's fairly common to be angry when someone you care about leaves you like that. It's not exactly rational, but it happens. To be honest, I was somewhat pissed off myself when I found him. It was so unnecessary. He did it to himself, you know."

"Yeah. Drank himself to death, I guess," Ray speculated.

"Yes, something like that. And, now that I think about it, he was always fond of a drink, but it never really went to excess until the last few years." Jay Pee fell silent and just shook his head for a moment before continuing. "There was something that was troubling him deeply, but he would never share what it was. I know his newfound friendship—or, rather, romance—with your aunt gave him great joy. But even so, the anxiety—and the drinking—never ceased."

"You two were close friends, I take it," Ray speculated, striking a high E.

"Good buddies since junior high school," Jay Pee stated, proudly. "Actually, we were like brothers back then," he said a little wistfully.

"Gee, I didn't know," Ray murmured.

"I digress," said Jay Pee, composing himself. "I should save it for the eulogy. Are you planning to say a few words?" Jay Pee gestured toward the microphone, forgetting that Ray couldn't see it.

"No, I'm the assigned musician for the event. Besides, I'm not that good with words," Ray confessed.

"I'm sure your musical contribution will say it all. By the way, Ray, I'm wondering about your vision. Isabel tells me that you're experiencing a relapse."

"That's right, Doc. It sort of comes and goes. Right now, it's pretty much gone."

"That must be very frustrating."

"You can't even imagine." Ray shook his head. "You know, that's something else I'm gonna miss about Freddy. He was always making jokes about my blindness."

"Jokes—and you miss that?"

"Yeah, it made it seem less serious—made it hard to feel sorry for myself, you know?"

"Like you said," Jay Pee replied, "I can't even imagine. Well listen, I made some time to examine your eyes tomorrow, but you need to call my service to find out the exact time. Right now, it escapes me."

"Sure thing, Doc. Thank you."

Jay Pee rose to leave. "By the way, your high E is more than a little sharp."

"I know. I'm just waiting for it to fall off. It'll be flat by the end of the first song."

"Nylon strings are a pain that way," the doctor remarked as he started toward the bar.

"Hey, Dr. Mort!"

Jay Pee stopped in his tracks. "Yes, what is it?"

"Do you pick?" Ray asked.

"I fool around on an old twelve-string. Of course, I'm certainly not the virtuoso that you are—but yeah, I pick some."

"Twelve-string, eh? Why don't you bring it by sometime so we can do some jamming together—yes? C'mon, it would be good fun."

"Yes…yes, I'd like that very much." Jay Pee smiled. "I could use a little more music in my life—fun too."

———

Rosa returned, dutifully carrying the white top sheet and pillow that Isabel had requested, but something more as well.

"I saw these dark blue curtains hanging in his room, and it struck me that we could fashion some kind of skirt with them if we drape them just right," she offered hesitantly. "In the dark, they might appear to be black…well, almost black, anyway."

"Hmm, yes. That was very resourceful, Rosa," Isabel muttered as she held one of the dark cotton panels up to the cardboard casket, "but they'll be too short if we use this table for a pedestal."

"I saw some picnic tables out on the patio," said Rosa. "One of those wooden benches would be the perfect height, I think."

"Good!" Isabel agreed. "Go and grab one and set it over on the raised platform next to Ray's setup. That's where the presentation will be—to the left of that microphone stand/podium thing…whatever you call it." She spied Manny serving Jay Pee a drink at the bar. She cupped her hands around her mouth and trumpeted for another group of recruits in monotone, as if through a megaphone: "Attention! You two at the bar—I need some strong backs to lift a corpse—but just a little one!"

Manny drafted the kitchen help again, including the hairless Negro fugitive otherwise known as Curtis, and Maria. The four descended upon the lifeless body like distant-family scavengers, hoisted Freddy upward, and placed him face-down on an adjacent table at Isabel's direction.

The skeletal mortician, Mr. Hackett, materialized suddenly in his uncanny way with a look of horror on his dreadful face. "You must handle him with great care and gentleness," he cried. "You might disturb his cavity seal!"

"As I said before," Isabel stated firmly, "that's why we kept you here, *señor*. If his poop dam springs a leak, you're the professional *plomero* on call. Besides, if you hadn't brought him here in a goddamn shoebox, we wouldn't be in this mess, *Harold Hackett*." It was a double throat thrasher, and apparent to everyone that the hard *h*'s were intentionally stressed by the queen of hyperbole. "So," she continued unmercifully, "if you still want a place in the buffet line, I'd keep a low profile, unless and until we call you for your professional help."

The macabre apparition bowed away and seemed to melt into the woodwork.

"Goddamn rooster," Isabel murmured. "How the hell did we end up with that weirdo for a mortician, anyway?" she asked Jay Pee. "He gives me the creeps; he looks a lot like that spooky actor, John Carradine, don't you think?"

"Yeah, well, he's the brother of the county coroner," Jay Pee informed her. "I try to steer business his way when it's within my influence. Makes it easier to ask favors of his brother—such as his waiver of an autopsy and toxicology examination in Freddy's case. You know, it occurs to me that you might want to ease up on him a little, Isabel—at least until Freddy hits the happy-trails bakery tonight."

"Uh…okay. Sure. Why didn't you tell me that sooner?"

"You were fine up to this point. I wouldn't want the Hackett brothers to get too smug either. That's why I didn't let him take us to the cleaners on that whole casket swindle. Besides, I think you're okay as long as his olfactory sense continues to possess him."

"Huh?"

"You've got him eating out of your hand—almost literally." Jay Pee chuckled.

"The food…yes. And I'm worried about the food, Jay Pee. Do you think there'll be enough?"

"Between you and Manny, I think you've made plenty for all the guests, with enough left over to feed the starving hordes of the world."

"What's that smell?" Isabel wondered aloud.

"Empeñadas?" Jay Pee guessed.

"No, it smells like rubbing alcohol."

"Probably Freddy," Jay Pee mused. "He always smelled like alcohol to me."

"How's this, señora?" Rosa interjected, pointing to her arrangement of the sheet and pillow in the box. She had also quite tastefully attached one of the curtain panels with a stapler she'd purloined from a cashier's station.

"That's fine, Rosa; thank you very much. Everybody else, put Freddy back in his box and carry him over to that bench that Rosa set up over there on the stage," Isabel directed.

The others who had lingered there did as they were instructed. As they hefted Freddy and his "vessel of departure" over to the stage, Jay Pee took a sudden interest in the Woody Strode look-alike on the opposite side of the box—the one who'd been hired as temporary kitchen help.

"Hey there, son—your name wouldn't happen to be Curtis, would it?"

Taken by surprise, the boy responded reflexively. "Yes, sir! But, hey, how did you know that?"

"Just a hunch." Jay Pee chuckled. "They call me Dr. Mort, but don't you worry about me; I'm on the good guys' team. Your secret's safe with me."

Godspeed

Father Frank Cullen cleared his throat and spoke with the practiced tone of authority.

"Far be it from me to question your driving skills, Joe." He said it loudly to be heard over the rumble of the wheels on the washboard road. "However, I seriously doubt if Mario Andretti feels threatened by your need for speed. So can you maybe drop it down to a velocity more suitable for a dirt track—say, forty-five, maybe?"

Sergeant Joe Garcia was indeed pushing his Ford Galaxie 500 cruiser to questionable limits for an unpaved desert roadway. He could feel the steerage begin to float as the car's trajectory drifted from side to side. But he resisted easing up on the accelerator pedal nevertheless as he answered his friend and parish priest.

"We need to get to Curtis while we still have a fix on him. I swear that boy disappears and reappears more than Harry Houdini." The sergeant focused his gaze straight down the road and tightened his grip on the wheel as he spoke. "Also, that undersheriff from San Pedro County didn't sound too keen on calling off his manhunt when I spoke to him on the phone. Knowing some of these yahoos down here, I'd say Curtis could be in danger. That's why I took this shortcut."

"Curtis can be as slippery an eel, no question. And I don't disagree with your sense of urgency," Father Frank replied. "I just want to get where we're going in one piece. You know, we won't be much good to him if we get into a rollover. Besides, my upper dentures are starting to rattle loose from the wheel chatter."

"Sorry if I'm scaring you, but I need to get there before any harm comes to that boy," Sergeant Joe said grimly.

"It's all very personal for you, isn't it?" Father Frank observed.

"You better believe it is. Curtis wouldn't be in this mess if I hadn't coaxed him to cop a plea. The hell of it is, I had a hard time imagining him trying to start that fire in the sports annex in the first place."

"Why did you advise him to plead no contest?" Father Frank asked.

"Several reasons. First, because he did trespass and steal some shirts, so I felt he had some dues to pay. Then, too, I thought thirty days in juvenile detention might keep him from going south on us. He seemed to be drifting in a bad direction. But, Father, I never reckoned on a year at Fort Grant," Sergeant Joe said.

"What else?" Father Frank probed.

"I thought his story about who he saw trying to start that blaze was not only pretty lame, but would bring the whole city government down on him like a pack of hungry coyotes."

The priest chimed in. "But as soon I told you my story about that other boy trying to start a fire in my church, suddenly Curtis's tale had the ring of truth to it, I suppose."

"Absolutely. And with all those other little trash fires popping up at churches all over town—well, it's pretty clear that that other boy is the culprit, not Curtis." Joe paused as if to compose himself. "Needless to say, I feel pretty guilty about not believing him in the first place."

"Well, I don't think you need to beat yourself up over this," declared Father Frank. "You didn't do anything deliberately—it was just a mistake."

"Are you absolving me, Father?" Joe asked, only half joking.

"Of what, a poor judgment call? Hardly. Besides, you have much graver sins to confess to me, Joe."

"Like what?"

"Like endangering the life of your parish priest with your reckless driving. Now, slow this thing down, Joe. *Right now!*"

Early Guests

La Cantina Vieja was the perfect venue for a wake, as Isabel had determined. The eight booths that lined the south wall were reserved for close friends and local dignitaries—Alberto Montoya, the current mayor of Oracle Mesa, Frankie Quintana, San Pedro Valley Constable and sole member of the local police force, three county commissioners with their families, Freddy's distant and only surviving relative, the Honorable Natchez Mendoza, with his entourage, and Pete Alvarado, the undersheriff of San Pedro County. The final booth closest to the raised platform, where Freddy lay in state, was set aside for Isabel, Jay Pee, Ray, and Rosa.

Rosa had assembled a makeshift presentation that completely disguised the cardboard casket and picnic bench bier: the skirt she fashioned from Freddy's bedroom curtains was fastened to the box in pleats. It was just the right length for the necessary concealment and, in fact, looked quite elegant. She had also confiscated a couple of empty wooden kegs from a storage room and positioned them one on each side of the casket, covered each of them with a white tablecloth, and crowned each with a tall, brightly burning candle. The whole arrangement, but especially the improvised candle stands, put Rosa back in Isabel's good graces.

"I couldn't have done better if we'd had the time and spent a thousand dollars," the widow commented in compliment.

A phalanx of rectangular wooden pedestal tables, each accompanied by a complement of six rustic pine chairs, traversed the remainder of the roomy dining hall in regimented rows, as opposed to the usual random clusters that Freddy had favored for casual dining. Each table and each booth was covered with a white linen tablecloth and adorned with a single votive candle, a modest floral centerpiece, and a small embossed posterboard memorial placard that read:

Alfredo Mendoza Hightower
1918–1963
Beloved Mayor of Oracle Mesa, Dear Friend,
and Loving Husband

Blinds were lowered and curtains drawn to mute the daylight and to enhance the candles' glow. Isabel was still lighting the last of the votive candles when a spattering of guests began to arrive prematurely. Things were falling into place, and Isabel was beginning to feel that perhaps the curse of the midnight rooster had been dodged.

Dave Randall, the disc jockey from Tucson, was one of several early arrivals. He hesitated at the doorway and stroked his well-groomed Vandyke thoughtfully as he surveyed the inner sanctum of the event. The radio man's ulterior motive for overruling his aversion to such inane events was to delight in some fine musical entertainment and, possibly, strike up a business arrangement with its author, one sightless and flawless guitar virtuoso and vocalist, Raymond Cienfuegos. Freddy's boastful promotion of Ray to the sometime talent scout had proven to be an understatement in Randall's professional opinion. In fact, Dave's take on Ray's previous performance was that it was "way outta sight," as he'd related it to Freddy just a few nights earlier. Randall, unconventionally clad in indigo denim trousers, a black turtleneck tee, black leather jacket, and Cuban-heeled boots, strode into the venue, turning a number of heads.

"Hello," Isabel greeted him with an outstretched hand, not six feet from the door. "I am Isabel Cienfuegos Hightower, Freddy's widow. *Bienvenidos.*"

"Thank you, and please accept my condolences for your loss. My name is Dave Randall," he replied, awkwardly, "and I must confess that Freddy and I had only recently become acquainted while discussing some business possibilities."

"Yes, Freddy had mentioned that the two of you had talked about my nephew, Ray. I think it concerned something about recording some of his music."

"That's right. I heard Ray perform last Saturday night, and I was quite impressed with the originality of his style. In fact, Freddy and I had been discussing some basic terms to start things moving when Ray disappeared rather abruptly." The disc jockey's focus, which had been riveted on Isabel's enchanting face, suddenly drifted. "All very strange," he mused.

"Not so strange," said Isabel. "Ray and I had a sudden urgency arise regarding his condition that unfortunately required us to leave in a hurry before the end of his performance."

"I wonder if I could have a word with your nephew, madam," Randall inquired.

"You can, but he is set to begin the funeral music right about now." As if on cue, Ray commenced with a quiet instrumental rendition of "I'll be Seeing You," alternating the melody line with finger-plucked chord fills. "Looks like you'll have to catch him between sets," said Isabel.

"That's fine. I came to listen to his music as much as to talk to him. And, by the way, given the circumstances," Randall speculated, "I suppose you will be assuming Freddy's managerial role for your nephew."

A minor but audible disturbance at the front entry drew their attention.

"Yes, I suppose that's right," Isabel muttered distractedly. "We'll talk again before you leave today, but, right now, I really should welcome some of these other guests. Please excuse me for the time being."

"Of course."

As Isabel approached the main entry, she observed a man in the doorway who seemed to be struggling with something. He had his back turned to her, but the voice was familiar.

"Tip it back so he doesn't fall out. That's it. Okay, on three, give it a heave!"

The voice belonged to Dr. Case of the Desert Shadows Nursing Home, and Isabel could see what the struggle was all about. He was tugging on an occupied wheelchair—lifting it, with the help of two strapping orderlies who were pushing from below, up the two steep concrete steps that rose from the street level to the cantina's threshold.

"There!" Dr. Case breathed as the group burst from the entry and into the room. "Nice job, boys…way to go."

"Such a *production* for a couple of little steps!" a gravelly voice rang out. "You boys need to start eating your spinach!" the old man in the chair admonished. "Next time I'll just get out of this contraption and prance right on up those stairs myself—lighten the load for you sissies."

He reached over and snatched a white cane from one of the orderlies, then jerked one of the wheels on his means of mobility, causing it to whirl and face Isabel. She beheld in his upturned countenance the very epitome of senescence. Pleated facial skin sagged from the high cheekbones like leathern drapes, thin lips were drawn tight into a perpetual purse, and a wisp of white at the crown of an almost perfectly round head resembled cobwebs more than hair. The only characteristic that distinguished the man's craggy face from that of a cadaver was a pair of large ebony eyes, which sparkled with the dazzling light of life. The man was obviously Natchez Mendoza, Freddy's great-uncle…or something like that.

Dr. Case stepped briskly toward Isabel, looking quite dashing in a black three-piece, Milano-fit suit, and shook her offered hand. "So nice to see you again, señora," he intoned as he stared at her, entranced. "I…I am truly sorry that, once again, it is under such…such lamentable circumstances."

"*Bienvenidos,* Doctor," she recited mechanically. Her own gaze flashed right past him and rested on the remarkably animated centenarian, who was wheeling toward her under his own steam, eyes like bottomless pools of awareness, drawing her in.

"Don't wait for him to introduce us, señora," the ancient fossil rasped as he tapped his cane on the wooden floor. "He'll stand there stammering like some love-struck schoolboy all day if you let him." He shifted the cane to his left paw and extended a quaking right hand. "I am…"

"The Honorable Natchez Mendoza!" Isabel exclaimed, as if awestruck by his presence. She took his withered hand, and it steadied, gripping hers with a surprising tightness.

"And you must be Lucrezia," the judge remarked.

"No, I am Isabel Cienfuegos Hightower, sir—Alfredo's widow."

"Of course you are. I am truly enchanted, my dear," the old curmudgeon smiled, presenting a vacant pair of gums. "You are even lovelier than the doctor here described you. Of course, being a man of science, his poetic prowess is quite handicapped by a cold, therapeutic vocabulary, and so his incapacity to thoroughly describe your phenomenal beauty must be excused."

"You are too kind, sir." Isabel beamed, her eyes transfixed by his.

"Not *too* kind," Dr. Case muttered.

"Whereas I am, to the contrary," Natchez Mendoza continued as he reluctantly released Isabel's hand, "a man of letters, and am more likely to charm my way into your affections than the younger, more attractive competitor who, as the attendant evidence attests, is stricken dumb, and can only stand and gape."

Isabel glanced at Dr. Case, who indeed had to shut his open mouth to elude the image conjured by the old man. "Listen, Nat," he interjected in a fluster, "I know you're just being your cantankerous self, but don't you think it's a little too soon to be flirting with your nephew's widow? I mean, you can't even wait until the funeral's over?"

"Yes, my grand-nephew—or something like that. I think we met a couple of times at family reunions. Hardly knew the man, but having now met you, my dear, I can say that he was one lucky guy—if only for a few hours of conjugal bliss."

"All right, Nat—that's quite enough!" the young doctor declared. "You're behaving quite inappropriately and making our hostess uncomfortable."

"No, Doctor—it's quite all right," Isabel interposed, shooting a slightly annoyed look at the younger man. "He doesn't make me uncomfortable at all. In fact, he seems oddly familiar." She turned back to the old man and again became lost in the depths of his obsidian eyes. "It's like we've already met before, isn't it?"

"Yes, and there's a reason for that sense of déjà vu," Natchez Mendoza replied. "We share many things, people, and even places in common—Alfredo Hightower and the nature of his demise perhaps being the least of them."

"What do you mean, sir?" Isabel inquired, obviously intrigued and a little troubled.

"We must talk, my dear, when we can be alone," he replied in a hushed tone. "The words that I have to say are for your ears alone." He turned to the doctor and raised his voice. "In the meantime, we should pay our respects and have a gander at the man of the hour." He made a chin gesture toward the open casket on the raised platform. "Maybe his face will jolt my hazy recollection of him."

Isabel was so bewildered by the old man's appearance and words that she'd momentarily neglected to monitor the entry for more arrivals. It was Jay Pee who rousted her from her fugue state.

"Hey there—you with the stars in your eyes! Don't look now, but the mayor and his wife are standing in the vestibule, waiting to be greeted. Of course," he taunted, "you could just ignore them and be the talk of the town for months."

"Thanks, Jay Pee." Isabel sighed and started for the door. "I think maybe I am already the talk of the town. I don't need a cardinal social sin to add to it."

She dutifully greeted first Mayor and Mrs. Montoya, then the undersheriff, and then the constable, Frankie Quintana. Isabel knew Frankie quite well from church, and he was a regular patron at the café. The constable made no secret about his loyalty to the former mayor and, since his passing, his widow.

"My condolences, señora. As you know, Freddy was my good friend, and if there is anything I can do to help you through this difficult time, I am at your service."

"Thank you, Frankie. That is very comforting," Isabel replied, guiding him and his wife to their booth. "As a matter of fact, there is something you can do, my friend. I need you to extend your professional courtesy to a couple of strangers who will come in that door in about an hour. They will state their business to you, and I hope you will assist them in any way you can."

"Of course I will, señora, but there is something else. I am hearing from my sources that the county deputy who was at the inquest Sunday has been harassing you, Isabel," the constable noted. "You just say the word, and that will cease immediately." He lowered his voice. "You know, that son of a bitch was suspended last year for faking a traffic stop so he could force himself on some young girl. Word has it that it wasn't the first time either."

"Really? So what ever came of that?" Isabel asked.

"Goddamn county mounties closed ranks and cleared the bastard. Creeps like that give cops a bad name. If he bothers you at all, Isabel, I'll run him in and give him the *special* tour of my jail."

Isabel was well aware that the San Pedro County Sheriff Department and most other municipal peace officers held each other in mutual contempt, and she knew that occasional scuffles had even resulted. She'd deliberately separated Frankie's and the undersheriff's booths by several spaces in the name of keeping the peace.

"I don't think that will be necessary, Frankie, but, if it gets to be a problem, you'll be the first to know, believe me."

As if on cue, Deputy Sheriff Myron Aycock clomped up the vestibule steps and strode confidently into the room as if he owned it.

"Goddamn rooster," Isabel muttered.

A Backward Glimpse
(Interlude Four)

"Natchez Mendoza!" I exclaimed loudly enough to silence the bleating crickets and the yipping coyotes. "I remember him—he's the Tucson municipal court judge who saw through Harvey Huish's fiction about his uncle's 'accidental' drowning," I added excitedly.

"Jesus H. Christ, Vince! Try to keep the volume down, will ya? Sound carries in the dead of night. You're gonna bring the cops down on us, and, out here in the boonies, it's the county cops. I don't know about you, but I don't have any friends among that bunch, so, please, try to stifle anything louder than a heart-stopping air horn, okay?"

It was a gentle reproach, softer than I expected for having broken my vow of silence once again.

"Sorry, Curtis. It's just that it hit me all at once. It's like when I'm reading something really good, and I make a surprise connection. I've been tossed out of libraries for my reflexive outbursts."

"Yeah, well this ain't no library, so put a sock in it. Old Mr. Natchez Mendoza just might tease another shriek out of you down the road," Curtis said.

"How so? Tell me more," I begged.

"All in due time."

"C'mon, man—don't string me along," I whined.

"Nah—you're never gonna get me to jump ahead again. Now, let's see…Isabel was fightin' battles on every front when we left off."

"Yeah, that lowlife Deputy Aycock had just come back into the picture," I added.

"That's right. By the way, Vince, you really *are* a good listener, aren't you?"

"Best there is," I clucked proudly.

Requiem for a Featherweight

The buzzing room went silent as the brash deputy weaved his swaggering way among the assembled tables, leering maniacally in Isabel's general direction. The purple bruises that dappled his face had actually darkened over the past couple of days, lending him the unmistakable image of an inexpert prize fighter—one who leads with his mug.

Frankie Quintana bristled. "Please, Isabel," he pleaded in a hiss. "Let me throw the bum out before he starts something."

"Now, why would we do that?" Isabel replied, cool and collected. "That would be starting something ourselves, and our guests would surely wonder why we would be so disrespectful to a would-be mourner of the deceased. No, better to hold off and let him make a fool of himself first. Then you can throw him out in the street with my blessing, Frankie."

Stetson hat in hand, Aycock was decidedly out of uniform and inappropriately dressed, given the occasion. His chosen togs consisted of blue jeans, a denim-blue, pearl-snap western shirt, and roper boots with heels that clomped loudly on the hardwood floorboards. Judging from his casual attire, it was apparent to all that his attendance was on impulse. His step was swaggering, and his body swayed in an ungainly manner as he walked. Isabel guessed that the deputy had recently downed at least a couple of glasses of courage to reach that level of audacity.

He made a courtesy stop at his boss's booth and exchanged a few pleasantries, but he maintained a distance that kept his toxic breath from wilting the table's flower arrangement. He then made his way in Isabel's direction, who was still standing at the barely restrained constable's booth. She anticipated his approach and was already moving to meet him halfway.

"Good afternoon, Deputy Aycock," she announced loudly for all to hear as she extended a welcoming hand. Then, more quietly, she said through a fabricated smile, "I hope you're here to pay your respects, and nothing more."

"Of course, ma'am," Aycock half smirked, emanating fumes of whiskey. "As I said before, Mayor Hightower was a friend of mine, and I have come to see him off. As for the 'nothing more' part, well, that's kind of hard to say. You see, I can't predict the future like some who have that reputation. But, you know, I do have an uncanny sixth sense about certain things like hidden motives and concealment of evidence—just one of my many professional skills."

The room began to buzz anew with heightened activity as new guests began to arrive sporadically. Ray launched into an instrumental version of "We'll Meet Again." Isabel's frozen smile broadened.

"Clearly, Freddy would have welcomed you despite your improper outfit. You see, we chose to suspend any kind of dress code for this ceremony because we knew that Freddy, in his good-hearted nature, sometimes fraternized with entirely tasteless people such as yourself, and we simply refused to discriminate against the socially handicapped."

"Bitch!" The deputy spat.

Isabel turned and beckoned to Jay Pee, who was watching intently from the bar.

"Bitch?" she replied. "Why, Deputy Aycock, you completely underestimate me in that regard… because, *you ain't seen nothin' yet.*"

"What's up, Isabel?" Jay Pee asked as he got within earshot.

"Your Honor, would you please *entertain* our guest, Deputy Aycock, while I greet these new arrivals?"

"It will be my pleasure." Jay Pee grinned. "Why don't you join me over at the bar, deputy? You know, a good buzz is wasted if you can't maintain it."

"That sounds just fine, Justice Morton. But first, I'd like to visit with Mayor Hightower for a bit. He was a friend of mine, you know," the deputy said.

"That's a fine idea. Mind if I join you? After all, he was a friend of mine as well," Jay Pee countered.

"I'd be pleased to have your company, sir."

"By the way," Jay Pee quipped as the two made their way toward the open casket, "who *is* your wardrobe consultant?"

"Huh?" the deputy did not follow.

"I mean, who advises on what to wear on certain occasions?" Jay Pee continued to poke. "Because I could issue a bench warrant for him for a felonious fashion violation on your behalf, if you like."

"What does that even *mean*?" Aycock sputtered.

"Never mind." Jay Pee snickered. "It was just a little joke. I'm warming up. You know, Freddy always enjoyed a little sarcastic humor, even when it was at his expense. So pay me no mind if I indulge in a few digs today. There's no offense intended. I just feel like it's up to me to inject some levity into an otherwise somber atmosphere." Jay Pee gestured toward Freddy, who was only an arm's length away. "He would have insisted that there be humor."

"I get it, Your Honor. Hell, you can take a good-natured poke at me any time. Folks say I'm pretty thick-skinned," Deputy Aycock offered.

"Pretty thick-skulled as well, I imagine," Jay Pee muttered.

"What was that?"

"Nothing—just mumbling to myself."

"My goodness!" Aycock exclaimed as his eyes rested on Freddy's corpse. "Just look at that face!"

"I was about to comment that the healing process has not been a friend to you," Jay Pee remarked, again unable to resist.

"Not mine, *his*." Aycock pointed to Freddy's ghoulish countenance. "He looks so *peaceful*."

"If you ask me, he looks absolutely ghastly—but that's a topic for another time."

"And he smells like a locker room," the deputy observed. "What *is* that smell—some kind of liniment?"

"Yes, I believe you're right—it smells like rubbing alcohol. Must be the embalming fluid."

"What is this? Hells bells, it looks like *he pissed his goddamn pants*!"

The tipsy deputy had unwittingly raised the volume on the last five words, and the buzz in the room fell off. Isabel strode over immediately, visibly annoyed.

"Really, Jay Pee, can't you keep him quiet for five minutes?" she snapped.

The chatter in the room resumed and masked the ensuing dialog.

"I bet you'd like that," Aycock chuckled. "I bet you'd like to shut me up before I have my say."

"Don't worry, Isabel. Myron didn't mean to be disruptive," said Jay Pee in defense. "I think the sight of Freddy just overwhelmed him a little—especially that wet stain around the crotch."

Isabel peered into the casket, and her mouth went agape. "*Dios mío,* Jay Pee! Freddy's sprung a goddamn leak!" She hissed. "Get that creepy undertaker over here, pronto!"

Eerily, Hackett the mortician had already materialized in their presence as if summoned, and he was instantly casketside, taking stock of the awkward situation before her words left her mouth. "There's really nothing I can do without taking him back to the mortuary," he determined after studying the problem at length. "However, I can guarantee that this unfortunate failure poses no hazard to any of your guests, dear lady. That body is absolutely devoid of any natural body fluid or any pathogen known to man, for that matter. There's enough methyl alcohol in him to eliminate a resurgence of the black plague."

"That's good. It's a real comfort to know that the people who will file past Freddy won't be joining him as a consequence." Isabel growled through clenched teeth. "Now, what do I do about the clearly noticeable flaw in the presentation?"

"I suggest that you simply cover his lower half with a sheet to conceal the problem and continue the ceremony as if nothing happened," Hackett offered whimsically.

"What about the smell?" The irate widow fumed.

"What smell?" the undertaker wondered earnestly. He sniffed. "I don't smell a thing."

Isabel rolled her eyes. "What about the smell, Jay Pee?"

"Let's just do as Hackett suggests. Pull a sheet up over the accident, and I'll run across the street to Buck Yee's Chinese Emporium for some incense to mask the odor. Do you have a preference?" Jay Pee inquired of her.

"What?" Isabel blurted, incredulously.

"Do you have a preference of fragrances? They have sandalwood and jasmine and—"

"Oh, for God's sake—*cow dung* would be better than this locker-room smell. Some junior-high coach is going to jump up any minute and try to give Freddy a farewell rubdown if we don't do something in a hurry!" Isabel shrieked.

"I'll be back in a flash," Jay Pee offered, "but someone will need to bay-yay…*entertain* Myron in the meantime."

Manny appeared as if he'd been summoned from the kitchen. *"Perdoname, señora, pero me quieres traer las comidas ahora?"*

"Not yet, Manny. Wait for fifteen minutes or so while more guests arrive. We don't want the later arrivals to get cold food. But you could show the deputy over to the bar and fix him a drink, if you don't mind."

"El gusto es mío. Venga, Señor Deputy," Manny said.

Isabel turned and approached the casket as Manny led Aycock toward the bar. She loosened some folds in the top sheet that Freddy was lying on and draped it over his midsection as the mortician had suggested.

"You don't give up, do you, Alfredo?" she whispered. "I sensed your lust for revenge when the rooster crowed at midnight. You know, I am doing my best to forgive you for what you did. Why don't you try to do the same? I don't want to live the rest of my life with a vendetta, but you should know that I won't be bested, and there are still worse things that I could do to you than what I did. Stop trying to get even. You'll only make things worse for yourself."

"I heard all that!" Aycock had broken away from Manny and slipped up behind her. "I knew it. You did him in for the inheritance, didn't you? It's the oldest motive in the book. Tell me, señora, how did you do it? I knew it that very morning. Your story was about as solid as a Hershey bar in hell. You poisoned him, didn't you?"

Isabel was genuinely surprised. "No—of course not. You misunderstood what I was saying."

"Look, Isabel, I know what I heard. I might not be able to prove anything, but I can sure as hell plant the seed of suspicion with a lot of these people gathered here—maybe even delay the cremation. How do you like them apples?"

Isabel cast her gaze upon the room: the mayor, police, friends, and fellow parishioners. Then, presciently, the twilight image of the state penitentiary she'd observed on her trip to Jacobs Well surfaced in her consciousness. She turned back and faced her accuser with an imploring expression.

"You judge me wrongly, señor, and you cannot give proof for such a lie," she whimpered with a pouty mouth. "You are right about one thing: you could do serious injury to my reputation with these people. It would seem that you have me in a very compromising position, Deputy. Is that the sort of thing you like?" she taunted a bit seductively. "Perhaps I misjudged you too. I think maybe you're just the kind of man who likes to be on top of things, so to speak. Am I right?"

"Could be," Aycock responded, a little flustered by the sudden change in behavior.

Isabel deliberately turned her backside to the deputy, striking a subtly provocative pose. She continued to speak to him over her shoulder. "Why don't you join me for a drink at the bar, and we can discuss more pleasurable ways for you to humiliate me, other than just injuring my reputation?" she murmured with a sultry look. "After all, I should think that a man like you would prefer to degrade me in private rather than in public."

Aycock wondered, but only for a few seconds, at that abrupt reversal of attitudes—that sudden capitulation of hers. Predictably though, his outsized ego eclipsed any healthy suspicion he might have entertained. *Typical woman: changes her entire manner with the slightest shift in the wind direction.* Of course, he had the drop on her, and how else could she respond except with complete and sweet surrender? But, despite that cavalier rationalization, he followed her less like the man in control and more like a lovestruck puppy as she began to sashay toward the bar, his spellbound gaze riveted on the gentle sway of her shapely rump.

Ray's playing shifted into a rhythmic version of "I Only Have Eyes for You." The tempo suspiciously matched her movement.

———

Curtis finished filling the rack with dirty drink glasses and fed it into the dishwasher as Maria had shown him. None of the food had gone out to the tables, and so mounds of clean white plates were still sitting, pristine, in the warming ovens along with a veritable truckload of assorted *comidas*. There was little yet for a dishwasher to do, but it was not just out of boredom and curiosity that he drifted to the order window and looked out at the growing crowd. He was drawn there. The lighting was dim, but the boy picked out a few familiar faces. Ray was perched atop a barstool on a raised platform, hunched over his guitar with Rosa standing by his side, apparently giving him a running commentary on developing episodes. Isabel was engaged in conversation with someone wearing jeans—someone that Curtis did not recognize from a distance—and Dr. Mort, the guy that he'd just met, but somehow trusted.

Curtis saw a face that was both familiar and strange. It belonged to a frail-looking, decrepit old relic in a wheelchair, and the face, a leather mask stretched over a round skull, wasn't really familiar at all—at least, not in the sense of an acknowledged history connected with it. It was a message in the eyes, warm and dark, staring across the room and right into Curtis's soul that somehow signaled a prior but unrecalled acquaintance or encounter. The eyes were, therefore, the source of that inexplicable, mutually familiar sense that made no sense whatsoever.

"You shouldn't be standing there at the window," a voice from behind him admonished. "Señora Cienfuegos…I mean, Hightower…told me to keep you away from the window as much as possible." It was Maria, and her tone was stern. "I don't know why, and I don't care. I just do as I am told, but I'm sure she has good reason. She always does."

"I have a pretty good idea why, and she does have good reason, but I can tell you that wild horses couldn't drag me away from this window right now," Curtis retorted.

"Why's that?" Maria wondered.

"Because somethin', or some *things,* are a-buildin' up inside that room. Can you feel it?"

"What I see building up is the number of people coming in the door. Looks like a lot more than the señora planned on," Maria commented.

"That may be part of it, but it feels more like that dinin' room is fillin' up with steam than with people—like in a pressure cooker that's about to burst. You're right," he continued. "There sure are a lot of people comin' in that door. Man, that guy Freddy must have really been popular," Curtis speculated.

"I never thought he was *that* popular," Maria suggested.

"He's sure gettin' a twenty-one-gun send-off," Curtis observed. "And, after all, he was the mayor, wasn't he?"

"*Used* to be mayor," Maria corrected. "Yeah, mayor of Oracle Mesa. Big deal. It's like being the Duke of Dogpatch."

"Still, he must've been a real heavyweight for the señora to marry him—and for all these people to come and pay their respects. Looks to be over a hundred of 'em out there."

"Listen, kid," Maria declared, "I know most of those people out there, and I can tell you that three-quarters of them are here for the free food and the open bar. Sad, but true. And I knew Freddy Hightower too, and I could never understand what the señora or Ray ever saw in that sleazy little guy. I hate to speak ill of the dead, but a *heavyweight*? Don't make me laugh. I used to work for him before I went to work for the señora. He paid cheap, made obscene suggestions to the waitresses, and stole their tips. Then, for whatever reason, the guy crawled into a booze bottle a couple of years ago and never came out. He was a featherweight, if anything."

"Ray and his aunt, they seem so smart—so 'in the know' about everything. I can't even imagine anybody puttin' one over on them."

"Me neither." Maria shrugged. "That's what doesn't make sense. But I do know that something came along just lately that scared the hell out of them too. Maybe they were just distracted and couldn't make a good judgment about the mayor." Maria's eyes narrowed. "Hey, kid, you talk like you know Isabel and Ray. But you're supposed to be a hired temp out of Tucson. What's going on here?"

"Never mind about that," said Curtis, sidestepping the question. "Just you watch the show. Look what's happenin' out there."

Isabel was making her way toward them, coming up to the bar with the jeans-clad stranger in tow. Curtis could see that his face was dotted with bruises and cuts.

"Man, just look at that guy," Maria remarked. "That's Deputy What's-His-Name out of uniform. He looks like he picked a fight with the Tasmanian Devil." She giggled.

Curtis turned his back to the window. "I'm not sure, but I think I know who the devil it was he picked that fight with," the boy muttered sheepishly.

"What's wrong with you?" Maria taunted. "I thought you wanted to watch the show."

"Not anymore."

"Why not?"

"'Cause I suddenly got the feelin' that the show's gonna start watchin' *me*."

<hr>

"What're you drinking, Deputy?" Isabel inquired as she situated herself opposite him behind the bar. "Manny's getting busy, so I'll be your barmaid."

"Bourbon on the rocks, please," said Aycock, as he laid his hat crown-down on the bar.

The *dueña* produced two barrel-shaped drink glasses and filled them with ice. "Kentucky bourbon?"

"Is there any other kind?" the deputy asked rhetorically.

She splashed double shots of the amber libation into each glass, placed them on the bar top, and moved to the stool next to him. "Your choice is appropriate. It was Freddy's drink too." She raised her glass as if to propose a toast, but the deputy cut her short.

"Put the glass down, Isabel," Aycock demanded.

"But I was just about—"

"Just do as I say," he insisted.

Isabel obliged him, and he reversed the placement of the glasses on the bar top.

"There." The deputy chuckled. "Now, I can enjoy your drink, and I hope you enjoy mine."

Isabel shook her head in wonder. "You're going to have to give up this silly notion of yours that I'm some kind of homicidal maniac. Even if that were so, which it's not, would I really have the nerve to poison you in front of all these people? Don't be foolish." She stood and raised the glass again. "To Freddy!" she exclaimed, loudly enough to be heard above the buzz of the room.

"To Freddy!" the room thundered back, as dozens of glasses were hoisted.

"May he rest in peace," she murmured after taking a long sip of the cold liquor. "So tell me, Deputy," she inquired as she sat back down next to him, "how is it that I've never seen you at my café before this week? Most of the sheriff's men stop in for breakfast or lunch from time to time. But you've been a stranger to me up until now."

"You can call me Myron, to begin with," the lawman retorted with a toothy grin. He took a long pull from his glass and continued. "I live up in Florence, and the northern half of the county has always been my zone of operation. I only come down this far south on the rare occasion that some incident draws more officers here. The manhunt for that escaped inmate from Fort Grant is what brought me here at the end of last week. Since then, I've developed another interest."

"Myron, how did you know Freddy?" Isabel wondered aloud.

"The mayor was a good friend of my boss, the undersheriff, and I provided his transportation whenever he visited the county seat."

"I see. So you weren't exactly what you could call close friends, I take it."

"No, not exactly." Aycock sighed impatiently. "Listen, enough of this small talk, Isabel. Let's get down to you and me meeting up in private, like you said."

"So much for the courtship." The widow chuckled wryly.

"I'm not one for wasting my breath or my time." The deputy smirked. "And your suggestive talk from just before has still got me wound up tighter than a ukulele string."

"I see that patience is not your strong suit, Myron. But, surely, you don't expect me to leave the ceremony with you. That would be…wait a minute. Speaking of courtship, here's Jay Pee."

Aycock turned and glanced toward the casket. "Yeah, so what? He seems to be pretty busy with something over there."

They watched as Jay Pee took an ashtray from a vacant table, placed it on one of the candle stands next to Freddy, and placed in it a small conical object. He lit a match and held it to the tip of the cone until a wisp of smoke emitted from it. Like magic, a sweet fragrance like juniper smoke instantly filled the entire room. He turned, his face lit with a self-congratulating smile, and strode briskly to the bar. He held the package of incense in his hand like it was a prize.

"I chose cedar," he announced proudly. "Listen to this." He began to read from the wrapper. "Cedar fragrance has long been used as a remedy for nervous tension, stress, and related disorders. Also, it is often used as an insect and vermin repellent."

"Hope it works," Isabel remarked drily, "'cause we've got our share of them."

"What's that supposed to mean?" Aycock demanded, sounding a little peeved.

"Tensions and stresses, I mean," Isabel returned evasively.

"I see you finally made it to the bar," Jay Pee said to the deputy. "What are you drinking?"

"Bourbon and bourbon." Aycock chuckled before draining his glass.

"Let me freshen you up while I make mine," Jay Pee offered cheerfully as he wrested the glass from the deputy. "I'm with you on the bourbon, but I like to dress it up as a Manhattan. Would you like to try one?" he asked as he slipped behind the bar.

"Why not?" Aycock grunted. "Just as long as it's not that Canadian crap."

"Wouldn't dream of using anything but good Kentucky bourbon for a Manhattan—although I seriously doubt if *you* would notice the difference if I poured isopropyl alcohol." Jay Pee chuckled.

"What's that?" Aycock asked, puzzled.

"I said I need some ice and the proper alcohol for the mix."

"That's what I thought you said," the deputy concluded.

"Isabel, I see you're still nursing—your drink, I mean," Jay Pee jibed.

"I need to keep my head clear," the *dueña* explained. "There is so much going on here to keep straight."

"Clarity is an elusive thing, my dear," Jay Pee quipped as he filled a cocktail shaker with ice and bourbon. "For some of us, a drink or two actually enhances the mental processes—loosens up the cerebral soil, so to speak. For others, it's just an anodyne that dulls the senses. Now, where did I put the vermouth?"

"I hope it's not dulling your senses," Isabel remarked. "You've got to give the eulogy in just a few minutes."

"Don't you worry about me, my dear. This is only my second drink, and I'm still as sober as a priest," said Jay Pee. "Now, a splash of grenadine, a couple drops of bitters, and we're ready to shake, rattle, and roll!"

"Jay Pee, I think you're having too much fun," Isabel admonished. "This is supposed to be a funeral, you know."

"Technically, it's a wake," Jay Pee replied as he strained the mixed libation into two chilled martini glasses. "Anyway, I knew Freddy as well as anybody here, and I can tell you that he would want us to have fun at his wake." He placed one of the glasses on the bar top next to Aycock and raised the other to his lips. "Man, that's good stuff. How about you, Myron—are you having fun?"

"About as much fun as a tornado in a trailer park," the deputy retorted as he hoisted the martini glass.

"Ah, *Dios mío*," Isabel muttered.

◆

"Dios mío!" Maria squealed. "I can't believe what I just saw!"

"I'm almost afraid to ask," Curtis muttered, still cowering with his back to the pass-through window. "Is that deputy gone yet?"

"No, but I've got a feeling he's going to be leaving us pretty soon."

"What are you talkin' about?" Curtis inquired.

"I'm talking about what I just saw."

"Which is?"

"First, I saw the señora break a little capsule and put it in the deputy's drink when he was distracted by something," Maria revealed.

"Holy shit—she slipped him a Mickey!" Curtis blurted.

"That's only half of it. Then, Dr. Mort made the guy another drink, and he put something in it too!"

"Are you sure?" Curtis asked in a skeptical tone.

"Sure as I'm standing here talking to you," Maria asserted.

"I told you this was a show. It's like Alfred Hitchcock or somethin'!" Curtis squealed.

"It's more than a show now," Maria observed. "It's turned into a regular circus. Now some pachuco-looking guy is talking to Ray."

"Pachuco?"

"Yeah—well, maybe not a real pachuco, but he's dressed like a real bad boy, with a black leather *chaqueta*, a Wolfman Jack beard, and Elvis Presley hair."

"What else?" Curtis prodded her.

"This really creepy-looking character is coming over to the bar. I know him! It's the undertaker over at the Peaceful Passage Mortuary. He's ordering a drink; I bet it's absinthe or something weird like that. Now, Dr. Mort has gotten up and gone over to talk to this ancient fossil in a wheelchair. Looks to be about a hundred years old. Probably gonna take his pulse and give him a business card. Man, you should be watching all of this, kid. It's a real performance," Maria declared.

Curtis succumbed to the temptation and turned around to take in the entire scene as Maria had described it. He scanned the room, grinning as his gaze passed over each little drama. Then, his eyes met with those of Myron Aycock. He was staring right at the boy, wearing an expression of focused curiosity.

"My God." Curtis sighed. "I've been had!"

———

"Isabel," Aycock muttered. "Who is the nigga boy in the kitchen?"

"The *colored* boy," Isabel corrected, "is temporary help from Tucson for washing dishes. Most of the regular kitchen help and waitstaff from La Cantina are out here attending the ceremony."

"Go tell the kid I want to have a word with him."

"Not now. He's busy, and so am I."

"He doesn't look busy," the deputy groused. "And, now that you mention it, neither do you."

"That's because I've been spending time with you. But, now that the room has filled up with people, I'll have to start directing things," Isabel explained.

"Like what?"

"First, I have to have Jay Pee deliver the eulogy."

"Then what?" Aycock pressed

"I'll have Manny bring out the food for the buffet line."

"Then what?" the deputy continued to prod.

It was like a conversation with a second-grader, but Isabel was relieved that he'd been so easily distracted from his interest in Curtis.

"I have to circulate and chat with the guests." Isabel waved to Jay Pee, who was deep in conversation with Natchez Mendoza, and beckoned him over.

"Then what?" The deputy giggled stupidly.

"I'll pour you another drink," Isabel responded absentmindedly.

"Whad I'm gedding at is the part where we get together—yoo an me." Aycock was apparently starting to forfeit his questionable power of pronunciation to a yen for liquid loudmouth.

"I thought we could meet at my nephew's house out in the boonies after the ceremony. You know the place. It's very secluded," Isabel suggested.

"Ah…the purrfeck rendezvous. RON-day-voo. Wow, isn' thad a weird word?" Aycock slurred.

"It's French, Myron. All French words are weird," Isabel stated.

"Come to think of it, *weird* is a weird word. Issit Frenj too?"

"I've gotta say," Jay Pee broke in as he strode within earshot, "that old man is absolutely fascinating. He must be over a hundred years old, and he's as sharp as a razor."

"Yes, I'm sure he is," said Isabel. "And, considering the time you spent over there, I imagine you took in his entire life's story."

"Just the condensed version." Jay Pee chuckled. "But I was able to determine, in the course of our brief exchange, that he is quite amenable to our plan for the estate. I'm going to announce it as part of the eulogy."

"Do you think that's proper?" Isabel asked.

"Under the circumstances, I think it's not only proper but quite necessary," Jay Pee advised.

"Whazzizz 'bout 'n ess-state?" Aycock demanded through a spray of nebulized saliva.

"You'll hear about it presently, Deputy," Jay Pee replied.

"Presently is right, Jay Pee," said Isabel. "Because I want you up there *ahorita*, mister. Now, and make it good!"

"Don't you worry. There won't be a dry eye in the house when I've finished," said Jay Pee.

"I *hate* yoo-loo-jees!" Aycock whined.

"So do I, my friend, but this one promises to be a bit different," Jay Pee assured.

The good doctor drained his Manhattan, which had languished half-consumed on the bar top until that point, and strode toward the microphone stand situated on the raised platform just a few feet from the deceased. Ray hurriedly wrapped up an improvised version of "You'll Never Walk Alone," as if on instinct, but actually cued by Rosa. Jay Pee seized the mike stand as he reached it and tapped the screened mouthpiece. Four loud pops confirmed that it indeed was live and also signaled his intention to address the crowded room. The dominant chatter fell off accordingly.

The Eulogy

"Good afternoon to you all, and *bienvenidos*."

His voice reverberated slightly through the amplifiers. He held the mike a bit farther from his mouth to correct the problem.

"It is indeed heartwarming to see so many faces here. As you all know, we are gathered today to commemorate the life and acknowledge the passing of our beloved friend and mayor, Alfredo Hightower."

He paused and glanced over at Isabel to confirm that the volume was right. She nodded.

"I originally wanted this eulogy to be a testament to Freddy's many noble attributes. But, unfortunately, I was told that I had to speak for at least three to five minutes, soo…"

He held up his wrist to his face, as if checking his watch, and glanced over at Isabel. She was grinning widely.

"Those of you who knew him well remember what a joker he was, even when the joke was directed at himself and his own shortcomings. Come to think of it, most of his jokes were self-deprecating, because he was his own best source for material—a veritable treasure trove of vulnerabilities just waiting to be mocked and ridiculed."

Faint laughter rippled through the group.

"Okay, for instance, everybody here knows what a penny-pincher Freddy was. He made Jack Benny look like Andrew Carnegie. You know, I said this would be a heartwarming experience, and I think you'll agree. Do you feel it—that warmth inside? Or maybe that's because we actually put a full shot of tequila in your margaritas."

Subdued laughter continued.

"Now, I don't believe the vicious rumor that Freddy watered down his drinks, but, if you ask Manny, he'll tell you that when Freddy was training him to tend bar, he suggested that an eyedropper is a bartender's most valuable instrument."

Hearty laughter rippled through the crowd.

"I find it supremely ironic that Freddy's claim to fame was that this bar served Tom Mix the Bloody Maria that killed him. I do believe that Tom Mix did stop by here for a morning libation. But consensus opinion has it that he died racing his way up to Florence, where he knew he could find one that actually contained some alcohol."

Pada-dop, chunk! Ray's impulsive imitation of a vaudevillian snaredrum rim shot executed with finger pops on the guitar top was spot-on. Jay Pee turned toward Ray and bowed slightly.

"Thank you, maestro, for the punctuation. Ladies and gentlemen, Ray Cienfuegos has been gracing us with the musical backdrop for this somber occasion."

Thunderous applause ensued as Isabel rolled her eyes. The eulogy was becoming too much a performance—too reminiscent of a celebrity roast for her liking. Aycock leaned back on his stool to join in the applause and barely recovered from tipping completely over.

"Ray," Jay Pee continued as the applause fell off, "I don't have to tell you that Freddy was pleased that you've become such a local success—pleased in the pocketbook, that is. But you realize he didn't hire you just for your talent, don't you?" Ray's perplexed expression was in earnest. "He told me he just couldn't resist hiring an entertainer who couldn't keep an eye on his own tip jar."

The crowd groaned their disapproval at the cruel joke at Ray's expense and a smear on the deceased's character. But Ray, grinning like a cat eating hair out of a brush, waved to the crowd, signifying his good-natured acceptance of the humor. And so Jay Pee finished mining the vein.

"C'mon, we're talking about the real Freddy here, people—not some folk hero. Oh, he quite candidly told me that managing a blind musician was an agent's dream. Of course, I'm not suggesting that Freddy was doing a little extra skimming in Ray's case." He paused. "But then, he *did* tell me that 'the kid couldn't tell a sawbuck from a C-note if it was printed in braille.'"

Pada-dop, chunk! Ray's vaudeville knock-off absolved the crowd of their uneasiness with Jay Pee's edgy humor, and they laughed long and hard.

"I see that most of his devoted staff is here, wearing that shared look of disbelief on their shocked faces. Shocked at their *patrón's* untimely death? Umm, I really think it's because I just informed them that, yes, with Freddy's passing there will, no doubt, be a substantial wage increase."

Pada-dop, chunk! The audience was laughing almost nonstop.

"Let's not overlook Freddy's better attributes. His entrepreneurial spirit was legendary and an inspiration to us all. He once told me that there is a fine line between a brilliant salesman and a weasel in the henhouse. Which brings to mind the time just last October—it was during that anxious month we now call the Cuban missile crisis—that he angled the most marvelous con…er, *conversion* of his entire career. It seems that the purchasing agent for his construction business had made a procurement error which rendered Freddy the owner of an excess of some half dozen concrete septic tanks. But Freddy—always on the prowl to change misfortune into opportunity—seized upon the prevailing angst of the hour by pawning off…er, *characterizing,* the giant concrete vessels as *atomic bomb shelters.* You remember this? He easily unloaded…I mean, conveyed, the surplus poop tanks—pardon me, *sewage receptacles*—for twice their market value to hungry consumers whose neighbors were clamoring for more." The group erupted with laughter. "Okay, most of you are laughing, but some of you—I think six of you at least—are cringing, because you're still trying to find the door to the damn things."

The mirth that was resounding so loudly throughout the room at the questionably accurate tale made Isabel frown her disapproval at Jay Pee. Sure, a couple of jokes to lighten the mood was a good approach, but he was really getting carried away with it. It was supposed to be a memorial service, not the debut of Shecky Morton's stand-up lounge-lizard routine, and, for her, his extended caper was no longer amusing.

With one eye constantly trained on her every facial nuance, he sensed her displeasure and tacitly agreed that it was time to change the tone.

"I've had a bit of fun at our old friend's expense, but I know he's looking down and laughing along. Looking down? Freddy? You may wonder about that. Speaking of which, if you missed Freddy's funeral Mass earlier, don't worry. He missed it too—mostly because there wasn't one. Okay, it's no secret that our friend and mayor was never a familiar face down at Saint Jerome's. In fact, when he showed up at Mass just last week, I had to prescribe a double dose of heart medication for Father Miguel as a consequence."

He shot a look at Isabel that he hoped said, *Look, I can't pull an instant U-turn when I'm going ninety miles an hour. People will get whiplash.*

"As his closest friend and confidante, I can tell you unequivocally that he was a believer. I know that not by his not-so-regular attendance in church, but by his anonymous acts of kindness and self-sacrifice. Yes, that's right. Freddy contributed generously to several worthy charities. You wouldn't know that because he always kept his generosity a secret—didn't want to spoil the Scrooge myth, I suppose. And, as mayor, he worked tirelessly behind the scenes to help improve our town and our lives. Where do you think our favorite gathering place, Pioneer Park, came from? Freddy donated that land and obtained a federal grant to create that much-loved sanctuary. I urged him to name it after himself, but he wouldn't hear of it. Again, I think he was protecting the Jack Benny image because the irony brought him a chuckle."

Or maybe it was something else, Isabel wondered to herself. *Wasn't it our Lord who told us that when we give not to let the right hand know what the left is doing?*

"By now," Jay Pee continued, "you may be wondering how it is that I was allowed these glimpses of his inner life that I've been describing. Many of you know that Freddy and I were boyhood friends. But I'm going to tell a short story concerning my friend and me—an event that explains the depth of our friendship. Of course, there were plenty of those cliché occasions where we stuck up for each other in the midst of some threat or other—a bullying classmate or a particularly oppressive nun or brother. But there was one defining event that cemented us together for life."

Jay Pee was concerned that he was on the edge of going too long, but a quick scan of the room made it clear that every pair of eyes and ears were keenly fixed upon him, particularly those of Isabel Cienfuegos Hightower.

"We were thirteen, buddies and classmates at St. Mary's School. It was mid-May, as I recall. We were riding our bicycles home from school. Freddy had a sleek new bicycle—fire-engine red with streamers coming out of the handlegrips—a real dream bike that put my rusty old two-wheeler to shame. We always took the shortcut along the canal-bank road up by the Vasquez orange grove—that stretch of canal near the diversion gates. Being late spring, the canal was really full, and the sluices at the diversion were running full force. As typical thirteen-year-old boys, we would dare each other to skirt the edge of the canal bank as we rode along. As you can guess, on this particular day, we pushed the envelope a bit too far. The dirt under my rear wheel crumbled, and I was pitched into the drink, bike and all. Man, I shiver to this day when I think about how cold that water was!"

An empathetic murmur from the crowd rose and fell.

"Well, I was wearing this pair of big clunky desert boots as a defense against snakes and scorpions. Needless to say, when I hit the water, I sank like a stone. I may as well have been wearing cement overshoes. Now, the undertow immediately began moving me toward the diversion gates at a very alarming rate. You see, we all knew that both of those two big sluice gates were raised only about a foot at bottom—just enough to allocate the proper amount of water to each of the two secondary canals they fed, but too narrow to allow the passage of a body, even that of a skinny kid like myself. That's why that particular stretch of canal was avoided even by the most foolhardy of swimmers. I was backpedaling along the bottom, but that was pretty useless. My feet were slipping over the slimy rocks on the canal bed. I soon lost hope, prayed a silent Hail Mary, and resigned myself to my fate as I was pulled ever faster toward those sucking sluices."

The room held its collective breath in suspense as Jay Pee paused.

"When I didn't surface right away, Freddy instantly grasped the desperate nature of my predicament. He immediately kicked off his shoes and jumped into the middle of the shrinking distance between me and the gates. He dove down, somehow finding me in that muddy swirl and, just few feet short of the sluice, pushed me upward above the force of the undertow. My head broke the surface, and I took a life-saving breath of air. Freddy's upward heaving of my body, of course, pushed his own down into the bottom-hugging rush of water. Just as the gentler downstream current at the surface delivered me to the salvation of the gatehead, Freddy's legs were sucked into the narrow opening of the sluice and, predictably, he became stuck at the hips. Now, ironically, I was saved, but I was sure my friend was a goner."

At that point, a glass hit the floor and shattered, breaking the silence that ensued as Jay Pee again paused to take a breath and gather his emotions. Annoyed pairs of eyes were cast in Aycock's direction as he stooped to pick up the pieces, then the audience focused once again on the eulogist.

"Then," Jay Pee continued, "as I scrambled up onto the concrete gangway, certain that Freddy was drowning and powerless to do anything about it, a true miracle caught my attention. Apparently, the ditch boss who maintained the gates had absentmindedly left the chain on the control wheel unlocked. I dashed over and struggled to turn the wheel. The big iron screw that raises and lowers the gate was pretty rusty, and it took all the might that a scrawny kid could muster, but I got it to move. I guessed that turning it clockwise would raise the gate, and my guess turned out to be right. I saw a lump of flesh and torn clothing bob up in the white water on the downstream side of the sluice. Freddy, or at least his body, had shot through. I can't express right now the overwhelming sense of relief that seized me when I saw him clawing his way up the near-side canal bank. I raced over to him. He was pretty scraped up, but still in one piece. He was still huffing to get his breath back, but he spoke up nevertheless, and I strained to hear over the roar of the rushing water the profound utterance of one who had just experienced a near-death experience: 'Helluva backhanded way to rig yourself for a new bike, wasn't it?' he gasped between breaths. We laughed until we cried, both of us overcome with the joy of just being alive.

"We made a pact that afternoon never to tell this story, but, given the circumstances, I think Freddy would approve of what I just divulged. You see, it tells a lot about the value and the nature of our friendship. But, more to the point, it's a testimony to Freddy's true character. Despite of all his flaws, I'll always remember him as the kid who risked—no, for all intents, *sacrificed*—his life to save mine. I'll always love Freddy as my brother, and, behind all the joking, my heart grieves that he has been taken from us…from me…too soon."

My God, what have I done? Isabel's mind suddenly cried out in silent self-reproach, as the words of Christ in John's Gospel came crashing in: *Greater love has no one than this: that someone lay down his life for his friends.*

"I'll wrap this up with one last quick thing—the icing on the cake of this remembrance," Jay Pee choked out, fighting back the tears. "Lest anyone here take Freddy's Ebenezer Scrooge persona too seriously—I should mention that his widow and his nearest blood relative approve—his last request regarding the disbursement of his estate will be honored. All holdings will be divided between his two favorite charities: Saint Vincent DePaul Society and Saint Jude's Children's Hospital. All holdings, that is, with the exception of the cantina, which will be conveyed to his faithful servant, Manny de la Torre."

A surge of applause arose as the entire throng stood for an extended ovation. It was hard to tell if they were cheering Freddy's memory or Jay Pee's eloquence, they were both so intertwined. The good doctor modestly bowed his head and waited for the acclaim to die away.

"I now relinquish the microphone to any of you to say a few words about Freddy."

Thunderous applause sounded again as he strode toward the bar where Isabel was waiting, tears streaming down her blushing cheeks. Aycock rose from his stool as Jay Pee drew near.

"That was wonderful!" Isabel cried over the commotion.

Aycock opened his mouth, but turned toward the bar and vomited into his upturned Stetson.

Jay Pee placed a hand on the deputy's shoulder as he retched once more into the hat.

"So, was it my speech or the vermouth?"

A Tangle in the Web

At Manny's command, Curtis and Maria began the frenzied shuttle between the kitchen and the buffet. They loaded the tables with more than a dozen piping hot chafing dishes overfilled with scores of cheesy shredded beef enchiladas, pork tamales, chile rellenos, deep-fried red and green chili burritos, little golden half-moon empanadas, *rollitos de pollo*, and a choice of chorizo or chicken quesadillas. There were panfuls of refried beans skinned over with layers of melted Colby cheese, and spicy Spanish rice boiled in chicken broth. It was a Mexican gourmet's smorgasbord of gastronomical enchantment.

The heavenly aroma of steaming meats and cheeses mingling with the bouquet of delightful spices was enough to entice the guests to the buffet without any verbal encouragement. No sooner had the food been placed than a queue began to form. It was only a matter of minutes before the better part of the assembled throng had served themselves and was heartily partaking of the feast.

Isabel breathed a contented sigh, finally pleased that all of the exhaustive food preparations were paying off in the simple pleasure of seeing all of the enjoyment saturating the room. It was as she expected—the cantina was the perfect venue for an exceptional event that was sure to be the talk of the town. She was pleased, too, to see Jay Pee rather forcefully escorting Deputy Aycock to the men's room to allow him, in a more private setting, to expel the remainder of his questionable stomach contents. It seemed that all of the sad nostalgia invoked by Jay Pee's eulogy and all of the distraction of Aycock's revolting performance were eclipsed by the apparent delight that the funeral banquet provided.

"*Todo es pacífico,*" Isabel whispered as she strode about the room seemingly unnoticed.

"Yes," said a rasping voice that seemed to come from everywhere, "a profound peace can be experienced in the midst of such bedlam, if one can just focus on the power of a single moment suspended in the present."

Isabel turned and found herself gazing at the leathern face of Natchez Mendoza. He was standing, supported precariously by an ivory cane, as his legs were visibly trembling. He held her there for a moment in his gaze, his dark eyes resembling two vacuous pools, thirstily drinking her in.

"Yes," she agreed, "and it was just such a quiet moment as this that I was waiting for to have a private word with you."

"Then, by all means, please join me in my booth over here, Lucrezia. I can stand, but only for a few minutes at a time." He turned, waddled the few steps to the booth, bent stiffly, and slid into the bench seat. Isabel seated herself opposite the ancient jurist. "Privacy is important," he continued, "and it is fortuitous that my handlers have all adjourned to the buffet line."

"Why do you call me Lucrezia?" Isabel probed. "You know my name is Isabel."

"My apologies. It was a mere slip of the tongue. You see, I am currently reading a fascinating biography of that captivating woman, Lucrezia Borgia, and your enchanting good looks just naturally bring her to mind. Most certainly your life can be measured by hers."

"Thank you, I think. Lucrezia Borgia—wasn't she some sort of queen or princess or something?"

"Duchess of Ferrara, actually. She was the illegitimate daughter of the infamous Pope Alexander. Are you familiar with her background?"

"No, not really," Isabel said.

"She was the notorious femme fatale of the politically ruthless Borgia family of Italy during the Renaissance period. Notorious not only for her profound beauty but for her pernicious habit of poisoning her enemies—including, they say, some of her suitors."

"And you are comparing my life with Lucrezia's? Your analogy is somewhat interesting, I suppose, but seriously misplaced, don't you think?" Isabel muttered dismissively.

"Why so defensive, my dear? I was correct to think the reference might pique your fascination, but did not expect such resistance." Mendoza continued. "They say Borgia's poison of preference was a substance known as cantarella because it was as deadly as it was difficult to trace."

"You don't say!"

"Yes, I do say." The old man smiled cunningly. "I suspect that oleander tea was not available in her time and place."

A long silence ensued, as Isabel was taken aback. She continued to protest that such subtle implications were being leveled against her, especially at Freddy's funeral. Mendoza's piercing stare would not waiver. Isabel soon could no longer bear the strain and began to tremble. "How could you *possibly* know?" she demanded at last in a voice muted by fear.

"Like you, my dear, I learn much about events and circumstances through means other than the normal sensory channels. As I said before, we have more in common than a relationship with my grandnephew," Natchez Mendoza said.

"Then you know about the situation I was in?"

"I know what your motivations were. I know of your supposed justifications. I even know about the previous slaying that led up to Alfredo's homicide. By the way, I hope the irony in your act did not escape you. After all, killing Freddy accomplished the purpose of the man you call Ezra. You extinguished the final life in the line of the Mendozas for him."

"What about you?" Isabel shot back, sweating and nervously twitching.

"I was adopted by that family at the age of twelve. They treated me like a son, but I'm not a true blood relative. That partly explains why the old coyote never made an attempt on my life."

"Partly explains?" Isabel inquired.

"You listen well for a woman in such distress," the old man observed. "Yes. I also believe that he stayed his hand with me because I once knew him—that is, I knew him as his former self before evil completely consumed his humanity. His name was Ezzymandias. He was a great warrior chief of the Aravaipa Apache."

"You speak of him with respect." Isabel desperately attempted to regain some calm.

"Like most of us, his spirit was tempered with a unique balance of good and evil—of virtue and vice. His most evident virtues included legendary courage and a keen sense of justice. I like to believe that I inherited some of the good that was in him."

"I surmise that you, sir, now have come here to expose me."

"Heavens no, woman!" He recoiled in surprise. "At this point, that would clearly do more harm than good. What makes you think I would even contemplate such a thing?"

"To avenge his killing—that, and the killing of Alfredo."

"Ah, I see. No. Vengeance is an evil distortion of justice that I reject. It poisons the soul and corrupts the mind, as you very well know firsthand. It is an overpowering scourge sent directly from hell, and I avoid it like the plague. Besides, the monster that you slew bore no resemblance to my father whatsoever. That thing was the very incarnation of vengeance. It was pure evil, merely exploiting my father's mortal shell as a facade—an abomination to the memory of the man who once wore that mortal armor. Its slaying was more than justified as an act of self-defense and a favor to mankind. The murder of Alfredo, Isabel—well, that's another matter."

"But, if revenge isn't your purpose, sir, then what brings you here today?"

"Among other things, I came to hear you out. You see, I have this overwhelming sense that you have something to say—something more than mere rationalizations for your wicked deeds. You need to relieve your guilt. You need to set yourself free."

Isabel nervously noted that a line of mourners had formed before the casket, and admirers were tossing flowers—albeit, flowers from the table settings—upon Freddy's corpse.

Feeling intense pressure to confess, Isabel finally cracked. "You're right—I do have something I need to say, and, as strange as this may sound, it is something that I think I want you, of all people, to hear."

"Then, by all means, speak freely, my dear," the old man encouraged.

Isabel glanced around to make certain that no one was within earshot. The prevailing buzz of contented mealtime conversation and Ray's finger-picking interpretation of "You'll Never Walk Alone" would provide a sufficient veil for her muted words.

"What you say is true," she stated in sotto voce. "I was driven by an irresistible thirst for vengeance when I killed Freddy. In fact, if you had asked me yesterday, I'd have told you that if he were to be miraculously resurrected, I'd gladly kill him all over again. He plotted with Ezra to kill me and my nephew. I hated him with every fiber of my being."

"But that has changed?" Mendoza pressed.

"Yes, and dramatically so—and just over the course of the past hour, although I'm not altogether certain what prompted the change of heart. I think maybe it was a combination of things," Isabel confessed.

"As is often the case with such emotional transformations," the old relic observed. "What 'things' prompted this epiphany?"

"The first prod came about an hour ago, when a young man informed me that Freddy had made definite arrangements for Ray to make some recordings this week."

"Ray Cienfuegos—your nephew over there playing the guitar."

"Yes. It became apparent Freddy went to a lot of trouble to make an appointment for someone he was plotting to kill beforehand. It didn't add up, but it started me thinking about all the effort Alfredo put into helping Ray cope with his blindness—the music venue, the joking and teasing, the money—again, all very inconsistent with someone conspiring to murder him, wouldn't you say?"

"Perhaps he was simply fabricating a cover so that he would not be suspected."

"I suppose that's possible, though I doubt it. If that were true, the charade was wildly overplayed, and Freddy's performance should win an Academy Award for Best Actor. No, I think it is much more likely that he was driven by Ezra's influence and the constant threat to his own life into a sort of emotional conflict—a divided personality."

"A sort of Dr. Jekyll and Mr. Hyde phenomenon?" Mendoza pondered.

"Exactly! That would also go a long way toward explaining what prevented my strongest intuition from penetrating his deception. The Dr. Jekyll that we experienced was kept somehow unaware of, or disconnected from, Mr. Hyde's treachery."

"Hmm—a plausible theory, but not quite compelling enough by itself," the old man muttered.

"Perhaps, but then came Jay Pee's eulogy. The kind and generous person he described was consistent with the Freddy we knew, not with the monster that I was obsessed with for the past few days. After all, someone whose first instinct was to save the life of his closest friend isn't likely to be one who's contemplating the brutal murder of his next two dearest friends. When Jay Pee described Freddy's heroics, it hit me: I was fixated on the man's criminal aspect, but God sees the totality of a life—the good and the bad—when He makes His final judgment. That is why we, who see so narrowly, are admonished by Him not to judge."

"Yes, I can see how your reversal in thinking might be explained, taken in context. You know, justice and mercy are not contradictory aspects of our Lord. So…you're now willing to give Alfredo the benefit of the doubt?"

"Yes, I am. I believe that, best case, Freddy was so conflicted that he was in denial of his darker side. And, worst case, he was a frightened little man who was so overcome with fear, he abandoned his better instincts. Either way, I must forgive him and give up this terrible obsession with revenge. After all, he was only human."

"I am greatly gladdened, my dear Isabel, to hear all of this from you. I sense that you are emerging from a great darkness that might have consumed you. Still, I sense that it is a darkness that you may never completely escape, now that you have been tainted by it. You will spend the rest of your life dishonestly maintaining the false front of your innocence. Your nephew is completely oblivious and would be devastated if he ever learned the truth. And your new friend, the doctor—he mostly believes you, and he represses any suspicions to the contrary because of his affection for you. But, despite this deception, you must reconcile with God. These other matters are secondary, and their effects may be diminished over time."

"I must confess that you are undoubtedly right. That is why I need the Lord's grace—because my repentance will never be sufficient or complete."

"Truer words were never spoken, Isabel. Now, there are two others to whom you must tell all of this."

"Oh?"

"Yes, one is a priest and the other may or may not be able to hear you, but his remains are right over there in that box. Don't delay, my dear—he won't be there for long."

"Thank you, Your Honor, for the kindness of hearing me. Now, please tell me, what 'other things?'"

"I beg your pardon?"

"You said you came today to hear me, 'among other things.' What other things?"

"You *are* a good listener!" The ancient curmudgeon chuckled as he tapped his ivory cane on the floor. "I came to pay my respects to Alfredo, as distantly related as we might be. I also came to dine on some of the best food in all of Arizona—although you may have to put mine in a blender. Most importantly, however, I came to revisit a former acquaintance. Do you suppose I could have a word with your colored busboy?"

◆

"I tell you, Doc, thad fuggin Messcn bish poysnd me!" Myron Aycock spat as he knelt before the open maw of a porcelain toilet. He retched long and hard, bringing up only a tiny cloud of putrid air. "I've never feld so fugging mizzrabull innahluvmy fugging life." He groaned.

"That's pretty far-fetched, Myron—especially considering that all of your symptoms are indicative of overindulging in adult beverages." Jay Pee chuckled.

"Izz thissthehendformee…Doc?"

"No, it's my professional opinion that you won't be dead tomorrow morning, although you may wish you were."

"Dammit, Doc—evrythig is fugging zpinnig roun," the polluted lawman choked out. "I juz wan evrythig to hole stil. *Hole fugging stil, evrythig!*"

"Ah, the proverbial spins—classic symptom of extreme inebriation. How much did you have to drink *before* you came here, Myron?" Jay Pee asked rhetorically as the deputy retched again. The revolting sound of Aycock's innards violently convulsing reverberated throughout the porcelain chamber of the water closet like the guttural wailing of a sow in heat. "And now, predictably, here come the dry heaves: nature's stomach pump—the body's instinctual effort to purge the offending toxins," Jay Pee narrated.

"Togzinz—'nother werd fer poyzn. Poyzn! The fuggin bish poyznd me!"

"No, toxin as in the word in*toxic*ated, Myron."

"I'm dyin'!"

"You are not going to die, Myron—that is, unless you drown face-down with your head in the toilet. Is that how you want to go out?" Jay Pee asked.

"No."

"Then pull yourself together, man. Now, what's all this drivel about poison?"

"Zhe *poyznd* me-hee." The drunken deputy gasped for breath.

"And who might 'she' be?"

"Yizzabel."

"*Jezebel*?"

The deputy gagged once more, again ejecting only stomach gasses.

"Save me, Doc." Aycock whimpered as he recovered from a wave of convulsions. "I'm fuggin' dyin'."

"You're going to be okay, Deputy," Jay Pee assured him. "Why do you keep insisting that you've been poisoned. Good God, man—haven't you ever had too much to drink before? All these symptoms are consistent with that, and nothing more. You're drunk, Myron, otherwise known as smashed, bombed, crocked, pissed, plastered, and polluted. In other words, you're fucking hammered, my friend, not poisoned."

"No, she poyzndme, jez like she poyznd the mayr," the deputy went on.

"Just who do you mean, deputy?" Jay Pee's tone instantly shifted from jocularity to gravity.

"Izzabel, the Messcn bish frum hell. She poyznd Mayr Hite-towr."

"Myron, I suggest that you keep such ravings to yourself, or you'll regret it. You're shit-faced drunk, and you don't know what you're saying. You'll wind up disgracing yourself and your entire department with such preposterous accusations."

No reply came from the stall.

"Do you hear me, Myron?"

More silence. Jay Pee peered into the confines of the metal partitions. As suspected, Aycock's face was submerged in the toilet water. The doctor quickly lifted the lawman's head from the cavernous commode, closed the lid, and propped him upright, wedged between the "porcelain pony" and the metal partition. Jay Pee anxiously checked his breathing. It was shallow but steady. He had finally passed out, but apparently hadn't yet inhaled any water.

That was close—too close for comfort. The small amount of Seconal that Jay Pee had slipped into Aycock's Manhattan was nowhere near enough to harm him, but combined with the effects of alcohol, it was sufficient to turn his lights out for a while and get him out of Isabel's hair. In doing so, of course, he had violated his oath as a physician and his integrity as an officer of the court—neither of which he had ever done before. But he had never been entranced by a woman like Isabel before. And, although he hoped he would never again have to stoop to such a lowly act, he knew that he was capable of any nefarious errand in the course of protecting her, the newfound object of his affection.

He had just begun to take stock of the present situation—the task of moving Aycock's sleeping hulk out of the building—when Curtis Jefferson entered the restroom. The sight of the deputy slumped in the stall and the anxious expression on Jay Pee's face froze the boy in his tracks, and his eyes widened.

"Thank God you came." Jay Pee laughed nervously. "Did Isabel send you?"

"N-no, sir—I just came in to take a leak." He gestured toward the crumpled Aycock. "Is he dead?"

"No, Curtis, he just passed out."

"You know who I am?" Curtis asked.

"Yes, son, I'm the JP around here. Your name came across my desk the day you slipped away from the fort. But don't worry. If Isabel has been giving you refuge, I'm sure she has good reason; so mum's the word, okay?" No sooner had the words left his mouth than the thought struck him that he'd compromised his pledge of honesty once again by volunteering his silence.

"Yes, sir," Curtis answered

"*Iherdahlathahd!*" Deputy Aycock sputtered from inside his stall. "Iss th' fuggin' nigger boy I bin trackin'!"

Curtis recoiled in horror as the clearly impaired deputy attempted to scramble to his feet. "You keep away from me you son of a bitch, or I swear I'll dot your eyes for you all over again!" the boy shouted as he clenched his fists.

The threat was unnecessary as the tipsy lawman barely made it past a crouch before collapsing again—that time face-first onto the urine-slicked tile floor.

"You see that?" Curtis chirped. "The sucker fainted dead away at the very thought of facin' me again!"

"I see you two have met," Jay Pee quipped. "That's nice. I hate making introductions."

"We met all right, but it was pitch black, and he didn't see anything but stars." Curtis turned again to the crumpled figure. "Hey, *honey gun*, what happened to your sidearm?" he taunted.

"Honey gun?" Jay Pee wondered aloud.

"Yeah. See, when I knocked him into dreamland, I didn't know what to do about his gun."

"Please, spare me the details for now, son." The doctor sighed. "And don't worry about our friend here. He'll tune in and out of consciousness for a while, but he's not likely to remember anything about you tomorrow—or anything else, for that matter."

"If you say so, Your Honor."

"I say so. After all, I'm his physician."

Curtis rolled his eyes. "If you say so, Doc."

"Now, Curtis, I need you to perform an errand for me, please."

"Yes, sir," said the boy, rising up onto his toes. "But can I pee first?"

"Of course you can, Curtis, and bravo for your solid grasp on the priorities at hand."

The boy unzipped and unleashed a torrent into a wall-hung urinal.

"Go ahead, Doc. This might surprise you, but I can pee and listen at the same time."

"Very funny. Okay, do you know who Frankie Quintana is?" Jay Pee asked.

"No, which table is he sitting at?" Curtis inquired.

"The third booth south of the entry."

"Ahhh…good to the last drop." Curtis grunted as he shook off.

"Are you listening?"

"Third booth south of the entry. Got it. What should I say?"

"Very quietly tell him that I need help in the men's room."

"Won't he think that's kinda weird?"

"Okay, tell him I'm in the men's room with the deputy."

"That doesn't sound much better." Curtis snickered as he zipped up.

"Just tell him. He's a cop—he'll get it. Now, *scoot!*" The boy was half-way to the door when Jay Pee barked the contradiction: "Stop!"

"You're supposed to say 'green light, red light,'" the boy remarked

"Curtis," Jay Pee retorted drily, "aren't you going to wash your hands?"

"What for?" he grinned, "I didn't pee on my fingers. Besides, I've got *priorities!*"

He was gone in a flash, leaving Jay Pee muttering lines from a Sir Walter Scott poem in his wake. More than a minute passed before Frankie Quintana entered and sniffed the rank air.

"I smell the foul odor of a sheriff's deputy, Jay Pee." He chortled, glancing into the toilet stall. "And there's the worthless sack of shit in the flesh. Man, is he out of it or what?"

"Yes, I'm afraid our county mountie has strayed just a few steps over the edge, Frankie."

"A few steps my ass. Looks like he took a flying leap," Frankie observed.

"Be that as it may, I'm not sure how to dispose of him—and I'm going to need a hand getting him out of here."

"I have just the place for our sleeping guest—my *jusgado*."

"Hoos-gow?" Jay Pee repeated phonetically.

"That's what I said, *jusgado*. Of course, my cell makes the county slammer look like a posh resort hotel, but it does have a great big clay pot in the middle of the floor where he can toss his cookies all night. That'll make the cockroaches happy. They haven't eaten in over a week. Now, I'll unlock the rear entrance and bring my car around to the back, so we don't attract too much attention. But he's going to have to nap in the back of the patrol car for an hour or so. I don't want to miss any more of this *funeral magnífico* than I have to over the likes of this bottom-feeder."

"Can't say as I blame you, Frankie. It is turning out to be a splendid event, isn't it?" Jay Pee mused. "Let's just be sure to leave the window open a crack on your car. We wouldn't want the deputy to suffocate."

"We wouldn't?" Frankie quipped.

"It's going to be tough enough living with the nickname you people have given me as it is. I wouldn't want folks to take it too literally, you know," Jay Pee retorted.

"Okay, a little crack it is." The constable grinned. "But just a little one." He held a pinched thumb and forefinger before his face and squinted. "A gap about the thickness of a cigarette paper. After all, we wouldn't want him to get too comfortable either."

"Agreed. So, hurry up, Frankie. I want to get some food before it's all eaten," said Jay Pee.

"Okay, but keep your guard up. He's starting to move around in there."

"Don't worry—he hasn't had much success with getting past hands and knees."

"You know, the señora should have let me throw the bum out to begin with." The constable spat on the tile floor. "That *pendejo*'s not fit to mix with decent *gente*." Frankie sneered.

"My goodness, Frankie. Don't hide your feelings," Jay Pee remarked. "But, please, get moving."

Okay, okay—I'm going. I'll be right back." The local lawman ambled to the door but hesitated there. "Listen, Doc, why don't you clean him up a little while I'm gone. He's got puke in his hair, for God's sake. Makes me sick to my stomach."

"I'll take care of it," Jay Pee barked. "Just go!"

The doctor took note of Aycock's condition as Frankie Quintana exited. The deputy had crawled on his belly a couple of feet to the threshold of the stall, but fell motionless again.

"All right, Myron," Jay Pee announced loudly. "As your attending physician, I am prescribing an overnight admittance to the hoos-gow as the antidote to your peculiar toxification. No need to thank me. My service will bill you by the end of the month." The doctor's sardonic remedy drew a low groan from his "patient," who otherwise remained as still as a corpse.

Jay Pee pulled several sheets of paper towel from a wall-mounted dispenser and strode purposefully to the center of three wash basins. Turning the cold faucet handle, he splashed some tepid water into his face and patted it dry. Then, gazing curiously at his own reflection, he regarded the visage as that of a stranger.

"Oh, James Patrick," he murmured to the mirror, "what are you doing?" He narrowed his gaze to the bright eyes that stared back at him and fixed it there for a long minute. At length, his mouth fell open and, in a thespian's baritone, spewed the poetic lines he had muttered earlier.

"Oh, what a tangled web we weave / When first we practice to deceive!"

The spoken sounds rang hollow against the cold tiled walls. It was a common quote, but one frequently attributed in error, and Jay Pee, a voracious devourer of English literature, knew well that the real source was an epic poem by Sir Walter Scott. He turned his gaze to where Aycock lay, still a lifeless lump on the toilet floor.

"I'm sure you've heard those words before, Deputy—everybody has," the doctor trumpeted quite stridently. "Those lines would be a perfect fit for that or any tale of a fool who enters into a web of deception just for the scant hope of finding favor with the alluring object of his affection. Lady Macbeth, Clara de Clare, Bathsheba, Señora Cienfuegos—the names are synonymous with enchantment and...and intrigue!"

He turned his eyes back to the mirror. "Who would have thought that I, after all these years spent as a workaholic and contented bachelor, would suddenly become game enough to throw in with the likes of King David, Macbeth, and Lord Marmion. But here I am, a fool for my lady's mere glances of approval—a sophomoric clown, performing for the hint of a smile. And yet...I've never felt more alive than I have these past few days spent in her company. Deputy, I know you can't possibly..."

He turned again toward Aycock and was startled to find him not only sentient but standing bolt upright at the threshold of the stall.

"Cahoots!" the deputy shrieked. "Yorn *cahoots!*"

"No, listen, Myron," Jay Pee sputtered, shocked, "you've got the wrong..."

"No, yoo lissen, Doc!" Aycock shouted. "Yorn fuggin' cahoots, an' I'm blowin' th' wissel on y'ahl—yoo n' the Messcn bish, her pussy-bline nefyoo, 'n' tha' lil nigger fyoojtiv tha' sheez bin stashin' 'way. Oh, boy!"

"Myron, you're not thinking straight," Jay Pee advised in his most reasonable tone as he stealthily inserted himself between the deputy and the door. "You've got things all confused."

"No, I've god it ahl straid now, an' I'm gwing out there an' tell ahlthospeeple 'bout this whole nest uv ratz."

"Deputy, I insist that you're in no condition..."

Aycock shuffled menacingly toward Jay Pee. "Get out of my way, Doc!"

The doctor had not noticed until then that the deputy outsized him quite considerably. Nevertheless, Jay Pee held his ground as Aycock lunged at him clumsily.

"I sed ged the fuck..." He seized the doctor by the throat with both hands and slammed his head hard against the tiled wall with a thud. Jay Pee reached out to fight back, but could only flail aimlessly. Aycock pulled the smaller man toward him until their chests touched, then thrust him away again with all his might, once more ramming his body against the unyielding partition like a rag doll's. Again, the back of Jay Pee's head struck the tile with such blunt force that his eyes rolled back and his knees buckled. Aycock released him with a leering grin and staggered out the door as Jay Pee slumped to the floor in a lifeless heap.

Funeral Pyre

Isabel waylaid Curtis the moment he emerged from the restroom and conveyed Natchez Mendoza's request to have a word with him.

"That creepy old fossil with one foot in the grave? I think I'll pass, señora. He gives me the willies. Somethin' about those dark eyes. He's a walkin' corpse. The only creepier character in this whole room is that smelly undertaker, and just the sight of the old duffer is givin' the mortician a woody. Just look at that death-dealin' lech. He looks like he's gonna go check the old man's pulse any minute," Curtis mused.

Indeed, Hackett appeared transfixed by Mendoza's cadaverous appearance.

"What's a woody?" Isabel asked innocently. "Something to do with Woody Strode?"

"That's it. Anyway, I've got *priorities*: I'm carryin' an important message from your friend, Dr. Mort, to Constable Quintana, whoever he is. I don't have time to socialize," Curtis declared.

"The constable is seated at the third booth from the door," Isabel directed. "I suppose Jay Pee needs some help subduing the deputy."

"Yes ma'am—the dumbass, pukin', fallin'-off-the-face-of-the-earth-drunk deputy, that is. The doc needs a hand movin' his miserable passed-out honky carcass, is what the deal is," said Curtis.

"You go over and pay our guest, Judge Mendoza, a visit just as soon as you pass Jay Pee's message on to Frankie Quintana, *joven*," said Isabel.

"Oh my God! He's a judge to boot? Now I'm even more creeped out. I've had some experience with judges, and none of it's been good," said Curtis.

"He's a retired judge, Curtis, and he's a delightful old gentleman.

Now, be a good *muchacho* and don't disappoint me," Isabel requested. "I need to have a quiet moment with Freddy before they take him away to the crematorium."

Eager to please his guardian angel, Curtis quickly relayed the doctor's request to the constable, and, in less than a minute, he was standing in front of His Honor's booth.

"There you are, young man," the ancient adjudicator croaked. "Please, have a seat. I've been wanting to talk to you all afternoon."

"About what?" Curtis heard the disrespect and suspicion in his terse reply as he slid into the booth, and sought to correct it. "I mean, what is it you wanted to talk about, Your Honor?" There was still trepidation in his voice.

"Many things, Curtis." The old man's deep obsidian eyes were probing him. "But first things first: I sense that you are hungry—isn't that right?" The judge's gravelly voice reminded Curtis of Andy Devine's gargling larynx.

"Now that you mention it, I *am* half starved. But how…how did you know my name?"

Curtis met the judge's penetrating stare with an expression of deep puzzlement.

"Justin!" the old man called out like a bullfrog as he beckoned his doctor over from the bar. "Please bring a plate of food over for my companion here. What, particularly, would you prefer, Curtis?"

"The enchiladas smelled scrumptious," said the boy, suddenly comfortable.

Dr. Case enlisted the aid of one of the orderlies and obediently adjourned to the buffet.

"No disrespect, sir," Curtis pressed, "but you dodged my question…Your Honor."

"Not entirely. I was getting to that. You see, Curtis, I know much more about you than just your name."

"Here we go again. So much for the busboy disguise, I guess."

"No, that was a clever enough masquerade to cloak your identity from most of the folks here—at least well enough to evade arrest. It's just that you and I have some history."

"You know, I got that feelin' when I first laid eyes on you a while ago. I can't for the life of me place you. Still, your eyes look so familiar…"

"I shouldn't expect that you would recognize me at first. I have aged a bit since our brief, one-time encounter. That and it was getting pretty dark, as I recall. However, this is not the first time that I've asked you to dine with me. The trouble then was that you misunderstood because I asked you in another tongue. Do you recall?"

"I really don't have a clue…"

"Then let me give you one by apologizing for hitting you in the face with that fish."

"What?"

"Yes, and I hope you'll accept my excuse for such bad behavior, Curtis. After all, I was only around ten or twelve years old at the time."

Once the line of mourners had dwindled, Isabel took up an empty chair and seated herself beside the elevated casket that enveloped her deceased husband's earthly shell. She sat in silence, assuming the traditional posture of the widow's vigil. She maintained a reverent stillness for what seemed like an hour, but was actually no more than a couple of minutes before she leaned in and heard her own voice speaking in a hushed tone.

"I don't quite know what to finally say to you, Freddy. Clearly, nothing that I can say or do will ever even begin to earn forgiveness for what I did to you. It was beyond brutal, I know. Forgiveness is now a matter between my Lord and me. All I can do is forgive you your betrayal of Ray and me."

She glanced around, tears streaming down her face, noting that the guests were conversing among themselves and paying her little mind. Most were milling about the room, cocktails in hand.

"Taking in all that I have seen and heard today," she continued, "I am now convinced that you acted more out of fear and weakness than out of malice, Alfredo. I recall how living under Ezra's beguilement and his constant threat twisted the way Ray and I behaved. I can only imagine how enduring that curse for years must have corrupted your mind."

She reached over and took the handkerchief from Freddy's jacket pocket, dabbed her tears, and carefully returned it, taking care to arrange it so that his embroidered initials, A. H., peeked over the top.

"Anyway, Freddy." She sighed. "Your accountability for whatever actions you took are now under God's judgment, as are mine. My penance on earth will lie in the concealment I must perpetuate with falsehoods. From that chain of sins, I will never be freed until my death, and I accept that fate. I refuse to carry in my heart any longer the burning contempt I held for you when I discovered your duplicity—that all-consuming hatred that drove me to murder you in that most monstrous way. Your last memory in this world was that of my face, twisted into an expression of wicked enjoyment at your final throes of agony. I am so sorry, Freddy. I now purge myself of that obsessive hatred by telling you that I no longer despise you, my sad friend. I hope you can hear me, somehow. I forgive you, and I am truly sorry for your suffering over all those awful years of living under that cloud of evil."

A sudden sense of alarm intruded on Isabel's fleeting moment of serenity—a presentiment that something dreadful was about to happen. She abruptly raised her head at the sound of shouts from the back of the dining room where the rear entrance was located. It was Frankie Quintana shouting for Aycock to stop.

"Surely you believe your own eyes, don't you Curtis?" Mendoza inquired.

"Beggin' your pardon, sir, but it's *your* eyes that's got me believin', not so much mine,"

Curtis returned, blinking. "And, after all I've seen, and heard, and been through over the past couple of months, I don't have much disbelievin' left in my person anymore. No, sir—I'm just more *amazed* than anything. But I do remember those same eyes starin' me down in the twilight along that creepy-ass path that led me into the past."

"And it was your good fortune—or Providence, more precisely—that you did not understand my invitation to come to our camp. I am certain now that it would have ultimately been the death of you," the old man speculated.

"I had some help from a friend to get me out of that fix too," Curtis muttered. "Randy led me back to the present."

"Yes, and you should feel confident, Curtis, that there will always be friends in your life to keep you from straying too far from the right path. Though I hope none of them will have to hit you with a catfish."

"Amen to that, sir."

"You can drop the formal address, my friend. After all, when we last met, I was at least four years your junior. They call me Natchez now, but my name was Nachise on that fateful eve upon which you traveled back in time. You—and you only—may call me by that name, Curtis."

"Thank you, sir…I mean, Nachise." Curtis's wide smile morphed slowly into a thoughtful gaze. "You know, Nachise, seein' you here today makes me wonder a lot."

"Wonder about what?" inquired Mendoza.

"About a lot of things—like I wonder…do you think it was Providence, as you call it, that you survived that massacre?" Curtis pondered.

"In a certain respect, yes," the old judge replied. "When I say Providence, you know I certainly don't mean anything like predestination. You see, I was compelled to learn at a very tender age that the world is a dangerous place, and evil lurks at almost every corner. Fortunately, we are blessed by the Creator with the free will to navigate through the dangers with right, or sometimes wrong, decisions. In a sense, our lives consist of little more than a constant series of such choices—tests, if you will, small and large. But make no mistake: our lives are not determined in the stars. Our choices are our own, and we must live by them—for good or for ill."

"That's what my mama says too."

"Your mama is a wise woman," the judge said with a nod. "Anyway, I believe that on that dreadful morning, when so many others perished,

I was spared as a consequence of my attempt to warn my tribe of the assailants that were upon them. My first impulse was to run away, but I stayed in the thick of danger to shout out the alarm instead. It was the greatest tragedy of my life that my warning came too late. I survived, however, and was given the chance to be tested further, much like you were in a different but related arena where you served an important purpose."

"I'm not exactly proud of what I did there," Curtis confessed.

"Good that you're not. But neither should you be at all ashamed," Mendoza stated firmly.

"Then you know. You know that I led—" Curtis began.

"I know that you resisted being tempted to a confrontation until you thought that a comrade was being attacked. Only then did you raise your hand against that murderous young fiend. And, when you finally acted, you did so with great courage, Curtis. Despite the danger to yourself, you goaded Mister Harvey Huish to a place where he was rendered incapable of harming anyone ever again—to his, pardon the cliché, 'just deserts.' The way I see it, you made the best of a very difficult and complex moral dilemma."

The old man related in brief the tale of young Harvey Huish's first murder, that of the boy's uncle.

"Whew! How can you possibly know so much?" Curtis wondered at length.

"Like you, I was granted the gift of vision at a young age—an endowment that was compounded by an unnaturally long life in which to develop it—a long life that has been a blessing, but has left me rather spirit-weary in the last few years," Mendoza confided.

"A good friend once told me not to forget about a second wind," said Curtis wistfully.

"I think maybe I've used up all the second wind I was afforded. Still, I sense that there is still at least one more test—"

"So, if you can see beyond here and now, do you see the future?" Curtis asked.

"I see a number of paths, but only the individual travelers can determine which ones are taken." The old man smiled broadly. "I see

where this is leading, and I can answer your question quite defini-
tively."

"You can?" Curtis asked.

"Yes, Curtis. Your running and hiding from the law is about to
end… today. In fact, it is about to end right now!"

Their attention was seized by a shout from the rear of the dining
area. It was Deputy Myron Aycock.

"Sumbuddy grab thad lil spook there!" he cried. "Heeza fyoojtiv
from Fordt Grandt!"

Weighing an escape, Curtis impulsively shot a look at the front entrance. At the threshold of the vestibule, seeming to block his perceived
avenue of exit, stood two very familiar figures who had just appeared:
Sergeant Joe Garcia and Father Frank Cullen!

"Stay right where you are, Curtis," Natchez Mendoza directed in a
grave and gravelly voice. "Like I said, your running days are over."

———◆———

Isabel could see that Aycock's angry glare was aimed in her direction
as he made his way through the milling crowd toward the raised platform. He raised a right fist menacingly as he neared the podium and
the microphone. But, just at the edge of the platform, he stumbled over
the step, flailed to right himself, and pitched headlong into one of the
candle stands. Reflexively grasping the cloth cover as he fell, he jerked
the lighted candle off the stand and sent it sailing. Astonishingly, that
smoldering waxen missile followed an airborne arc directly into the
gaping yaw of the open coffin! The crowd gasped in disbelief as the
exuding fumes from the ethyl alcohol that soaked Freddy's trousers ignited into a huge ball of flame—a hell-inspired flare that seemed to
engulf the grieving widow's tearstained face.

"Oh my God—the *humanity*!" Harold Hackett cried out.

Screams instantly enflamed the panic that ensued as many guests
surged to the front and rear portals to escape amid loud shouts of
"Fire!" Undaunted by the blazing casket that was issuing flames rival-
ing those of a ritual bonfire, and oblivious to the seared flesh on her

left cheek, Isabel spontaneously seized the cloth from the other candle stand, cast it over the conflagration, and pressed her own body against Freddy's, instantly smothering the flames. The premature cremation, as some came to call it, was doused just as suddenly and just as amazingly as it had begun.

Fits of coughing broke out among the remaining guests as an acrid stench, one that local lore would later testify bore the distinct smell of sulfur, permeated the air, although the fire had been completely extinguished by Isabel's instinctual act. Overcome by the fumes emanating from the casket, however, the heroic widow swooned and rolled onto the hardwood floor, unconscious.

Aftershocks

Maria was thrilling to the scene unfolding at the pass-through order window. It was better than Hitchcock's *Rear Window*. Dr. Case was kneeling at Isabel's side in an instant, checking her vital signs and administering smelling salts to bring her around, while Frankie Quintana cuffed Aycock's wrists behind his back. Curtis seemed to be transfixed by his dialogue with the ancient judge, Natchez Mendoza. It was almost too much simultaneous activity for a young girl to assimilate. Almost.

Harold Hackett, the undertaker, appeared at the casket, wringing his pasty white hands. The opportunity to wax dramatic was too enticing, and he pounced on it like a hungry puma on a speckled fawn.

"Just look at how these cretins have spoiled my lovely handiwork with all of their careless roughhousing." He moaned as he peeked under the tablecloth that Isabel had used as a fire blanket and cringed at the sight. "No one appreciates the delicate nature of preservation art these days. *Please*," he implored loudly with a sob, "someone help me carry the deceased out to my hearse. We mustn't allow him to be viewed in this disheveled state. If his dignity is to be maintained, the final incineration must be performed at once. I am compelled to finish the job these hooligans started."

Natchez Mendoza happily volunteered his two burly orderlies for the task. They were joined by Dave Randall and Mayor Montoya, who all served as makeshift pallbearers in an ad hoc procession out to the parking lot. Isabel sat up in time to witness the less-than-somber march. The four chatted noisily about the unscheduled entertainment and the quality of the food with a level of reverence they might have shown had their burden been a gunny sack of russet potatoes. Ray, who was oblivious to the entire episode because Rosa was dumbstruck by the spectacle of it, was playing "Smoke Gets in Your Eyes," which seemed wholly inappropriate. Constable Quintana and Undersheriff Alvarado were escorting Deputy Aycock to the rear exit, each holding one of his arms and both quibbling over jurisdiction. Guests who had taken flight from the threat of fire were drifting back in, and social cliques were reforming in standing clusters, some folks coughing from the caustic air, some tittering at the vaudevillian atmosphere that Aycock's antics had generated. For Maria, it was a lifetime treasure trove of gossip.

But it was all too unceremonious for Isabel's liking. She rose to her feet and began to smooth her skirt in an effort to regain her dignity. Only then did the fire in her cheek begin to heat up.

"You need to join me over at the bar, señora," Dr. Case commanded.

"My goodness, doctor, you've certainly gotten bold in a hurry," Isabel observed.

"No, we need to get some ice for your cheek quickly," the doctor stated matter-of-factly. "That burn you sustained is beginning to blister. It may leave a nasty scar if we don't get a cold compress on it immediately."

"Let's do that!" she yelped with a sudden urgency. She started for the bar, then stopped dead in her tracks. "Wait a minute," she said to herself as much as to anyone else. Glancing around, a slight panic seized her. "Where is Jay Pee?"

—◆—

Sergeant Joe Garcia spotted Curtis the moment he and Father Frank entered La Cantina. He removed his hat, and Father Frank crossed himself as the ragtag, chattering quartet of pallbearers processioned past them with their half-baked encumbrance, the gaunt mortician bringing up the rear with his oily head bowed.

Curtis, too, had his eyes lowered as the pair approached the booth where he and Natchez Mendoza were seated. His downward gaze fell on the anticipated pair of black leather high-top duty boots and a brown pair of dress oxfords. The boy kept silent.

"Now, what kind of greeting is that for an old friend, Curtis?" Sergeant Joe cajoled.

Curtis slowly raised his head. "Hello, Joe. Hello, Father," he chanted mechanically.

"Nice hair style, little cousin," Joe quipped. "Is that the standard appearance code at Fort Grant these days?"

"There is no code at Fort Grant," Curtis retorted, "unless craziness is a code."

"Gentlemen," the old jurist chimed in. "Please have a seat." He scooted aside and offered a hand. "I am Natchez Mendoza, a friend of Curtis's as well. Forgive me if I don't stand. It takes an act of God and two orderlies to get me to my feet these days."

"Starting to feel that way myself after a measly half hour at the gym." Joe grinned as he shook the old man's hand. "Curtis, I know you're surprised to see us, but don't get too excited," he said to the boy drily. "Y'know, I broke the land speed record getting down here as soon as I heard you were in Oracle Mesa."

"I can attest to that," Father Frank confirmed, as he, too, shook the old man's trembling paw. "I prayed the rosary repeatedly the whole way."

"It doesn't take a brain surgeon to figure why you're here, Joe," Curtis said sulkily. "And it's good that you brought a priest."

"Why's that?" Sergeant Joe inquired.

"'Cause you're gonna have to shoot me before I'll go back to that loony nut farm you guys call a reform school," Curtis declared, only half joking.

"You're jumping to the wrong conclusion, son," Father Frank announced with a smile. "We've come to take you home."

"*What?*" Curtis hissed. "How's that work? I haven't served my time, I jumped the fence, and now they suspect me of starting a fire that killed four people. It would take a miracle to spring me, the way I see it."

"Miracles are right up Father Frank's alley." Joe chuckled. "Of course, he also twisted a few arms, but between the two of us, we managed to get your conviction reversed—at least on the arson part."

"I don't get it," said Curtis, still perplexed.

"Some new evidence emerged that pointed to another perpetrator, Curtis," Father Frank explained. "We used that new evidence as leverage to get some backroom deals done."

"The downside of the deal is that none of us will divulge the name of the suspected firebug," Joe added. "The evidence is pretty circumstantial, and he has agreed to undergo psychiatric therapy…"

"No juvenile court for the city manager's kid?" Curtis interrupted.

"I guess not," Joe continued, "but the upside is that you no longer have to take the fall. And, since you were exonerated for the locker room fire, you're no longer a suspect in the Fort Grant fire. Besides, there's this funny thing about the disappearance of those staff members."

"Funny like 'ha ha,' or funny like 'weird?'" Curtis posed.

"Funny like 'weird beyond belief,'" Joe replied. "First of all, forensic officers could find no human remains in the aftermath of that building fire. It did burn to the ground, so the fire was extremely hot, but there should have been some skeletal remnants and teeth. There was nothing. Now, that's strange in itself, but there's more."

"Doesn't surprise me a bit," Curtis asserted. "Go on."

"When the Bureau of Prisons guys followed up on the four—the lieutenant, the doctor, and the two guards who went missing—their identities were missing too."

"Huh?"

"They can't explain it at all. They all had employment files, but beyond that, nothing—no social security cards, no drivers' licenses, no identities at all. It was like they never existed."

"Fort Grant is the site of many phenomena that defy explanation," Judge Mendoza interjected. "Or, should I say, they elude *rational* explanation."

"You ain't a-kiddin' about that, Judge," said Curtis.

"Anyway," Joe continued, "the petit theft count sticks for now, but that's negated by time already served. You keep your nose clean during a six-month probationary period, and that prior can even be expunged."

"What about my escapin'? Won't there be a charge for that?" Curtis wondered aloud.

"Generally speaking," Natchez Mendoza broke in, "if an escapee is found to be wrongly imprisoned in the first place, that charge will not apply if no one was injured as a result of the breakout. But that will be up to the discretion of the judge in this jurisdiction, I believe."

"That's correct," Sergeant Joe agreed. He pulled a letter from his inner jacket pocket and scanned it for a name. "So we need to speak with a Justice J. P. Morton to secure a valid release. I hope it's just a formality. I don't do very well with red tape."

"Hmm," the old judge pondered with a wrinkled brow. "Under normal circumstances, I'd say it would be a breeze. But something tells me that's not the case here. What say you, Father Frank?"

"I am sorry to say that I share your pessimism, sir," the priest averred.

"Yes, I dare say we are of a like mind in many respects," the old man rejoined with a wry smile.

<hr>

"He seems to be coming around this time," Dr. Case muttered as he withdrew the broken inhalant of ammonium carbonate from under Jay Pee's nose. Indeed, Dr. Mort's eyelids began to flutter.

Isabel stepped forward, blocking the glare from the examination room light.

"Jay Pee!" she called loudly.

He heard her faintly, as if from a great distance. Not surprisingly, he experienced a peculiar serenity in being distant but not entirely cut off from her. He closed his eyes and began another slow, floating descent from consciousness.

"*Jay Pee!*" Isabel shouted again, more sharply than before. "Don't you slip away from me!" She landed four rather forceful palm slaps to his pale cheek in a staccato salvo. "Wake up!"

"Pfft," Jay Pee sputtered, his eyelids fluttering again.

Isabel raised her hand to slap him further awake when another hand firmly intervened.

"There's no real hurry, señora," Dr. Case averred as he slowly relaxed his grip on her wrist. "He's not showing any symptoms of severe concussion, or I would have insisted on a trip to the U of A emergency room instead of his own little clinic here. We can take our time bringing him around—unless, of course, you're in a hurry to get back to the wake."

"That goes without saying," Isabel retorted impatiently. "An important social event like that needs the guiding hand of an experienced hostess to keep things from getting out of control. Just look at the crazy commotion that broke loose when I relaxed to have a simple moment of peace with my dear departed husband."

"I see your point." The doctor nodded in agreement. "My orderlies will be happy to return you as soon as you like—right now, if you prefer."

"Yes, I would prefer that, except that I want to make sure that Jay Pee is all right first."

"I can assure you that he'll be just fine, Isabel," Dr. Case said. "Of course, I'll have to stay with him until he regains complete consciousness."

"I don't want him to think I abandoned him. I want mine to be the first face he sees when he comes to."

"I understand your frustration," said Dr. Case. "Speaking of your face, let me see what kind of development we have with that burn of yours."

Isabel cautiously withdrew the ice pack she had clutched to her cheek since leaving the wake to accompany Jay Pee on the fifteen-minute van ride to his home office. Dr. Case could not conceal an expression of astonishment at the unveiling of her injury.

"What is it, Doctor? Is it that bad?"

"No, of course not," he managed in a fabricated tone of assurance. "It's actually quieting down rather nicely. "It's just…" He hesitated, struggling to find the words.

"Just what—*hideous*?" Isabel demanded, shrilly. *Repulsive? Unsightly?*

"No, I guess I would have to say, um, *extraordinarily defined*."

"Oh no, mister, those are weasel words if I ever heard any, and spoken in your practiced bedside voice too. What the hell does that mean, *defined*? You need to tell me the truth right now!"

"I don't know how else—" the doctor began.

"Forget it. I'll see for myself." Isabel nearly spat. "There's got to be a mirror around here somewhere."

As she was glancing around the room, the telephone at the reception desk in the connected waiting room where the orderlies sat patiently rang loudly enough to startle them all. Isabel strode over and picked up the receiver.

"Yes, Manny, what is it?" she barked, then paused to listen. *"Dios mío!"* she exclaimed at length, "You can't be serious!"

"What is it, señora?" Dr. Case asked uneasily.

"Manny, put Judge Mendoza on the phone right away." Isabel held the phone aside and faced the doctor. "Everyone's left La Cantina— everyone except Judge Mendoza."

"What…where did they go?"

"They all went down to town hall," Isabel said.

"What the hell for?"

"From the way Manny tells it, the jail is under siege."

"That's insane!" Dr. Case cried.

"Goddamn rooster," Isabel mumbled.

Battle of the Bullhorns

Town Square or, *La Plaza*, in Oracle Mesa was a peculiar collision between traditional and contemporary influences. Located off the main highway that passed through town and a three-minute walk from La Cantina Vieja, the central plaza consisted of a block-square historic park. The southeast corner of the park presented a babbling three-tiered fountain—a typically Sonoran-style affair with a seven-foot plaster column spouting a generous flow of *agua fría* from the top, splashing into a trio of descending stone bowls, each bowl successively greater in diameter than the one above it, the lowest spilling its fizzing deluge into a waiting pool. The circular catch basin, stretching some fifteen feet across, consisted of a two-foot-high white stucco retaining wall with a twelve-inch band of colorful ceramic Talavera-style tiles and a plaster bottom lined with turquoise mosaic tile. The entire design of the park was apparently an effort to pay homage to the life-giving water that facilitated the founding and development of the town. That blessed liquid life derived from the miraculously north-flowing San Pedro River.

A turn to the east-facing elevation presented onlookers with a taste of the antiquated, Spanish Colonial look of Old Town Hall, a complex that housed the town council chambers, justice court, the mayor's office, the office of the city clerk, and the constabulary and jail.

That momentous day—a day beginning, as Isabel Cienfuegos had noted, with a rooster crowing at midnight—was marking the close of its daylight hours with deepening shadows reaching out from stately cottonwoods across the park to the west-facing storefronts. Curtis could see from the front window of the constabulary that those deep-purple shadows were extinguishing the solar glare from the glass fronts of the modern shops at the opposite end of the square. The diminishing glare gave way to an array of pulsating ruby-red lines slicing across the glass like the flesh-rending slashes from cold steel fencing foils. The throb of light emitted by the rotating beacons of four San Pedro County patrol cars positioned curbside at the perimeter of the park was beginning to mesmerize the boy.

"I don't get it, Joe." Curtis whined. "If the charges against me were dropped, why in the hell…excuse me, Father…why in the heck does that clown out there want to arrest me?"

"I told you before," Joe replied with uncharacteristic tension in his voice, "the reprieve is not official until it is countersigned by the justice of the peace in this jurisdiction."

"Can I see that paper of yours?" Curtis asked.

"I left it back at the cantina on the table. I tried to reason with the undersheriff, but he wasn't having any of it. Then, the whole thing with the crowd happened so fast, I didn't have a chance to pick it up."

"Brother." Curtis moaned. "Out of the fryin' pan and into the fire."

"Anyway," said Joe, "why this undersheriff wants to make a federal case over a technicality is beyond me."

"I can shed some light on that," said Constable Quintana. "See, the sheriff of San Pedro County is retiring next year. Pete Alvarado, the undersheriff out there, has to win an election to get the job."

"What does that have to do with me?" Curtis wondered. He gazed out the window again and marveled at the throng of townspeople that had amassed at the gates. It reminded him of the torch-wielding mob in the Frankenstein movies in reverse—that is, they were not facing the building and clamoring for its occupant. Rather, they were facing outward with arms locked together, forming a human barricade to prevent the undersheriff and his deputies from reaching the doors of the constabulary.

"Son, we have two things in here that are fueling the fire—one thing old Pete Alvarado wants and one thing he doesn't want," Frankie Quintana replied to Curtis's question.

"Can you be a bit more specific?" Father Frank entreated.

"Sure can. It's this way: Pete wants the attention from the press that arresting this boy, who is, by the way, still the subject of a statewide manhunt, will get him, no matter that the boy will be exonerated the next day—a detail that will be buried on the back pages. He's hungry for the kind of name recognition that wins elections," said Frankie.

"And the thing he doesn't want?" asked Sergeant Joe.

"He doesn't want the kind of scandal that will spread if his deputy, the guy I've got in the can there, is tried in a jurisdiction other than San Pedro County Court—the court that always covers up for these county mounties," Frankie replied.

"CONSTABLE QUINTANA—BRING OUT THE BOY RIGHT NOW!" a voice boomed, echoing against the buildings.

A spotlight on one of the cars directed a beam toward the fountain across the way to illuminate a tall figure standing atop the fountain's retaining wall. Pete Alvarado had a bullhorn in hand, and, from what Curtis could see in the semidarkness, it was tethered to a large amplifier of some sort. His voice was apparently quite deep to begin with, but with the volume and reverberation that the amp afforded, it was downright majestic. Another spotlight fell on the speaker and the side lighting from both directions lent an ethereal effect to the figure. The undersheriff looked and sounded much larger than life and quite intimidating.

"FRANCISCO QUINTANA—BRING OUT THE BOY AND THE DEPUTY, OR I'LL START ARRESTING THESE TROUBLEMAKERS FOR OBSTRUCTION," the voice thundered again.

"Then there's this third thing," Frankie Quintana muttered almost inaudibly.

"What third thing is that?" Joe demanded.

"When we got out to my car with the deputy, old Pete and me had sort of a disagreement about who Aycock was going to go with," the constable said, stifling a grin.

"And?" Joe prodded.

"I don't believe there were any witnesses, but, if there were, they might tell you that there was a tussle of sorts, and that I knocked old Pete on his ass and left him lying in the parking lot eating the dust from my squad car. I suppose there might be some personal hard feelings figuring in as well," Frankie confessed.

Curtis imagined an hour-long ride up to Florence in the back of a county patrol car with his hands cuffed behind his back alongside his copassenger, Myron Aycock, uncuffed. It would be a long ride.

"CONSTABLE QUINTANA—YOU ARE ACTING IN VIOLATION OF THE AUTHORITY OF SAN PEDRO COUNTY. SURRENDER THE PRISONER AND THE DEPUTY AT ONCE, OR I WILL HAVE YOU ARRESTED AND TRIED FOR OBSTRUCTION!" boomed the reverberating voice again.

"Anybody else up for a short prayer?" Father Frank offered.

———◆———

"Can I get you anything, sir?"

Natchez Mendoza looked up from the table. It was Manny de la Torre, the newly endowed proprietor of La Cantina Vieja, addressing him in Spanish.

"Yes, sir," the ancient judge replied in the same tongue. "As a matter of fact, you can bring me a Brave Bull, if you please."

"A tequila and Kahlúa?" Manny asked.

"Yes, please, on the rocks and with a lime wedge. I can use a little fortification," Mendoza said.

Manny nodded, hurried to the bar, and returned in a trice with the Mexican cocktail as ordered. The old man thanked him before taking a sip. He closed his eyes and smiled with a sigh. "Please sir, have a seat," he continued, still speaking Spanish. "It seems I have been abandoned, and I don't care to drink alone."

It was as he said: the premises were eerily devoid of any human occupation save the two of them and Maria, who was diligently puttering in the kitchen and occasionally appearing in the pass-through window. The sudden vacancy was in stark contrast to the carnival atmosphere of the funeral just a short time ago. Manny slid into the booth opposite old Mendoza, hailed Maria, and had her bring him a cold bottle of beer. The two sat sipping their drinks in silence for a moment, the judge submerged in astonishment at the event he had just witnessed.

"I wonder, my friend," Mendoza asked at length, "if you can explain to me just what it was that happened here ten minutes ago, eh? Wait, let me be more precise: I have a pretty good idea *what* happened; I'm having more of a tough time comprehending *why* it happened."

The event he referred to entailed a spontaneous incitement and mass exodus of the entire throng that had occupied the building just moments earlier. The incident was sparked when Undersheriff Alvarado entered the room and loudly demanded custody of the erstwhile fugitive, Curtis Jefferson. When Sergeant Joe Garcia just as loudly declared himself the authorized custodian, several attendees impulsively inserted themselves between Garcia and Alvarado. As the argument escalated, more and more bystanders assumed an active role by swarming around Sergeant Joe, Curtis, and Father Frank. The patrons actually formed a protective buffer around the trio that the undersheriff could not possibly penetrate by force. Then, amazingly, the human cocoon slowly moved toward—and eventually out of—the door, bearing their protected subjects with them. Judging from the shouts from the rest of the crowd that followed behind, the entire throng was adjourning to the town hall and the constabulary to deliver their sheltered captives into protective custody.

"You have to understand how the people of this town feel about Pete Alvarado and his county mounties in order to comprehend that little demonstration," Manny replied to Mendoza's inquiry.

"Anyone could see it was no love fest," the judge croaked, still speaking Spanish, "but why all the animosity?"

"It's a long story, Your Honor, but I'll try to give you the short version. You see, for years, the San Pedro County Sheriff's Department has subsisted on traffic fines, both real and contrived. The people of Oracle Mesa know that they can't drive on the main highway without getting pulled over and cited by the county mounties for a broken taillight, an unsafe lane change, or a California stop. The traffic stops are ridiculously excessive and mostly bogus. The fines are inflated, and Florence is a long way to go to fight a citation, so people pay, if they can."

"If they can't?" Mendoza asked.

"The deputies come for them and take them up to spend some time in their county slammer. My patron, the mayor, tried to reason with Undersheriff Pete, and he seemed to make some headway for a while. But still, whenever the county comes up with a financial shortfall, it's back to the old game of highway robbery," said Manny.

"So it's no mystery why the undersheriff is disliked," Mendoza remarked.

"Disliked is quite an understatement. He's about as popular around here as Fidel Castro. I was surprised to see him show up today, given the local sentiment. People get tired of being bled. Tempers are short, and memories are long," Manny told him.

"I guess this little rebellion here was a prime example of that hostility. In any case, I'm glad the crowd protected my friends, even if it did get a little ugly," said Mendoza.

"The enemy of my enemy is my friend," Manny sagely observed. "But you don't think this incident is over, do you?"

"No, I suppose it's not, although I really can't fathom why this undersheriff is so bent on arresting Curtis. This paper here clearly exonerates him. All it lacks is a signature from Dr. Morton, and the boy is no longer a fugitive."

"Pete Alvarado has a very high opinion of himself, and every arrest is like a trophy to him," Manny commented. "He drags a local newspaper reporter around with him and stages arrests. What's more, he is not one to concede gracefully once he has been confronted. If anything, he is likely to stoke the fire. I would not be at all surprised if he had a whole swarm of his deputy dogs down at town hall right now with rifles trained on the jail."

"Yes," Natchez Mendoza agreed, "given your understanding of the local temperament, I wouldn't doubt your prediction one bit." The old man pondered thoughtfully for a moment, nursing his drink. "Listen, Manny," he said at length, "may I impose upon you for a favor…? Actually, two?"

"What can I do for you, Your Honor?"

"A phone call, please, to Señora Cienfuegos…er, I mean Hightower…at Dr. Morton's office."

"Of course. And the other favor?" Manny inquired.

"First, let me ask you: How far is it to town hall?" the old judge asked.

"Just around the corner—less than three hundred meters," Manny replied.

"Then another one of these, please," Mendoza grinned as he drained the last of his libation. "It's helping me forget what my limitations are."

———

"Maybe I should go over there and try to reason with him, Constable," said Sergeant Joe. "He doesn't have a personal beef with me, and, after all, I did bring the release papers for Curtis. He ought to extend me the professional courtesy of safe conduct, don't you think?"

"Reason with a maniac like Pete Alvarado? Just take a good look out there," said Francisco Quintana. "You see over by that stand of cottonwood trees?"

Sergeant Joe peered through the glass-and-steel-mesh window, across the lane, and into the gathering gloom of the plaza. He made out the shadowy forms of three deputies skulking among the trees and bushes of the park.

"Two of 'em have scatterguns; the other's got a tear-gas launcher," the constable observed.

"Man, this guy is certainly making a stink, isn't he?" Joe remarked.

"That's Pete for you. The man's definitely let the position go to his head. He's really kind of scary, when you get right down to it. Do you have that release paper on you?" Frankie wondered.

"No," Joe confessed. "I left it back at the cantina. The crowd just kind of swept us out of there before we had a chance to grab our things."

"I think you'd be wasting your time trying to talk," Frankie advised. "Pete's got his mind made up, and he'll go to any extreme to make this look good for him in the Florence newspaper. Hell, if my windows didn't have the security mesh on them, he probably would have lobbed a gas canister in here ten minutes ago."

"What can we do, Constable?" Father Frank chimed in.

"You can call over to La Cantina and see if someone can run that release document over here. Other than that, you can sit tight for now, Father," the constable replied as he opened the door of a wall-mounted locker. "I already put in a call to the state police, but it will be awhile before they get a car up here from Tucson. Meanwhile, I can keep the undersheriff busy talking." He pulled a large bullhorn of his own from the locker. "Pete loves a good argument, and, as long as he's talking, I don't think he'll have the county mounties make a move. Besides," Frankie added as he holstered a long-barreled revolver, "it can't hurt to put our side of the story out there on the street."

He opened the hollow metal front door to the constabulary and stepped confidently into the cool of the evening.

"How long has he been gone, Manny?" Isabel demanded. "*Cuánto tiempo?*"

"*Diez minutos, señora,*" he replied. "*No más.*"

"Hell, I didn't know he could walk at all," Isabel said, directing the comment to the orderlies who had just brought her back to town.

"He can walk a few steps, is all," one of them offered. "At least, that's what I thought. I mean, for God's sake, the old man is over a hundred years old. Who'd have thought?"

"He apparently had us all fooled. And he took the release paper, you say?" Isabel asked, turning to Manny again.

"*Si, el viejo firmó el papel y despues salió,*" said Manny.

"Which road did he take?" Isabel inquired.

"*No sé,*" Manny replied with a shrug.

"We need to find him quick," the orderly said, "or we're gonna catch six kinds of hell."

"There are two streets that lead to town hall. One of you needs to stay here in case he comes back; the other should take La Calle Bajo, the second right turn, just across the highway," Isabel directed. "I'll take La Calle Alta. Manny, get on the phone and call Dr. Case—let him know what's happening, and find out how Jay Pee is doing."

"*Sí*, señora."

"All right, then," she shouted, "*ándeles todos!*"

"Señora!" Manny suddenly exclaimed. "*Qué pasó a tu mejilla?*"

"What about my cheek, Manny?"

"*Me parece que…es como una media luna!*"

"That's the strangest compliment I've ever gotten, Manny. Too bad there's no time for explanations. We gotta go, right now—*ahorita!*"

———

Natchez Mendoza halted the seemingly endless march to Town Square and rested his weight on his ivory cane with both hands. His chest was heaving in spasms. A loud wheezing like some annoyingly atonal bursts squeezed from an antique concertina escaped his dry throat. An audible heartbeat that pounded out an excited Bo Diddley rhythm joined in the self-produced cacophony that assaulted the old man's ears. He looked upward. The sky had still been golden with the sunset when he'd started his trudge, but only a residual brassiness clung to the tile rooftops as the deepening purple of twilight crept in to smother a diminishing glow in the shadows. He wondered at the spontaneity of his decision to deliver the paper in person. Certainly a personal delivery would have more impact, but would he arrive too late to make a difference? Would he even be able to close the distance to the park at all? The powerful sense of urgency notwithstanding, that brief rest was no convenience; it was a necessity.

And the heart must pause to breathe,

The words suddenly occurred to him as if by telepathy. Where did that line come from? He shifted his cane to his right hand, pulled a handkerchief from his trouser pocket, and wiped his perspiring brow. He'd wisely left his suit jacket back at La Cantina, but even his silk vest left him feeling weighted. He unbuttoned it, taking care that the folded paper in the breast pocket did not fall out. His breathing gradually became less labored, and he began to take in long draughts of the cool evening air through his nose. The fragrance of a freshly cut lawn wafting on a warm evening breeze filled his head, as did some more remnants of the poem the respite had conjured.

For the sword outwears its sheath,
And the soul wears out the breast,

A mourning dove called plaintively from the peak of a nearby roof. He could see its tiny silhouette against the pale gray band at the western horizon as it hooted a sad but familiar refrain for its missing mate, "Where ARE yoo-hoo-hoo-hoo?"

Then, a different sound piqued his attention. Shouts arose from down the street, and the woof and squawk of amplified voices boomed from a short distance.

"The spirit is willing, but the flesh is weak," he muttered. "No, there is one more mission, and it is a vital one," he countered, "and it does seem that I am getting my second wind!"

He stepped forward, slowly, teetering a bit as he began the last leg of his journey toward the sounds coming from the park.

"The spirit is willing!" he cried aloud in his raspy voice. "The spirit is willing!"

He made each trembling step with great effort. With his mind fixed on his ordeal and the victory of each agonizing tread, he made his indefatigable way—a step at a time—toward the developing fray. It was a good five minutes or longer before he reached the intersection where he could see lights and people.

He shuffled past Harold Hackett's lighted storefront and briefly peered through a giant pane of polished glass at the morbid display of funereal accoutrements inside. *Not yet*, he thought, *but soon.*

He turned and began to cross the avenue toward the commotion, but, as he approached, the noise he had heard suddenly abated. The eerie quiet made him feel as if he were stepping onto a stage. And, of course, he was.

———◆———

The high-pitched squeal from audio feedback called everyone's attention to the raised stoop in front of the constabulary. A tinny voice rang out from a dimly lit form.

"SHERIFF ALVARADO—HAVE YOUR MEN STAND DOWN. THERE

IS NO GOOD REASON FOR THIS EXCESSIVE SHOW OF FORCE. THIS IS A PEACEFUL TOWN."

The volume and tenor of Frankie's medium were decidedly less magnificent than the undersheriff's, but the tone in the voice itself projected a confidence that Pete Alvarado's seemed to lack.

"CONSTABLE QUINTANA—YOU ARE HOLDING TWO PRISONERS WHO HAVE COMMITTED CRIMES IN MY JURISDICTION—YOU ARE HARBORING A FUGITIVE AND ARE REQUIRED BY LAW TO RELEASE THEM BOTH INTO MY CUSTODY *IMMEDIATELY!*"

Again, the voice came booming across the avenue as if it originated from the likes of Oz, the great and powerful wizard. The volume lent the message an unquestionable air of authority, but an authority based only on its own insistence.

"SHERIFF ALVARADO—YOUR DEPUTY IS IN VIOLATION OF A STATE STATUTE, AND WILL BE TURNED OVER TO STATE AUTHORITIES. THE BOY HAS BEEN RELEASED INTO THE CUSTODY OF THE JACOBS WELL AUTHORITIES BY WRITTEN REPRIEVE. I HAVE PROMISED TO PROVIDE SAFE CONDUCT FOR HIM AND HIS CUSTODIAL OFFICER WHILE THEY ARE PRESENT IN MY JURISDICTION."

The tinny voice was replying in strong tones of self-assured defiance. The amplified discourse began to sound like an electronic dialogue between David and Goliath. Frankie Quintana surveyed the crowd assembled below at the gates of the front wall. Several of the townspeople were nodding their heads in agreement with his declaration.

"CONSTABLE QUINTANA—A CHARGE OF DRUNK AND DISORDERLY IS NOT A STATE VIOLATION. YOU MUST HAND DEPUTY AYCOCK OVER TO COUNTY AUTHORITIES TO DISPENSE WITH THIS MINOR MATTER. AS FOR THE BOY, I HAVE SEEN NO EXECUTED RELEASE FORM, AND, UNTIL I DO, HE IS A FUGITIVE FROM AN INSTITUTION IN MY JURISDICTION AND SUBJECT TO ARREST BY ME."

A hint of frustration crept into the speech of The Great Oz as the exchange devolved from declarative to argumentative and the voices rose from bass to baritone.

"SHERIFF ALVARADO—YOUR DEPUTY HAS BEEN CHARGED WITH ASSAULTING AN OFFICER OF THE COURT, A FELONY. HE WILL BE TRIED IN STATE COURT. THE RELEASE FORM FOR THE BOY IS COMING HERE BY COURIER. IT SHOULD ARRIVE ANY MINUTE. AT THAT TIME, WE WILL PERMIT YOU TO COME UP HERE AND VERIFY ITS INTENT AND ITS AUTHENTICITY."

The crowd began to murmur its agreement with Frankie's line of reasoning, and he recalled that the better portion of his authority derived from the townspeople's assent.

"FRANCISCO, YOU FUCKING *PENDEJO*!" the undersheriff screamed. "YOU GIVE ME MY GODDAMN PRISONERS THIS MINUTE, OR I SWEAR I WILL BURN YOU AND THIS WHOLE MISERABLE LITTLE RATHOLE OF A TOWN TO THE GROUND!"

A cry of defiance went up from the crowd as at least a dozen middle-finger salutes replied to the undersheriff's shrill threat.

"I'm sure that little tantrum just won you a truckload of votes, you stupid ass," Frankie muttered to himself. He lowered the bullhorn and stood reticent for the better part of three minutes, allowing the lack of response to act as his answer to the undersheriff's ultimatum.

Just as the crowd began to quiet, someone across the street shouted out a military-sounding command, and, with nightsticks drawn, four tan-clad deputies wearing gas masks crossed the avenue and stood a few feet before the crowd at the gate. Three more emerged from the darkness of the park with lowered shotguns, ensuring against any possible resistance. Behind them, a solitary officer brandished a tear-gas gun. The deputies froze in position and held their poses like plaster of Paris statues crowned with white Stetson hats.

Frankie unholstered his revolver but kept it lowered at his side. Sergeant Joe Garcia stepped outside and drew alongside the constable.

"This is some serious shit," the sergeant whispered. "I've never seen cops act like this before."

"It's a whole different world out here on the fringes from what you're accustomed to in the suburbs. Question now is: which cops are you going to stand with?"

"You should know that me and that kid in there have a lot of history, most of it good. And, truth be known, if I'd been a better man a few months ago, he'd never be in this pickle today." Joe drew his own sidearm. "There's no question about who I'm standing with."

"Hope you don't need that," murmured Frankie.

Sergeant Joe nodded in agreement. "What are you expecting, Constable?" Joe asked at length.

"Name's Frankie, Joe," he asserted. "Maybe nada, maybe all hell. I know all those people out there at the gate, and I'm pretty sure some of them are packin'. Hard tellin' what to expect. Maybe nada, maybe all hell."

"My money's on all hell," Joe said, "but my life's ridin' on nada."

"It all depends, doesn't it?"

"On what?" Joe probed

"On whether there is or isn't some armed moron out there with a case of the nerves, either side of the street," the constable replied.

"Like I said, my money's on all hell," Joe quipped wryly.

"Shhh…listen!" Frankie whispered. "Do you hear that?"

"Hell, it's so quiet, I could hear a gnat farting in the key of G. Hear what?" Joe wondered.

"Listen—sounds like a clock ticking, only slower," Frankie replied.

"Yeah, I do hear it now—a strange clicking."

"Look!" Frankie exclaimed. "Down at the end of the park."

Joe squinted, and, sure enough, there was movement at the start of the brick-paved walkway. The dim light of the antique street lamps illuminated a bent figure ambling slowly toward the fountain where Pete Alvarado made his stand. A closer scrutiny revealed the source of the mysterious clicking: the bowed figure made his tedious way up the path with the aid of an ivory cane that sounded out a tap on the brick pavers with each agonizingly drawn out step.

Isabel arrived at the plaza just as an inexplicable hush fell over the crowded square. She strode hurriedly through the darkened park toward the lighted fountain, the apparent focal point of the unstable assembly, but was cut off by one tan-clad county mountie who blocked her way, scowling and hissing a command that she halt her advance or face some dire consequences. Stifling an almost irrepressible urge to swat the white Stetson from the deputy's head, she opted to obey and, instead, scanned the crowd across the street for a glimpse of Ray. She saw him standing with Rosa a safe distance from the suppressed uprising that was evidently brewing at the gate to the constabulary.

Satisfied that her nephew was not in any immediate peril, she drew her probing eyes away to seek out the source of the sudden ubiquitous silence. They quickly focused on the only movement in the entire plaza. She was transfixed by a slow-motion image that commanded her complete attention: an almost absurdly ungainly figure of a man progressing at a turtle's pace along the cobbled sidewalk toward the fountain where Pete Alvarado was perched atop the catch pool's retaining wall. The frail-looking form teetered precariously, almost comically, with each tentative step aided and punctuated by the stroke and support of a radiant white cane. The cane seemed to pulsate with a strange luminosity as it reflected the lambent glow of the overhead street lamps with each wavering tread. Isabel stood, breathlessly amazed as Natchez Mendoza made his step-by-step approach to the wayward lawman's illuminated venue.

His Honor

It was out of a profound astonishment that Undersheriff Pete Alvarado cut off his amplified tirade and held his command in abeyance—astonished that the old man he'd seen confined to a wheelchair at the funeral was actually walking toward him, tentatively but sturdily, as if driven by some internal mission. Even more riveting was the human relic's expression of grim determination, which became more clearly evident with each approaching step. More than anything, it was that aura of resolve that gave the brash undersheriff pause and blunted his bravado. The image of a plodding cadaver solely animated by the pure and unadulterated spirit of conviction left him somewhat uneasy.

Despite Judge Mendoza's agonizingly gradual progress, his approach nevertheless eventually came within twenty feet of the fountain. From his raised vantage point, the undersheriff could see that the old fossil was panting and perspiring profusely from his fatiguing trek. He stepped down from his makeshift platform on the wall to hail the bedraggled figure.

"*Oye, viejo!*" he called out. "Don't take another step. You're tired. I'll come to you."

Mendoza immediately struck a motionless pose, resting both hands on the glowing white cane. The salutation was disrespectful and patronizing, but the instruction to rest was welcome. The undersheriff stepped gingerly toward the judge's hunched-over form and frowned.

"I don't know what kind of notion brought you here, old man, but it's really not safe for you. I'll have a deputy drive you back to the cantina or to your motel, whichever you prefer," Alvarado announced loudly. "Right now, this is a dangerous place to be," he informed the judge in condescending tones.

"I always wonder," Natchez Mendoza rasped between labored breaths, "why some people speak to the elderly as if we're little children. Nevertheless, I am curious. Maybe you can explain to a bewildered old man why this peaceful little park has suddenly become a dangerous place."

"Really, it's much too complicated to explain to you right now," Alvarado muttered, glancing around. "Let me just say that we have a standoff situation here. Now, let's get you in that car before you get hurt."

"Your offer is very kind," Judge Mendoza breathed hoarsely, "but you assume that I am here by some mistake. That is not the case, and, therefore, I will decline."

"Now, listen, *viejo*—" Alvarado started scathingly.

"No, *you* listen to me!" the judge asserted in a low but gravelly voice. "You speak of a situation. If this situation concerns the boy you believe to be a fugitive, then I have the resolution to all of this unnecessary confrontation right here." He pulled the folded document that was Curtis's reprieve from his vest pocket. "You must have somehow missed this order from the Maricopa County Court during the commotion back at La Cantina," the old judge croaked as he handed the paper to the undersheriff. "It should settle matters quite thoroughly."

Pete Alvarado scanned the paper in a cursory manner. "This is not an official document," he declared dismissively. "The countersignature was not executed by an authorized justice of this jurisdiction."

"You see, that is *my* signature." The old man smiled innocently.

"Yours?" Alvarado asked.

"Yes—let me explain. I don't like to boast, but I am a retired justice of the Arizona Supreme Court. I was made Honorary Justice for life upon my retirement."

"What does *that* mean?" the undersheriff demanded skeptically.

"That means my signature conveys legal authorization in any jurisdiction in the state. It means that the document you hold there is a valid exoneration and an order for the boy to be placed in the custody of the Jacobs Well officer to be transported home," the judge said.

Alvarado glanced again at the document and glowered silently.

"I guess that settles the matter," the ancient justice concluded glibly. "What do you say, Sheriff?"

"What do I say?" The undersheriff growled. "What do I say? I say you are a senile old coot masquerading as a judge of some sort. I've never heard of you, and, as for your signature, it is worthless—as worthless as this scrap of paper." With that he wadded the document into a crumpled ball and tossed it onto a passing breeze which bowled it across the grass for thirty yards before it came to rest at the feet of Isabel Hightower Cienfuegos.

"What do I say?" Alvarado continued. "I say that the boy is a fugitive in my county. As such, he will be arrested and incarcerated by me unless and until a higher authority advises me otherwise. Now, for the last time, *viejo*…"

"AND I SAY THAT YOU SHALL NOT!" Gone was the gravel in the Andy Devine voice. The words rolled out of the judge in a clear, commanding baritone, as they had once issued forth from his lofty judicial bench. The sudden change in tone was startling, and Pete Alvarado stared in wide wonder at the old man's smoldering obsidian eyes, as they, too, widened in righteous indignation. Mendoza's knuckles whitened from a surge of pressure that he exerted on his brilliant white cane, and his bent spine slowly and miraculously straightened. Rising up to the proud stature of a younger year, the elderly jurist spoke again in a booming voice that required no electronic assistance for its magnificence.

Isabel, even at thirty yards, was nearly bowled over by the powerful volume. She pondered for a fleeting few seconds on the way Jesus Christ had preached from a mountainside and how the multitudes all heard that voice as strong as the coursing current of the Jordan River and as deep as the Sea of Galilee. It was no Christ defying the embodiment of corruption before her, but neither was it the decrepit old gentleman she had conversed with at the funeral. The image she beheld was electrifying.

"You have been authorized to enforce the law, young man!" Natchez Mendoza roared as he raised his luminous cane toward the darkened sky and took an unsupported step toward the incredulous undersheriff.

Looking on from the shadows, Isabel gasped at what she saw: the old man's glowing white cane took on the appearance of a radiant crosier as he held it aloft like a bishop in procession.

"You shall NOT abuse that authority!" Mendoza roared again as he took another step toward Alvarado, who took two wobbly steps backward. "You shall NOT bend that power to feed your outsized arrogance!" He suddenly struck the bottom tip of his cane-cum-crosier on the pavement to punctuate his emphasis on the word *not*, and, at that instant, a terrifying clap of thunder shook the square. The crowd of onlookers scanned the skies for clouds, but there were none. The larger-than-life Natchez Mendoza strode quite powerfully toward Alvarado, who was backpedaling a proportionate retreat to the old man's intimidating advance.

"You stay back, *viejo*," the undersheriff yelped as he stepped rearward. "My men are trained to protect me."

"You are a *peace* officer," Mendoza declared loudly. "Command your men to stand down—NOW!" Again, he struck the cobbled pavement with his crosier-cane. Again, a mystifying thunderclap pealed through the night air. "I swear you shall NOT bring harm to any of these people!" old Mendoza boomed again as his forward treads quickened.

"Blessed are those who hunger and thirst for righteousness, for they shall be filled," Isabel muttered the scripture by rote, starry-eyed and transfixed.

Stricken by the menacing miracle before his eyes, Pete Alvarado backed into the retaining wall of the fountain. As if choreographed, his heels met the short stucco obstruction at the same instant that the ancient judge struck out another inexplicable clap of thunder. A reflexive shout escaped the undersheriff's lips as he tumbled backward into the fizzing pond.

For a brief moment, the only visible remnant of Pete Alvarado was a white Stetson hat that floated and bobbed comically upon the bubbling sheets of white water. One of the spotlights was trained on the water where the coughing and sputtering undersheriff finally broke the surface. A roar of laughter and a smattering of jeers and catcalls went up from the crowd assembled across the street as Alvarado stumbled and fumbled in the catch pond in search of his unholstered pistol.

Mendoza cast his fiery eyes toward town hall, settling upon the deputies who still wielded their nightsticks threateningly. He brandished his cane and shook it in their direction, and they immediately lowered their batons as if they'd been silently commanded to do so. He turned and made a similar gesture toward the armed forces at the edge of the park. Remarkably, they opened breaches and lowered their weapons.

At that very moment, three state police units rolled into the plaza with red and blue beacons blazing. Department of Public Safety Captain Ron Wheelen emerged from the first cruiser to arrive at the sidewalk in front of Frankie Quintana's constabulary; his gun-metal blue uniform and gray, flat-brimmed "Smokey Bear" hat starkly distinguished him from the tan-clad deputies in their Stetsons. Five more similarly clad state troopers climbed out of the cruisers and assembled in a tight formation behind Wheelen. Constable Quintana holstered his sidearm and descended the steps to greet the captain and his entourage.

"Evening, Frankie," the trooper intoned as the two shook hands. "It's been a while."

"Evening, Captain," Frankie returned. "Yeah, too long—about a half hour too long."

The trooper pulled a pack of nonfiltered cigarettes from his shirt pocket. "Mind if I smoke?" he asked in jest as he lit up with a gold-plated butane lighter.

"Be my guest." Frankie grinned.

Captain Wheelen took a long, thoughtful drag from the cigarette before speaking again. His cool, rather loose demeanor contrasted with the stoic postures of the troopers standing frozen at attention behind him. "In your phone call, Frankie, you mentioned something about a little jurisdictional dispute?"

"That's right, sir—a minor difference of opinion about the law."

"Looks more like the makings of another Mexican Revolution, if you ask me," Wheelen mused as he glanced around at the throngs clustered about the plaza.

Undersheriff Alvarado stepped out of the fountain pool and made his waterlogged way across the street, raining a personal torrent onto the pavement and making squishing sounds with his snakeskin boots.

"Yes, sir, I guess things got a little carried away," Frankie confessed.

"So it seems. Well, then, when you told me that Pete Alvarado was involved, I decided to bring the cavalry here with me." He cocked his head toward the five statue-like figures amassed behind him.

"Glad you decided that, sir. The more the merrier," Constable Quintana quipped.

"Hey there, Pete." Wheelen chuckled at the undersheriff's sodden approach. "You decide to take an evening dip to cool off that hot head of yours?"

"Hey there, Ron," Alvarado replied with his hand out, still shedding droplets profusely from his stringy black hair. "And no, I just lost my balance."

"Lost your balance." Captain Wheelen chortled, retracting a bit. "That's a good one. Hope you find it someday, Pete. And whoa—don't get too close, now. You'll put out my damn cigarette with all that dripping," he huffed. "Hell, you're a walking cloudburst!"

"Sorry," the undersheriff responded sulkily.

"Tell me, boys," demanded Wheelen, "what have we got here?"

The two took turns telling their conflicting versions of the long and short of things, starting with the drunken Deputy Aycock barging in at the funeral, through Sergeant Joe and Father Frank's surprise entrance, to the exploding corpse and mass exodus to the plaza. Between the two of them, few, if any, details escaped the telling.

Captain Wheelen shook his head in disbelief at the conclusion of the story. "Only in Oracle Mesa could a simple funeral deteriorate into a full-scale uprising." He chuckled. "Now, Frankie," he continued in a more serious tone, "you say there is a legal document releasing the boy?"

"That's correct, Captain," Sergeant Joe broke in as he approached the trio. "Pardon me, but I am Sergeant Joe Garcia of the Jacobs Well PD. I brought the order from the Maricopa County Court to release Curtis Jefferson into my custody for safe passage home. He has been exonerated of the charges originally brought against him."

"Can I see the order?" Wheelen asked, casting down the half-consumed smoke and crushing it out with his boot heel.

"That's a problem, Captain," Joe responded.

"Not anymore!" Isabel sang out as she strode up. She smoothed the crinkled paper and offered it to the state trooper. "I saved it after that *cabrón* of a sheriff wadded it up and tossed it away."

"And who might this attractive lady be?" Wheelen asked Constable Quintana, hinting for an introduction.

"I am Isabel Cienfuegos Hightower, widow of the recently deceased Mayor Alfredo Hightower," Isabel offered herself. "And I am sole proprietor of La Cocina Café," she added proudly.

Wheelen pinched the brim of his Smokey hat as if to tip it to the lady. "My condolences, ma'am, for your loss, and my thanks to you for salvaging this paper." He squinted, then scowled as he scanned the document. "This looks pretty official, Pete. Is it true you crumpled it up?"

"It's not worth the paper it's written on, Ron. It has to be countersigned by a judge in this jurisdiction."

"Where's ol' Jay Pee Morton—why didn't he sign it?"

"He was unavailable at the time," Frankie Quintana retorted.

"Knocked unconscious by that *pendejo* Deputy Aycock," Isabel added.

"Whose signature is this at the bottom?" Wheelen asked pointedly.

"They had some old fossil sign it just to make it look official." Pete Alvarado sneered. "Just some geezer guest at the funeral."

"That old geezer would be me," a gravelly voice piped up. No one had noticed his approach, but the old jurist was standing in their midst, once again bent over and resting precariously upon his ivory cane. "I am an officer in good standing with the court, and I happened to be available," he declared. "That signature rightly validates the document, although I think it should be notarized, if you want to get technical."

"I am having a hard time reading your signature, sir," said Captain Wheelen. "Can you help me out here by telling me who you are?"

"My name is Natchez Mendoza. I am a retired justice," the old man announced proudly.

"Wait a minute," Wheelen retorted, "you're not *the* Natchez Mendoza of the Arizona Supreme Court, are you?"

"I was the last time I checked," the old gentleman quipped.

"Why, hell, I'll be a fritter dipped in bacon grease!" the trooper exclaimed as he stretched out a hand to grip the judge's withered paw. "Captain Ron Wheelen, and I am pleased, sir, to make your acquaintance. My grandfather was Henry Wheelen, member of the last installment of the Arizona Rangers—later became sheriff of Pima County. You and he were colleagues of sorts, or so he told it."

"Yes, I remember your grandfather quite well. Henry Wheelen was an extraordinary lawman, and one of the finest public servants I've ever met in this lifetime," Mendoza stated emphatically. "It's a crying shame that all peace officers can't be as high-minded as he was." He cast a disparaging look in Pete Alvarado's direction.

"Yes, sir," Wheelen agreed, "I hear that a lot. And he spoke very highly of you as well, sir. He said you were by far the toughest but most fair-minded and honorable judge this state has ever seen. I gotta say, old Henry has been dead for more years now than I can recall. I can hardly believe that you…well, I mean…"

"It's plain to see that the Lord has blessed me with the longevity of the ancients." Mendoza sighed. "I must confess that I am growing rather weary these days…" His voice trailed off.

"I can only imagine," Wheelen muttered. "Anyway, Pete," he continued, turning to Alvarado, "that pretty much settles the matter of the boy. It's quite clear to me that this is a completely legal directive, as His Honor can validate anything he puts his hand to, as far as I'm concerned. Curtis Jefferson is to go with Sergeant Garcia here back to his home in Jacobs Well."

"Thank you so much, Officer!" Isabel cried out. "That boy has been through hell for no good reason, and he misses his mama in the worst way."

"No thanks necessary, ma'am. I'm just following the court order. But, if I've greased the wheels in any way for a mother-and-child reunion, well, that's an incidental blessing."

Pete Alvarado grimaced. "What about my deputy," he asked with a slight whine in his voice.

"Yeah." Captain Wheelen pondered. "What about that deputy, Pete? I hear he's something of a troublemaker."

"Then let me deal with him, Ron. He's my problem, not yours—and he sure as hell isn't Frankie's."

The trooper turned then to the constable. "Frankie, I'm gonna have to ask you to turn the prisoner over to Pete here. I know it galls you to do it, but we have to respect the courtesy we always observe among cops. Y'know, that each department sees to their own? If the tables were turned, I'd do the same for you. You understand, don't you?"

"Captain," the constable finally replied, almost choking, "I'll do it, of course, out of respect to you. But I don't believe for all the tea in China that anything like justice will be served up in Florence, sir—not in this case."

"We're just gonna have to trust that the folks up there will do the right thing, won't we?" He turned to the undersheriff again. "Pete, I assume you're gonna suspend that deputy of yours and turn this matter over to the county attorney, is that right?"

"He'll be relieved of duty, pending a thorough investigation," Alvarado assured in his most persuasive tone.

"I'm not convinced," Constable Quintana mumbled.

"Listen, Frankie," Wheelen commanded sternly, "I want you to go up there, bring your prisoner out, and turn him over to Pete, and I want you to do it *now*."

The constable reluctantly turned on his heel, trudged up the steps, and disappeared inside.

Pete Alvarado smiled broadly. The warm evening breeze had already nearly dried him off, rendering his appearance less comical. "You're doing the right thing, Ron," he tutted. "You know we take care of our own."

"Listen to me, Pete. If you so much as breathe a word that sounds even remotely like gloating, I'll run your boy down to Tucson so fast, you'll be talkin' about it in your sleep for a month. Now, wipe that goddamn smirk off your face before Frankie gets back!"

The undersheriff mustered a look of contrition that was almost convincing.

Sergeant Joe edged his way over to Captain Wheelen's side and spoke under his breath, taking care not to be heard by Pete Alvarado.

"I understand the even-handed approach, Captain," he murmured, "but I think you're making a big mistake with this one."

"That so? What's fair isn't always what is just, is it? Maybe you should hold your thought, stranger, and watch how this all plays out," the trooper replied furtively.

"Jus' loogit awl these beaners out here to greet me!" a familiar voice called out from the top step of the constabulary. "Three cheerz folks for my 'manseepayshun!'"

A unanimous groan arose from the crowd to dispute Deputy Aycock's arrogant self-congratulation. With propping from Constable Quintana on the right arm and Father Frank's support on the left, the tipsy deputy, hands cuffed behind his back, descended the short flight of steps somewhat precariously. A handful of county officers pushed a few aggressive onlookers aside, clearing the gate for Aycock and his handlers to pass through.

"Frankie," Captain Wheelen directed, "take the cuffs off the deputy."

"Yeh, Frankie—take the goddamn cuffs off th' dep-yoo-tee ride the fug now, like ol' Smokey sez."

Frankie Quintana complied as he hissed in the deputy's ear: "You ever show your ugly face in my town again, it'll be the last time."

"Did everybody hear that?" Aycock hooted, rubbing his wrists. "I thing I wuz jus' threadnd."

"Not so," the constable countered. "I just passed on a little geography lesson to my fellow officer—that's all."

"I got yor number, Barney." The deputy sneered. "So you bes' keep your bullets in your gun from now on, cuz I'll be payin' you a vizzit real soon."

"Pete, I'm doing my damndest to ignore your deputy's mouth," Wheelen broke in, "but you better cuff him and get him outta here before all my patience gets used up."

"He's no problem for me, Ron," the undersheriff replied. "I don't need to cuff him."

"Since when did San Pedro County start neglecting to handcuff accused felons?" Wheelen demanded.

"Hell, Ron—it's just a drunk and disorderly charge." Pete Alvarado chuckled uneasily. "A little too much to drink, is all. It's no capital crime."

"Let me remind you, Pete, in the most courteous way I can, that your deputy here is accused of assaulting the justice of the peace in this town. Now, I guess I'll have to check on any recent revisions to arrest procedures in San Pedro County, but, in the meantime, humor me and cuff the boy," the captain directed.

"Turn around, Myron," Pete muttered reluctantly. "It appears that I'm gonna have to put the cuffs on you."

"Wat?" Aycock protested. "Wad th' hell'r yoo peeble thinging?" He gestured with his chin toward Isabel as Undersheriff Alvarado clamped the handcuffs onto his wrists. "If ennybuddy needs arrested iss thad Mess-cn bij over there. She poyznd Mayr Hightowr, and she tried to poyzn me!"

"Pete, I know you can't gag him, but if you don't shut your boy up, he's headed for Tucson, not Florence," Wheelen warned.

"Okay, shut the fuck up, Myron, and get in the back of the patrol car." Alvarado prodded his deputy with a finger in the ribs.

"Hell no!" Aycock shouted in defiance. "I'm nod gowing ennywhere without my little spear-chucker buddy. Thad little fyoojitiv was my fuggin' collar, y'know? Therz gotta be some big payback cummin' to thad black boy."

"Okay, that does it." Captain Wheelen fumed. "Boys," he commanded loudly, "escort this loudmouthed deputy to the back of one of our cruisers, please. He's headed south tonight."

The quintet of troopers instantly broke formation, rushed past Pete Alvarado, brushing him aside, and surrounded Deputy Aycock.

"Wow!" the deputy exclaimed. "Loogit all th' Smoagee hatz. Shouldn't yoo boyz be fightin' a foress fiyer sumwheres?" he taunted as the five herded him to a state police car.

"Don't worry, Pete," Wheelen offered his crestfallen colleague in mock consolation. "Your boy will get a fair trial in superior court, although I'm told there's a prosecutor down there who's got a thing for rogue cops. You might want to think about hiring a replacement." Then, turning to the constable: "I guess that about wraps things up, Frankie. Maybe you ought to do something about dispersing this crowd."

"Ten-four, Captain." The constable grinned. He sprinted to the top of the steps and retrieved his bullhorn. "THE EXCITEMENT IS ALL OVER, FOLKS. TIME TO HEAD BACK TO THE CASA," he blared into the night air.

Wheelen nodded toward Isabel and pinched the brim of his had again. "Ma'am, I'm pleased to have made your acquaintance."

"*Igualmente*, Señor. And be sure to stop by my café for breakfast or lunch the next time you're up this way—my treat."

"I'll make a point of it," the trooper replied. "And, Sergeant," he added as he shook Joe's hand warmly, "I would wait until morning to transport that boy. I don't think Pete would try anything, but some of his boys are pretty headstrong."

"I believe I'll take your advice on that, sir—and *vaya con Dios*." Sergeant Joe said.

"*Igualmente*." The captain grinned, then turned heel and exited.

Isabel glanced around and noticed that the crowd seemed oblivious to the constable's admonitions, as people were still loitering about. She mounted the stairs and relieved Frankie of his bullhorn.

"THE FOOD IS STILL HOT, AND THE BAR IS STILL OPEN AT LA CANTINA, FOLKS. THE CORPSE IS GONE, BUT THE FUNERAL ISN'T OVER UNTIL I SAY IT IS!"

A hearty shout of concurrence went up from the crowd, and a mass exodus toward the restaurant ensued. From her elevated vantage point, Isabel saw Jay Pee's jeep enter the plaza and thread its way through the milling mob toward the town hall. She descended the steps and rushed to meet the off-road vehicle. It rolled to a stop just as she reached it, and Dr. Case emerged from the driver's side. Isabel sidestepped the young doctor, hardly acknowledging his presence, and peeked inside the cab to see Jay Pee buckled into the passenger seat, smiling weakly.

"Welcome back to the land of the living, Dr. Mort." She chuckled. "Good to see you awake and alert."

"At least awake," Jay Pee agreed, "but still a little woozy. However, seeing your lovely face again invigorates me immensely, my dear."

"Sorry to intrude on this syrupy reunion," Dr. Case broke in, "but has anybody seen His Honor anywhere?"

"Yes," Isabel replied pointing toward the gate at the constabulary. "He's right over…well, he *was* right over there." A puzzled expression contorted Isabel's features. "You know, that old man gets around a lot better than you would suspect."

———

Natchez Mendoza paused at the edge of the cobbled walkway at the far side of the park. He turned and gazed one more time at the commotion across the way. He had done his part: Curtis would be given safe passage home. One by one, the beacons on the police cruisers went dark as, one by one, they departed. Isabel's amplified voice rolled across the grassy greenbelt, enticing the throng to reconvene at Manny De la Torre's bar and grill. He smiled broadly and wondered wistfully about joining them for just one more Brave Bull and a good laugh with some new friends…but no. A gentle tug at his heart led him elsewhere.

Yet we'll go no more a-roving
By the light of the moon.

He turned and teetered his way across the deserted avenue to a dimly lighted storefront. The door would be locked, of course, but he tapped it lightly with his cane, and the deadbolt clicked open.

———

The search party broke into three contingents. Dr. Case and the two orderlies combed the north side of the darkened park on foot. Sergeant Joe, Father Frank, and Curtis took the south end, and Isabel and Jay Pee circled the plaza in Jay Pee's jeep. By Isabel's best reckoning, the old man hadn't been out of her sight for more than five minutes and, therefore, couldn't have gotten beyond the plaza perimeter at his turtle's pace.

Isabel drove, cruising in low gear, steering with one hand and working a side-mounted spotlight with the other, much like those included with standard patrol-car equipment. Jay Pee, riding shotgun due to his lingering impairment, scanned the park side of the street while Isabel meticulously illuminated each storefront they passed and aimed the luminous shaft down each narrow alleyway between stores.

There was no sighting of the ancient judge on the first two sides of the square that the pair explored. Then, at the end of the third quadrant, Isabel brought the vehicle to an abrupt halt in front of a conspicuous establishment that occupied the corner space. She killed the motor.

"Why are we stopping here?" Jay Pee wondered aloud.

Isabel played the beam onto the glass storefront, but the polished panes only reflected the glaring eye. Even the dusky widow's probing hawk's-eye vision could not penetrate the interior of the store.

"I have a bad feeling about this place, Jay Pee," Isabel murmured with a shudder.

"I guess that could have something to do with the nature of the enterprise," Jay Pee mused. "After all, it is Harold Hackett's casket emporium. Not exactly a dispensary of mirth and merriment."

"No, it's not just that," she replied, biting her lower lip. "We need to check this place out a lot more closely. You wait here; I'll go have a look-see."

Isabel got out, crept over to the storefront, and peered through the glass, open hands cupped to her temples to ward off any collateral glare cast by distant lights. She immediately returned to the jeep, reached inside the window opening, and issued two long blasts on the car horn.

"*Goddamn* rooster," she muttered one more time.

"You've apparently uncovered something of interest here, my dear," Jay Pee surmised.

"Y...yes," Isabel returned in a quavering voice. "Jay Pee, I know you're still feeling kind of weak from your ordeal, but I think you're going to want to get out and see this for yourself, regardless."

"See what? Don't be so mysterious."

"Here, I'll come around. You can get out and lean on me."

"That sounds rather enjoyable, actually." He followed her directions, and they approached the glass together. Jay Pee peered in and immediately recoiled. "Oh my God!" he exclaimed. "That is by far the most bizarre sight I've ever laid eyes on."

Dr. Case and the two orderlies, summoned by the horn blasts, trotted up with the other trio of searchers close behind.

"Did you find him?" The doctor panted. "Where is he?"

"Look in there," Isabel replied.

Inside, a subdued light played on the interior exhibition—a soft glow designed to enhance the macabre elegance of the morbid wares. The assortment of Harold Hackett's most opulent vessels of the hereafter lay presented before them like ships in a harbor prepared to set sail on a sea of eternity, the wheelhouse doors thrown open to display the various pastel hues of their velvety confines.

And there, at front and center, lying in the most exquisite casket of all, a black walnut number with polished silver hardware, Natchez Mendoza reclined, as if sleeping in that silken repose. The subtle lighting, so meticulously adjusted to exalt the display, instead lent a ghastly pall to the old man's frozen features.

"How'd he get in there?" Curtis voiced the question they were all thinking.

Dr. Case pressed the thumb latch above the entry handle and, to everyone's amazement, the glass-paneled door swung wide, admitting the octet of trespassers who instantly surrounded the occupied casket. Case quickly clasped the centenarian's limp wrist.

"There's no pulse," he announced with a note of sad resignation in his otherwise professional voice, "but he's still warm. He can't have gone any more than a few minutes ago. Still, I think we're too late to try to revive him, much as I'd like to."

"Yes, I think it's proper that we spare him that indignity," Jay Pee concurred. "He apparently knew better than anyone when the Lord was finished with his earthly mission."

"And, speaking of the Lord, as we always should at moments like this," Isabel broke in, "I suppose it's also too late for last rites, Father Frank?"

"Yes, for the traditional Anointing of the Sick, it would be most inappropriate," the priest replied. "But they say that when the body is still warm, the soul remains close by. We can certainly pray that his spirit be commended unto Our Lord."

At that, the eight bowed their heads in reverence as the priest knelt before the elevated casket and offered a few chosen prayers, some in Latin, some in English, some in Spanish. He closed in English: "Lord Jesus, we pray that, by Your loving grace, You will absolve our friend of all earthly sins, and that his cleansed spirit may join You in Your Father's hallowed house for all of eternity."

"Amen," they all murmured as one, falling into a long, reverent silence.

"Since some of us probably won't be able to attend the funeral," the priest spoke up at last, "maybe someone would care to say a few words of remembrance?"

Dr. Case took the cue. "He had an extraordinarily long life and a full one, of which I was blessed to be a part, if only for a small fraction of it." He paused, as if mulling over some decision, then continued. "Now that he is gone, I will divulge a detail that he had me keep in confidence for the several years that I've known him. Having been the last in line of an old established family of merchants and landowners, Justice Mendoza was a profoundly wealthy man, whose generosity was only exceeded by his humility. As executor of his estate, I can say that he was, and is, the benefactor of many worthy charities, all extensively researched and found to be most effective in reaching those with the greatest need. In fact, he owned and funded Desert Shadows, the nursing home in Tucson. At his request, we fabricated and maintained the myth that it is a corporate-owned, for-profit enterprise, while Nat actually subsidized the great majority of the expenses so that working-class people can afford a quality of care for their elderly loved ones that is really beyond their means."

"The anonymous humanitarian," Jay Pee observed.

"Quite," Justin Case agreed. "What's more, he insisted on living in the same facility at the same level as the other residents to ensure that they receive the best care and comfort money can buy, even though he could have easily afforded to live out his years in the lap of luxury. In any case," the doctor continued, "I only share all of this because I feel he is among friends right now—some very recently made, but friends nevertheless."

"I've known him since he was around eleven or twelve years old," Curtis piped up spontaneously. The others stared at him as if he'd just claimed the next right of succession to the royal crown of England. "And I can tell you that he was the last survivor of the massacre at Fort Grant in 1871, and, most likely, the last of the Aravaipa Apaches on the face of the earth."

"How could you possibly know all of that, Curtis?" Sergeant Joe demanded. "And what do you mean that you've known him since he was twelve?"

"All I can say is that a stay at Fort Grant can leave a boy with some strange notions that you just can't explain away," he replied. "But you already know that, right, Joe?" he added with a narrow-eyed, probing expression. "What I do know is that the last thing that my friend Nachise did in his life was to save me from a back-seat ride to Florence with a loony deputy bent on snuffin' me. For that, I'll be forever thankful."

"I believe that almost anything was possible with His Honor Natchez Mendoza," Isabel broke in. "We only just met today, and he told me things about myself that no one could possibly know."

"Me too!" Curtis exclaimed. "He could tell I was hungry when he first laid eyes on me."

"Doesn't take a seer to peg you with that, Curtis," Sergeant Joe muttered. "You were born with a craving for food and a hungry look to go along with it."

"He was more than a mere seer," Isabel continued. "Given everything I've seen and heard of him today and tonight, I am convinced that he was nothing less than a mystic, no doubt about it—a Christian mystic in our midst if ever there was one."

"That would explain how he penetrated this, the inner sanctum of my finest presentation of otherworldly wares," came a strangely familiar voice from behind the group. "I am absolutely certain that I locked up tight as a drum before I left to attend to poor Mayor Hightower," Harold Hackett attested in his characteristic rasp as he glided into their attendance. "But the silent burglar alarm that transmits to the funeral home tipped me off that someone had opened the door here less than fifteen minutes ago. I parked down the block and crept up, expecting to surprise some teenage pranksters. You can imagine my own surprise to find you all here, huddled so cozily with my next client."

"Justice Mendoza apparently selected one of your finer caskets, Harold, for his rather sudden departure," Jay Pee explained. "We found him here like this just a few moments ago."

"I must say he certainly had the most impeccable taste. I only hope he had a hefty life insurance policy, because he has selected the most luxurious, top-of-the-line vessel of my entire showroom, rendered most exquisitely from the highest quality materials by the finest crafts-men in the trade, and with a price tag to match," Hackett declared.

"His Honor could buy and sell this entire emporium with his pocket change," Dr. Case declared rather haughtily. "And, yes, he will require your services, Mr. Hackett, but only the initial preservation needed for transport. He will be returning to Tucson for his funeral and final in-terment."

"You speak with some authority in this matter," the mortician spec-ulated, rubbing his pointed chin.

"I am His Honor's physician, executor, and companion," the doctor stated. "I hold his power of attorney, and all transactions will be carried out with my approval."

"Then an invoice will be made out to you, and payment will be made by you at the time you claim the body for transport—say, late tomorrow morning?"

"Yes, of course," the doctor said with a dismissive gesture. "Tell me, sir, do you always conclude your terms in the presence of the deceased while he is still warm?"

"Ours is a very competitive profession," Hackett replied with an oily expression.

"I swear I've heard that before, but it beats the dickens out of me where," Jay Pee remarked with a peculiar grin.

"I suggest we get moving before any other vultures descend," Dr. Case directed sardonically.

"Yes," Hackett agreed. "The sooner I can get started with the pro-cess, the less drastic measures will be required. This will be my first centenarian, and I expect his advanced physical state will challenge all my learned skills. But I welcome the challenge. My hearse is parked less than a hundred feet down the block. How fortunate that we have so many able-bodied men to bear the vessel," he remarked.

With that, Father Frank closed the coffin lid, and he, Dr. Case, the two orderlies, Sergeant Joe, and Curtis hefted the container and moved toward the door. The undertaker led the way, and Isabel brought up the rear, propping up the still-weakened Jay Pee. She drew near the priest as the procession slowed to negotiate the narrow doorway.

"Father Frank," she murmured. "The last thing the judge told me was to have a word with you in private—the sooner the better."

"Yes, I sensed that you would come to me before long. We'll talk in a moment. I'll meet you over at the plaza fountain."

"Jay Pee, do you think you can drive yourself over to La Cantina Vieja?"

"Yes, I think I can manage that."

"And take Curtis with you, please."

The darkness provided a cloak to conceal a number of tears as the loss of the man who made better the world he was born into began to take hold. When the sad, ad hoc procession reached the sidewalk, Ray, led there by Rosa, was standing at the curb. As the somber march slowly passed by, he spontaneously offered a song, a capella, in a clear tenor that pierced the fragrant spring night:

I'm just a poor wayfarin' stranger
Travelin' through this land of woe;
And there's no sickness, toil, or danger
In that bright land to which I go.
I'm goin' there to meet my Savior,
I'm goin' there no more to roam;
I'm only goin' over Jordan,
I'm only goin' over home.

Homeward Bound

It would be the last time Curtis would awaken in strange surroundings for quite some time. He soon came to the vague realization that he'd spent the night in Ray's vacated loft bedroom above the café, Ray having finally coaxed his sweetheart Rosa into a sleepover out at Hayseed Heights. Curtis recalled, while ascending through several hazy levels of consciousness, how he had persuaded Sergeant Joe and Father Frank to allow him to leave La Cantina Vieja with his friends the night before while the two guardians sought their own repose at the same edge-of-town motel where Dr. Case and the Desert Shadow orderlies were staying.

In another moment of gradual awakening, he relived the sweet memory of sharing a table downstairs in the café with his friends Ray, Rosa, and Isabel. They'd stayed up most of the night, chatting feverishly, sipping coffee laced with a hint of Kahlúa, and snacking on bizcochitos, catching each other up on their various perspectives concerning the week's events.

Curtis had taken his audience from shock to hysterics with his recounting of the inevitable pummeling of Deputy Aycock and of his brilliant stratagem of dunking his adversary's gun in the honey tin to render it useless.

Finally, the story to top off the night: Ray had previously tried to convince Rosa that he had left her at the cantina the prior Saturday night only because his life was threatened by the stalking presence of an Apache *brujo*. Her dark eyes widened to the size of poker chips as the other three told how Isabel dispatched the old monster and described the method in which the trio had disposed of the corpse. It was Rosa's initiation into a somewhat bizarre family.

"After that story, I don't think I'll ever eat bacon again," Rosa whined, as they finished the tale.

"Whoa, let's not get too carried away," Curtis returned, and they all laughed.

Curtis and Isabel had lingered at the table awhile after the pair of young lovers had bid them good night and adjourned to their remote love nest. The mood and the conversation took a serious turn as Isabel waxed transparent and, in hushed tones, confessed her responsibility for Freddy's death, along with a plethora of details—some directly related, others more remotely so. Curtis listened intently before informing her that he was already aware, on an intuitive level, of her secret offense. He told her that he also knew that she had slipped away earlier in the evening to make her confession to Father Frank.

"Sometimes, I think you forget that I'm a seer, just like you," he reminded her.

Despite that confirmation of his worst misgivings about the image of his flawed angel, Curtis sensed that she was somehow less tainted than when he'd first suspected her crime. It was then, in a hopeful bid for some sort of an affinity with her, that he felt compelled to divulge his own implication in the taking of the life of another evildoer. He described the ugly deed in great detail, still not certain whether it was heroic or horrendous.

"We are kindred spirits more than I had imagined," Isabel surmised when he had finished.

"I sensed that the moment I laid eyes on you," he returned.

Curtis then boldly reached across the table and gently touched her jawline just below the well-defined burn on her cheek. She reflexively turned her head and pulled her black tresses back to better expose the mark to him.

"Is it dreadful?" she asked.

"No," he answered matter-of-factly, "but it sure is, well…*peculiar.*"

"How so?"

"The shape of it," he returned. "It's a perfect half moon, you know."

"Yes, I've heard that already." She sighed. "I just hope it doesn't scar."

They both knew that it would, and that it would be the symbol of a profound penance she would endure for the rest of her earthly life. Curtis noted that the lunar image was on the left side of the terminator: it was a waning half moon. He kept his fingers touching her face for slightly longer than he should have, and his hand began to tremble almost imperceptibly. She took it into hers and gave it an affectionate squeeze.

"Curtis," she said, gazing into his eyes, "you are a very special young man, and in a very short time I've grown *very* fond of you."

"*Igualmente.*" The boy grinned.

"I mean, I feel like you're already part of our family—like Ray."

"Oh, sure, sure—I, I know what you mean," Curtis stammered, withdrawing his hand and doing his best to conceal an embarrassed expression.

"So I am going to confide in you about something else," she continued, "and I hope you don't think too lowly of me for it."

"What is it?" he inquired earnestly, wondering what could be less forgivable than murder.

"I know it seems improper of me, being less than a week into my mourning," she whispered, "but, Curtis, my heart already belongs to another man."

"Dr. Mort?" Curtis asked.

"Is it that obvious?"

"Maybe not to him," Curtis observed rather astutely, "although I have to say, it's pretty clear he has those feelin's for you."

"I guess it's time I let him know how I feel about him before he gives up on me."

"If he does, he doesn't have the brains I give him credit for. No, he's a lucky guy." Curtis yawned.

"Even with this?" Isabel once again struck the pose that exposed her burn.

"Even with that," Curtis assured her. "Maybe even *especially* with that."

The two continued to chat, filling in gaps in each other's stories until the wee hours.

"I think perhaps it's time we got some sleep," Isabel suggested. "Five o'clock is only a few hours away."

"The sandman's been beatin' on me for about ten rounds, and he's closin' in for the knockout," Curtis admitted.

So the exchange was ended, but it came back to Curtis so clearly in the morning that it made him feel like it had transpired only minutes earlier.

Then, he remembered something else that made him sit bolt upright in the bed. That morning, he would be going home—*home!*

———

It was nearly 8:30 a.m. before Isabel and Maria finished serving hot plates of huevos rancheros to all the guests at the exclusive "special breakfast" Isabel had promised to a select few friends on that morning. Dr. Case and the two orderlies from Desert Shadows arrived first, followed soon after by a steady stream of folks: Ray and Rosa (Ray grinning like the cat who ate the canary), Jay Pee (apparently fully recovered), Sergeant Joe, Father Frank, and even Frankie Quintana, who showed up rather unexpectedly but was warmly welcomed nonetheless. Finally, Carol Farnsworth appeared in the vestibule with the paralegal Betty Wood in tow. The two had to be coaxed inside by Isabel.

"I feel like we're intruding," Carol stated rather timidly.

"It's just a casual gathering of drop-in friends," Isabel assured her, "and you were invited and expected, so please join us."

Mrs. Farnsworth and Miss Wood hesitantly took an empty table a little bit away from the others while Isabel brought out three steaming plates of food and joined them. Maria continued to refill coffee cups and delivered plates of seconds on demand—the first taker, of course, being Curtis. Isabel sensed right away that her widowed guest was somewhat taken aback by the joviality of the present company, as it seemed to her an ill-suited atmosphere for her decidedly somber mission.

"I hope you like huevos rancheros for breakfast," Isabel spoke up over the din of frenetic conversation coming from the adjoining tables. "This is a single-entrée café this morning."

"To be honest," Carol responded, "I skipped breakfast this morning to get up here early and beat the heat. But, having tasted this, breakfast is now a priority. These eggs are heavenly! If I could cook like this, I'd be the size of a water buffalo inside of a month."

"I am so pleased that you appreciate my work." Isabel chuckled. "Most people do enjoy it, but some don't care for real Mexican cooking at all. I never know."

"Some people don't have the sense God gave them," Carol Farnsworth declared between mouthfuls.

"In that case," Isabel returned, "I invite you to dine here at my café anytime you like, compliments of the house. It is small compensation for the kindness and courage your late husband showed me and my family."

"Once again, I must say that it is very strange that you say that, señora, because my husband never spoke to me of you and your family, although I know that he visited this area regularly on business. And I can say pretty confidently that he never ate at your café, because, if he had, I'd never have heard the end of it."

"Carol," Isabel said softly, "may I call you Carol?"

"Yes, of course you may."

"Then I should explain, Carol, that the circumstances surrounding our case were very *delicate*," Isabel told her in a lowered voice. "Now, I don't know much about lawyer-client privilege, but I think Mr. Farnsworth would have kept the specifics of our situation in the strictest of confidence, at least in this instance," Isabel said.

"You're saying this was a quiet pro bono project that he worked on after hours?" Carol speculated.

"Yes, it was definitely an after-hours kind of effort." Isabel grinned.

"You know, my husband was a very ambitious man—always trying to get ahead," Carol stated innocently.

"I could sense that."

"So it is comforting to hear that he apparently began to listen to his heart over his head."

"You might say that, yes." Isabel stifled a chuckle.

Betty Wood, who had remained silent up to that point, chimed in. "I was Will's assistant, and I knew nothing of this side project either."

"Excuse me—I don't want to intrude," Ray interrupted, "but there's something I need to tell you, *Tía*—immediately, before you get it secondhand." Ray was standing at their table wearing a wide Ray Charles grin behind his signature Ray-Bans.

"*Mijo*, I am speaking with Mrs. Farnsworth, Will Farnsworth's widow, and Miss Wood, his assistant," said Isabel.

"I can see that. Pleased to make your acquaintance, ladies." Ray reached out and shook hands.

"What did you just say?" Isabel demanded.

"I said, *pleased to make*—" Ray started.

"No, no—right before that."

"I said, *I can see that*—because I can!" Ray snatched off the sunglasses, and his eyes were riveted on his aunt's beaming face. "That's right, *Tía*. I've got my vision back—one hundred percent, and I think for good this time."

"Oh, *mijo!*" Isabel cried as she sprang from her chair. "That news is a joyful sound to my ears!" She wrapped her arms around her beloved nephew and squeezed until he protested.

"Urrgh." He groaned. "You're crushing me like a boa constrictor, *Tía*. You're gonna make me fart."

Curtis and Rosa appeared at the table, with Jay Pee close behind.

"I'm sorry," said Isabel, "but I'm so overwhelmed by all of this that I've forgotten proper introductions. Everyone, this is Carol Farnsworth, widow of the recently deceased Will Farnsworth, our counselor."

Rosa and Jay Pee looked puzzled.

"Carol," she continued, "this is my nephew, Ramón Cienfuegos. All of this fuss is because he has just regained his eyesight after a terrible ordeal that left him temporarily blind."

"I am forever in your husband's debt for his intervention with the party responsible," Ray added.

"Now, I am the one who is overwhelmed—" Carol started to say.

"But let me finish with introductions before we *all* get overwhelmed," Isabel interjected. "Now, this is Rosa Moreno, my nephew's fiancée."

Rosa looked shell-shocked as she offered a limp hand to the widow. "How could you possibly know that?" she directed the question toward

Isabel. "Yes, Ray proposed to me just last night, but it was after we left here. We were going to announce it this morning."

"Please." Isabel chuckled. "You've got a thing or two to learn about your new *tía*, my dear." She turned then to Jay Pee. "And, this is my *novio*, Dr. J. P. Morton."

"Your *novio*?" Jay Pee gasped. "Your *boyfriend*?"

"Any objections, Judge?" Isabel quipped.

"None whatsoever," Jay Pee returned. "Just pleasantly shocked, is all."

"And this is our newly adopted *primo* who is about to leave us, Curtis Jefferson," Isabel announced.

"I am so pleased to meet you, ma'am," Curtis cried as he seized the woman's hand and began pumping it. "I am truly obliged to your husband for all he did for us."

"My goodness!" the widow exclaimed. "Is all of this gratitude connected with Will's work in Ray's situation?"

"That and the fact that he picked me up out in the middle of the desert when I was lost, hounded, and dyin' of thirst," Curtis stated.

"Again, it's very odd that Will never mentioned such an incident to me. When did this happen, young man?" Carol inquired.

"Less than a week ago, it was. I don't recall exactly what day it was. I was pretty out of it."

"You must be mistaken, Curtis," Carol asserted. "My husband was killed in a car accident several weeks ago. I came here today to erect a cairn memorial at the site of his collision."

"No, ma'am. I'm not mistaken about this. I know when he was killed. I heard about it while I was an inmate at Fort Grant when it happened. Even so, he picked me up out in the middle of nowhere less than a week ago—right after my escape."

"You must have him confused with someone else." Her voice was quivering.

"I don't think so. Your husband drove a black slab-side Lincoln, later model, right?"

"Yes, but…"

"He was, or is, a Mel Tormé fanatic?"

"How could you possibly—"

"Oh, and I almost forgot," Ray broke in, as he reached into the front pocket of his jeans. "He left this with me, and now I know why." He produced a Saint Thomas More medal, dangling it before her on a delicate chain. "He meant for me to get it back to you."

She took the medallion and acknowledged with tears welling up in her eyes that it was indeed the one that she had given to Will to keep him safe.

"What is this? Some kind of cruel joke?" Carol whimpered as she clasped the trinket in a closed fist.

"No, ma'am—anything but," Ray responded, feeling more than a little awkward. "I just wanted you to know how grateful I am to him for saving my life. I am truly sorry if I upset you in some way by telling you so."

"Carol," Isabel interjected, "what Ray and Curtis have said in their blunt sort of way is a truth that I was skirting around. We don't have the slightest notion why or how, but it seems that God, in His infinite wisdom, has empowered your husband with an afterlife mission of rescuing desperate folks from grave danger. He saved both Ray and Curtis from certain death."

"But how can this be?" Carol sobbed.

"I don't know," said Isabel in a most sympathetic tone, "but I hope that when the shock and disbelief wear off, you will take some comfort in knowing that your departed husband Will is *heroic*. He is a heroic savior-soul, intervening as a check on the evil Ezra."

"A noble knight if ever there was one," Ray added. "The Don Quixote of the netherworld."

"Carol," Betty Wood broke in, "all that's being said here is giving me shivers. It seems that I have something in common with Ray and Curtis."

"What do you mean?" Carol asked, surprised.

"I have to tell you, it was told to me that when I was left for dead out on the reservation, I was brought to the hospital by an anonymous stranger—one who drove a black slab-side Lincoln," Betty disclosed.

"Left for dead on the rez?" Isabel remarked. "This sounds like a tale that begs to be told."

With no further coaxing, Betty Wood launched into her story regarding Kenny Armenta, her friendship with Eduardo Cruz, and her near-fatal encounter with the *brujo* Ezra, finishing by repeating the mention of the black Lincoln and the unseen driver.

"I can't help thinking now that it was Will who saved me that night," said Betty, her voice trembling.

"Oh my God—then it's true!" Carol cried aloud.

"It's true, Carol," said Betty. "Ask yourself—how or why would we have made all of this up?"

"Yes, but it seems so impossible," Carol implored.

"Why does it seem so impossible, Carol?" said Isabel, now almost whispering. "Saint Augustine said that miracles are not contrary to nature, but only contrary to what we know about nature. God's ways are above our ways," she added. "And, after all, purgatory is just a halfway house for souls who still have some hope for salvation."

Carol considered Isabel's observation for a moment. She knew the Augustinian quote quite well, and had pondered it herself on several extraordinary occasions in the past to help rid her mind of doubt when her faith was tested. After all, she had lived all of her life believing in the unseen: God and heaven, angels and saints, miracles, and magic. She'd nearly had her life taken by some twisted form of voodoo. She had been presented with the suggestion that her deceased husband, who was certainly no saint in life, had been granted in the afterlife a chance to atone for his shortcomings as an earthly creature in the afterlife. Why doubt that apparent grace, however bizarre? A willing suspension of disbelief began to intervene on her late husband's behalf.

"I…I don't know what to say," Carol stammered.

"There is only one thing to say that sums it all up," Isabel offered: "With God, all things are possible."

"Amen to that!" Curtis exclaimed. "Now, is there any dessert? I think I heard somebody mention pie."

———

"Front or back?"

They were the first words Curtis had spoken to Sergeant Joe since he and Father Frank had arrived at La Cocina that morning. It had finally come time to transport Curtis back to Jacobs Well. The brevity of the goodbyes to the Cienfuegos family was tacitly understood to avoid any tears, and Joe regarded the terseness of the question to be a remnant of that emotional evasion.

"You can ride in front, Curtis." Joe grinned. "You're not a prisoner anymore. Besides, Father Frank might want to enjoy the experience of the rolling cage."

"I don't mind," the priest agreed cheerfully, easing into the low back seat, "but it does smell kind of peculiar back here."

Curtis slid into the passenger side of the front bench seat, planted a canvas duffle bag that Ray had given him in the footwell between his knees, closed the heavy door, and dutifully buckled his seat belt. The black-and-white Ford Galaxie eased slowly across the gravel lot and fishtailed slightly as it entered the two-lane blacktop. After a couple of northbound miles, Joe finally broke another long silence.

"How'd you do it, Curtis?" he inquired. "How did you manage to escape?"

Curtis glared at the sergeant defiantly but managed to maintain his stony silence.

"I'll ask you one more time, Curtis. How did you wind up getting out?" Joe asked.

"Good behavior," Curtis answered wryly.

"Give me a break!" Joe exclaimed as he rolled his eyes upward. "There's no provision for good behavior in reform school."

"You ought to know—you're a proud graduate of Fort Grant yourself, aren't you?"

"That was a long time ago, kid. I was pretty wild in my day, and I made a lot of stupid mistakes," Joe confessed.

"But you *knew!* You knew how loony, how *twisted* that place was, and you didn't warn me!" Curtis blurted.

"So that's what's eating you. Look, Curtis, I gave you the best advice I knew of to help you get by, but nobody can predict what will happen on the inside," the sergeant said defensively. "I even gave you an exercise regimen to help keep you focused," he continued. "What more could you want from me?"

"A warnin' about the curse would have been nice," Curtis returned coolly. "At least I could have taken some comfort in knowin' I wasn't losin' my damn marbles."

"I don't know about any curse, kid. I just remember that a lot of weird stuff would happen after dark, and I avoided it all like the plague. I don't like to talk about it—even to this day."

"Even hearin' *that* would have helped," said Curtis.

"Maybe," Joe conceded, "but up to now, I think I'd pretty much convinced myself that I just imagined it all. You know how active a thirteen-year-old's imagination can get."

"You'd have to have a *fuel-injected* imagination to dream up the stuff I saw and heard," Curtis remarked.

Another long silence ensued, but Joe thought he had brought the boy's defenses down enough to try one more time. The curiosity was killing him.

"C'mon, Curtis, be straight with me. How did you get out?"

"Long story short, I went over the wall—that's all," Curtis answered.

Another deliberate pause ensued. Joe was being cautious.

"If you want to roll your window up, I can turn on the reefer," he offered at length.

"I like the outside air, if it's all the same to you."

"No matter—saves on gas, anyway. Father?"

"I'm okay," the priest replied. "The air smells good—better than the smell back here."

Joe endured another pause before pressing his juvenile passenger further.

"Curtis, what *are* you going to tell the Bureau of Prisons investigators about the…uh…*events*?" he prodded. "You know that the state legislature is appointing an investigative panel into this whole incident, right?"

Curtis cleared his throat, his custom before launching into a dissertation.

"I'll tell them the truth, of course—I plotted with a dead kid to tempt a killer inmate down to a massacre place where he would be gobbled up like a human dog biscuit by the revenge-hungry souls of a hundred and forty-four victims of a mass murder that happened ninety-two years ago, and that the headmaster and part of the staff were really survivin' veterans of the Civil War and the Indian campaigns. Their deaths were somehow held up by the Fort Grant curse, but they rose—or fell, as the case may be—into the afterlife when they burned themselves up in a fire that burned the infirmary to a cinder. That's when I escaped. I was then hunted by a vigilante posse and was dyin' of thirst until a headless lawyer picked me up in his jet-black Lincoln and gave me an air-conditioned ride with Mel Tormé blarin' on the stereo all the way to La Cocina, where the Cienfuegos family took me in and hid me away." Curtis gasped breathlessly.

Sergeant Joe let out a low whistle. "Man, where'd you learn to talk like that?"

"From the dead kid, mostly." Curtis grinned. "But you shouldn't be surprised at my new, improved language skills. After all, a reform school's first mission is *to educate*—isn't that right?"

Joe burst into a laughter so hysterical his whole body convulsed, and the patrol car swerved dangerously.

"Man!" Joe exclaimed when the laughter faded and the car straightened. "You know, it's the warped *truth* in what you said that makes it so funny."

"Yeah, man," Curtis returned, reaffirming an old sense of familiarity. "You and I are probably the only ones left in this world that would get that sick joke at all—twisted as it is."

"Anyway, what the hell *will* you tell those investigators about what happened back there?" Joe asked. "I know you can't feed them that horror story you just told me, or they'll be having me transport you to the state hospital in a heartbeat. No kidding, if you spin them that yarn, you'll be waking up in a rubber room the next morning. And let me clue you, Curtis, Fort Grant is a junior-high skating party compared to the state hospital."

"Very funny. So, what do *you* think I should tell them, huh?" Curtis asked.

"I don't know. I guess you should tell them something that makes sense and satisfies all of their questions with answers that won't confuse them or make them think you are lying—answers that you think they can believe. You know, stuff they want to hear," Joe replied.

"Let me get this straight—you're telling me to lie to them so they don't think I'm lyin'. Is that it?"

"Don't be so smug, kid," Joe retorted. "You know what I mean."

"Please forgive me for sayin' so, but this great advice you're givin' is way too familiar. If you remember, it's the same advice you gave me when I went before juvenile court a few months ago. A lot of good it did me then," Curtis recalled.

"Seemed like good advice at the time, Curtis. If you had gone running off at the mouth in open court about a town councilman's son starting that fire, no one would have believed you. I figured your silence on that matter might have bought you a suspended sentence. So did your lawyer."

"So much for that brilliant strategy. I would've been better off just tellin' the truth," Curtis concluded.

"Hindsight is always twenty-twenty, isn't it?" Joe quipped.

"Trouble is, Joe, I don't think even *you* believed me when I told you—even though it was the truth," said Curtis.

"Excuse me for intruding on this rather testy exchange," Father Frank broke in, "but it seems to me, Curtis, that you need to get straightened out on a couple of things. First, I want to remind you that you were no innocent bystander at the scene of that incident. No one believes you started that fire anymore, but you were at the scene, trespassing and up to no good. You know as well as I do that once you cross a very distinct line into the realm of wrongdoing, you subject yourself to the effects of whatever other evil lurks there."

"You got me dead to rights there, Father," Curtis admitted. "You're not the first to remind me of that."

"Good—then I hope it sinks in. The other thing I should inform you of is that Sergeant Joe really went to bat for you to get you released. He even risked his own job when he defied some of his superiors over this matter and took it straight to town hall. I'm telling you, Curtis, his voice was instrumental in your vindication. So, if I were you, I'd direct any more finger-pointing away from him."

Curtis sat silently for a moment, absorbing the priest's words. "I...I guess I owe you an apology, Joe," he stammered at length. "Guess I was just gettin' rid of some of the poison that's gotten into my blood lately."

"No apology necessary, kid." Joe smiled. "If I'd done better by you in the first place, maybe none of this would have happened."

"It's over now, and, now that I look back, it wasn't *all* bad," Curtis observed. "I will miss Isabel and Ray, but I miss my mama and my friends back home even more. Man, I can't wait to get home so I don't miss any other stuff. Can we go a little faster?"

"I don't want to tempt any county mounties with an excuse to pull us over. However, I do know a few back-road shortcuts that will get us to the south approach quicker than going through Florence. You guys game?" Joe asked.

"Whatever gets us there faster," said Curtis.

"The scenic route is fine for me," said Father Frank.

In a matter of minutes, Joe eased the Galaxie onto a wide gravel road in a westerly direction. "By the way, this road will take us past the fort, Curtis," Joe mentioned as an afterthought. "Hope you don't mind."

Curtis remained silent on the matter, making his ambivalence apparent until a bend in the road brought the sun-bleached ramparts of the fort into view. A sharp intake of breath was audible to the other two passengers in the car.

"Even in broad daylight, just the sight of that place gives me the willies," Curtis murmured. "I know it don't seem possible, but all of that stuff I said earlier really happened."

"We believe you, Curtis," Father Frank intoned softly. "With God, all things are possible."

"I know, Father. But the devil has a few tricks up his sleeve too, and the fort seems to be a stage where he likes to perform those tricks," Curtis observed.

"I, for one, have no doubt that the devil has some favorite places— sites that are cursed by an evil history. Very rational people have reported eerie disturbances happening in places where atrocities occurred, places like battlefields and concentration camps. But don't you think that the most recent events have perhaps broken the curse of Fort Grant?" Father Frank wondered.

"I'd like to think so," the boy returned, "but I really can't say for sure."

A fearful Curtis Jefferson continued to be riveted by the sight of the old fortress and could not take his eyes off it until it vanished behind a veil of shimmering summer air and the dust of their own wake. At length, after several side roads joined their gravel thoroughfare, a great hump changed it to a two-lane blacktop highway. With the blink of an eye and a bend in the road, they were headed north again.

"By the way, Curtis," Joe wondered aloud. "Did you call your mama to tell her you're coming home?"

"Nope," Curtis stated bluntly.

"Going to be a big surprise then, huh?" Father Frank guessed.

"No, she knows I'm comin'," said Curtis.

"How?" Joe wondered.

"She just knows," Curtis stated emphatically. "Which reminds me— I should invite you two to my homecomin' dinner."

"When is that?" asked Father Frank.

"Just as soon as we get there." Curtis grinned knowingly. "And, hey, she's fixin' *Cajun*."

Loose Ends and Ashes

The story weaver's voice trailed off. We sat there, the two of us, in silence for I don't know how long. I glanced at my watch, something I'd refrained from doing for hours, and was surprised to see that it was ticking away again, the luminous hands indicating 5:12 a.m. The tale was coming to an end, and Curtis had been right about how long it would be in the telling. The last segment of the story had not only told itself, but had carved itself out a refuge from the grasping tentacles of time so that it could be told in its rambling entirety within a single phase of a dusk-to-dawn passing. We were still sitting cross-legged on that cultivated mound, and the once mild night air had chilled considerably. I was facing east. From my perspective, I could see that the inky black of the night was, once again, slipping into a faint purple glow. The familiar outline of the Superstition Mountains loomed against a deep-azure sky where the sun would soon burst onto the horizon.

We rose and started walking in the lifting darkness to where our bikes were parked—a good quarter mile away.

"Can I ask a couple of questions?" I asked, breaking the silence. "There are some serious loose ends I want to tie up for myself."

"Ask away—I might even answer." Curtis chuckled.

"According to Randy, Harvey's death was supposed to lift the curse, but it sounds like it didn't," I guessed.

"Nope—that didn't lift the curse, at least not for the most part." Curtis sighed.

At the end of the field, we hopped over the ditch and searched for the glint of chrome that would be our bikes.

"Just one more thing," I begged. "Whatever happened with Isabel and Jay Pee? And what about Ray and Rosa? I bet they all got married and lived happily ever after."

"Well, you're partly right," Curtis confided. "They got married in a double wedding ceremony late last summer. It was a big event—bigger than Freddy's funeral, if you can believe that. Luckily, there were no explosions or fistfights."

"I take it you went to the wedding?" I probed.

"No, but Father Frank did, and he gave me a pretty good play-by-play."

"Why'd you skip it?" I wondered.

"I try to stay out of San Pedro County for health reasons," Curtis replied. "See, that moron Myron Aycock has a killer grudge against me that he'll cling to till his dyin' day, I swear," Curtis explained.

"You mean the state cops didn't put him away?"

"Nah—they got him fired all right, but if you send a cop to the slammer, it's a death sentence," Curtis observed. "Jay Pee had 'em drop the charges against that honky as long as they took his badge and gun. Dr. Mort didn't figure knockin' his lights out was a capital crime. Anyway, somebody told Father Frank that they saw old Myron lurkin' around outside the reception—lyin' in wait for me, no doubt. Then there's ol' High Sheriff Alvarado and all his brown-shirt county mounties who still harbor a warm spot in their hearts for me. No, I probably dodged a bullet takin' a pass on that joyous event."

"Too bad. So, do you ever see any of them at all?" I inquired.

"Matter of fact, I saw the señora just last week."

"No shit?"

"Yeah, no shit." Curtis grinned. "She came up to confess to Father Frank last Wednesday. She called the house and met me at the bowlin' alley afterwards for a soft drink and to catch up. She looks kind of different."

"Different, how?"

"Not sure. She looked kind of *...tired.* And that scar on her cheek—man, it's really taken hold," Curtis explained kind of wistfully. "Anyway, she told me that Ray and Rosa are expectin' their first little one in a couple of months."

"Cool. Wonder why she came all the way up here to Jacobs Well for confession?"

"I got a pretty good notion why," Curtis divulged in a low voice. "Anyway, we had a lot of catchin' up to do. All in all, it was a real nice visit."

———

Isabel awakened to the familiar sound of a squeaking tread from the stairs outside her open bedroom doorway. Ignoring the distant crowing of a rooster, she turned and glanced at the clock on her nightstand: 12:15 a.m. Dr. Mort had attended to a late-night at-home birth at the Gomez ranch several miles south of Oracle Mesa. Isabel was still struggling with his irregular hours.

"I hope you got yourself something from the kitchen, because I really don't want to get up," she croaked in her bedroom voice as his quiet footsteps entered the room. "And don't you dare turn on the light, whatever you do," she added. "I have to get up early."

She moved from the center of the bed to the far side to make room for her mate as she watched his movements in the darkness. Isabel detected the strong smell of smoke as he seated himself on the side nearest the open door.

"Jay Pee, you reek of cigar smoke again," she declared loudly.

But instead of answering her, he pulled the top sheet away from her and she felt a strange chill on her naked flesh.

"*Isabel.*"

She gasped. The voice was as soft as the darkness that carried it. It was not the voice of Dr. Mort.

"Isabel…it's time to consummate the marriage."

Abject horror choked her. It was a terrifyingly familiar voice.

"Alfredo!" she managed to squeak out with a little cry.

A ghostly arm stretched out through the deep gloom, and an icy hand clawed at her bare breasts. A wave of fear turned her muscles to stone as she felt his cold, cadaverous weightbearing down on her. With a mighty effort, she freed her right arm, seized a small table lamp from the nightstand and struck her phantom assailant repeatedly. But, alas, the blows, though well aimed, served only to evoke a spate of eerie laughter from her spectral assailant.

Just as the strength began to wane from her arm, the bang of a door closing downstairs and a dim light from the dining room filtered through her doorway.

Dr. Mort was home.

"Jay Pee!" Isabel cried out, "Come and help me—*ayúdame!*"

"Isabel?" Jay Pee rushed up the stairs, dashed into the room, and switched on an overhead light. He gasped at the scene before him. Isabel was lying on her back, eyes closed, naked before him, her entire body writhing on the bed as if convulsing from some seizure as she flailed in the air with a table lamp.

"Isabel!" Jay Pee shouted. "Wake up—you're having a nightmare!"

He rushed to her bedside and wrested the lamp from her.

"It's Freddy—get him off of me!" she screamed and then suddenly went limp.

"Isabel," Dr. Mort repeated, "wake up!" He patted her cheeks, gently at first, then more sharply. Her eyelids fluttered at length. Then, opening her eyes wide, she sat up and drew the sheets up over her naked breasts.

"Jay Pee," she murmured, "Freddy was here…here in my bed. I…I thought it was you at first, but then…"

"There, there," Jay Pee cooed as he sat down on the bed next to her. "You're still dreaming, sweetheart—still half asleep. You don't know what you're saying."

They sat in silence for a moment as Isabel gathered her wits.

"Can I get you anything?" Jay Pee eventually asked.

Isabel blinked a few times, and her eyes narrowed. "Yes, you can," she declared with a new sternness in her voice. "You can hand me my robe. There's something I need to do before morning."

She wrapped herself in the white terry cloth gown and marched downstairs, her confused but deferential husband trailing in her wake. She strode across the dining room to the fireplace and pointed at the mantle.

"There, Jay Pee—look at the goddamn urn. Why is the lid off?"

Dr. Mort gaped. It was as she said: the shiny cap lay faceup next to the brass urn perched on the mantle.

"I don't get it," Jay Pee muttered. "That's a twist-off lid. Someone had to deliberately…"

"Never mind that," Isabel snapped. "Take a look inside," she demanded.

The dutiful husband carefully lifted the urn from the mantle and peered into the open mouth. "Ashes are still in there, Isabel," Dr. Mort announced. "Freddy's still at home," he quipped.

"Very funny. Let me see."

Indeed, the vessel was about two-thirds filled with Freddy's powdery remains, as it had always been.

"There you have it—no risen Freddy." Jay Pee snickered. "Although, I must say that just the image of you lying in bed naked would be enough to animate even a dead man."

"Jay Pee, this is no joke. How did the urn get opened?"

"I'm sure there's a reasonable explanation. Perhaps one of your customers did it earlier in the day as a sick prank. You just didn't notice it until now."

An expression of skepticism crept over the lady's face.

"So, Isabel, are you satisfied?"

"No. You stay here with that goddamn jar—I'll be right back."

She disappeared into a closet space under the stairs and reappeared carrying a coffee can.

"What's that?"

"Never mind—just put the urn over here on this table and hold it steady."

He did as he was told, and she carefully poured the contents of the coffee can into the urn, thus filling it nearly to the rim. "Are you lonely, Freddy?" she chuckled maniacally as she tapped the edge of the can on the lip of the urn, emptying the last few grains of dust from the can. "Now, hurry, Jay Pee," she urged, "close it up tight!"

Jay Pee dutifully screwed the lid on the brass jar and tightened it.

"Isabel, what was—"

"*There*, you sorry son of a bitch!" Isabel nearly screamed at the urn. "Isn't that cozy? I sure hope you like your new playmate, 'cause you two are gonna be *compadres* now for eternity. I don't imagine you'll have much time to bother with me anymore, 'cause you're gonna have your hands full with your new companion from hell." Looking at Dr. Mort, she ordered: "Drive me down to Hayseed Heights, please, Jay Pee."

"Now—in the middle of the night? Whatever for?" Jay Pee asked.

"Yes, now—I want Ray to braise this goddamn lid shut so the devil himself can't get it open again," she explained.

"Isabel," Jay Pee implored again, "what the hell was in that coffee can?"

"Nothing much." She chortled, wild-eyed. "Just Ezra's ashes!"

———◆———

"Makes me think that curse is just gonna live on and on forever," I mused as I mounted my trusty Huffy.

It was odd, but we both sat there on our bikes for a while—sitting starry-eyed and silent by the canal bank, as if reluctant to leave the place where we'd shared so many hours under the spell of the story. It was that moment just before the muted grays give way to copper—that vaporous juncture between daylight and darkness when the air is still and heavy with the fragrance of the earth. The coyotes had ceased their crying, and the doves in the eucalyptus branches above us had not yet begun calling to one another. It was as if the world was holding its breath in that endless moment.

My Catholic upbringing must have kicked in at that point, because I thought of the old judge's mighty wielding of the power from above to head off a potential bloodbath. I thought of the noble deeds of the headless lawyer. I thought of Veronica's postmortem animation. I thought of Isabel's Rite of Reconciliation. There was no denying that divine intervention was a recurring theme in Curtis's tale. I was about to question Curtis about all those heavenly references in the story, but he spoke first.

"Seems like," he stated bluntly, finally returning to and agreeing with my contention that the curse was perpetual. "So, Vince, are you thinkin' about hittin' the canal today? It's gonna be a hot one." I could tell he was eager to bring us back to planet earth and out of the twilight zone.

"Actually," I said, "I'm thinking about going home and getting all this down on paper—at least some notes. That is, unless you object."

"Nah, I don't mind. I kind of figured you'd want to do a book some-day—maybe two. I bet it'll take you a year to get it all wrote out, anyways."

"Probably longer," I speculated.

"That's gonna be a lot of work," Curtis concluded.

"I don't mind. Hey, it'll probably get me that Pulitzer Prize for fiction. After all, it is a whale of a tale, my friend."

"Now, listen," Curtis declared, "you go winnin' some kind of big ol' whoop-de-do prize, you best be sharin' some of the glory."

"No problem. I've got this notion to write it so you're the teller."

"That suits me just fine. That just makes you a ghost writer and me the author, doesn't it?"

"Ah, shit, Curtis—I'm not going to—" I started.

"Don't sweat it, pal," Curtis assured me, shaking his head. "I was just foolin' with ya. You gotta know I'm not about to steal your thunder." He chuckled and added, "You will be a writer of ghosts, though."

"Man—you got me again."

"Hey, Mr. Author, just one more thing," Curtis requested.

"What's that?"

"Don't forget to mention in your book how strong and fast and pretty I am."

"Oh, *brother*." I rolled my eyes.

"And smart," he added proudly.

"Consider it done, Curtis. With God, all things are possible."

About the Author

Vince Bailey grew up in Central Arizona, starting in the late nineteen-fifties. His youthful experiences there contribute significantly to the nostalgic aspect of his fiction writing. *Merging Paths* is the final book in the award-winning *Curtis Jefferson* series. Book one in the series, *Path of the Half Moon*, was the Winner of the Arizona Authors' Association Literary Award and the Chanticleer International Book Awards for Paranormal and Supernatural Fiction. Book two—*Courses of the Cursed*—was a Finalist in the 15th Annual National Indie Excellence Awards.

Vince has also been published in several college and local newspapers, and for the past ten years he has penned a column for a nationally distributed trade periodical. Mr. Bailey currently resides in Peoria, Arizona, with his family.

IngramElliott Publishing

IngramElliott is an award-winning independent publisher with a mission to bring great stories to light in print and on-screen. We publish stories that will translate well into film, broadcast, and streaming television projects across many popular genres. We look for a great story, unique voice, and the author's ability to build a strong platform. Please review our current submission guidelines for more information.

IE Snaps! by IngramElliott

Our IE Snaps! imprint features novella-length genre fiction in favorite genres like action, thriller, mystery, romance, and young adult. These titles are designed for a quick read on the go. Visit our website for all of our IngramElliott and IE Snaps! titles and to follow us on social media.

www.ingramelliott.com

www.ingramcontent.com/pod-product-compliance
Lightning Source LLC
Chambersburg PA
CBHW061052190726
48286CB00006B/1721